About the Author

Originally qualified in archaeology and conservation, Rae Andrew spent twenty years working in the heritage profession until in 2001 she conceived the plot for *The Lay of Angor*, and retired from her museum consultancy business in 2005 to concentrate on writing.

Now married and living in Wakefield, Rae works as a full-time writer, lecturer and living history interpreter. Under her maiden name, Helen Cox, she has published two non-fiction accounts of the Battle of Wakefield, and articles on Wars of the Roses history which have appeared in various county magazines and historical journals. An active member of Towton Battlefield Society and Secretary of its affiliated re-enactment group, the Frei Compagnie, she is currently working on a visitor guide to the Battle of Towton and Book 2 of *The Lay of Angor*, both scheduled for publication in 2012.

For further details about Rae Andrew and Herstory Writing & Interpretation, see www.helencox-herstorywriting.co.uk.

GW00722740

THE LAY OF ANGOR

BOOK 1

GONDARLAN

Rae Andrew

First published in 2011 by Chipmunkapublishing
Revised 2nd edition published in 2012 by Herstory Writing &
Interpretation, www.helencox-herstorywriting.co.uk

ISBN 978-0-9565768-3-5

Cover Illustration: Heraldic emblem of Elinor, Princess of Gondarlan,
by Rae Andrew

Printed & distributed by:

York Publishing Services,
64, Hallfield Road,
Layerthorpe,
York YO31 7ZQ
Telephone: 01904 431213
Email: enqs@yps-publishing.co.uk
Website: www.yps-publishing.co.uk
Internet orders: www.YPD-books.com

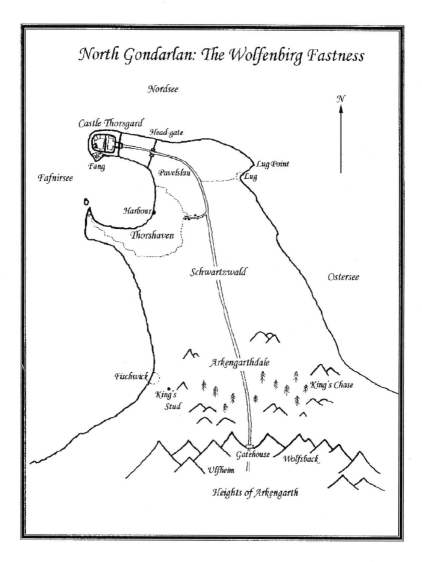

Map of Castle Thorsgard and its Environs (Rae Andrew)

Principal Characters:

Gondaran:

Thorund IX, High King of Gondarlan
Princess Elinor, his daughter
Berthe Olsen and Fran Fischer, Elinor's ladies-in-waiting
Loki, Elinor's lapdog
Hakon, Warlord of the King's Armies and Admiral of the Royal Fleet
His Grace the Archbishop, Sigismund Wolfsbane
Maris, one of Sigismund's monks
Lord Hel, the Head Torturer
Ragnar Thoralson, the Master Mountaineer
Loric Sorenssen, Head Gentleman of the Royal Household
Rupert Endriksson, King Thorund's Chief Clerk of Accounts
Haral, Captain of the Gard
Elf, Sergeant of the Ingard
Skala and Karl, Ingard Privates
Baron Ulfar, Keeper of Arkengarth Gate
Ferdi Mickelsprech, Town Crier of Thorshaven
Radnor Wolfblest, a Merchant-Venturer
Freya Fedricson, senior tart at the Mermaid Inn
Freyling, a prostitute-in-waiting
Anna, Else, Gretel and Ingrit, the other Mermaids
Ecbert Ecbertsson, the Mermaid's proprietor

Angorian:

Jehan Sol-Lios, Elect of Angor
Oratoria Nerya Aul'aia, Speaker and First of the Kalaia
Oratore Nikos Aul'ios, Speaker and First of the Warriors
Perikleia, Next of the Kalaia
Iris Kali-Ra (lit. 'Eye of Kali'), the Seer
Floria Zafia, a Healer and Minister for Health
Iamis, Captain of the *Breath of Gaia*
Thesis, the Mouthpiece of Naume, High Priest of Angor
Iactus, Highest of the *Hai*, Steward of Upper Angor
Eque'la Florian, a groom
La-Hai Dimitri and Dario, general assistants to the Angorian Counsel
Constable Kaa, a Flying Messenger

Glossary and Pronunciation Notes:

Gondaran is a Germanic-sounding language. The *ch* is soft, as in loch; *J* prounced *Y*, for example *Neujahr* (New Year) as Noy-yar; *W* as *V*; and *V* as *F*, for example Thorshaven sounds like Thorss-harf'n.

Angorian has a Latin sound. The *J* in Jehan is hard, as in John; where given as *I*, it is pronounced *Y*, as in Iactus and Iamis (Yack-tuss and Yam-iss). *Ai* is pronounced *I*, as in *Hai* (High) or Kalaia (Kal-*i*-yah).

Arkengarth – high mountainous region of northern Gondarlan
Aleia! – Angorian exclamation, akin to 'Alleluia'
Aquavit – Gondaran strong spirit, akin to schnapps
Ausgard – guards of Castle Thorsgard's Outer Bailey
Aum – light, life, warmth; sacred monosyllable corresponding to Yang
Ave (pronounced 'Ah-vay' - lit. 'Hail') – Angorian greeting
Charo, *chara* – dear, beloved
Choca – cacao, chocolate
Fang, Mount Fang – tall conical mountain, the look-out tower of Castle Thorsgard
Floria – a scent-healer, masseur and aromatherapist
Fusion of Naume – badge of Angor, represented as Yin-Yang
Elect, Electa – elected representatives, governors of the Angorian Republic
Fafnir – Gondaran Wolf-God (in Archbishop Sigismund's New Theology)
Fafnirsee (pronounced 'Faff-near-zay' – lit. 'Sea of Fafnir') – sea west of the Wolfenbirg Fastness
Gaia – Goddess of Life, personification of the planet, sister of Kali (Angorian theology)
Gondarlan – the northernmost kingdom of Urth
Grunewald – formerly an independent country, now southern province of Greater Gondarlan
Hai, High – respected Angorian working-caste; *la-Hai*, workers with animals and humans; *na-Hai*, workers with plants; *su-Hai*, workers with earth, stone and water
Ingard – guards of Castle Thorsgard's Inner Bailey
Kalaios – rank of the Oratore (lit. 'Speaker'), Warrior spokesperson
Kalaia – Angorian elite troops, the Elect bodyguard
Kali – Goddess of death and destruction, personification of Nône, sister of Gaia

Kali-Mara (lit. 'Red Mist of Kali') – a battle cry

Kali-Ra (lit. 'Eye of Kali') – surname of Seer Iris

Kali't'aia (lit. 'Blades of Kali') - mixed battle formations of Kalaia and Warriors

La-, *na-*, *su-* - Angorian prefixes corresponding to animal, vegetable and mineral

Lios, laia – son, daughter

Luna – Moon-Goddess, daughter of Gaia and Sol, name of Elinor's horse

Lung – chasm between Castle Thorsgard and Mount Fang

Maia – Great Mother, used by Angorians in reference to goddess or parent

Mit'winter (lit. 'Midwinter') – last month of Gondaran year

Mocha – Angorian beverage, coffee with a hint of chocolate

Naume (pronounced 'gnome') – force of Universal Creation, Fusion of Aum and Nône, represented as Yin-Yang

Moon-tag – first day of Gondaran week

Nône – dark, death, cold; sacred monosyllable corresponding to Yin

Oratore, Oratoria – Speaker, spokesperson

Passionata – Angorian national plant, widely used for medicinal and culinary purposes

Pit – Lord Hel's domain, the dungeons beneath Castle Thorsgard

Pyro-teknia – fireworks, explosives

Seehalle (pronounced 'Zay-halluh' – lit. 'Sea-Hall') – original name of the Mermaid Inn

Schnee, Schneeball, Schneeballkrieg - snow, snowball, snowball fight

Siva – God of death and destruction, spouse of Kali (Angorian theology)

Sol – the sun, Sun-God, spouse of Gaia (Angorian theology)

Sol-Invictus – the unconquered sun, name of Jehan's horse

Sudheim – major port on the southern coast of Grunewald

Tantra – the Arts of Love

Tantr'aia (lit. 'Daughters of Tantra') – exponents of the Arts of Love (Angorian); prostitutes (Gondaran)

Tantrissima – female expert in the Arts of Love

Thorsgard – King Thorund's castle on the Wolfenbirg Fastness

Thorshaven – Gondaran capital on the Wolfenbirg Peninsula

Urth – the planet (Gondaran theology)

Vale (pronounced var-lay) – Angorian farewell

Wolfenbirg Fastness, the 'Birg – peninsula off north Gondaran coast

Wolftag (lit. 'Wolf-day') – Gondaran day of rest, last day of the week

GONDARLAN

Chapter 1: Kaa's Mission

Constable Kaa flew steadily into the keen ice-flecked wind. He had travelled a thousand leagues with the cloud-snagged teeth of Gondarlan snapping under his wings, but now, with the foothills of Arkengarth receding at his tail, journey's end was in sight.

The Wolfenbirg Fastness was aptly named; the dark promontory thrust off the northern coast in the rough shape of a wolf's head, gaping to swallow the sea. Kaa made for the extremity of its upper jaw, where the buttressed hulk of Castle Thorsgard lurked in the shadow of a tall rocky spire. Observing the royal standard, black with a silver wolf's head, flapping from the keep to signal His Majesty's presence, the Constable swooped into a steep dive and landed on the inner battlements by a trio of idling soldiers. Two were Ingard privates dressed in leather jerkins stitched with metal rings, iron-banded wooden helms, and black mantles blazoned with a white wolf. The third boasted a solid iron helm with brow and nose guards, and the wolf on his cloak was blood red.

All three spun in surprise at Kaa's hail. Grinning slyly, one eased the bow from his shoulder.

"Hold, Skala - *look*!" his mate hissed. "It's got a gold collar - *and* summat strapped to its leg! Don't shoot it back off the wall, or the Ausgard'll get 'em."

"Great Wolf - so it has!" Skala's eyes glinted. "Could we catch it? It'd buy us good sport at The Mermaid, would that lot!"

"Catch it? Huh - you useless buggers couldn't catch the pox," scoffed Sergeant Elf. "Leave it to me – my Cousin Ulrik's taught me somewhat of raptors."

Skala and Karl exchanged glances.

"Hark at Master Falconer," said Skala. "Try it, then - but lose us our shag-money and I'll take it out on *your* flabby arse."

Elf deigned not to notice. "Ready your blades," he whispered. "Finish it off when I grab its collar." He sidled forward, arm extended, making kissy sounds with his pursed lips. "Who's a good boy, then - come to Uncle Elfie."

To his gratification and secret surprise, it hopped obligingly onto his forearm. To his even greater surprise, it tapped thrice with its bill on the gold disc hanging at its breast, and fixed him with meaningful gaze. Elf went cross-eyed. Belatedly recalling the role played by eyeballs in a raven's diet, he surreptitiously stretched out his arm to its fullest extent, drew back his head, and dry-mouthed, with infinite precaution, his free hand crept forward...

The second his fingers struck gold Kaa launched into the air, squawking protest. A thrashing wing caught Elf in the face; he staggered, slipped on the icy flagstones and sat down hard, legs waving aloft. Chuckling, the Constable flapped out of reach and adding insult to injury, dropped an accurate splat of guano onto the Sergeant's helmet before resuming his perch on the wall.

The Gards leaned helpless on each other's shoulders as Elf struggled cursing to his feet.

"Fetch me Ulrik Falconer," he spat, "Now! Then get back on patrol. You can both do double watch today - aye, and a month of fatigues afore you stuff your fat tart again! Not laughing now, eh? Be off with you, then - *at the double!*"

Grumbling under their breath the pair trotted off, returning shortly with the falconer. Kaa took willingly to his gauntlet, amazing Ulrik in turn with the pendant-tapping gesture. What did it mean? Falconer reached cautiously for the golden tube strapped to the bird's leg, but it shifted away with a warning click of the beak. Prudently, he withdrew.

"I've never seen aught like this," he murmured. "I daren't interfere with it, Cousin – I should take it straightway to the King."

"Daren't risk it'll peck you, more like!" snapped Elf, bitter at losing his prize. "Go on then, if you'll hazard naught else!"

In his Presence Chamber, King Thorund was wrangling with his two chief ministers while a respectful distance away, the sole surviving fruit of his twenty-year marriage sat quietly sewing with her ladies. Princess Elinor had been motherless for a decade, and so she looked set to remain. The losses of three infant boys, two girls and at last his unhappy Queen had chilled the King's loins till the thought of remarriage, of renewing his quest for a prince, filled him more with distaste than desire.

Lacking sons in blood, Thorund's only recourse was to get one in law – a prospect Elinor viewed with numb resignation at best, and at worst, with mortal terror. Deprived of choice in the matter of her bridegroom, she nonetheless harboured certain romantic fancies; and desperate to glean whence the marital winds might be blowing, exploited her every chance to eavesdrop on affairs. But today she had no need to strain her ears - the men's rising voices enabled her to catch the full sense of their exchange.

"... and what if the Faals track a pirate back to port?" her father had angrily demanded.

"Then they'll get a hot welcome!" retorted Warlord Hakon. "If they waste their navy chasing our *Seedrakens*, so much the better - more prizes for us while the second fleet's building at Sudheim! Only think, Sire... the sooner our ships rule the Faalian Straits, the sooner we can take those soft little islands," his eyes glinted, "And with 'em, gain a toe-hold on the South!"

The Princess kept her countenance with difficulty. Please God, she thought, not war with Faal – 'twould be the end of all hope! Her spirits sank lower as Archbishop Sigismund echoed,

"Indeed, Sire, the strategy has great potential! So many poor benighted Faals ripe to heed the Call of the Pack... so many abbeys to found, and indulgences to sell... why, the revenues-"

"What's that?" Thorund cut His Grace off abruptly. Without, there were sounds of commotion: scuffles, expostulations, a yelp of pain and another cry, harsh and inhuman. Then the door burst open and an ashen-faced captain, wringing his gashed hand, thrust past Ulrik Falconer.

"Sire," he cried, "I tried to stop Ulrik bringing this carrion into your presence - whereupon it struck at me, and-"

"So we see!" Thorund said testily, "Then he doubtless has good reason, and we wish to hear it. Haral, go tend your wound - quick, man, you're fouling our floor!

'Well, Falconer," he went on, as the disgruntled captain retraced his blood-stippled footsteps, "What means this intrusion?"

"Begging your pardon, Lord King, but this carrier bird's just arrived. It'll let none touch its burden, so I fetched it here, Sire - forgive me, but I didn't know what else to do..."

As Falconer trailed off Kaa launched from his glove, flew to the table and alighted in front of the King. Tapping thrice on his pendant he presented an expectant leg; then finding Thorund too surprised to react, teased little leather straps undone as a blackbird might tug a worm from its hole, caught his message tube deftly in his beak, and held it forth with unmistakeable meaning.

The astonished Princess snatched up her quivering lapdog to forestall any whining - or worse. Whippet-shaped, game as a terrier, smaller than a cat and equally inquisitive, her Faalian Seekhound possessed a more fearsome weapon than his sharp little teeth: a piercing yap humans found unbearably annoying, and which at its highest frequencies made four-legged aggressors flee howling. Seekhounds were popular in Faal as guard and tracking dogs, but their winsome

13

appearance also made them sought-after pets for noble ladies... so Elinor's delight at this recent diplomatic offering from the Emperor – and at what it might portend - had been boundless. When the pup erupted from his transport and danced round her in joyful release, all silvery hair and pink lolling tongue, she was instantly besotted and dubbed him Loki, an Old Faith allusion that irked the Archbishop but perfectly suited a creature so akin to that naughty pagan god. Loki himself greatly preferred it to 'Tiny', (short for Augustinus Maximus VII of Linnaise, his pedigree mouthful); or even worse, 'Silkie', which his mistress was wont to use in moments of private affection.

That was what she whispered now, constraining him to her bosom - "Hush, Silkie." Thus balked of closer investigation Loki flared his nostrils, sucking in the scents wafting from the strange visitant's feathers: salt wind and snow, carnivorous breath, the round heavy odour of gold...

Oblivious to such subtleties, all human attention was bent on King Thorund as he extracted a tiny scroll from the golden tube.

By Kaa's Wing: Hail Thorund Thorssen, he read. *The Doleful Intelligence has lately come to us that Pyrates are wreaking great Woe upon the High Seas; and upon Angorian lands; and upon our Kindred & Allies elsewhere. Trusting that ye will join us, and All Civilised Nations, in putting an End to this Menace, we propose a Delegation led by Me, Jehan, to forge Alliance against this Common Foe – an Alliance we would further Cement by Uniting with the Princess thy Daughter. We have therefore embarked for Gondarlan, and our Arrival should follow this Message by some Score of Days (dependent upon Wind & Tide).*

I do look forward to the Hour of our Meeting,
Felicitations! Jehan Sol-Lios

Thorund's jaw clenched. Such presumption... yet there were undeniable advantages in wedding Elinor to an Outlander prince, a desire she seemed to be hinting at lately. Could this unlooked-for prospect be the answer?

Recovering from the immediate novelty, his audience was agog. Hakon broke first.

"Who's it from, Majesty? What does it say?"

The King turned instead to Ulrik. "Give the bird meat and drink then release it - the messenger's return shall be response enough to its sender." Even as he spoke, Kaa took off for the window sill and tapped on the lattice with his beak. "Hah – so the Angorian envoy declines our hospitality! Let it out then, Falconer – quick, man, afore it breaks the glass - and leave us."

Hastily, Ulrik obeyed. The Constable dived from the window, swooping and twisting to evade the darts of any watching soldiers, and setting his beak to south-west, was soon lost from sight. When the falconer too had departed Thorund, choosing his words carefully, addressed their Lordships.

"Angor's ruler seeks to wed, and craves permission to pay court to Her Highness – a proposal we are minded to consider."

Elinor gasped. "No, Father, please," she cried involuntarily, "Pray do not wed me to Angor!"

Thorund was astounded; his daughter had never so defied him in private, let alone in public. As he rose, glowering reproof, the Princess sank weak-kneed to the floor. Her ladies cowered alongside, Loki diving into their puddle of skirts to hide from the King's basilisk glare.

"Retire, Madam," he said icily, "Prepare to receive the Angorian Lord's suit, while we devise some means of ensuring you do not repeat this… unfortunate behaviour. We would not have you shame us so before the Outlanders.

'And don't argue, My Lords," he snapped as the women fled, "We'll brook no more rebellion this day! Begone, both of you. Archbishop, consider a suitable *regime* for Her Highness's improvement - and on your way out, bid Loric attend me."

Alone, Thorund cleared the table with a furious sweep of his arm, scattering documents, platters and empty goblets abroad. The papyrus roll he threw down in disgust, stamped the golden tube underfoot and kicked both aside. Then subsiding in his chair, he expelled a long breath and buried his head in his hands.

At that moment Loric Sorenssen, Head Gentleman of the Household, entered with a tray of refreshments. Taking in the situation he quietly cleared up the debris, slipping the crushed tube into his jerkin while its cap and contents lay buried in the rushes, and he passed them by unaware. Next he took a small box from his pouch, extracted a pinch of brown powder and dropped it into a beaker of hot spiced mead. Giving the mixture a swirl, he handed it wordlessly over.

Thorund supped gratefully. Warm tendrils unfurled in his gullet; his strained face softened a fraction, and sighing deep, he laid aside his massy silver coronet. Then, as Loric kneaded away the red indentations it had left in his brow, the King sighed afresh. What a body-servant this man was, the envy of any monarch on Urth – how easy he'd rest if he could leave the realm in *these* hands! Physically, Loric could have passed for his son, being nigh as tall and well-made, as dark of hair and complexion. Alas, he would not be *accepted* as such, however highly Thorund might ennoble his service. The barons would never stoop to be ruled by a common sailor's son – least of all one from the troublesome province of Grunewald, a region still haunted by dissent more than twenty years after its absorption into Greater Gondarlan.

Sorenssen had been raised far away from the efforts of Sigismund's Brethren to extinguish the flames of Old Faith in his homeland. Then at nineteen, concluding his talents might be best employed at court, he duly set sail for the Fastness and secured a lowly position in the royal household. He set about his new duties with diligent good humour, uncomplainingly relieving his fellows of the heavy, dirty, unpopular work. Some took advantage, loading him with ever-more onerous labours, but others were grateful and sought to repay him in kind. Within a few months he had become indispensable; many were pleased to call him friend, while the rest allowed that he was useful and kept to his place.

In due course Olaf Steward remarked to his wife, "That young Sorenssen's wasted as a dogsbody. And now there's a vacancy among the Junior Gentlemen-"

"Aye," sighed Mistress Steward, "Since Thren Garssen fell off the Stair, foolish boy! Drank a gallon of ale and climbed it for a bet, says his poor mother, you can imagine how distraught *she* is – such a tragic waste of her fine son-"

"-I'll recommend him for it," Steward stemmed her rising emotional tide. "He seems a steady lad - unlike the late Garssen."

So after a testing interview, Loric won admittance to the most envied elite of Thorsgard servantry, the jostling clique where intimate proximity to the monarch conferred status and prestige. Here again his humble, willing ways gradually endeared him to the rest even as they did to King Thorund, who began calling for him more and more. Sorenssen shared the resulting perquisites with a generosity disarming to the prickliest ego; and as delicacies from the King's table, coins and rich items of apparel continued to flow at a steady and satisfying rate, it behoved the other Gentlemen to maintain his favoured place as much for their own benefit as his. Rapid promotion inevitably followed, to Senior then Head, a meteoric rise closely observed by the Archbishop. Who *was* this young Grunewalder, mused His Grace? Discreet, personable, not given to brawling, boozing or whoring; never causing Hel to exercise his instruments; always where he should be, performing his duties with grace. Sigismund was on principle suspicious, yet even the Wolfsbane dared not lay hand on one who had broken no law, transgressed no rule and against whom a trumpery charge would be unlikely to hold, thanks to his friends in high (and low) places. But every man had his secrets – and every man his price, the Archbishop believed, wondering what Sorenssen's might be.

So the Household ran smoothly and the King was content. But even Loric's best care could not stave off his encroaching middle-age, the loss of fullness from his face and colour from his hair, the hoar-frost that sprinkled his beard and the white icicles that drooped from the corners of his mouth. Only his eyes were unchanged, deep-set beneath brows still youthfully dark, and possessed of an unsettling quality. The green irises were shot with filaments of crystalline grey, ringed with a darker corona, and normally looked cold and glassy as an ocean in winter; but in wrath, the pupils dilated to meet their charcoal rim, driving out the green till they appeared blank, black and inhuman. With the white fang-like streaks in his beard adding to the effect, Thorund's royal mystique was greatly enhanced in a land where the wolf was so deeply revered it had been hunted well-nigh to extinction.

His lupine metamorphosis was uncanny enough to loosen the most stalwart of bowels, as it evinced a temper which could have ghastly consequences - and incidentally provoked Sigismund's furious envy (being altogether shorter and better-fleshed, His Grace needed high heels, a prick-eared cowl and a silver wolf mask to effect such a semblance). Of all things, Loric dreaded having this Eye of the Wolf fall upon him; it would mean that some failing of care had pained his lord into fury. To avert this possibility he strove to anticipate Thorund's every need and whim, hoping to lighten his eyes with a smile, the image of the good and faithful servant.

Today's ministrations had soothed a decade from the King's countenance; yawning, he stretched luxuriously.

"I shall rest before dinner… Loric, ready my couch."

Loric drew aside the arras screening Thorund's private sanctum. The rock-hewn chamber, its single dawn-facing window giving scant light at this hour, had once been dank and cheerless, but under Sorenssen's influence it had softened into comfort. Its cold black walls were cloaked with heavy tapestries and the floor with rich rugs, and the window and bed draped with fresh crimson velvet to match the upholstery of a low couch. Otherwise the furnishings retained their former simplicity – a desk, sundry carved wooden chests and cupboards, a high-backed armchair with a footstool, several small tables, and a nightstand.

Sorenssen closed the curtain, shutting out a view of snowflakes whirling hectically against the thickening twilight. While he stoked the fire and turned up the lamps, Thorund changed his robes for a loose fur-lined mantle, reclined on the couch and accepted a second cup of mead.

"Bide here and talk to me a while."

Pulling the footstool to the head of the couch, Loric sat. "Gladly, Sire; what about?"

Thorund supped thoughtfully. "Tell me of Angor."

Loric hesitated. "Um... I fear you'd think me a traitor, Majesty - my account would so contradict common belief."

The King smiled. "I won't condemn you for telling the truth – pray speak freely."

"In that case, Sire... well, if you recall, many years ago my father Gunther was shipwrecked in a storm, and would surely have died if an Angorian vessel hadn't chanced to pick him up. Then they helped restore his trading fortunes, and when I came along, Angorian tutors schooled me in the arts I now employ to your comfort. Thus my family stands indebted to that land; indeed, I owe it my very existence! So I can only speak of it kindly, even though the Brethren call it a dangerous, decadent place."

Thorund nodded. "Say on."

"Well... it's a prosperous country, and Aumaia, the principal city of its upper province, is very large and fine. The people are fair and decent, fond of travel and adventure, and naturally jocund and light-hearted for all that they love learning. Our Lore calls them loose-living heathens - but I found them to be devout in the ways of their own faith."

Innocuous enough, thought the King; commendable, even. "Hmm... now, as to their ruler, this Jehan Sol-Lios: did you ever see, or meet him?"

"Sadly not, Sire, although my parents know him. They say he leads a popular government and that he's shrewd and learned, a great athlete, and bold in battle when the need arises."

There was vast dissonance between Loric's observations and the rancid preaching of Sigismund's Brethren (who had never ventured farther south than Sudheim, as far as Thorund knew). The King's

18

eyelids drooped. How barbarous could this Jehan be? At the very worst he must be a *rich* barbarian, and there would be ways of bending a wealthy son-in-law to his advantage...

"One final question, my friend," he murmured, without raising his lids. "A marriage of my daughter to Sol-Lios... would you say such a course is well-advised?"

Loric's heart leapt. "I believe so, Sire," he said carefully. "Allowing for differences in our habits and culture, I'm sure that every courtesy would be extended to the Princess, and that Lord Jehan would come to cherish Her Highness as dearly as I do myself."

Thorund smiled faintly. "Then one decision I can make, and carry with an easier heart. Elinor *shall* wed the Angorian – and perchance I'll live long enough to see a grandson for Gondarlan's throne." He shifted on the couch. "But for the nonce, see no-one disturbs me... I would sleep for an hour."

Sorenssen watched the steady rise and fall of his chest as the adulterated mead finally drew Thorund into slumber. With his silver hair spread out upon the cushions and face in repose the King looked beautifully serene. Loric regarded him tenderly, and when he was sure his Lord slept deep, he gently kissed Thorund's brow, then feather-light, the parted lips. Tasting with his tongue a mere instant, he inhaled hungrily, and holding his breath, tiptoed quietly out.

Chapter 2: Devices

The import of Kaa's message spread quickly thanks to Hakon's drunken maunderings in the officer's mess, and by morning, rumours of an imminent royal betrothal had infected the Thorsgard like plague.

Meanwhile Elinor had spent a doleful night, mourning the death of a long-nurtured dream and trembling over the possible consequences of offending the King. Frowsty and red-eyed over her morning posset, her mood was not improved by receiving a note from His Grace.

Highness, it said, *According to His Majesty's command, you are charged to proceed with rigorous instruction in Angorian language and custom so that you might discourse with the Lord Jehan in a suitable manner. The task being so urgent, from the morrow you will rise at sixth glass. You will not break fast but spend two hours at grammar and court Angorian. Next week the study period will increase to four hours; in the third week six hours, and so on till the Delegation arrives.*

Put to her lessons again! That was no great hardship, although rising so early would be irksome. Elinor was not terribly proficient in Angorian, but she enjoyed languages and was not averse to the notion of bettering her skills.

Even so, "Odious man," she exclaimed, "How I despise his fat little dewflaps! But I won't let this spiteful cleric best me. I'll study and strive – two hours a day? Pah! I'll begin straight away! Fran! Berthe! Fetch my Angorian dictionary."

They duly obeyed; Elinor set Loki down in her lap, dismissed them and turned to her books. Moments later she sat back and expelled a long breath, absently stroking his ears.

"Ah, Silkie," she lamented, "Why, *why* didn't Father act sooner? I so *longed* to go to Faal... and from Sudheim 'tis only a few days voyage to Linnaise, where I would have found one to love me and woo me as befits my estate...

'But now – O, Loki, Angor is *weeks* away! And there are pirates, and sea-monsters... and what if we're shipwrecked? O, woe and alas," she was weeping a little now, "To be subjected to such fear and danger for some pagan Outlander's sake... denied even the meanest right to follow my heart's inclination! It's not fair!"

She leapt up, sending Loki diving from her lap as self-pity gave way to scalding defiance. "But if I *must* go, I'll show those bloody men! I'll astonish this oaf Jehan with my learning; aye, and slap it in Sigismund's face!" She tossed her head, black ringlets flying. "Damn them all to Hel! I'll array myself to dazzle the Jehan - then spurn him! I'll go with him to Angor if there's no help for it, but he'll not have *my* love, O no – he shall pay dearly for robbing me of hope!" Picking up Loki, she buried her face in his silky hair. "But my precious darling," she said into his neck, "At least I'll have thee! And Berthe and Fran, they must come too if none else."

Next morning at a quarter of six there came a perfunctory rap at the anteroom door and in swept Sigismund, accompanied by a small rat-like monk.

"Good morrow - I trust Her Highness has arisen?"

Berthe flushed. "You're too early, My Lord – my mistress isn't dressed yet. She'll be ready at sixth, as instructed."

"Nay indeed, she's ready now - bid her come forth in her nightgown."

Elinor had betimes leapt into slippers and dressing-gown, and crammed a velvet hood over her sleep-disordered hair.

"Ah, Highness," the Archbishop forestalled her complaint, "I'm come to see His Majesty's instructions carried out. As you're doubtless aware, King Thorund was deeply dismayed by your, shall we say, *unfortunate lapse*, and desires that you should be firmly taught to remember your rank and dignity. And so..."

He produced from his sleeve a device comprising two iron rods some eighteen inches long and a half-inch thick, connected with a link of chain, both terminating at either end in circular bands of flexible iron fastened with small padlocks.

"This instrument will remind you, while you harness your mind in study, that bonds of self-restraint must likewise harness your behaviour. You will sit upon this stool under the eye of Brother Maris, and not assume your daytime apparel until the study period is ended and the rods removed."

"This is outrageous!" she cried. "I can't believe my Royal Father requires me to sit unclad before your snivelling minion!"

Maris scowled as his master replied unperturbed, "Madam, I have His Majesty's full dispensation to act as I see fit in this matter. And I'm reliably instructed by Lord Hel that the device must be worn close to the skin for you to reap its fullest benefit - but you may resume your mantle once it's in place."

Elinor strove for a careless tone. "So be it – then I am ready."

The sooner we start, the sooner it will be over, she thought, giving the Archbishop her back and shrugging off her robe.

"Excellent! Woman, take this," he ordered Bea. "Open out the straps fully, place the vertical rod against Her Highness's back and secure it with the belt and collar. Now, turn out the cross-piece and fasten its loops round the shoulders. Lock it in place, thus, every morning until our guests arrive."

Berthe replaced Elinor's mantle to shut out the horrid sight. The Princess turned slowly, investing her rigidity with all the grace she could muster.

"Don't let me detain you, Holy Father," she said steadily, "I would be about my studies." She sat down and reached for her lesson book, ignoring Sigismund as he handed Maris the key and departed.

As the metal gradually warmed against her body, the full implications of the device made themselves felt. Without the whalebone stays which had supported her torso since adolescence, Elinor's spine and untried muscles had to bear the full weight. Discomfort increased rapidly to pain as the heavy rods chafed the ill-fitting straps against her shoulders and throat, and she parroted her Angorian alphabet by rote.

"Dear Gods," she thought, daring a glance at the hourglass and feeling a stab of horror when she saw how little sand had trickled through, "I can hardly stand another minute, let alone another two hours." She fought back tears of pain and despair. "And not just for today, but for weeks on end – O, Great Fafnir, grant me strength to bear this burden and confound mine enemies!"

The lesson droned on. Fran and Berthe busied themselves around the chamber keeping a suspicious eye on proceedings. Somehow, Elinor managed to repeat her letters and verbs without error until Maris turned the first glass and smirked.

"My Lord Archbishop, in his great consideration for your wellbeing, has instructed that you may now walk about for five minutes and take a cup of water."

Berthe hurried to Elinor's side and led her tottering around the room, supporting as much of her weight as she dared.

"Here, Madam," she murmured, "Lean on this chair – I'll fetch your drink."

Elinor bent stiffly from the waist. The changed position gave a modicum of respite to her back and shoulders and she let her head droop as far as the collar permitted, turning it from side to side and feeling her neck tendons crunch. Then she sipped a little water while Berthe bathed her temples with the dregs until Maris called,

"Highness – it's time to resume!"

The hour passed with excruciating slowness. At last the girls were free to half-lead, half-carry their mistress to bed and lay her down, drawn and faint, oozing tears from beneath her closed eyelids. Bundling her in furs they chafed the hands and feet frozen from sitting so long lightly clad and motionless, rubbed her brow and lips with *aquavit*, and forced a little hot mead into her mouth.

Gradually she revived, and began to cry in earnest. "Never did I suspect I'd be punished so! I can't stand it, I'm like to die with pain – how can I bear this over and over, for longer and longer each week? I'd rather throw myself down the Lung!"

"Nay, Madam, say not so," Fran reassured, "You'll feel better when you're rested."

"Aye," said Berthe, "and we'll pray for fair winds to speed the Angorians, that your torment might be ended the sooner!"

Elinor moaned and tossed on the bed. "No, no, I can't do this again, my back will break. Go, beg Hel for poison! If he won't give it, I'll cast myself from the battlements. Then they'll be sorry," she added bitterly, "but I don't care. I *will not* be used in this way! I'd rather die by my own hand than submit."

With that she turned her face to the wall, and responded no more to their pleas and blandishments.

They left her, trailed by Loki with his head down and tail drooping.

"I've never seen Her Highness like this before!" said Fran. "What shall we do? One of us should bide with her always lest she make good these threats of self-destruction."

At that moment came a tap at the outer door. Berthe's face lit up to see Loric, smiling on the threshold.

"O Loric, well met indeed," she cried, throwing her arms round his neck, "If anyone can aid us, surely 'tis you!"

"A strange coincidence, since I'm here to beg for *your* aid - or rather, for the noble Seekhound's. But if you're in trouble, my little quest can wait."

Briefly, Berthe apprised him of the morning's events. "And so, dear Loric, we stand in fear for her very life... and ours too, for we'll suffer Hel's uttermost torments if she puts an end to herself!"

Loric kissed her brow. "Fear not. Every problem has a solution, if we bend our minds to it. Pray ask Her Highness to grant me private audience..."

Elinor responded with a bare shrug that could have signified assent or dismissal; Bea chose to believe the former, and soon Loric was kneeling by her bedside.

"Madam, I'm come to offer my small skills as a healer - and to help you endure, mayhap even profit by His Grace's regime. May I speak freely? I wouldn't sully your honour for worlds, yet this proposal could see me gelded for its mere utterance."

"I'm past caring, Sorenssen," she sighed. "For a cure to this woe, I'd endure five of His Grace's sermons, end-to-end!"

"Naught so dire, Highness," he smiled, "Though must we take precautions." Gathering up Loki and one of his playthings, he opened the door and threw out the leather ball.

"Watch and ward! Tell us if anyone comes."

Loki skittered away, catching up with the ball at the junction of those corridors leading to Elinor's apartments. Lying down with it between his front paws he settled to a steady worrying, eyes and sensitive nose scanning the approach routes.

Meanwhile Loric made all secure and returned to the bedchamber. "Bea, pray stoke the brazier and turn up the lamps. Highness, may I examine your back?"

Elinor smiled faintly. "I seem fated this day for all and sundry to lay hands upon me! At least you're benign in intent, Master Loric - do as you must."

Slowly and painfully she sat. Loric kneaded her back with his thumbs, turning her head this way and that, working down each vertebra in turn.

"Happily, the spine is undamaged, Madam," he said after some minutes. "Your pain is purely muscular, and I can relieve it with massage. Pray, come to the couch."

Sitting up had rekindled her hurts. Desperate for surcease she did as he bade and lay down on her face. Loric covered her legs with furs, and unfastened her night-gown to the waist. Lubricating his palms with an oily perfumed unguent, he slid them smoothly over her spine, ribcage and the muscles of neck and shoulders, then down to the lumbar spine and the swell of her hips. Joints emitted sudden staccato cracks causing her to cry aloud, and then her pain began to dissipate under Loric's practised hands.

Slowly she relaxed, even though under Gondaran law the penalty for such an outrage would be immediate incarceration followed by summary execution: of Loric, for touching the royal flesh; of the Princess, for letting him; and of her women, for aiding and abetting. Yet she could not help enjoying the strangely healing hurts this forbidden novelty engendered. Unfamiliar sensations were stirring elsewhere too, as her bosom and pubis pressed against the couch with his weight bearing down on her back...

"Enough, Master Sorenssen, thank you. I feel greatly eased," she said unsteadily. "I shall go back to bed for a while."

Loric fastened her nightgown, giving no sign he had divined the reason for her sudden discomfort. She stood up and stretched.

"What wonder - the hurt's truly gone!" She wrung Loric's hand, a piercing look in her crystal grey eyes. "My heartiest thanks – how can I recompense this service, and the great risk you ran to perform it? Pray name your reward."

Sorenssen bowed low, kissing her hand. "Madam, your release from pain is reward enough! Though there is one boon I would ask: the loan of Augustinus, to find a lost item."

"Granted," she replied, "Loki is at your disposal – but watch him well, he's naughty and apt to run off.

'O, but Loric, my heart still quails to contemplate the coming days! However can I withstand it?"

"Well, Highness, I have a plan! 'Tis pure fallacy that noble ladies are too feeble to bear their own weight, as is taught hereabouts - but your back needs strengthening to do so without corsets. You must follow a diet, and I'll attend after your lessons to soothe your hurts and teach you healing exercises.

'Aye," he continued thoughtfully, "I'll send hearty soups for your lunch, with good bread and cheese. You should eschew alcohol, save a little red wine or dark beer, but drink freely of water and dandelion tea. Dine on salads and oily-fleshed fish, curds and milk puddings and fruit. At bedtime you'll have a soothing night-cup, and a posset on waking to sustain you till fast-break."

The Princess regarded him doubtfully. "How will that help? I'll get fat as an old sow - my stays will burst asunder! And how will you contrive a release from your duties to attend me?"

"Consider the diet as medicine to develop your frame. As to your attire: ladies, fit the back seams of Her Highness's gowns to the natural waistline. Leave off the stays save for public appearances, then lace only for support, not constriction. This will help you endure until Angor arrives," he went on as she grimaced, "And its lasting benefits will prepare you for your journey.

'As to the last: evince perfect submission to His Majesty. Express an earnest desire to study conversational Angorian that you might profit to the utmost from your grammar lessons." He grinned. "Humility, application and good sense - even His Grace can't raise any reasonable objection. Nor can King Thorund refuse, since the Thorsgard holds no more qualified tutor than me!"

Seeing no alternative to this perilous flouting of convention, Elinor inscribed a note to her father pleading ill-health, assuring him it would soon improve if he acceded to her request. This Loric delivered along with the news that Loki had found the golden cap, which had been reunited with its somewhat crumpled carrier tube and put safely in the Treasury.

Thorund chuckled. "By Fafnir's Mane, the proud mettlesome cub - verily, she is mine own child!" He flashed an emerald glance at Loric. "Behold, Her Highness swallows my rebuke, defies the Archbishop's diktat, and demands extra studies to boot! Well, so be it – let her labour like a clerk if she so choose.

'Loric, you're a linguist – go to the Princess each afternoon and converse with her, as long as you're back to attend me for evening. Inform Madam we shall continue the discourse over dinner, when I expect her progress to amaze me."

"Gladly, Lord King," Loric replied, bowing low to hide his amusement, "Shall I begin tomorrow?"

Repairing forthwith with his glad tidings to Elinor's suite he stationed Fran and Loki to keep watch and sent the Princess to rest on her bed. To Berthe he said, low and rapid,

"Let Her Highness sleep extra warm from now on. Put a wool chemise and hose next her skin, under the thickest night-gown she possesses. Last thing at night serve a cup of warm mead and a pinch – a *pinch*, mind - of powder from this black pouch.

'For morning, steep oatmeal and almonds in milk. Add a measure of cream, one of honey, and a pinch from the white pouch. See she sups it, warm, afore Maris arrives. It will somewhat dull her pain – which I daren't numb altogether lest she appear stupefied, and my trick be detected. Set cap, slippers and furred gown over her night-robe, and a fleece under her stool to keep cold from her feet."

He smiled reassuringly at the anxious face before him. Berthe was a lovely little dumpling of a girl, flaxen-haired with eyes blue as Grunewald gentians and a plump white bosom that reminded Loric obscurely of his grandfather's favourite nanny goat. He knew she trembled to lift her skirts for him; and had his heart not belonged to another, would have been glad enough to woo and wed her. The prospect of exposing her to such danger filled him with misgiving; yet what choice did he have?

"Dear Bea, we must conceal this herbal art - even from Fran. If our scheme's somehow uncovered, innocence may spare her much grief. What say you? Can you keep silence?"

As Berthe nodded gravely, there came a scuffle and a yip from without. The door opened and closed. Fran called urgently,

"Alarum - someone comes!"

Quick as thought Sorenssen stuffed the pouches under a chair cushion, commanding Loki to sit and stay. The Seekhound curled up on it, nonchalantly grooming his tail, while Berthe checked nothing was amiss round the room and Loric went to stoop by the keyhole. He glimpsed Sigismund rounding the corner, proceeding majestically towards Elinor's suite with robes a-swishing, his wolf-headed staff striking sharp against the flagstones.

Loric rose, gesturing quiet with finger on lips and a mischievous light in his eyes. Timing the moment to perfection, he swept the door open just as Sigismund made to rap upon it with his staff. The Archbishop stumbled forward in undignified haste, the maids stifling giggles as Loric side-stepped in counterfeit surprise.

"A thousand pardons, My Lord! Pray excuse me - I was on the point of leaving. Ladies, pray thank Her Highness for Loki's assistance - and now I must bid you farewell. Good evening, Your Grace." He bowed out and returned to King Thorund, his sober face belying the lightness in his heart.

And so it went that every morning, the Princess underwent her tortuous lesson; and afterwards, Loric soothed her aches with massage and her mind with conversation. In the first days he found her weeping, for notwithstanding his best efforts, the hours of sitting erect in the device left her joints and muscles screaming. On these occasions, Loric administered a second tiny dose of night herb, numbing her back with ice from the water butts packed in a cloth; and by way of distraction, had her repeat the morning's lesson to lodge it firm in her memory.

He alternated his spinal manipulations with exercises derived from the Angorian *Way of Water*; then when Elinor's pain and stiffness had diminished, Fran and Berthe were released from guard duty to join the conversation. Loric sang songs and told simple stories remembered from childhood which they repeated line by line; or played word games, all shrieking with laughter as they tried to guess which object in the room he had named in Angorian. He also taught them salutations, small talk and polite courtly phrases, enabling the Princess to greet Thorund each evening, enquire for his health, and make apt remarks on the weather, the feast, and the progress of her ceremonial wardrobe.

By the second week, her muscles burgeoning in release from the crippling corsets, stomach likewise freed from constraint, she began to relish her wholesome meals. Growing strength made exercise pleasurable and she took to practising in her spare moments, flaunting Angorian relaxation techniques daily before the unwitting Maris (whose linguistic capability she fast came to outstrip). Soon the combination of regimes wrought a tangible change. Her pale complexion took on a soft lambency like a summer moon, her herb-dilated pupils darkening her irises to winter twilight. Her flesh grew firmer and more generous, while pain etched a poignant maturity into features previously somewhat smooth and bland; and as this new beauty waxed, from certain angles Elinor showed such resemblance to her father in wrath that folk began dubbing her, 'She-Wolf', though her public manner remained as restrained and demure as ever.

Sigismund, balked of tearful pleas and entreaties, writhed at her docile acceptance and unaccountable wellbeing. Longing for reason to increase her punishment, he periodically invigilated the sessions in hope of detecting her in rebellion or error. Divining his purpose, Elinor feigned a suffering she felt less by the day, faltering over odd words and making minor mistakes – albeit nothing sufficient to warrant further penalty. Her consciousness had gained the ability to gather up its metaphorical skirts and withdraw to sit in comfort, observing as if from afar her physical remnant, erect and tranquil, making its responses. Thus she was spared much torment even when the sessions doubled in length. Loric simply doubled her herbal intake, and to the Archbishop's unspeakable ire, she continued to endure with dignity and without complaint.

The Princess herself was immeasurably relieved to discover she was less badly off than she had feared; proud in her achievement, she wore the harness lightly on strengthening shoulders, almost welcoming its discipline as she chanted her verbs and declensions.

When release came, she practised movements to ward off stiffness, broke fast most heartily, and awaited Loric's arrival. Then one day towards the end of the second week, struggling to master the bends and twists of the *Dance of Ocean,* her feet entangled in the hem of her night-gown and she fell headlong to the floor.

"O, to Fafnir's Arse with this thing – I'll wear it no more!" She flung the gown onto the bed, leaving her clad only in a sleeveless, thigh-length chemise and a pair of knitted hose. Her exposed flesh was translucent, whiter even than the fine virgin wool, with firm arms dimpled at the elbows; her unbound hair, disordered by exercise, streamed down her back like an inky waterfall.

Fran's cry of, "O, My Lady!" brought Berthe scurrying from her station to gape at her mistress's impropriety. Loric meanwhile fell to his knees as if pole-axed. Elinor's girlhood seemed fled; she suddenly appeared more as a Priestess of Angor than a Princess of Gondarlan. Dropping his eyes in hideous embarrassment, Loric tugged surreptitiously at his jerkin, frantically directing his mind towards cesspits, pustulent sores – anything but Elinor's bosom, glowing under its chemise like twin moons behind a drift of cloud.

"Pish, ladies, affront me not with thy mimsy mouths!" she cried. "I will *not* wear this cumbrous garment in the privacy of mine own apartments, where there is none to see, or to tell!" adding deadpan, "For thou art servants, and thy opinions of no account!" At Berthe's wounded look, she collapsed giggling onto her bed. "O, Bea, I meant it not! I hold all of you dearer than any in the world, save my darling Silkie. But your faces! And Loric, what in God's Name ails you, Sir? Are you moon-struck?"

"Aye, forgive me, Highness, it is even so – your beauty smote me down like a storm on the Fang." He knelt by the bed and kissed her hand. "Angor's gain will be Gondarlan's great loss! Surely Jehan is the most fortunate of men; may the Universe rain joy upon thy coming union!"

It was Elinor's turn to look discomfited. "Arise, Loric, for the love of Fafnir." She withdrew her hand, blushing, uncomfortably aware of the expression that flitted across Berthe's face at the sight of Loric paying this homage. "And don't be so presumptuous! I've not even *met* the man yet... doubtless there'll be much politicking to undergo before any such union takes place."

Chapter 3: Arrivals

For reasons he did not entirely comprehend, King Thorund let himself be borne along on the wave of patriotic fervour that washed over the 'Birg as news of the impending visitation spread abroad. He commanded the Thorsgard scoured from Pit to Fang-tip; the visitor quarters to be sweetened, hung with tapestries and embellished with costly items prised from the Treasury; and put his chefs to sweat over the menu for a splendid Welcome Feast to receive the guests in suitable style.

Meanwhile his daughter's demeanour seemed underpinned by a new steely resolve as if the iron cross was imparting its qualities to her very character. Her rapid linguistic advances obliged Thorund to return furtively to his own grammar books, and engage Loric in Angorian conversation when he was not so occupied with Elinor. By God, she's becoming a woman, thought the King; Wolfsbane, I should have turned to thee sooner!

The Warlord's gaze now followed Elinor like a moonstruck calf, his expression that of a man beholding a great prize shortly to be removed forever beyond reach. His sufferings occasioned Thorund a good deal of private amusement, and the King warmed somewhat to Jehan as he reconciled himself to the potential advantages of this match. Moreover, he savoured the prospect of revealing the full import of Sol-Lios' message to their Lordships, vacillating between a dignified prior briefing and a wholly irresponsible, unkingly desire to withhold the intelligence and see them wrong-footed at the parley-table. This impulse surprised Thorund mightily. Not given to puckishness, he feared he might be experiencing the onset of dotage; but concluded that if it *were* so, he may as well indulge himself whilst he still retained wits to enjoy.

So, lighter of heart than for many long years, the King set flag-makers to work on bunting and pennants in the sacred colours of black, for Fafnir's pelt, white, for his rending teeth and scarlet, for the blood of his victims; and despatched squadrons to clear corpses from the scaffolds and dung from the roads of Thorshaven, where an unaccustomed carnival atmosphere spread through the streets even as stately bunting spread between its buildings.

For Skala and Karl, the Angorians could not come quick enough. They were heartily sick of the irksome duties continually assigned them by Elf, not to mention the extra drills ordered by a Warlord swinging between lethargic self-pity and bouts of violent action when the Gard were harried day and night and set to polishing weapons and armour until they gleamed. Sigismund was similarly impatient, having been compelled to recall many of his Brethren from their usual work and apply them instead to preparations. Hel, thereby deprived of new prisoners to torment, passed the weeks cleaning his instruments and adding the final touches to a splendid new garment for the welcoming feast.

Thus the days passed until the twenty-first morning dawned cold and clear, with an intense, colourless sun lighting the monochrome sky and peaking the pewter waves with quicksilver. Master Mountaineer Ragnar Thoralson, gazing from the south-west window of Fang-tip, clapped a telescope to his eye. His heart leapt into his throat. Lunging for a roll of scarlet cloth, he knotted it to a stout staff, opened a roof panel and thrust it out, bracing the butt in a socket designed for that purpose. A long pennant unfurled on the wind, snapping its warning to the Gard far below while Thoralson grabbed his whistle, flung aside the vent cover, hung head-down on the iron ladder and blew thrice with all his might.

This done he scribbled, *9th glass: 2 sails sighted SSW. Expect docking by Noon* on a scrap of parchment, dropped it into a bucket, tied a red streamer to the handle and winched it down the shaft. He continued blowing periodic blasts on the whistle until a distant echo signified his report had been picked up, then hauled in the flag and made ready to descend for the ceremonies of welcome.

The ensuing hubbub penetrated even to Elinor's chamber. Her heart thumped – it had come then, her last day of torment! A sickening plunge followed hard on joy's heels. Perforce it was also the day her dangerous suitor would step from the realm of imagination, where he had dwelt uneasily alongside Eduard of Faal, and into the harsh land of reality... Distracted, she stumbled badly over the past historic of '*To Unite*'. Maris smirked maliciously, but before he could open his mouth in rebuke Fran rushed in.

"Madam, they're here! Come, Brother Maris, the key – you must let my mistress go!"

Stung by her peremptory command he retorted, "Not until noon, woman – Her Highness must complete the lesson."

"O, fie!" snapped Elinor, "If the barbarians are at our gates, I must be at my *toilette* – or should I greet them clad thus? Bethink what my Father would do if I disgraced him so, after all our toilsome efforts to the contrary!"

"Nonetheless, I am bound to His Grace – we shall continue until he bids me otherwise."

The Princess sprang up and cast off her mantle. "Maris," she growled, "Remember that I outrank His Grace, and command mine own household as absolutely as my Father does Gondarlan!" Heedless of the iron cross striking hard on her scapulae, she paced back and forth declaiming in clear, perfect Angorian, "Behold how lightly I bear thy punishment – and how I've mastered his tongue, just as I shall master Angor himself! Remember, I'm to be Queen there - shall I prevail on my husband to wrest Gondarlan from the Jaws of the Wolf?" Her voice became sly and insinuating, "You know I've a good memory… consider how I might repay any that ill-served me, from the head of our conquering armies!"

She spun to face him, eyes burning; so like The Fafnir did she look that Maris fell to his knees in an access of terror. "Now, monk," she hissed in Gondaran, "Last time, I command thee: give over that thrice-damned key."

Maris proffered it in nerveless fingers. Berthe unfastened the hateful device and dashed it clanging to the floor as her mistress continued in a honeyed snarl,

"What care I now for the Brethren's edicts, when I'll be soon beyond reach of thy Claw?" Grasping the neck of her night-gown she rent it to the waist, exposing her chemise. "So make no complaint to your master, or Berthe will take this straightway to my Father, and inform him that filthy lust provoked *thee* to tear it. Now begone, I say - or I'll make good my threat upon the instant!"

As an image of the penalty for such assault rose into Maris's mind, shameful heat gushed on his thigh. Clutching his habit he fled, leaving a urinous tang.

Fran and Berthe gazed after him open-mouthed. At last Fran said, "Well done, Madam!"

Berthe nodded. "Truly thy Father's Daughter, Highness - you'd best not show *that* face to Lord Jehan!"

Elinor relaxed; her stature seemed to diminish, the She-Wolf receded and she smiled ruefully.

"Indeed – I didn't know it was in me to behave so… I hardly recognise myself at times. But the hour is upon us - fetch me hot water and ambergris, my jewel caskets and new costumes. I must be arrayed in such splendour as to strike the barbarian dumb. Go, quickly - we haven't a moment to lose!"

With Sol in Splendour blazing from their mainsails, the Fusion of Naume flapping from their masts, the Angorian vessels sailed into Harbour-mouth just as the sun rose to zenith, and slid smoothly up to the principal moorings. Anchors were dropped, sails furled and sloping ramps run down to the holds. The equine passengers duly emerged, blinking and shaking their manes in the cold fresh air, and filed off the gangplank to gather in a snorting, stamping herd on the quayside.

Their riders appeared, tall and well-made, long-nosed and merry of eye. With many a good-natured wave to the onlookers, they saddled their chargers and mounted up in travelling formation. Ten dappled grey stallions brought up the front and rear, ridden by warriors in black leather breeches and boots, chain mail coats with bright-burnished breastplates, and pointed iron helms surmounted by white horsehair plumes; a red and white Fusion encircled with crimson was worked on the back of their midnight-blue cloaks, and the Sun of Angor shone from the pennants of their spears. Between them rode a squadron of eight elite Kalaia whose helmet plumes, and their horses' manes and tails, were all dyed crimson with madder, and whose cloak devices were bordered in black.

Within this protective cordon sat six unarmed riders led by, (the gawking crowd presumed), Princess Elinor's bridegroom-to-be, mounted on a palomino stallion and leading a white mare laden with panniers. His long, nut-brown hair was bound with a gleaming gold fillet, and he wore a richly jewelled breastplate under a sky-blue cloak with its emblem haloed by a burst of golden sun-rays.

Behind Sol-Lios rode an older man with flowing silver locks, wearing a violet cloak with a circle of rainbow round its black and silver Fusion; this was Thesis, the High Priest of Naume. At his side was Iamis, the *Breath of Gaia's* Captain, in his cloak of ultramarine with a blue and white yin-yang surrounded by azure waves; to further proclaim his profession, his white stallion's mane and tail were dyed indigo save at the tips, and rippled on the breeze like foam-capped billows.

The next two were a middle-aged man and a pretty young woman clad alike in brown leathers and riding chestnut horses. Iactus, the Highest, had close-clipped grizzled hair, his creased leathery face lit by green-grey eyes dancing with impish good humour; his cloak was the deep green of a mature leaf, its device a stylised golden tree cradling the Fusion in its branches. His companion Zafia gazed curiously about with warm, honey-brown eyes, advertised as a *Floria*-Healer by the circlet of amethyst flowers on her sun-gilded curls, and

33

her crimson cloak bearing a great phallic plant with a purple and red Fusion on its bulbous root.

Last came a coal-black mare whose rider was muffled from head to foot in black, its face concealed by a deep cowl, its cloak device an Eye with a black and silver Fusion for the iris and silver crescent moons for the lids; a raven, (Kaa, relishing his second sight of Thorshaven), was perched upon its shoulder. Nearby the crowd was subdued, the figure so reminiscent of Sigismund's Brethren that some pressed away to lose themselves in the throng, muttering and forking the sign of the Claw.

Captain Haral dourly watched the party ready itself, vastly annoyed with Gard and burghers alike for their open-mouthed gawping, and at the lowborn crowd for presuming to converse with the dignitaries. Said crowd, meanwhile, was enjoying itself immensely. Normal work had been abandoned; the *thegns*, merchants and artisans, their plump wives and chattering households were arrayed in their finest, lining the streets and craning from windows and rooftops to view the procession. Most gleeful of all was the merchant Radnor Wolfblest, who had contrived himself an invitation to the coming feast, and swaggered through the streets resplendent in cloth-of-silver with sable furs.

Sundry remarks detached themselves from the general hubbub and made their way to Haral's ears:

"Look at them big buggers, then! Be they Men or Giants?"

"Nay, wi' that hair they look more like maidens to me!"

The sniff of ribald banter had lured Freya and her colleagues away from baiting Skala and Karl, stationed glumly behind the Gondaran cavalry with dung-pails at the ready. Squeezing through the throng they arrived on the quay in a grand swell of bosoms and gaudy-dyed furs, raising speculative eyebrows over the possible contents of breeches and purses.

Freya called brazenly, "Ho, my Lord! If your member's as great as your spear, pray come to The Mermaid tonight!"

His warrior comrades greeted her sally with laughter. The one at his side rejoined, "Nay, you'd be sadly disappointed – shall I come instead?"

Nikos, the soldier she had addressed, shook his head. "As my spear? Not I, Madam - or Nery here, despite these braggart words! Which is well, for who could accommodate me then - not a fresh Bud like you, surely? Yet were I not otherwise engaged, I'd as lief put it to the test!"

He winked. Freya flushed like a silly virgin, a delicious twinge in her privy parts as she read the plain invitation in his eyes. Surely The Mermaid would prosper as never before with these vessels in dock!

This was too much for Haral. He spurred his stocky pony forward, rigid with embarrassment as the eyes of the crowd turned to him.

"Welcome to Thorshaven, My Lords," he cried. "I'm Haral, Captain of Thorsgard, here to conduct thee to the castle."

The afternoon glass had turned twice. Elinor paced, frenziedly. From the tower window she had seen the ships at their moorings, people thronging the harbour-place like ants in the distance; but while she dressed, had lost sight of the delegation's progress through the heaving streets.

On nervous pins she complained, "Where in the Wolf's Name are they? 'Tis not so very far from Thorshaven, the Jehan should be here long since! God rot his barbarian soul for keeping me afoot like this... my gown will be all over creases if I sit."

"Aye, Madam," replied Berthe, "It's a puzzle – how can these last minutes seem as long as the past score of days?"

Elinor sighed. "I know not. I know nothing, in fact. Not how this Jehan looks, or is, or what will become of us. I feel all a-churn - one moment I wish it wasn't happening, the next that it already *had*, and was over and done with. How shall we like it in Angor, d'ye think? O, I *do* wish we were going to Faal instead – 'tis not so foreign there, or so far away!"

Berthe shook her head. "A pity indeed, My Lady... but at least we'll see somewhat of Urth, as Loric has done – and have our own traveller's tales to tell!" She smiled, wistfully. "It'll be some solace to visit places he's been... for my heart's so sore at leaving him I daren't dwell on it overmuch."

The Princess embraced her. "Ah, Bea, don't lament – you'll be reunited one day, I'll make certain of it."

Berthe's face brightened. "O, Madam, I pray so! Then I'll endure our... temporary separation... as best I can." She twinkled mischievously. "And mayhap we'll *both* have a wedding, if Lord Jehan proves to be your heart's desire!"

"Mayhap... mayhap not. He may be coarse, or ugly, or cruel. Or smell bad – if he washes his hair in urine, or chews on raw garlic, or some other such horrible practice, I shall run away!"

"Well, Highness, we'll all know directly," Fran cried, her

voice rising with excitement, "Look, they're coming at last!"

The Princess rushed to the window. Yes! Down there, at Wolfsmaw Gate! There was the cavalry troop, the Gondaran standard flapping at its head; and behind, what could only be the Angorian delegation within a thicket of raised spears.

"O God," she exclaimed, hand to mouth, "I feel sick…"

Alas for Elinor, despite all Haral's barking, the delegation's progress had been sorely impeded by jostling, curious hordes which several times brought it to a complete standstill. Then with the city behind them, the peninsula opened out into dry-stone walled fields. The scent of scrubby winter grass made the horses' nostrils flare, and they began to whinny and prance.

"Captain, pray halt!" called Jehan. The cavalry reined in their ponies, and the whole group milled uncertainly on the roadway. "Our companions are chafing to run, and they've been cooped up so long it seems cruel to thwart them.

'Hail, Farmer!" he went on to a grimy peasant engaged in repairing the wall, "May our horses stretch their limbs in your field?"

Falling to his knees, the *ceorl* glanced from Jehan to the Captain and back again, his lips working soundlessly.

"Get up and out of it, fool, or feel my whip across your back!" Haral snapped. To Jehan he said, "Very well, Sir, but not for long – I do have my orders."

The Angorians dismounted and swiftly unharnessed their neighing, stamping mounts. The instant Jehan's horse was free he bolted for the broken wall, cleared it in a stride and galloped across the ridged field, silvery mane streaming and hooves ringing on the frozen ground. His brethren followed suit, plunging across the breach and leaving poor *ceorl* Knut reeling with the rush and thunder of their passage.

Zafia's heart melted; she went to Haral and laid a hand on his knee as he sat fretting on Lumpi.

"O Captain: as you must perforce wait, might not your horses join ours, just for the littlest while? Even if you say me nay, we'll get there no quicker!"

Haral could not withstand her pretty face and pleading eyes. "Gard! Dismount and let the ponies roam," he cried, adding, "And mind, Ladyship – it must be for the littlest while."

Soon the whole herd, foreign and native alike, was racing around in ecstatic liberation, bucking and rearing, or rolling on the brittle frosted grass. Jehan grinned.

"Thank you kindly for this, Captain Haral. It's good to see them run after so many weeks of confinement." He shifted restlessly. "And my own muscles are so stiff I'm minded to do likewise…"

He gave a shrill whistle. Sol Invictus trotted up steaming and expectant, and Jehan leapt aboard crying, "Hai!" The stallion galloped off while Haral watched aghast, praying the Elect would not fall and break his neck on the iron-hard earth - a dire eventuality for which he himself would surely be blamed. His dismay increased when Captain Iamis and several others joined in, taking the horses turn and turn about. Meanwhile the Gondaran cavalrymen, after a certain amount of shuffling and whispering, approached the Angorian party to beg for a ride and before long, half the troop was riding bareback around the field on borrowed steeds.

Somehow Captain Haral could not summon the words to bring back order even though discipline had broken down quite.

"Ah, bollocks," he muttered, seeing no immediate prospect of progress. "I yield; the King of Angor isn't mine to command." He stumped off to join a trio of soldiers sitting on the wall, loading his clay pipe as he went.

"Ho, Captain," hailed Jenia, a tall, smooth-faced youth, "A fellow smoker - come share a pipe with us! Peri, shift your arse."

Haral heaved himself into the space vacated on the wall, accepted an intricately cast silver pipe, and gratefully inhaled.

Fifteen minutes later Skala and Karl panted up with their dung-pails, glad to stop for a smoke-break. Each coughed and wheezed in his turn.

"What's *that*?" choked Skala, "It's made my head spin!"

"Only *wayblend*," Haral proudly displayed his new knowledge. "Aye, 'tis good stuff – c'mon, you'll soon get the taste. Here, take another pull-"

Leaning forward to proffer the pipe, the Captain overbalanced, plunged headlong from the wall, stumbled into Skala and knocked him down. Like a tortoise on its back the Gard waved his legs, unable to right himself for giddiness. Haral, in no fit state to assist, collapsed upon him and the pair lay in a writhing heap, red-faced and screeching witless laughter.

When Nikos had recovered from his own amusement and hauled them to their feet, still voiceless and streaming at the eyes, he said to his comrades,

"Our *wayblend* must be more potent than the herb they smoke." He noticed that Zafi, amid a gaggle of admirers, was also lighting up. "Hurry - we must remedy this before more of them succumb!"

Vaulting onto the wall he whistled and waved at the riders. The chattering groups by the roadside dispersed, and by the time Jehan and Iamis jogged up with the last of the ponies, their companions were busily engaged with buckle and strap. The Captain beamed on them beneficently, weaving gently from side to side as Nerya deftly caught Lumpi and made a fair fist of saddling up with the unfamiliar Gondaran tack.

More than an hour had elapsed. The Angorians, struck with remorse, now made all speed, bundling the unresisting Captain up onto his pony and putting Skala between the mare Luna's panniers, where he sat frozen in terror at her unaccustomed height. Karl fared somewhat better, for to the envy of the rest Nikos hoisted him up behind Zafia, where he snuggled into the Healer's cloak, arms about her slender waist and face buried in her curls.

At long last, the party set off for the Wolfsmaw at a steady canter. They left *ceorl* Knut gazing after them, then down at his heavy hand, in wonderful amazement. Blazing in his dirty calloused palm was a golden Sun of Angor, the tip bestowed by Jehan for his labour in minding the gate.

Chapter 4: Into Wolf's Maw

"Faugh!" The Warlord cast aside his spyglass and red-faced, thunderous of brow, clanked from the battlements in his best parade armour. "Exercising their horses - they're exercising their *horses*!" he repeated in rising tones. "The barbarian bastards are *exercising* their *horses*! The entire Thorsgard on tenterhooks, the Gard on alert, I stuck in this bloody rig – and they're *exercising their fucking horses!*

'Who does this thrice-damned Outlander think he is? And Haral, letting his cavalry play like gypsies at a horse-fair!"

Elbowing a hapless sentry aside he stamped into the Gardroom, snatched up a wax tablet and inscribed a hasty message.

"Elf!" he bellowed. The Sergeant appeared at the double. "The minute he gets here, take that useless sod Haral to the Pit and give this," thrusting the tablet into Elf's hand, "to Lord Hel."

The Sergeant snapped a hasty salute and departed. Hakon followed him out, muttering, "Only wait till His Majesty hears of this!"

At the King's apartment, the door-guards fell back at the sight of his blood-rage. The Warlord pushed roughly between them and flung open the doors. A startled Gentleman leapt to his feet.

"No-one's to enter, My Lord - His Majesty's engaged."

Hakon replied by knocking the man off his feet with a backhanded blow from his gauntleted fist. Bursting into the suite, he found Thorund wrapped in a loose mantle in his big chair with Loric behind him, comb in hand. The King's feet were immersed in a basin of steaming, scented water and his hands, aglint with rings and freshly manicured nails, lay relaxed in his lap. His beard was trimmed and his hair gleamed like new iron, damascened here and there with small braids terminating in silver-bound wolf fangs.

Opening one eye he said coldly, "What's the meaning of this, Warlord?"

Hakon shot Loric a glance of distaste – he disliked seeing Thorund's grey mane bedecked like a maiden's, albeit with trophies of the hunt.

"'Tis the barbarians, Lord King, perpetrating a gross affront - instead of hastening to pay homage they frolic in *Thegn* Pavel's meadows, making their horses run about! Sire, grant me leave to drag the discourteous curs here on leashes!"

The King raised a quizzical eyebrow. "If by *barbarians* you mean our noble guests, I'm ready to receive them, am I not? Claw take thee, Warlord! I'll not be dressed this half glass or more – what odds is this to me?"

"But Sire! Surely it's for the... the *Angorians* to wait on your convenience, not arsey-versey?"

"Hakon, they've sailed far; no doubt their beasts are mettlesome. Indeed, I deem it a favour – the horses will be less frisky in our stables."

Hakon scowled. Thorund was getting old and daft, he thought, and the fire gone from his belly. "But Majesty, the insult!" he protested. "Gondaran pride is at stake!"

"Enough!" snapped the King. "Insult, say ye, who comes crashing into our privy chambers to rail at us undressed? You're lucky we don't have you flogged!

'Utter one word of complaint to our guests and you'll not find us so forbearing! Now *get out* – and when they arrive, mind your manners."

Bowing out Hakon stormed from the suite, so swollen with temper his armour chafed, his eyes bloodshot as the cabochon garnets on his breastplate.

"I am mistreated," he said furiously under his breath. "What price duty? What price loyalty? Here am I, ready to lay down my life in defence of his honour, and how does the ungrateful dotard repay me - with the hand of the Princess? Nay! He invites the Jehan to pay her court instead!

'And when that southern fop keeps My Lady..." he paused, choked with ire. "When he keeps Her Highness, us all, hanging about for the sake of dumb beasts, what then? Does The Fafnir appear in righteous wrath and smite them down? Does he allow me to chastise the pagan? He does not! O Thorund, my heart's turning from you... You're no longer the King I once knew."

Wolfsmaw Gatehouse yawned from its crenellated wall like a gigantic black Head of Fafnir, its ears formed by twin lookout towers and its eyes by a pair of tall arched windows with glaring red lamps for their pupils. The delegation trotted through its snout-like barbican, past stiff ranks of Ausgard and a goggling throng of lower servants, and on through the iron-clad gates of the Inner Bailey. As the last portcullis clanged down and the gates heaved shut, a band of minstrels struck up a stately air and scattered applause broke from the waiting crowd.

Sergeant Elf, flanked by two burly halberdiers, marched over and waved his orders in Haral's still benign face. The beatific smile dropped instantly from his lips as Gards dragged him from Lumpi and

40

frogmarched him towards the Pit, carrying the luckless Captain bodily when his legs failed in an extremity of terror.

Jehan urged Sol Invictus forward. "Hail, Warrior! Why is our good escort being so treated?"

Elf bowed. "With respect, My Lord, the Thorsgard has stood ready for your coming these last two hours. Warlord Hakon is sorely displeased, and has ordered Captain Haral held in custody, pending correction."

"Alas, this is our fault!" cried Jehan in dismay. "Pray take me to this Warlord - I must plead the poor man's case."

"Nay, My Lord – pray tarry no longer or I'll surely join Haral in the Pit! He's in no immediate peril, and Lord Hakon's wrath may cool – if he's not further provoked."

"Aye, leave it, Jehan," said Nikos. "We've offended our host before we even set foot in his House - for pity's sake, make matters no worse."

Relieved, Elf signalled the minstrels to blow a fanfare. Olaf Steward, chain of office gleaming on his breast, clinked forward with a phalanx of stable-hands who eyed the tall horses nervously.

"On behalf of Thorund the Ninth, High King of Greater Gondarlan, Master of the Fang and Chief Cub of Fafnir, I bid you welcome to Castle Thorsgard!" Steward's great voice echoed and rolled round the courtyard. "Pray dismount, My Lords, the servants will tend to your beasts."

Princess Elinor stamped her embroidered slipper. "God's Teeth, they're taking forever! What's happening, Fran, let me see – O, do get out of the way."

She yanked at the curtain so impatiently that its pole came unseated and fell clanging to the floor, dumping its heavy velvet load on top of them. To Elinor's unspeakable horror she was thus exposed in the window bay, all undignified, at the exact moment the delegation turned towards the Keep. With the greatest ill-luck possible, the flapping drapery caught the attention of a tall Lord in a gilded and bejewelled breastplate; he glanced up; their eyes met. Wailing, mortified, Elinor hastily withdrew her amorphous bulk of skirts and *passementerie*.

"Don't cry, My Lady," beseeched Berthe, scurrying to the rescue, "You'll raddle your eyes! Come, Fran, untangle yourself - we must put Her Highness to rights!

'There, there, Madam, don't fret – they'll never recognise you with your crown and veil on."

The Princess clenched her jaw. "O, Great Day!" she exclaimed sarcastically. "What a first sight for my husband-to-be! O, *husband*! Pestilence take him – did you see the ill-bred boor smirk? I hate him already!"

In an attempt at disguise, she insisted on exchanging her conspicuous white brocade gown for another new outfit, a dark grey velvet kirtle embroidered with seed pearls. Central panels of bright cloth-of-silver in the bodice and skirt drew attention from her waistline, whose increased girth was further concealed by a crimson brocade waistcoat faced with feathers resplendent as rubies in their shimmering iridescence, all edged with sable fur. She examined her reflection critically. The garments became her exceedingly well, her pale excited face luminous against their deep colours. Elinor bit her lips, pinched and slapped some pink into her cheeks and felt almost satisfied, yet still something seemed amiss.

"It's no good!" she cried. "I can't face the pagan like this – I'm fat as an old grandmother, and it spoils the hang of my dress. Tighten my stays, for God's sake!"

Berthe replied, "Now, Madam, remember what Loric said – for support only, not constriction."

"Fie to Loric - what knows he of *couture*? Come, there's still time – pull me in!"

They obediently opened the back of her dress, took hold of her corset lacings and heaved. Gasping, grunting, she endeavoured to suck in her stomach but to scant avail, having gained both fat and muscle, while her ribs protested with sharp stabbing pains.

"Enough! Tie me in and measure me!"

Fran ran a tape around her slightly diminished waist.

"Nearly two feet – ah, Sorenssen, what have you done? Alack, I've been so occupied with bloody Maris and my poor aching back, I'd not realised what ill your stupid regime had wrought!"

"No, My Lady," Berthe protested, "You look lovely, and your weskit's very flattering - no-one will notice! Anyhow, these visitors seem to pay elegance scant heed – didn't you see? There was a maid – at least, I think 'twas a maid – breeched, and riding astride like the men. So they cannot care much for high fashion."

The Princess gaped. "What - you must be mistaken, Bea. A lady of degree sufficient to ride with a monarch wouldn't consent to such indignity! With her… *apart*… no, I don't believe it."

Fran and Berthe exchanged glances. From their vantage point

it had certainly looked like a girl, yet it seemed safest not to insist lest Elinor fly again into frenzy. They fastened her up, bound her hair with a rope of small pearls, and set over it a veil of fine white tissue held by a dainty silver and moonstone tiara; a long sleeveless surcote of black velvet, figured with silver and trimmed with matching wolfskin, completed her ensemble.

"Every inch a Princess, Highness!" cried Fran. "I can hardly wait till the Lord Jehan sees you!"

The fanfare sounded. Two columns of Ingard marched smartly into the reception chamber and disposed themselves at attention along the walls, followed by the Angorian *Kali't'aia* escort who did likewise.

A herald announced in ringing tones, "The Oratores Nikos and Nerya, Speakers of the Angorian Host!"

The tall warriors advanced up the aisle, their sun-bleached ponytails bound with black ribbon, hands pacifically crossed on their breastplates, and made their bow to Thorund on the dais. Next were presented Thesis, the Mouthpiece of Naume; Questor Iamis, Captain of *Breath of Gaia* and Admiral of the *Marin'aia*; Iactus, Highest of the Counsel; and Zafia, the Minister to Health.

Then the herald proclaimed, "Counsellor Iris Kali-Ra and... er... Constable Kaa of the Messenger *Avia*..." The black-clad figure advanced, doffing mask and hood to reveal not the elderly man Thorund had somehow expected, but a woman in her late twenties, little older than the Healer. She was paler than her compatriots, with clear olive skin, amber eyes gazing catlike beneath determined black brows, and long wavy golden-brown hair, prematurely faded to silver at the temples. Hard on her heels, Jehan eagerly approached.

"At last - hail, King Thorund," he cried, "And well met, indeed – I have long looked forward to this day!"

Before Thorund could reply Hakon broke out gruffly, "Lord Jehan! Ancient custom demands that visitors high or low make obeisance to the King – and through His Majesty, to the Great Wolf Fafnir – on bended knee!"

Jehan regarded him levelly. "Angor bends the knee at no man's command, Sir. Although for my own part I'll gladly honour you, O Thorund: as man, and as monarch, and one day perhaps as my second father, grandsire to my children and the union of our lands!" He knelt. "It's a pleasure to make your acquaintance, Sir."

The King glared at Hakon. "The honour and pleasure are ours – arise, we implore," he said hastily. Drawing Sol-Lios to his feet, he met for the first time the eyes of a man tall as himself. Olive-brown, long-lashed with a piquant almond slant and rayed about with deep laughter lines, their expression under the curious spray of tattoo on Jehan's brow was direct and open, and he held Thorund's gaze without effort.

"You're most welcome in our House, er... how should we address you, Sir?"

"'Jehan' suffices, for it is my given name; 'Elect' or 'Sol-Lios', if you prefer a title."

"Then, Jehan Sol-Lios, noble guests, pray be seated; the Princess will join us shortly."

A messenger was duly despatched while the Archbishop and other senior officials were presented, then the King introduced Loric.

"Master Sorenssen has journeyed somewhat in Angor and speaks your tongue fluently, Sir. We place him at your disposal for the duration of your stay - Loric, we bid you serve the Elect and his folk with the same care you lavish on us."

As Sorenssen bowed in assent the trumpets resounded. All eyes turned to the door.

"Her Most Serene Highness, Princess Elinor of Gondarlan!" cried the herald.

Chapter 5: Moon-Daughter

Elinor paused on the threshold. On the dais beside her father stood a tall figure, his face as yet indistinct in the candlelit gloaming of late afternoon. She drew as deep a breath as her stays would permit then set out up the aisle, Loki looped over her arm like a white fur muff. A buzz of soft exclamations ran through the visitors as she passed, and catching their approving tone if not the words, she stepped forth with increasing confidence, silver beams flashing from her skirt.

This first sight of his putative Lunaia stopped Jehan's breath; with her dark surcote lost against the shadowy background, her white face seemed to float towards him like a moon veiled with cirrus cloud. Intently he watched her approach, noting her pleasingly upright carriage and graceful bearing.

Elinor's own gaze was riveted on the tapestry of Fafnir behind the thrones, praying the Great Wolf she would not betray her nerves by tripping over her hem. She took her place at the Angorian's side, glimpsing from the corner of her eye the blaze of gems on his breastplate; etiquette forbade her to inspect him more fully, much as she ached to. Fran and Berthe in her train had fewer scruples; frequently raising their eyes, they devoured every detail of his person and costume to chew over later in private.

"My Lord Elect, permit us to present Elinor, our well-beloved Princess," said Thorund.

She made a deep obeisance, peeping through the filmy tissue. The view was not displeasing. Sol-Lios was well dressed, his golden breastplate looking as if it might mortgage half of Thorshaven, and well-built, with a hawkish face she found comely enough. Less favourable points were his age, (he seemed quite old, at least thirty); the strange marks that disfigured his brow; and his darkness (Eduard of Faal was reputedly a fair blue-eyed blond).

Courtesy dictated she should now put back her veil. The Elect met her crystalline gaze for several long seconds.

"Hail, Princess! I'm Jehan Sol-Lios, and honoured to be at your service." Taking her hand he bowed low, kissed her fingertips and did not relinquish his hold as he straightened up, faint lines of irony bracketing his mouth. "Though I regret to say I've been grievously misled by the tidings I've heard of your beauty-" Elinor's fingers flinched indignantly, but Jehan held on fast. "For in truth, they are sad understatements – you're fairer than Luna herself!

'O Thorund, if you would truly part with this pearl, we must

45

offer some return for robbing your realm of such glory – though I fear no gift, howsoever rich, will be adequate recompense."

Flattered, obscurely annoyed, Elinor felt her cheeks pinking and blessed the candlelight. Inclining her head, she replied to his Gondaran in faultless, formal Angorian,

"Greetings, Lord Jehan. I am gratified ye do not find my person wanting, else thy long voyage would have been wasted."

Thorund shot her a sharp glance. "Come, Daughter, Sol-Lios - be seated."

Now order was given to admit the senior court. When drinks had been served and toasts exchanged, Jehan begged leave to present the items his pack-mare had carried, now temptingly arrayed upon the sideboard.

First he unfurled a silk wrapper, set an oblong golden casket before Thorund and unfastened its close-fitting lid. Out rolled a gust of mouth-watering fragrance from scores of tiny square cakes nestling in gold-foil cups, arranged like the tesserae of a mosaic in a yin-yang pattern, half golden, half chocolate brown.

"These are *staycakes* of the Upper province. The dark are named 'Pleasure', the light ones are 'Peace' - and given chance, they keep good for months in these foils."

Thorund bit into a 'Pleasure'. "Hmm… 'tis well named, Sol-Lios - good, very good indeed."

Finishing in a second bite, he took a 'Peace' and slid the heavy box to Elinor, who selected one of each for herself before Loric handed them out to guests, courtiers, Household and Gard alike. Expressions of delight broke out even as explosions of flavour broke out on all tongues. Elinor's stomach gave an undignified growl and saliva poured into her mouth.

"Quick, Fran," she whispered urgently, "Get me another before they're all gone!"

"As to your gift, Sir," went on Jehan as folk munched, "We wondered what to give a King that he does not already have. But since one of the greatest gifts is knowledge, we hope you may find this useful." He handed Thorund a large volume bound in gold-tooled leather decorated with gems and golden clasps. "It's the *Lay of Angor*, the story of our days; truly, all you might wish to know of our land and people lies within its pages."

"A noble gift – thank'ee, Sol-Lios. I'll peruse it with interest."

Next Jehan said, "Master Sorenssen, this comes with your parents' love and blessing. In the lid is a little pamphlet setting out the properties and uses of the substances within. Your mother bids you study it well before you employ them."

He handed over a cedar wood coffer, gold-sheathed throughout, the golden flasks and tools in its compartments worth a fortune. Speculative eyes turned to the Gentleman. Who would have thought his mariner sire to be a man of such means? But to Loric, the contents of this travelling pharmacy were worth more than their containers and his eyes blurred with tears as he read the inscriptions thereon, describing the rare essences and extracts they held.

"Ten thousand thanks, My Lord! Pray assure my dear mother I'll use the gift wisely and well."

The Elect clapped his shoulder. "Most willingly - and perchance sooner than you think," he added in undertone.

To Elinor he went on, "Wintermoon, the rest are for you. This first is a powerful distillation which will serve equally well in your homeland or ours." He proffered a decorative flask, bulbous at the base and tapering to a narrow neck, a likeness of the *passionata* blossom rendered in electrum with a sheaf of yellow gold stamens for its stopper.

Uncorking it in delightful anticipation, Elinor sniffed deep then hurriedly withdrew it from her nose. "An unusual perfume, My Lord! Whatever is it?"

Jehan laughed. "Not perfume, Madam, but *Quintessence*, or *Earthseed*. It's distilled from mainly, ah, vegetal sources, and a powerful agent of generation. Add but a drop to the soil and your plants, from a rose to a pine tree, will wax fecund."

"Thank you, Sir," she replied dubiously, resolving meanwhile to pour the horrid stuff away and use the flask for a more fragrant scent. But his next offering pleased her better: a sandalwood coffer containing layers of slippery white satin and lush, midnight-blue velvet, spangled here and there with scintillating gems; and nestling on top, a flat blue leather box.

"The raiment is in the Upper Angorian style and this suite of jewellery is designed to match it. There's a mirror set in the coffer lid, should you wish to try it now."

Elinor opened the box. Sparkling on a black velvet bed were a tiara, necklace and earrings of blazing diamond spikes, radiating from Fusions made of moonstone and star-sapphire.

"O, how beautiful! Majesty, please may I wear them?"

Thorund nodded. Berthe removed Elinor's crown and veil, unbound her hair and set the tiara and ear-rings to gleam among her glossy black tresses, while Fran slid off her high-collared surcote in order to fasten on the necklace and display its best effect.

Elinor turned in triumph to the room, beaming fit to match the diamonds. She saw her reflected image quiver as the hands holding the mirror began trembling, and Jehan's answering smile froze into rictus. Hah - this will be an easy husband to master, she thought smugly. Her gaze shifted to encompass the rest. All the Angorians were staring pole-axed, Iamis open-mouthed, a glass stilled on its passage to his lips. To her astonishment their expressions registered anything but mute appreciation. Indeed, Jehan had physically recoiled; all humour had fled his face along with its colour, leaving his countenance livid and ghastly. The moment lengthened agonisingly. She cried inwardly, what is it? What have I done? Name of God, why does someone not speak?

The silence was shattered by the fall of Iamis's goblet. "*Sol-Avia!* Shame on you, Madam, to flaunt such bloody spoils before us!"

Hakon leapt to his feet. "Infidel – that's no way to speak to Her Highness!" He drew his sword. "Apologise, Angorian, down on your brown face - or by the Wolf, I'll slice it from your skull!"

"*Kali-Mara!*" Nerya sprang up, a long, razor-sharp blade hissing from its scabbard. Nikos and the warriors followed suit, scanning round for the first sign of attack.

For a moment Thorund sat stunned and disbelieving. How, in the space of a minute, had they gone from gift-giving and amity to the brink of bloodshed? Then he too rose, menacing in black wolfskin and spiked silver crown.

"Stand down!" he thundered.

Sol-Lios bowed coldly and turned to his comrades. "Lower your swords, *Kali't'aia*. I beg pardon, King Thorund – but this," he gestured to Elinor's waistcoat, "has shocked us profoundly."

"Granted," said Thorund, equally cold, "provided you explain. Any lesser man's life would be forfeit for drawing blades in our presence. However," he glared at Hakon, "You weren't first to unsheath, and had some provocation – Warlord, hold thy peace!

'Yet we comprehend not the insult offered to our blameless Daughter. So enlighten us – or, by Fafnir's Mane, we'll see you banished from our realm never to return, no matter how compelling your persuasions!"

Elinor clasped her hands, praying that whatever her offence Jehan would cherish it, sweep out in high dudgeon and take his unpredictable folk back to Angor. In this prayer she was joined heartily by Hakon, whose rage diminished even as a wild, fresh hope bloomed in his heart - and by the Gard, holding their collective breath, fumbling for weapons and figuring their chances.

"I'll willingly explain," Jehan replied, "if I have your assurance that my company won't be molested. If so, we'll stand down. If not speak now, and we'll quit your House forthwith."

"Sol-Lios, whatever slight you've suffered, we swear it was unintended. Even now we can't conceive how the particulars of Her Highness's costume could precipitate such frenzy! But we give our word, as High King to Elect - no hand shall be raised against you and yours. Lord Hakon will pledge likewise."

Brows knit in fury, Hakon lowered his blade.

"Then come and give thy hand on it."

The Warlord complied with slow reluctance. Laying his palm atop those of Jehan and the King he rasped, "I too swear peace, by the Lair of the Wolf."

"And for abusing our guest Captain Iamis?" the King demanded, relentless.

Hakon's heart felt like to burst with rage as he made his bow and apology to the dark Mariner.

"Then let's smoke a peace-pipe," said Jehan, "And may I crave a boon? Pray, let that red jacket be removed. To speak of the matter is enough; to talk and look together, overmuch."

Elinor silently removed the offending garment. Gods, she raged, my prettiest new thing – now everyone can see how fat I'm become! She gave it to Fran, who rolled it up and slipped it under a chair; then in a sudden rush of temper, ripped off the new jewels and thrust them too into the startled maid's hands. Resuming her place humiliated and furious, she fixed the Elect with baleful glare.

Sol-Lios fired his bowl, held down a lungful for several long seconds and passed the pipe to Thorund, who likewise drew deep. The Angorian leaf was somewhat throat-tickling but deeply satisfying. Almost at once, the King felt his agitated pulse slow; he inhaled again and handed it to Elinor, who took a tiny sip for form's sake. Even that made her choke, and raising Loki to her face, she coughed discreetly into his coat. As the atmosphere thawed and thickened, a wild chatter broke out, punctuated here and there by bursts of hysterical laughter. Only the Archbishop abstained on religious grounds; no-one else dared refuse. Even Hakon was obliged to accept the pipe from his rival, though after a token puff he spat, rinsed his mouth out with ale and loaded his own bowl with honest Faalian leaf.

Suitably fortified, the Elect began. "To cut a sad story short:

that red garment is made from the breasts of a colony of *Sol-Avia* – or Sunbirds, in your tongue – their hue is uniquely distinctive. They were taken by vile pirates - and now we know by whom their plunder was received!" He sighed. "Aye, we knew the names and lineage of those birds, just as we knew the great cats whose fur trims their remains - *and* the many innocent Centrali, our allies and friends, who were murdered alongside.

'So to us, Madam, your waistcoat is a grim relic of the day when a whole community, from Elders to babes, was slaughtered with the foulest cruelty. I'll spare you the details – suffice to say, you'd do us great kindness if you wore it no more."

"I'm sorry to hear this," said King Thorund. "Be assured, we knew naught of the matter - nor of any offence Her Highness's garb would occasion. However, we can't speak the same for the procurer and supplier of these materials… and we would give much to know their source."

Elinor said haltingly, "A-all the rare stuffs for my wardrobe came from Merchant Radnor's emporium, M-my Lord King."

"Then we shall have words with Master Wolfblest," Thorund muttered under his breath; and aloud, "Well, Sol-Lios, let's not have our nascent friendship clouded. Our tradition of *were-gild* dictates the payment of blood-money for such offences - can we offer aught in reparation?"

Jehan bowed. "Thank you, Sir – indeed you can. Pray surrender the feathered garment for us to restore to the Centrali. They can best decide how to commemorate the fallen, and ensure that their dirge is not forgotten."

The Princess's humiliation reached a fresh nadir as Thorund obliged her to retrieve the waistcoat and present it to the Elect. Muttering dire imprecations under her breath she proffered the limp red bundle, which Sol-Lios passed reverently to Thesis.

"And now, My Lords and Ladies," said the King, "Let us retire - our guests will no doubt wish to rest before the evening's entertainment. See them to their quarters, Loric, and get the luggage stowed – we reconvene in the Great Hall at eighth."

Chapter 6: Meditations

"O, Madam! What did you think of Lord Jehan?" exclaimed Fran, the moment they reached the privacy of Elinor's suite. "And that one called Nery – I've never seen a man so fair!"

"Aye, but Lord Jehan's also fair, isn't he, Highness?" giggled Berthe. "If my heart wasn't already won I'd gladly give it to him, for all he has hair like a maiden's!"

"And his face is like a maiden's too," added Fran, "His cheeks are so smooth."

"Aye, Madam, you must make certain he's truly a man before your wedding night," Berthe teased, "Imagine the disappointment if his codpiece proves as empty as his chin is of whiskers!" The girls tittered rudely, cheeks pink and eyes streaming.

"Berthe Olsen, you're foul-mouthed as a fishwife and dirty-minded as a whore," snapped Elinor, disgusted. "I care not for the contents of the barbarian's breeches, for I will not have him!"

Their braying died abruptly. "What can you mean, Highness?" inquired Fran, "They're bonny big fellows - did you see how Lord Nerya leapt-"

"O, hush! No, I'll *not* wed Jehan! He's humiliated me, *ruined* my beautiful outfit and made a fool of me in front of the whole senior court! I'll go to the Warlord instead, and beg him make me safe from my Father and these Outlanders alike."

"Out of the cauldron into the fire-" Berthe broke off as a rap came at the outer door, announcing the delivery of Elinor's Angorian gifts. "O, but look, Highness, those lovely things… Lord Hakon could hardly woo you in such style!

'Pray, Madam, try on the gown – you could wear it this evening. And mayhap Lord Jehan will seem more agreeable now that the… er… misunderstanding's resolved. If not, there'll be time aplenty tomorrow to lay plans with the Warlord."

Elinor sighed. "O, I suppose so - and the jewels *were* becoming, weren't they? Did you mark the look on Baroness Ulfar's face?" she went on, brightening. "And there'll be minstrels and tumblers, and I'm so heartily sick of everlasting bloody roots and nuts… aye, why should the pagan spoil my fun? God knows I've laboured and suffered enough on his account to merit some reward!"

"That's the spirit, Madam," said Fran, busying herself with the chest. "Let's all dress up fine! I can't wait to see what the visitors will wear – I wonder what the ladies' gowns will be like?"

"Ho, you just want to see the Nery in tight breeks, I'll bet - as I do that Lord Nikos!" Berthe chuckled. "I hope it's not their fashion to wear long mantles- O, Highness, what a gorgeous satin!"

She held up a plain, close-fitting bone-white sheath, sleeveless and fastened up the back with small pearl buttons. It was clearly designed to be worn beneath the next item, a floor-length coat of midnight blue velvet, spangled all over with diamond stars and fastened with matching buttons. Keen seamstresses all, they fingered the beautiful fabrics, admiring the needlecraft and gems.

"Just look at the tiny stitches!" Berthe cried. "This velvet's as soft as moss – pray, Madam, put it on, else I shall don it myself! What a colour, what – O, what else is this?" She drew forth a suite of underwear in gossamer-fine white silk, lightweight yet warm: a chemise, stockings with silver ribbon garters, and a pair of short drawers. Another packet held a pair of little blue velvet slippers, buckled with diamonds to match the surcote.

A blush rose to Elinor's cheek. "Humph! The dress and shoes are lovely, but I can't wear these flimsy under-things – save for the stockings, they're nicer than my others. Fran, fetch my lightest stays, and a proper chemise and bloomers."

A little later, the three stood before her mirror wearing expressions of dismay.

"O, Madam, it's no use", panted Fran. "This robe fits so tight you can't walk unless we unbutton it to the knee - and the bodice is in the wrong place!" Indeed, it hung on the Princess like an ill-made sack, hemline askew, its glossy fabric pushed out awkwardly by her bulky stays.

"Dross and excrement!" she hissed in Angorian, savouring words privily coaxed out of Loric. Aloud, she replied, "Aye, it looks ridiculous, and doubtless the coat's cut the same... it seems I must after all don these indecent underclothes."

After they had unlaced her, Elinor shooed the girls out. Wriggling free of her stays she slipped on the silk chemise, pulled down her drawers, and stepped into the tiny Angorian version. Feeling all but naked she hurriedly threw the chill, slippery sheath over her head. Whispering over silk, it now moulded softly and perfectly to her contours as if it had been modelled on her very body. She flushed at her reflection, the lustrous satin emphasising the luminosity of her skin and jetty blackness of her hair. Gods, she thought in rising excitement, I look fantastical! On went the velvet coat and soft slippers, then with trembling fingers she plundered the jewel box, setting the tiara into her wild hair and fumbling with the necklace and earrings. Scintillating before the mirror in her new finery, an odd expression spread over her features.

"Hah!" she barked, "Look upon me, Sol-Lios, and weep! Fairer I am by far than thy countrywomen- I will vanquish thee quite, and then spurn thee! And I'll have none of that idiot Warlord, for all my threats and his dreaming on it. Nay, ye'll be poltroons before me - by the Gods, I'll have my fun tonight!"

Running gaily to unbar the door she cried, "Fran, Berthe, come see! O, come see the new Queen of Angor!"

"Come, friends," said Jehan when they were ensconced in the guest apartments, "we should take Counsel."

"Then, Sir, with your leave I'll retire," said Loric, "but if there's aught you need I'll be within call."

Jehan laughed. "No, Sorenssen - King Thorund bade you attend us, and I'll not gainsay him afresh this day! Nor have we made your acquaintance to let you go so soon - remain, and join our debate. Only tell me: is this apartment truly private?"

The Gentleman smiled. Knowing the Brethren's predilections, he had scoured the lodgings and sealed up several flues and vents they might have deployed for mischievous purposes.

"Privy enough, Sir - but if you'd prefer a sound-proof vault, follow me." Pulling aside a wall hanging he led the group through a short tunnel to a room carved deep into the Thorsgard's rocky heart, as sumptuously furnished as his master's private sanctuary and aglow with many candles. Leaving the Angorians to dispose themselves in comfort, he locked the outer doors then returned with a wide grin irradiating his features.

"So," said Jehan, "We're secured against surprise? Then well met, my friend – well met at last!"

When the general back-slapping and embracing had abated, the Counsel convened. All eyes turned to Iris, sitting cross-legged on a cushion with Kaa, almost invisible against her sable robe, nestled in her lap like a hen.

"Well, Seer, what did you make of all that?" asked Zafia.

She replied thoughtfully, "A good deal, by the grace of Kali's Eye… To take their greatest first: I See potential in King Thorund, for all that his aura's chill and drear. He's a man of good faith and good manners; his conscience is clear, Iamis - he knew naught of that bloody waistcoat's origin or meaning.

'As to the Princess, she burns cold and blue as hoar-frost! She craves to be the brightest jewel in a lover's heart; forsooth, the poor child has struck but a fitful gleam in her own father's. As yet untried, there is steel in her soul - and if she fuses her mettle with yours, Sol-Lios, what alloys you could cast! But she's young and wild, and there'll be a long road to travel betwixt now and then. Moreover, you have a rival... how the Lord Hakon detests you! His aura boils so bloody it blinds him to consequence; I've never seen such a jealous fury of a man. For the nonce, Thorund contains him; but left to himself, he'd kill you quick as thought."

"Pish," said Nerya, "He'd have to get through us first!"

Their discussions continued until Loric collected himself with a start and looked at the hourglass. "O no, I'm late," he cried, "I should be readying King Thorund for the feast!"

"Then tarry only to point us towards the Great Hall," said Jehan. "We'll make our own way there when we're changed."

"Aye," said Thesis, "But we've not heard the Seer's view on Lord Sigismund. Iris, what did you make of the Wolfsbane?"

The Seer's gaze came unfocussed, her eyes rolling back in their sockets as she spoke in strange, sonorous tones.

"It casts a black shadow, but it hath no aura. It is the Nadir."

Pinpricks of light crept over the causeway as lamplighters ignited torches along Thorshaven road. Before long, the Wolfenbirg was flickering like a golden serpent under the icy moonlight, crawling with folk who had followed an Angorian baggage train from the harbour then remained to watch local dignitaries making their stately progression up to the Castle. Tremendous excitement permeated the crowd; such was their desire to participate in the festivities that pockets of spontaneous revelry kept breaking out, especially in the vicinity of bottles and flasks, and they cheered most heartily whenever their *thegns* passed by.

Radnor Wolfblest was among the guests, waving in lordly fashion from the window of his fine wagon. I'm made for life, he thought, standing so high in old Siggi's favour! There will be Her Highness, magnificent in stuffs from my store... and all those noble ladies, avid to ape her... what a market there'll be for my goods by the morrow – that next cargo will sell like hot cakes!

His sense of self-importance inflated still further when a reception party at Wolfsmaw stepped forward to meet him. It gave way to affront as they hauled him down, and its sad remnant evaporated in loud and woeful terror when they clapped him in chains and dragged him off unceremoniously. The horses were turned about and his wagon, now containing only a squad of surly Gards sent to impound his stores, clopped back to Thorshaven amid amused jeers from the onlookers.

Poring over the *Lay of Angor*, King Thorund failed to notice the advancing hour. At first he had merely leafed through the illuminated pages marking sections of interest, intending to return to them later. But attracted by some apocalyptic illustrations, he became engrossed in the history of a bloody schism that had in ancient time brought Angor to the brink of utter ruin.

Chapter finished, he sat back and exhaled a long breath. "Sol-Lios, you spoke true; the soul of your realm *does* lie bared in this book," he murmured. His eyes turned involuntarily to the glass and he leapt up. "Ach, but I'm late!" He crammed the crown back onto his head as Sorenssen skidded into the chamber, red-faced in a flurry of apologies.

"Why, Loric," Thorund chuckled, "'Tis the first time I've seen you so out of countenance! Come, man, I've no time to change. Just fetch my mantle – we must bustle."

Others had been less cavalier about time. Marriageable noble maidens had long been preparing with tweezers and unguents, and by evening could hardly sit still for impatience. The most daring wore necklines cut low, their stays tightly laced to push up milky bosoms framed temptingly in swansdown or fox-fur, their comparatively wasp-like waists accentuated by jewelled chatelaines. Not to be outdone either by their womenfolk or the Angorians, the men sported knee-length tunics brightly dyed and enriched with embroidery, with chains of office hanging heavily across their breasts, and their hands weighed down with loyalty rings.

By seventh glass, knots of courtiers dripping furs, massy brooches and niello-inlaid, pattern-welded blades began to stroll, affecting nonchalance, towards the Great Hall. Here minstrels were tuning in the gallery and Gentlemen putting the finishing touches to long trestles creaking under the King's best plate and glasses while Endrik Treasurer hovered at the back, inventory clutched in his sweating hand, terrified lest any of the precious tableware be broken or misappropriated. As the hour wore on with no sign of the King or delegation, dignitaries from Thorshaven started to arrive and circle like wary dogs, scanning each other's finery with jealous eyes, and jockeying for position by the Great Door through which the guests should enter. The atmosphere became charged, the crowd tensing each time a fanfare blew and subsiding audibly when yet another local baron or *thegn* was ushered in.

In the meantime the Angorians had followed a short-cut Loric had shown them, entering the Hall through a small service door far removed from the main portal. They were immediately swallowed by the pack of lesser courtiers relegated to a normally poor view at the back. Folk flocked to greet them and by the time the royal fanfare sounded, the Hall was thick with merriment and fragrant smoke. It fell silent at Thorund's entrance, the throng parting for Jehan who strode up and swept a deep bow.

"Forgive us, noble host - we came a back way from our lodgings and arrived unannounced into the midst of celebration."

"There's naught to forgive, Sir; go where you will, and do as you please. And pray pardon my own lateness, though you've only yourself to blame – I was detained by your fascinating gift!"

Elinor watched the hourglass empty by another quarter. "Why am I not summoned – 'twill surely have started by now... let's to the Hall!"

"O, Madam, d' ye think we should?" said Bea. "King Thorund must be late, and that's why we're not sent for. It wouldn't be proper for us to arrive before His Majesty."

"Well, I *will* go!" the Princess cried. "There must be some error – I'll see his herald whipped for not fetching me timely."

They set off in nervous excitement, Loki, groomed to within an inch of his life, hanging in the crook of Elinor's arm. As they neared the Great Hall, sounds of merriment grew louder, but the anteroom was empty and no-one was manning the door.

Fuming, Elinor bade Fran peep through the crack. A few moments later she turned back, flushed with fun.

"O, Madam, the Door-staff are engaged with our visitors!"

"What d'ye mean? What on Urth are they doing? Let me see - O, do move aside, Fran!" She pushed the doors a chink wider and peered out. "Well, really – they might have waited!"

Within the party was in full swing, thanks to the courtiers gathered in animated, curious knots around the Outlanders. Closest to view she glimpsed Iactus, splendid in emerald-green doublet with a gold Tree of Fusion pinned over his heart, close-fitting brown hose, and brown calf-length boots. With him were three similarly-clad strangers,

High from the ships lately arrived with the baggage cart: Dimitri to care for his human comrades; Florian to care for the horses; and Dario, their driver and general assistant. These latter were responsible for her current predicament, having purloined the herald's trumpets which they were attempting to play, more for their own edification than that of their audience.

"Well, *really!* How dare they? Only wait till my Father hears of this," the Princess exclaimed furiously, "he'll have them all flog- O!" She broke off, rooted with astonishment. There! King Thorund was *already there* – through a shift in the crowd she had just seen his silver-crowned mane. "Great Wolf," she gasped, "How can he permit such laxity? Why, Sol-Lios, you've much to answer for – but first I'll put a stop to this nonsense!"

A moment later, one of the heralds felt a tugging at his buskin. The Princess's lapdog had fastened sharp little teeth on his boot and was trying valiantly to tug him towards the Great Doors, where a white finger beckoned through the crack.

Fran and Berthe winced empathically as their mistress's wrath descended on the luckless trio's heads.

"...now get back to your places - and if there's any such folly again I'll have the skin off your backs for a purse!

'What are you waiting for? Go play the bloody fanfare!"

Reeling from unfamiliar smokeweed and verbal assault, they rushed to obey. At long last the Great Doors swung wide and the heralds' trumpets, blown hard in pure terror, rang out.

Elinor arranged her features along more serene lines while the court resumed a semblance of its usual order. The central aisle respectfully cleared; interspersed down its length, Angorian Blades stood smartly to attention in their dress uniform of red coats, white breeches and black boots, their swords held upright in martial salute; and at its head waited King Thorund, with Jehan alongside.

In the gallery, minstrels struck up a slow and stately air. Having long contemplated this entrance Elinor had ordered the music specially, its tempo enabling her to proceed at such pace that all the ladies had ample time to envy her costume. She felt exquisitely smug. Her original gown for this evening had been fine enough, but this exotic rig was daringly unique – an unprecedented coup in the court fashion stakes! Taking a deep breath of lavender and orris-root from the body-warmed satin she set out in triumph, twinkling like a starry midnight sky.

"*Pulchrissima princessa!*" Elinor translated Captain Iamis's appreciative remark among the buzz of comments and scattered applause, and her spirits soared higher. But as she swished on down the aisle, to her astonished chagrin began discreet nudges and quickly-concealed smiles among the noble ladies. Even worse was a snort or two of mirth from their ill-bred maids, and in her train, Fran and Berthe hurriedly dropped their eyes for fear they might join in. For it seemed that while Angor's tailors had abundant fine fabrics at their disposal, they possessed a dearth of patterns. Save for colour and jewelled insignia, all the men wore identical doublet and hose; ultramarine and white with black boots for the Captain, with Thesis in violet and dove grey; and as the ladies stepped forward to greet her, she understood the laughter at her expense – they had fared no better! The Healer's outfit was the exact counterpart of her own, albeit in purple satin under a cote of rose-pink velvet enlivened with flowers of amethyst and pink diamond; even her jewellery was similar, only wrought in red gold with gems to match her coat and slippers. Iris alone bore an individual touch: a short cape of the finest feathers Magpie, Raven and *Sol-Avia* could donate, fastened with a diamond Eye, the iridescent blue-black plumes setting off her olive face and another huge diamond that blazed from her brow. Her sheath was black satin, her surcote a sleeveless net of jet beads punctuated by diamonds and fire-opals, scintillating in an ever-changing play of light-in-darkness as she moved. Kaa was perched on her wrist like a falcon; even the wretched bird, Elinor observed sourly, sported diamonds on its breast.

Pah, she thought; in Angor, gemstones must sprout from the earth like weeds, if even beasts can afford them! So much for Jehan's gifts; a flask of stinking compost; ornaments of commonplace type; and apparel of common cut, less rich than this black witch wears!

With the reverse of her discomfiture Zafi advanced smiling broadly. "Hail, Wintermoon!" she cried, "How lovely you look in the fashion of our homeland - behold, are we not fair?"

Hel take them, the Princess said to herself, but I shall outface them all! She stretched her lips in a fair facsimile of Zafia's expression and forced a glad tone.

"Good evening, Ladies. Aye, fair indeed - and what a rare compliment, to be styled as your twin." It was true enough, she grudgingly conceded, looking closer. The Healer had kohl-rimmed her eyes and enhanced the flush of her cheeks and lips with carmine, the little cabochons of amethyst, ruby and rosy diamonds that bloomed everywhere suiting her complexion exceedingly. The darkly smouldering Iris was beautiful too, her golden eyes made even more disquieting by their rim of black make-up.

Just then they were joined by the King and Elect. Next to her soberly-clad father Jehan looked bright as a sunny afternoon in boots and doublet of fine tawny leather heavily tooled with gold, a cloth-of-gold lining gleaming from collar and cuffs and welling through slits in the sleeves. Over his left shoulder hung a short cloak of sky blue satin, also lined with cloth-of-gold, clasped with a Fusion brooch of sapphire and diamond. He had gold rings in his ears, and on his head a gold fillet set with a mighty yellow-hued diamond in a burst of golden sunbeams.

"Good evening, Madam," said Thorund, a meaningful twinkle in his eye, "Angorian *couture* becomes you exceedingly well - eh, Sol-Lios?

'And now if you'll kindly excuse me, I should go and mingle. Daughter, you can entertain My Lord Elect until dinner, can you not?"

Chapter 7: The Great Feast

Irked by her father's transparent manoeuvre, Elinor took her suitor's proffered arm and they set out on stately promenade, watched by the speculative court. When they had strolled beyond earshot of the rest Sol-Lios said quietly,

"My apologies for this afternoon, Madam - I regret that under the circumstances, I couldn't admire your red waistcoat."

She lowered her eyes, annoyed and embarrassed. "Pray don't remind me – I find the matter too painful."

"Very well - then what shall we speak of? Come, Elinor-Lunaia, let's start afresh! Duties of State are upon us - we may as well make them pleasant."

"As you say, Sol-Lios – let's make the best of it," she replied, hardly flattered.

To change the subject, Jehan looked to Loki and tickled his silvery ears. "A fine animal – an Imperial Seekhound, is he not? Are ye not, *cheri*?" he slipped into Faali, "Thou art fair, my good boy!"

Loki pricked his ears at the tongue recalled dimly from puppyhood, and to Elinor's chagrin, licked Jehan's hand. Bloody little turncoat, she thought, bought cheap with a few foreign words!

"You've a way with beasts, My Lord! But Loki is undiscriminating curious – doubtless you smell strange to him."

"Doubtless, Lunaia," Jehan agreed, blandly. "Seekhounds are *connoisseurs* of aroma, so it's hardly to be wondered at."

Elinor looked puzzled. "What's this name you keep calling me, this 'Lunaia'?"

"It's derived from the name of a Goddess, Madam. Its literal translation is 'Moon-Daughter', the counterpart of my title, 'Sol-Lios'. However," he qualified in Gondaran, "'Sun-Son' sounds foolish in this tongue, so pray use the Angorian form!"

She nodded. "A pretty conceit... but the Moon is surely no goddess, just a stone like this Urth."

"And one of Creation's mightiest offspring! Isn't that worthy of veneration?"

"Hmm, I suppose... Who is this goddess, then? I would know what I'm likened to before assuming her title."

The Elect grinned. "Perhaps I shouldn't say, for fear your head will be swelled! But it suits you well, Moon-daughter; for your face, shining among your raven hair, appears to me like Luna Herself, glimpsed through a bare tree at midnight."

Elinor almost smiled; it seemed a genuine, if high-blown, compliment.

"Besides," he went on, "Luna is the female Quintessence, the very throb and pulse of life. She moves the Ocean and swells the river tide, calling the fishes to spawn and all creatures to come into season..." Warming with enthusiasm, he failed to notice the dawning horror in her eyes, "...just as She governs the tides in Womankind's bodies, making them fertile. Luna waxes as the ripening womb, the swelling breast and gravid belly; Her wane is the flow of life-giving milk, the letting down of finished blood-"

"Stop, for the love of God!" Elinor choked. "How dare you, *how dare you*, speak to me thus?"

Jehan looked nonplussed. "How 'thus'? You asked, and I answered. What's wrong-"

"Wrong?" she hissed, "Hardly 'wrong' – it's an abject disgrace! Some matters men do not speak of, should not even *know* of... ach, you are filthy! I *forbid* you to give me that horrible name - never address me in such wise again!"

The Elect guffawed. "Ah, Princess – if that's the tone you customarily take with your suitors, small wonder you've remained so long unmated!"

"Good evening, Sir." Iris stepped into the shadowy corner where the Torturer lurked, her eyes glittering fit to match her dress and a naughty smile twisting her lips. "My Lord... Hel, is it not? Since you've evaded our party all evening, it seems I must effect mine own introductions. I'm Iris Kali-Ra... and to pay for your discourtesy, you shall now greet me according to my station, and in the fashion of my homeland."

Before Hel could protest she cupped his face in both hands, drew him towards her with surprising strength and closed her mouth on his in a warm, generous kiss. She held it for several exquisite seconds; kissed the Torturer, in fact, until his legs buckled and he fell panting to his knees, crimson to the top of his dome.

"I'm delighted to make your acquaintance at last," she smiled sweetly down. "But be not so formal – arise, I implore!"

As she helped him to his feet her feathered cape fell open, baring her left upper arm and the swirling Eyes and triskele motifs spiralling round it from elbow to shoulder in a riot of indigo inks. Hel was enormously impressed. Bowing low, he pressed his lips to the vast diamond on her fourth finger; then muttering apologies and promises to

61

return, begged to be excused.

Leaning over the garderobe's gaping shaft he yanked open his breeches, his thunderous heartbeat and erection subsiding in the familiar ammoniac stench. She had kissed him! The beautiful lady he had covertly studied all night had deliberately sought him out and kissed him! Hel was quite overcome. Since rising to prominence in the Archbishop's service, his sex-life had been limited to raping the odd comely prisoner, or bribing a whore to endure his attentions; respectable womenfolk, down to the lowliest scullery-wench, avoided him like contagion. Indeed, the only creature not to shun him was Loki who, attracted by his powerful odours, would slip his leash and hunt the Torturer out whenever occasion permitted; and for the most part, Hel was entirely content with this state of affairs.

But the Seer had him shocked and disturbed, afire with furious, curious lust. She was barely even a woman as he understood the sex, standing there dauntless as King Thorund, displaying the needle-workings on her tender flesh - and capable of bringing the Head Torturer of Gondarlan to his knees with a simple caress! His groin twitched afresh at the memory. He quickly fastened his breech, crossed to the washstand and doused his freshly shaved pate with cold water; then loins duly girt, he drew a steadying breath and strode forth.

Iris watched him reappear, sliding his powerful bulk through the crowd as easily as a scalpel parts skin. Behind his dungeon pallor he was not unhandsome, she mused; and by Kali, what a prodigy he seemed! She grinned in the shadows as Hel sat down beside her with a leathery squeak, and accepted a pipe from her hand. The unlikely couple smoked in silence for some minutes, the Torturer's dark eyes raking in every exotic detail of her face.

"Well, My Lady," he managed at length, "Is the price for my want of courtesy now paid in full?"

"By no means, My Lord!" she dimpled. "For shunning us so long and so harshly, you must now sit with me and Zafia at table, and entertain us in a proper hostly manner!"

King Thorund surveyed proceedings at his High Table, wryly amused by the seating plan Loric had devised. Hakon's crony Baron Ulfar was sandwiched uncomfortably between two Kalaia; subdued by the separation from his entourage, he was contributing little to the talk. Predictably, the Archbishop and Warlord were also cold and taciturn, giving Thesis and the Speakers, their immediate neighbours, a hard time of things. To his right, Sol-Lios was faring little better with Her

Highness, and Thorund rolled his eyes at their perversity.

Luckily not all his subjects were in such ungracious temper. Ragnar Thoralson was deeply engrossed with Captain Iamis, and Olaf Steward proudly holding forth to Iactus on royal housekeeping. Even the servants looked cheerful, enjoying the novelty of exotic company; and to general astonishment Hel, a rare visitor to the Hall, was rising spectacularly to the occasion. Sitting between Iris and Zafi, he studiously ignored the Wolfbane's garnet stare, his eyes turning to the Seer with such keen interest and naked longing that for once he appeared almost human. And for once, that was how Hel felt – he was a Gondaran Lord, by the Wolf, noble, virile... attractive! As a romantic coup, his monopolising the two beautiful ladies was unprecedented, and gave him a sense of unusual power. Even if he was being made butt of some strange foreign joke, the Torturer cared not – he was enjoying himself.

Their conversation ran hither and yon. Hel responded with increasing confidence to the flirtatious banter, even managing a few unpolished compliments on the ladies' evening gowns.

To his intense discomfiture Iris responded in kind, laying wondering fingers upon his sleeve. "And this is a fascinating suit, Sir – how did you come by it?"

"What?" said Hel, starting guiltily, "This? O, this is... um, it was... ah – I think I had better not say."

"Not say?" Zafia giggled, "Why not? You should be proud of your tailor – it fits like a second skin, and the leather's surpassingly soft."

The Torturer swallowed. "Nay, Lady. Truly, you don't want to know – and I don't want to tell you."

This created an intolerable mystery; the Angorians teased and cajoled and reasoned and pleaded until eventually Iris laughed,

"Enough pointless evasions, My Lord – an' you love me, tell me where you got this bloody suit, or forever forfeit my regard."

Hel sighed. "That's what I fear will happen if I speak, Madam! I'd really rather not - but as you insist..."

Hel's suit had come from Arnor, chief of Grunewald's Druids; a preserver of the Old Ways, a focus for dissent among the common folk – and sworn enemy of the Archbishop. Sigismund's Brethren had tracked Arnor high and low through Grunewald, persecuting his disciples most ruthlessly until he was finally captured and dragged in chains to the Fastness. Hel was well pleased; he had been turning a concept around in his mind for some time, but lacked a suitable subject upon whom to experiment – until now. Arnor, a big, corpulent man, had been amply nourished in concealment by the Resistance. However, recent experiences had reduced him somewhat, and by the time he reached the Pit, shackled and filthy, the skin of his once-proud belly hung flaccid and loose.

At first, in a starkly clean cell with an ominous drain in the floor, Arnor endured nothing worse than ministrations with cut-throat razor and hot wax that left him devoid of all body hair. Thenceforth he was cleansed within and without, washed, shaved and plucked, lubricated with greasy unguents, obliged to swallow flagons of water, and fed on skimmed milk and thin gruel just sufficient to keep starvation at bay. His frame rapidly wasted and dwindled, its pampered skin gleaming whitely in the gloom of his cell. Hunger was an almost constant torture, but otherwise he encountered surprisingly little physical pain - until the day Hel commenced his long-planned Design.

The unfortunate Druid was chained motionless, flat on his face, while a ticklish brush applied some unseen image to his back; then his torment began in earnest as Hel cut it deep into his skin. After an hour that reduced Arnor to a shrieking curtain of blood, the Torturer judged his labour sufficient for the day. The Druid was sluiced clean and his wounds attended solicitously, some areas irrigated, others rubbed with stinging ointments while Arnor prayed for death, his back afire from neck to buttocks.

Alas, Hel was as skilful in the prolonging of life as he was in its taking, and day after day Arnor was subjected to the agony of the Design, sometimes for minutes and sometimes for hours while the Torturer painstakingly developed the image. At length, he enjoyed a brief respite while his final wounds healed; then Hel slit the skin around his neck, wrists and ankles, opened up his central seam and with a horrible ripping sound peeled him like a rabbit. The perfectly intact hide was taken away to be tanned and dyed black, while Arnor's screaming scarlet body was suspended in a bath of mild tepid brine. By dint of the most painstaking nursing, the poor flayed Druid survived to see the results of this project: his hide snugly tailored, adorning the Torturer's frame; and worst blasphemy of all, wrought in the bas-relief of scars worked up from his living flesh - a snarling likeness of the architect of all Grunewald's woes, Great Fafnir Himself.

For the benefit of his listeners, Hel summarised Red Arnor's tale in a line, then resolutely changed the subject. "*I* made the suit - from a man-skin I flayed and tanned myself."

The opening toasts given and returned, minstrels struck up a gay tune while diners fell to on the appetiser, a collation of breads, cheeses and cured meats with a shredded cabbage salad. Their next course was fruits of the sea: shellfish, soused herrings, caviar, baby eels, fried whitebait, smoked salmon and steaks of seal, whale and porpoise, with laver bread and a briny samphire pickle on the side. This was followed by roasted swans, geese, partridges, pheasants and pigeons accompanied by their eggs, coddled and preserved, all washed down with chilly white Grunewald wine.

Then to rapturous applause, a team of staggering scullions hauled in the *Prey of Fafnir*, a great bull moose stripped of its internal organs and stuffed with a reindeer, itself hollowed out and stuffed with pheasants and rabbits. The offal had been minced fine, mixed with barley and herbs and packed back into the body cavities, then the whole thing glazed with mead and slowly roasted. Golden and crackling, the tender moose now reposed majestically on a huge silver platter, shored up by ramparts of roast turnips and flat field mushrooms, and pouring forth clouds of mouth-watering steam.

Hampered by his silver wolf-mask the Archbishop enjoyed, in lieu of gluttony, ample opportunity to observe his fellow diners. The Thorsgarders he saw waxing loud, their faces red and brows moist; many had thrown off their cloaks and rolled up their sleeves not to soil their fine cuffs in the gravy. Hakon's ire had rather stimulated his appetite than otherwise, and beard shiny with grease he dismembered fowl after fowl, ripping the flesh as if it were Jehan's throat and cracking the bones between his teeth.

By contrast, the guests seemed poor, finicky eaters and Sigismund felt a creeping chill in his vitals. They had helped themselves only modestly to the earlier courses, taking their wine well diluted with water, while the *Kali't'aia* among them drank no alcohol at all. He shuddered, half in fear and half in sickening, covetous envy. What discipline – *they're* the Pack of Fafnir, not the soft topers Hakon calls an army, he thought bitterly. Do they plan to slay us all, and have the whole Fastness taken by morning? To be sure, the Warlord would leap to battle in an instant should they rise... but he's so foully drunk I dare say even their painted whores could best him. The rest are no fitter, save Her Highness, who still looks no more enchanted than I, but *she* can't wield a sword - what peril! Perforce I must trust their mealy-mouthed, pacific reputation; but I don't! Every man has his price - I'll lay this Jehan and his war-dogs are no different... His countenance lightened a trifle. Aye, they *must* have their weakness and I shall find it, if we survive this blasted feast! Could I but bend them to the Wolf, not a force left on Urth could withstand me - neither Hakon nor Thorund himself. O, curse this hollow festival! I need peace to ponder matters...

Meanwhile King Moose was rent asunder and devoured with unbelievable speed. Belts loosened, greasy chops a-glisten in the torchlight, the courtiers sat belching and replete, awaiting the coming entertainment. This interlude after the main course was an essential feature of Gondaran feasts. The sweating kitchen staff knew the worst of their labour was over, and while the carnage of the meat courses was cleared, they scavenged their own meals from the ravaged platters. The diners likewise required a period of recuperation following their protein overload and after a purgative pipe or two, the garderobes began to reek in preparation for the sweet courses. Minstrels played softly to soothe the court's digestive processes, and sleek junior courtiers more interested in romance than in gorging began to circulate, and some to dance a little. Others, among them the Angorians, were content to sit and converse. Hakon and those who liked them not withdrew further into sullen drunkenness; the rest, taking lead from their uncharacteristically sociable King, relaxed into merry bonhomie.

Iris, averting her gaze from Hel's ardent face, smiled at their rosy swirling auras, pierced hither and yon by the white radiance of her countrymen and the keen flames of the Warriors. She perceived no serious danger, culinary or otherwise, afoot for this evening. The puff of pure black ire emanating from the Archbishop was not lost upon her, though it concerned her little; she knew that however he might rage, Sigismund was powerless to move against them that night. Nonetheless, she could feel the malevolence of his stare through the garnet eye-pieces of his mask, and was unsurprised when the Wolfsbane rose to his feet.

"Majesty, I'm feeling unwell – have I thy leave to retire?"

The King eyed him shrewdly. "Certainly - I trust no tainted portion has slipped by your food taster, Sir! Happily no-one else seems to have taken more than the usual degree of harm from their dinner– but be assured, henceforth not a dish nor a glass shall leave the kitchens without it has the closest scrutiny!"

With Sigismund and his Brethren departed, the atmosphere perceptibly lightened. Thorund thought, I feel very kingy tonight. *Kingly*, he quickly amended, suppressing a chuckle. In honour of his guests he had bidden Loric serve him Angorian style, drinking only a few spoonfuls of wine and that in plenty of water, though he had smoked their fine leaf with abandon. He looked on the scene with satisfaction: his magnificent Hall, blazing with firelight, boards groaning under their load of fine plate; his courtiers, bless their scheming, avaricious souls; and ripe for alliance with this insanely rich foreigner, his beautiful, accomplished Daughter. The King rolled his eyes to the roof beams; said beautiful daughter was evidently piqued, ignoring the Elect in favour of her ladies and a feigned interest in the musical entertainment. Silly little vixen, he thought, there's no pleasing her; well, piqued or no, she *shall* go with Sol-Lios and must learn to bear it with better grace than this! Still, she's lovely in her new finery and Jehan does not appear too displeased, in spite of her behaviour…

Around him the discourse was far-reaching, peppered with jokes, puns and humorous digressions as it flashed from subject to subject. Angorian cuisine, its mainstay *passionata*, and the amusing consequences of overindulgence; the geography of their two lands; the curious differences in manners and mores; all these and more were debated. Engaged by their good-natured chaffing, (in which his own nobles were too stiff-necked to indulge), the King was emboldened to remark,

"Sol-Lios, will you make a fit husband for my daughter, or will it be the other way round? Truly, with your timid bibbing and girlish locks, I begin to wonder!"

Jehan drew himself up in mock hauteur. "If you seek to insult me, you fail pitifully – girls possess so many virtues I'm honoured by the comparison! In any event," he cheekily flipped one of Thorund's plaits, "Who art *thou* to criticise a fellow for the length of his hair, Master Wolfsmane?"

Amid general laughter, Nery added, "The reverse is true also! You can't insult an Angorian woman by calling her 'mannish', if that means she's confident and strong, practical and capable, rational and masterful, or whatever forceful characteristics are wrongly considered sole province of the male."

Awareness of a chance for legitimised hostility penetrated Hakon's clouded brain. "Then what if I called you a dunghill, Sol-Lios - a soft pile of Southron shite?" he demanded. "Wriggle out of that, you slippery worm - or prove the lie of it with your blade!"

Iactus leapt up. "I claim the right to answer *this* call! For your highest offence is our Highest compliment," he punned, "In explanation whereof I shall sing you the Song of the *Hai*."

As his companions clapped out the rhythm, he began in a light baritone,

"O sacred the shit- pile, the symbol of Naume,
Swarming with life, the transient home,
Of rot and decay, of maggot and fly,
Of worm and of beetle, of fungus and slime!
Thou art the Quintessence, the fountain of birth,
And source of all being on Gaia's green earth!"

Several verses followed in similar vein, and Iactus finished to generous applause.

"So I'm sorry to disappoint you, Lord Hakon," he smiled, with infuriating good humour. "Dross is a fact of life. If we couldn't void, we'd swell with meat and drink till we burst asunder; if we couldn't die and decay, Gaia would fill till we stood upon one another's very shoulders. And where would we be if 'twere not for the carrion eaters - drowned in a sewer of corpses and garbage!

'We *Hai* are devotees of such matters. We can't claim our labour sweet-smelling, and since we toil aboard *Quintessence* like scarabs on a dunghill, your comparison's not inapt. But no matter – all shit washes off at the end of the day."

Hakon glowered. "If the cap fits, then wear it! Though not even a Gondaran *lass* would bear such denigration."

Jehan shrugged. "What's the direst insult save a collection of syllables, a momentary wave of sound upon the ears? Life's too full of tangible concerns to waste time on such ephemera. Deeds, not words, cause the only true offence."

"More pretty words from the pretty fellow - you do but hide your cowardice behind 'em, the better to swallow grossness without challenge!" Hakon drew his sword and slammed the blade flat on the table.

"Witness my *deed* then - I call thee out, poltroon! Now act, or stand before Her Highness and this Court hoist by thine own petard."

Chapter 8: The Challenge

Elinor's nails dug into her palms – was she about to witness the Elect spitted like a pig by her unlikely champion? She glanced gratefully to Hakon standing unsteadily defiant and felt sudden wild hope drain away. He was drunk, he was bloated and slow and he was a head shorter than Jehan, who had by now risen and lifted the sword by the tip of its blade.

Hefting it easily, Jehan balanced it for a moment on his outstretched palm then flipped it up, caught it neatly by the hilt and sighted dangerously down its length.

"A fine weapon, Sir, if a trifle heavy for my taste." He slid it back across the cloth. "But I should scorn to wield it against a man in his cups. Do be seated, My Lord – let's not press the point."

"Cups or no," Hakon roared, "I'm the better man, needing no shield of fancy words to cower behind! Poltroon I called you, right enough – now stand and fight!"

"Peace, Warlord!" King Thorund snapped. "The Elect has made fair answer, fairer than you deserve, so let be. Even the Almighty Wolf doesn't harry his prey from the warmth of his den, with a bellyful of moose! Sit down and calm down - they're bringing the refresher, which God knows we all stand in need of."

"Nay, how can we leave this unchallenged?" protested Nikos. "Our Elect has been called poltroon and coward, and I'll not let such an untruth stand. Yet proof of valour doesn't necessitate bloodshed… what say you, Nery – instead of a duel, shall we show them our Way?"

"What Way is this?" asked Thorund, intrigued. "Show us, by all means - only partake first of this refreshment, I trow you don't have its like at home!"

The King was right. Frozen dishes were almost unheard of in Angor, and his guests exclaimed in delight over the lemon sherbets, mint water ices and frothy elderflower sorbets served to waken jaded palates for the final course. This consisted of rich trifles, syllabubs and custards, with the centrepiece of a prodigious wolf-shaped cake. Covered in blood-red marchpane highlighted with edible silver leaf, it glared with its glazed cherry eyes, snarled with its blanched almond fangs, and crouched as if ready to spring from the moat of blazing *aquavit* around its silver platter.

After a frugal spoonful of sorbet the Speakers withdrew to work out their routine. Hakon subsided in a rumbling sulk, and a speculative buzz ran round the tables. Ordinarily, this was Elinor's favourite part of the evening, affording opportunities for discreet gluttony while the court's attention was directed towards musicians, tumblers and fools. But tonight her nerves were so jangled she could swallow scarcely a mouthful, and she cursed Sol-Lios anew. She was further exasperated to see him utterly heedless of her emotional state, unaware even that she had ignored him this last half-glass, so engrossed was he in conversation with her Father! Still, at least there would be a new entertainment to watch...

A space had been cleared at the end of the Hall, and folk crowded round to get a better view. The Speakers doffed their crimson jackets revealing sleeveless singlets of black buckskin which allowed the onlookers to appraise them like bloodstock. The men laid mental wagers on which should prove the most able while their ladies simply palpitated, for in many respects they were equally matched: long legged and broad shouldered, with tanned skins taut over sculpted muscle and seamed here and there with silvery scars. Nikos was by far the most massive with clear advantage in terms of weight and power, but the lighter Nerya looked lithe and agile, likely to prove much the quicker.

After a bow to the audience and each other, the exercise began. The stylised moves, slow at first, gradually became faster and more complex, incorporating spinning and flying kicks that drew gasps from the crowd. As their battleground grew ever larger, spectators at the front backed away nervously but the violence remained under impeccable control, even when Nikos aimed a whirling kick of such ferocity at his opponent's groin that Nerya had to spring high in the air to avoid it.

Fran clapped her hands over her mouth to suppress a scream, a foot having whipped past her face close enough to stir her hair. But her hero was safe, seeming to hang momentarily suspended at the apex of his leap before lashing out a boot that would surely have broken the other's neck had it connected. Nikos instantly dropped to a squat then threw himself over in a back flip, landing poised on the balls of his feet to meet Nerya's next assault. With that, the contest swept away, and Fran breathed again. She greeted the end of their unarmed display with relieved and rapturous applause, only to gasp when the pair drew their swords and took up position once more. Soon the blades were flickering and dancing in whistling arcs and she held her breath anew, expecting either Speaker to lose a head or limb at any second.

Luckily, the Kalaia were so attuned to one another's fighting styles they could have given the demonstration blindfolded. Had their battle been real, it was hard to say which would have prevailed. On points, Nikos might have taken the victory in unarmed combat, while in swordsmanship, Nery's lightning reflexes and astounding agility carried the day.

When they were done, the court roared appreciation, Fran jumping up and down and blowing fervent kisses. What a man, she thought, strong as a wolf, graceful as a deer and fair as a beardless boy! She felt faint with joy when Nery caught her eye, winked, and blew a kiss in return.

"Bravo, My Lords," a sarcastic voice cried from the back. "A flashy show - huh! I'll lay those be dress swords wi' blades dull as your pricks! It suffices not for me – I still want to see what yon laddie-lass can do with a real weapon in his fist!" Hakon reeled into view, staggering under the weight of two broadswords he had lugged down from the wall. Dropping one contemptuously at Jehan's feet, he stifled a hiccup and appealed to Thorund,

"Sire, we've witnessed these… Guests flaunt their so-called prowess. Pray let me do the same, in the name of Gondarlan! Let this Sol-Lios try his skill with a doughty Gondaran blade, and prove he be a meet suitor for Her Highness!"

The King struck his brow with the heel of his hand. "Very well," he said coldly, "You've tried me beyond endurance this day - Sol-Lios, if you'll stand against this buffoon then do so, and slay him without compunction.

'There, Hakon; on your own head be it."

The Warlord bellowed triumphantly. Breathing heavily, he fixed smouldering eyes on Jehan and inflated with fury, his inebriation driven out to a degree by the pound of adrenalin. Lifting the broadsword with a grunt of effort, he began to swing it and courtiers pressed back in alarm. Carried by the weight of the weapon he lunged wildly at the Elect, who had not yet picked up his own blade. The encounter was over in a second. Jehan side-stepped, ducked under the steel arc and swept Hakon's feet from under him with an outstretched leg. The Warlord fell headlong, and landing heavily on his swollen belly, lost breath and dinner simultaneously while his weapon spun away harmlessly across the floor.

Jehan raised an eyebrow at Zafi and Loric. Together they hauled Hakon to a chair for the Healer to tend him while Iactus and his High comrades helped Gentlemen clean up the mess.

With order restored Nerya said, "Our point's made, My Lord. We're none of us cowards… and to refute your final accusation – Niki, if you please!"

With the flat of his sword Nikos flicked up a lock of Nerya's ponytail, and as the tress came down, turned the blade so its honed edge sheared through the hair with a whisper. Nery caught it as it fell and to the envy of other maidens, walked over to the flushed and trembling Fran. Bowing over her hand, the Kalaia kissed her fingertips then presented her with the sun-bleached lock. Fran clutched it to her bosom, starry-eyed.

Applause and laughter broke out all around. The Speakers returned to their squires, who stripped off their sweat-soaked singlets to rub down their glistening torsos. Fran gazed longingly at Nerya's supple brown back, beating her palms together along with the rest, begging for an encore.

The applause intensified as they reached for their weapons again and turned to the crowd. All noise abruptly ceased. The silence was broken by a soft thud; Fran had fainted, signalling an immediate eruption of feminine screams and masculine ejaculations. Gentlemen raced about with towels and cloaks; Berthe scurried anxiously to Fran's aid; and the Angorians, in utter confusion, got in everyone's way.

The object of this outcry stood swathed in draperies and incomprehension, sword still in hand. Jehan was the first to recover his senses. Striding into the centre of the aisle, he lifted his voice to a parade-ground bellow.

"Peace, Thorsgarders! For the love of Gaia, what ails thee?"

"That thing!" howled Baron Ulfar. "What manner of Monster is it, an Hermaphrodite?"

"Nay, Sir," replied Nerya indignantly. To a new outbreak of squeals and gasps she flung off her drapes, exposing afresh the small, high breasts all had previously taken for the bulging pectorals of a well-muscled man. "I'm female, like all my Sisters in Kali! Is not our sex writ plain enough on our faces? Moreover," she went on, a dangerous edge in her tone, "I fail to see what this commotion's about - my form is not unpleasing!"

"B-because, *Madam*, 'tis perverse, a foul distortion of all natural order!" exploded the Baron. "Womenfolk can't be soldiers!"

"What am *I* then, a seamstress?" Nery said frostily, throwing on her doublet to conceal the offending bosom. "Why can't we? You can't still misthink we're not strong or valiant enough, or that we lack skill in the Ways! Pah! You've not seen the half, not the *tenth* part, of what the Kalaia can do - but by the Mist of Kali-Mara, I'm minded to fucking well show you!" She made as if to advance on Ulfar, but Nikos stepped into her path and caught her sword arm.

"Hold, Oratoria," he said quietly, "Don't unleash! If you'd

offer further proof of your credentials, why not let me sing for them *Nerya's Lay?*"

Nery bared her teeth and for a second it seemed she might strike him. Luckily at that moment Fran sat up shakily from her swoon and their eyes met across the aisle. Struggling to her feet she threw her veil across her face, shook off Berthe's consoling arm, thrust her way blindly through the spectators and fled.

The Kalaia snapped brusquely, "You will not! I tell you once and in all seriousness – speak my *Lay* in this company and it'll be your last utterance!" With the briefest of bows to Jehan and the King and a final glare at Ulfar, she spun on her heel and strode out.

Nikos watched her retreating back and blew out a long breath. "A close call, Brother!" he remarked to Jehan.

"Perilous close - thank Naume the young maid took her attention, else I think you'd be carrion now, along with the Baron!"

King Thorund approached with amazement on his face.

"Sol-Lios, mean you to tell me – nay, I cannot credit this - that your personal bodyguard are *all women*? What of Lord Nikos, who's patently not? I've never heard of such a thing before!"

"It *is* even so - they are fine, are they not?" Jehan gestured to the knot of Kalaia contained wary and indignant behind a restraining cordon of male warriors. "Frankly, Thorund, I'd pit any of them against your wildest Berserker with complete confidence in the outcome. Nery's most puissant of all; me she can master with a hand tied behind her back, and in the fullness of her Blood-Rage I doubt even the Kalaios would take her on - eh, Niki?"

"Hah! Not without Scylla between my legs and a crossbow in my hand - and even then I'd feel safer with an army at my back!" laughed Nikos. "But look, Thorund, your people are frenzied and our Sisters not best pleased. Pray, call for order so that everyone can hear the answers to your questions."

The King raised his hands. The hubbub died down to a rustling of fans, ill-suppressed sniggers, and the occasional "Harrumph!" from such as Baron Ulfar.

"Noble guests, for the benefit of all would you please clarify: which of you are male, and which female? For to my lasting shame, it seems we can't tell." Aside he murmured to Loric, "Had you thought to prepare us for this, sirrah, much embarrassment might have been saved!"

Perikleia came forward. "As Next to the Oratoria I shall explain. All the Counsel save Zafi and Iris are male, as are all twenty

Warriors. And all the Kalaia are female, save only Nikos.

'You can tell by our names. Those of men typically end in 'S', and of women with 'A' – though there are exceptions, like Jehan and Iris. But our Marks," she touched her brow, "have no such ambiguity. At maturity, every girl receives her crimson Blood-Drop, every boy his white Seed-Leap. Knowing this, you'll never fall prey again to error."

"But if all Kalaia are female, what of your Speaker?" asked Thorund, still puzzled. "You're not gelded, Sir, surely- O, forgive me, that was most unconscionably impertinent."

Nikos roared with laughter. "I'm no eunuch!" He reached for the lacing of his breeches. "Would you have the proof on it?"

Berthe's squeak of excitement was gagged by the sharp arrival of Elinor's elbow in her solar plexus.

The King said hastily, "No, Sir, your word alone suffices!"

"Very well," replied Nikos, still struggling for gravity, "This is the way of it! Each Kalaian division has an Oratore to intercede between Sisterhood and Warriors at times when they find male company intolerable. I'm chosen by virtue of kinship with Nery. We've been hand-in-glove since childhood, I can manage her, (mostly!), and she, for her part, can endure me even in the grip of *Kali-Mara*. Thus lines of communication remain open always, without innocent Warriors hazarding their lives or their manhood."

"Hmm," said Thorund, pulling his beard musingly. "But since you arrived, I've heard the Kalaia referred to as 'him', 'he', 'Sirs', and so forth - yet neither objection have you raised, nor contradiction."

Peri replied, "Ah - we're so accustomed to it that we hardly notice. Nor does our sex have relevance for our foes when they see us bearing down on them, for then they have weightier concerns on their minds!

'In our triple-gendered tongue, occupational descriptors like 'warrior' are neutral. Sexless, you might say," she smiled. "Whereas in Faali, with its two genders, the words for 'soldier' and their variants take masculine form, as they do in Gondaran.

'So it occasioned no surprise to be addressed in such wise. Nor did we realise you understood not our Marks – hence this unfortunate predicament! But now misunderstanding's cast aside, let's return to table. I'm gagging for a pipe."

"Nay, Sire!" expostulated Ulfar. "Is this… this *perversity* simply to be borne? Are we to sit down afresh with these creatures now their abominable nature's revealed?"

"Well, what else would you have us do, Sir?" snapped Peri,

"Lay down our arms and don skirts just to save your discomfort?"

"Aye, Monster, that exactly!" the Baron spluttered. "*And* cook, *and* clean, *and* bear your man's bairns and mind your manners, as a normal woman should! Not ape your betters and vaunt yourselves publicly clad so improper – or, by the Wolf, clad hardly at all, like that other shameless harlot! Get back to the kitchens and nurseries, the lot of you! Take lesson from the noble ladies of Gondarlan, and meddle not in men's affairs."

The Next shook her head. "That will never happen – never! Warriors we are, and so we remain till *Nône* takes us. Accept this knowledge and live with it. Or accept it not, and die now – it matters not to me!"

"Pay no heed, Perikleia," said Thorund, "We *do* accept it.

'Thorsgard, hear us! We hereby bestow the freedom of our House upon our honoured guests to go where they will, do what they will, and observe the dress and customs of their homeland without hindrance. They shall all be treated with every courtesy and respect that hospitality dictates - this we swear, by the Name of the Wolf! So abide by our will. Transgression will be punished by banishment from the Castle, yea, from the very Fastness itself!"

Nerya sprinted from the anteroom in time to see the trim of Fran's gown disappear through an archway ahead. She followed swiftly to a small oaken door. Bending low to peep through the keyhole, saw Fran facedown on the couch of the Castellan's sewing room, her shoulders heaving convulsively. Happily she had not locked the door; Nerya slid in and closed it behind her.

"My Lady?"

Fran sat up with a jerk. "My Lor- er, er, Madam - O, I don't even know what to call you! But please, go away and leave me alone," she wailed, burying her face in hands that still clutched the lock shorn from Nerya's ponytail.

Nery sat down alongside. "No - Mistress Fran, pray explain. I would ease your sorrow if I can, perceiving myself to be in some way the cause."

Fran faltered, "You must know, surely… I thought you a man, the most handsome I'd ever seen! And… and when you kissed my hand and gave me your token I thought, well, I'm one of Her Highness's Ladies, why *shouldn't* I catch this fine soldier's eye? Other girls find husbands amongst our Gard officers – and as I'm going to Angor with the Princess, why shouldn't I look there for *my* spouse?

'But- you're a woman! Please, Madam, forgive me. *This* is what ails me – I'm the dullest ass that ever walked the Urth! So go now, I beg you - I can speak no more on it."

"Fran," said Nerya softly, "Look at me!" The other shook her head and turned away, but the Kalaia, relentless, pulled her chin round. "Come look, and tell me: am I less fair than when you first beheld me?"

Reluctantly, Fran raised her eyes. Nay, she thought, and the tears spilled down her cheeks again, you're ten thousand times more so, now I see you up close! Nery's brow was wide and clear, her turquoise eyes rimmed by thick corn-gold lashes. High cheekbones flared from a delicate aquiline nose; her firm square jaw was cleft at the chin by a poignant dimple and she wore a permanent half-smile, the left corner of her mouth being contracted by a thin puckered scar. Strong, even teeth gleamed whitely as her grin widened under Fran's scrutiny. Even under close observation she could pass for a man, young and clean-shaven, fresh-faced and comely.

"Well, then," she demanded, "*Am* I less fair?"

"O, why d'ye seek to make me say these things?" Fran sprang to her feet in a surge of temper. "Of course you're fair, as you must see whenever you look in the glass - or d'ye scorn such girlish vanities? Yet even now I can hardly take it in… look at you, tall as His Majesty and brawny as a blacksmith…" She squeezed Nerya's arm. "Your muscles are like bronze – you're not the same stuff as Gondaran ladies! What *are* you then, really?"

Nerya smiled. "I'm Kalaia! Angorians are generally tall, those of the Warrior castes loftiest of all. I've trained and sweated, ridden and run even as the lads, eaten the same rations, fought the same battles, endured the same hardships. So I've waxed strong, and am accounted somewhat as a fighter; yet I'm truly female, as you'd soon realise if you saw me off Duty.

'Now pray reciprocate - for I'm still at sea. You admit I'm fair, tall and strong. And I'll have you know that I am Oratoria, Director of the Kalaia and all the Hosts of Angor, an Adept of the Seven Ways – isn't that good enough for you? Indeed, there are only two things a man can do that a woman cannot: engender children, and piss standing up!"

Fran giggled. Then, "Commander of all the armies?" she gasped. "I thought that must be Lord Nikos!"

"Oho, for the love of Gaia don't tell *him* that - he'll get ideas above his station! No, the Oratore holds office at my behest. He's my half-brother, accounting in part for our similar looks; my oldest friend, my sparring partner, my sometime lover-"

"Lover – didn't you just say he was your kinsman?"

"What of it?"

"But that's incest, for a sister to lie with a brother!"

"Then it is not lawful here?"

"Indeed not!"

"Hmm… it seems there's great distance between my homeland and yours – but it'll not seem so strange when you come to know us better." She patted the couch and took a pipe from her pocket. "So let's take a smoke and further our acquaintance."

They passed Nery's pipe back and forth without further conversation until it was done.

"Now let's see if I grasp any better… at first you admired me… then discovering my sex, all delightful speculation turned to dust and ashes. Is that the way of it?"

Fran nodded mournfully. "Aye… O, how the others will mock! They looked at me so ill, the cats, when you singled me out – what fun they'll poke now!"

"Pish - why care, when you'll so soon be gone from this place? In the meantime if you wish, when your duties permit, we'll walk and talk together; you can speak to me of Gondarlan, and I to you of Angor. At the very least, we'll wax in understanding and friendship. At the very most, who can say?

'As to what you call me - he, she, or it will suffice - aught but 'Lady' or 'Madam'! Call me Nerya, or Nery; call me Kalaia; call me Speaker, in our tongue Oratoria, Ora for short. Call me what you will – just call me kindly. Does this soften your plight?"

It did. "Or-a," Fran said slowly, filling her mouth with the rolling new word, "Ora Nerya? I like that," she rolled the tress of hair into a ball and tucked it into her bodice. "But I'm still confused. You *look* like a man, you *speak* like one, you *act* like one… it's as if the Kalaia take girls to wife in the same way Lord Jehan seeks to wed with our mistress."

Nerya passed her hand over her mouth to wipe away a grin.

"That is so - in a way."

"But- O, but that's silly! If a woman's rich enough to have servants, what need has she of a wife? Besides, what could they do 'neath the covers with no babies to get? You're teasing me, surely!"

"Hast ever lain with a man?"

Like Berthe, Fran had known her share of drunken fumbling and stolen kisses but both girls had defended their honour vigorously, clinging to virginity as essential for their future prospects.

"Certainly not, I'm a good girl!"

"With a woman, then?"

"O aye, many times. Well, girls, at least – Bea and I share a bed, which is better than at home. There I had to sleep with two sisters *and* my baby cousin."

Nerya replied carefully, "Then you're in no position to compare what a man *or* a woman might do 'neath the covers, as you put it." She pulled off Fran's headdress, unloosing a platinum flood. "So what makes you think *I* should prove less apt to please you there than a man?" She worked her fingers through the shining mane, grazed fingertips over Fran's cheeks and temples, traced the line of her silvery eyebrows, the curve of her lips. "What makes you think," her voice darkened, "that *I* can't play the man - and a sight more ably than many that were born to it?"

Fran's heart hammered so loudly she was surprised Nerya did not hear it; surprised the whole *Thorsgard* did not hear it, and come running! She felt giddy, her body traversed with swathes of gooseflesh, her nipples erect inside her bodice. This was not like being pressed up against walls by the Gards, or grabbed by lecherous courtiers on the way to the garderobes. Nerya did nothing lewd, in fact she hardly did anything at all, the touch of her fingers as light as a butterfly's wing… but Fran's every nerve was alive with expectation.

Looking at her rapt face and heaving bosom, Nerya groaned inwardly; in a minute she would tumble this delicious bundle back onto the cushions and ravish her right there and then. To circumvent this imminent possibility she arose, hefting Fran with her as easily as she might have done an infant. The kiss, when it finally came, was bestowed chastely on her forehead.

Wild with anti-climax, Fran stood on tiptoe and flung her arms around Nerya's neck. "O, don't stop!"

The Speaker smiled ruefully and shook her head, disengaging Fran's arms.

"Were we in my House, by dawn you'd be spoiled for mere men forever! But we're not – so sleep on it, Fran. In Angor you can be my friend, companion, lover – whatsoever pleases you best. But for now we *must* return to the Hall - God knows what tales have been concocted in our absence. Pray compose yourself; I'll run back and despatch you an ally, so you're not obliged to re-enter the gathering alone - or worse, in the company of this unnatural Monster!" She tucked a stray wisp of hair behind her ear and tugged at the hem of her jacket. "So, am I decent?"

Fran drew back her head, looking full into Nerya's face. "Decent? Never! But beautiful – there's an apter word."

Their eyes locked. Fran slid a hand over Nerya's doublet, caressing the jewelled insignia over her heart, insinuating small fingers between the hastily closed fastenings and releasing a feral, civet tang. The Kalaia's heart was thudding; breathing fast, she met Fran's eyes with an expression of open lust so electrifying it made her tremble, if not falter. With a flick of her practised seamstress's fingers, she unhooked the frogs and slipped her hand inside to cup the slight, firm swell of Nery's breast.

"So thou *art* a woman, mighty warrior," she whispered, "The top half, at least!"

"Enough – stop, for the love of Gaia!"

"Then kiss me properly! How can I choose a path with you else, not knowing if I shall like it?" She hauled Nerya's head down by the ponytail until the Speaker met her parted lips with a kiss so sensual and intense Fran's legs turned to water. Nerya's mouth, so dissimilar to the beery maws of previous acquaintance, was meltingly soft, but her body felt as hard as any man's. Breathless minutes elapsed. Finally Nery broke free and lowered Fran to the couch, limp and gasping yet triumphant.

"There now!" she said, adjusting her garments, "See what you've done, Temptress - I'm lathered as if I've run a marathon! O, 'twill be a hard road back to Aumaia thanks to your teasing… but now we *must* return to the feast."

Fran threw herself down in much the same attitude she'd been first discovered in, albeit for different reasons. The memory of Nerya's kiss pierced her vitals with shivery chills; she thrust her fist between her thighs and moaned. It was thus that Berthe found her, having scuttled from the Hall as quickly as she could in response to the Speaker's directions.

"Fran! O, Great Wolf, Fran! What ails you? O Gods, you're not dishonoured – was it the Lor- I mean, La-? What's she done - what's *happened*?"

Fran sat up, smoothing her madly disordered *coiffeur*. "I hardly know how to tell you! O, Bea… I'm going to Angor."

"And for this shocking revelation you flee the Hall weeping and miss the best show we've seen in years? Of course you're going to Angor; I too, and Her Highness! Don't tell me the import of this last month has only just sunk in."

"You misunderstand – I go with the Princess or without. I'm going with Nerya, and if Madam scuppers my plans – commits some idiocy to escape Sol-Lios, like running off with the Warlord - I'm *still* going, if I have to stow away on their ship to do it."

"Fran, what are you saying? This is treason! Why do you speak in this lunatic way?"

"Lunatic? I've never been saner – though in a way I *am* mad, mad with love! *Now* I understand how you feel about Loric. She's everything I ever dreamed of, only better - handsome and strong and rich, and kind and funny and wise...

'What's for me here except drudgery - and the hope of one day catching a nice officer who wouldn't beat me or drink all our money away? I'd end my days as they began, tending others and labouring for my bread... either that or pensioned off to ply my spindle and shrivel in the corner like an old spider. But Ora wooed me as if I were a Lady and she a noble *thegn*... to what end I barely understand, but I tremble to wonder. And I intend to find out – so I'm going to Angor whether Princess Elinor comes, goes, or puts an end to herself!"

"Words fail me!" Berthe immediately gave herself the lie. "How can you be so bold and reckless, Fran, so wilful and deviant - why, a half-hour ago you swooned at the sight of her bosom, yet now you're planning to desert our mistress and fatherland in favour of becoming – well, I scarcely know what to call it, a, a *companion* of some sort, to her? And you say you've fallen in love? What of the recipient of this strange passion, what has she to say?"

"O Bea, that's the most wonderful thing! She feels the same, least, I think so... nay, I'm certain! For I felt the thunder of her heart, and looked in her eyes and *saw* how she wrestled with her desire to do... well, I know not, exactly." Her voice quavered as images of such explicit carnality, of Nerya's expert caress roving farther afield on her body, shot through her mind.

"But O, the kiss of her mouth," she resumed, "'Twas like drinking from a clear mountain stream, I still feel it tingle on my lips! I care nothing that she be a woman. She is of all things the best and noblest and most pleasing in my sight."

"Well, I never did!" Berthe said, in a low voice. "I'm sorry, Fran, 'tis too much to take in," her lip began to quiver and her eyes to fill, "to suddenly find you so wild and so... so resolutely altered!"

"O, Bea, don't cry – don't turn from me! I have but fallen in love... I can't help it."

"It's not that!" Berthe wailed. "She had the court fooled to the last, even King Thorund – and yours were not the only tears shed in consequence, Gudrun Ulfarsdottir was scarcely better!

'So now you'll be longing to go away with your love – while I leave mine behind. While you're being courted, I'll be pining alone… and who knows if I'll ever see Loric again? Truly Fran, I rejoice for you – but for myself, I'm so sad!" The trickle burst into a torrent, swelled when Fran joined in empathically.

By degrees, their lamentation died to hiccoughs and snuffles. Blowing her nose juicily, Berthe managed in stifled tones,

"Well, at least she'll not beget a babe on you, then deny fatherhood and damn you for a whore!"

"Indeed," sniffed Fran, "Leaving me to cast myself into *Fafnirsee*, like poor Gerda Linstrom when she was deflowered. Nor will she, (I trust), come home sotted of a night, and rut on me in a cloud of ale and sweat."

"Nay, nor piss in the ewer, mistaking it for the chamber-pot!" Berthe giggled, "And I'll lay she do not snore, or befoul the privy floor, or stink out the bedchamber with noxious farts!"

"Is it against the Lore for us, d'ye think?"

"I've never heard so. Then again, I've never heard of such a thing as… er…*this* at all! But it's bound to be, so for God's sake don't bruit it abroad – what if you're thrown out of service, or… or given over to Hel? Pray, be discreet till we're all safe away. O Fran, 'tis a queer notion to be sure… I'm with child to hear the full tale- but the feast, we must go back! Have you a comb, your hair's a fright – and you missed *such* a row with Baron Ulfar! I'll tell you as we go – hurry, Her Highness will wonder what's become of us."

They hastily made themselves presentable, Berthe appraising Fran the while of developments during her absence."And then in came the Kalaia and spake privily to Her Highness, who sent me off to find you," she concluded.

"Great Wolf, what d'ye suppose she said," Fran grimaced, "Shall I be in for it?"

Berthe snorted. "I doubt it," she replied dryly. "They stretch a nice point with their truth-telling, these Angorians! No word of falsehood did Lady Ner-"

"Not Lady - she likes it not!"

"Very well - no word of falsehood did *Speaker Nerya* utter, just that she'd 'found you in such-and-such a chamber, indisposed'. How long she'd *sought* before she found you, though, she forbore to mention," Bea gave her a shrewd glance. "And as we'd been much

81

preoccupied with all the arguments and whatnot, Her Highness didn't question it. She's in a fey mood this evening, and less impressed by Lord Jehan than you by his General – mores the pity, or she'd be the happiest lass in Gondarlan by now."

"Well, I think she's silly and spoilt!" Fran said, with a final tug at her neckline. "The Elect seems a fine man to me; indeed, I like him best of all, saving my Oratoria. Though your Lord Nikos is a splendid fellow too, and I can't believe that he – um…" She bit off the remainder of her sentence, turning to straighten the cushions.

"That he what?"

"Er… that he'd scorn to comfort you for your lost love, if the worst came to it," she recovered quickly. "But I've a feeling 'twill all come right in the end - have you even asked Loric, will he quit the King's service and join us?"

"Why no," replied Berthe, as they scurried back to the Hall, "For truly, I dread his reply! Surely if he wanted to he'd have asked me by now. But he hasn't."

"You goose - what if *he* waits to be asked? What if he fears *your* response? For God's sake, Bea, *ask* him - you've naught to lose. And we'll be leaving soon, so you'd better make haste."

"You're right!" Berthe's countenance brightened. "Then at least I'll know… and if he wants me not I shall have to endure it, and cast mine eyes elsewhere. Who knows where they might land – a mighty Kalaia like yours, eh?"

Baron Ulfar thrust through the crowd mustering his family and retinue. "Thorund Thorssen!" he bellowed, "These pagan travesties of womenfolk besmirch the clean rock of Wolfenbirg - my Lady Wife and I will not remain 'neath the same roof, nor suffer our innocent children to be contaminated!"

Gudrun Ulfarsdottir, seeing her prospects of a rich foreign match snatched away, fell to her knees imploring her father to reconsider, whilst her mother tugged at his sleeve and spoke up in timid remonstrance.

"See, Thorssen, 'tis not a moment too soon – already they're corrupted!" He dragged a silver ring from his left hand and hurled it, but it fell short and tinged away harmlessly at Thorund's feet. "Th'art not fit to be Ring-Giver - I renounce my allegiance!

'Come, Wife, Arkron - back to the purity of Arkengarth, far from this blasphemous stench!"

Ulfar dragged his family down the aisle, followed by their

subdued and frightened servants. Thorund let them go, jerking his chin at the portal-keeper to open the Great Doors, and causing Fran and Berthe, eavesdropping on the threshold, to jump hastily back.

"Does anyone else wish to throw back our favour like that ungrateful cur?" he demanded, "Come now, speak up!" His courtiers mumbled and shuffled their feet, but none replied. "Very well, back to your places - we'll speak of this discord no more. At least," he added *sotto voce* to Hel, "Not till the pious Baron is dragged back from his eyrie to explain himself... but for that entertainment we must wait till our Guests have departed."

"O, at last!" hissed Elinor, "What in God's Name have you been about, Mistress Fischer?" Luckily she did not wait for an answer, merely gesturing for them to follow her back to the table.

Before she had gone a dozen steps, a disagreeable acrid whiff announced Hakon's arrival at her elbow.

"Highness, may I speak on a matter of some import?"

"If needs must, My Lord. But pray be brief!"

Drawing as close to her ear as she would permit, Hakon murmured his proposal. Elinor's eyes widened, turning on the Warlord with such a glitter that his heart swelled triumphant.

"A capital suggestion, Sir – I can't think why my Royal Father did not moot it himself." She squeezed his arm gently, treating him to a dazzling smile. "I'll raise it at a suitable juncture – and remember who put it in my mind."

Swollen with pride, the Warlord bowed acknowledgement and handed Elinor into her chair; then settling himself down with a grunt of satisfaction, called for a flagon of ale.

Jehan looked round at the flushed, excited faces of his hosts. "So tell me: can I at last take my ease, or would anyone else have proofs of my manhood and capabilities?"

"Nay, Sol-Lios," laughed Thorund, "be seated – there'll be no more exertion of that kind tonight!"

But Elinor put out a restraining hand, her clear pale eyes pleading. "Pray wait, Majesty! My Lord Elect! O, 'tis not fair," she pouted, furrowing her brow with a pretty little frown. "All the feats of prowess we've seen thus far have been at others' behest, yet 'tis *I* that the Lord Elect has come to honour with his suit. And I wish to be wooed and won like a Northron Princess of olden times.... so I'd like Lord Jehan to perform some small feat, some service for *me*, as proof

83

not of his manhood but of his regard!"

Thorund chuckled. "Impudent cub, is not the King's ransom you sport on your back proof enough?"

Elinor ducked her head, peeping out through inky lashes and dimpling her cheeks engagingly. "Indeed, my Angorian gifts are wondrous fair - but it's not the same! In all the old tales a Prince must slay a dragon, or... or behead a giant before the Princess's Father gives her up to be his wife."

It was an enchanting performance. Jehan could not help smiling. "Fair enough, Madam. Yet what would you have me do? I'm at your disposal - only pray, do not ask me to fight you."

"There, Majesty! The Elect consents - please may I set him a quest? O, Sire, do let me, pray!"

Thorund shook his head in despair. "Foolish child, the wine and excitement have gone to your head! But if our guest wishes to indulge this whim, I'll not countermand him. Go on - name your task."

Head on one side she glanced coquettishly at Jehan, tapping her lips with her index finger as she affected to consider. Then the warmth drained from her eyes, leaving them grey and frigid as river ice.

"Jehan Sol-Lios, if you'd uproot me from my homeland and take me far away to be your wife, then do this one thing for me, to prove before my Father's court and the Mighty Fafnir that you'll be a fitting husband:

'Climb Mount Fang – tonight."

Chapter 9: Fang

Elinor bit her cheek to keep from laughing, while Hakon smirked into his beard. Timing the ruse to perfection, Her Highness had wiped the smile off the pagan's chops and no mistake!

"Climb Mount Fang," Jehan gasped, "What, yon black spike - by moonlight? Ye Gods, Madam, if that's your concept of a 'small service', I dread to think what you'd consider a great one!"

"Most amusing, Daughter," said Thorund carefully, "and out of the question, of course. Name something sensible, pray, or hold peace on your romantic fancies!"

"No, let it stand – I accept."

Thorund shook his head. "It's too dangerous – tell him, Thoralson."

"His Majesty's right, My Lord. It's not a typical ascent, and places strange demands on the climber."

"How so?"

"Well… physically, it takes little more than strong arms, a firm grip, and a good head for heights - every hold's manually placed, and every one sound, as I can vouchsafe. But it's perilous notwithstanding, and has cost many lives."

"No reason to hold back - indeed you do but whet my appetite, Master Mountaineer!"

"Preposterous," said the King, "Surely your comrades wouldn't wish you to pursue such a reckless course?"

Nikos leapt up. "O Thorund, for my part I'm *sorely* displeased, having thought to spend this evening in leisure, not adventuring high peaks by moonlight! Yet if the Elect is so determined, I'll accompany him."

Thorund groaned. "Say not so, Lord Nikos!" he implored. "Noble Guests, pray dissuade them!"

"We can't, Sir," replied Iris. "We could neither oblige Sol-Lios to undertake such an act against his will - nor forbid him now his heart's set on it, and Niki bent on sharing the glory. If the Challenge was declined, ever after we would wonder what the outcome might have been… but I believe they've too much to accomplish on this plane for the Goddess to let them drop them off your Fang tonight."

"Well said, Seer - that's good enough for me. Come, Niki, Thoralson, let's prepare."

"Hold hard, Sol-Lios! I think you're madmen… but I granted you freedom of my House, which I suppose includes the Fang. I give permission – reluctantly, mind! - provided only that weather permits. On that matter Thoralson alone can judge; I require absolutely that you stand by his guidance.

'What say you, Mountaineer?"

Ragnar thrust open a casement. The night was biting clear, bright with moonlight and myriad frosty stars; a keen steady wind blew, but conditions were as favourable as could be at such an hour.

"'Tis fine but cold, Sire – the climb *could* be attempted without undue hazard."

The King sighed. "Very well – then go, if you must!"

The Angorians went to change into outdoor garb and the special Fang gear Loric provided: sealskin buskins with soles of rough shagreen, their insteps thickened with whale baleen; close-fitting sealskin hoods; shagreen-palmed gloves; and goggles of leather and glass to prevent their eyeballs being seared by the cold.

Returning to the Great Hall they found festivities continuing in muted fashion, Thoralson, ready in his own gear, engaged in earnest debate with the King over a roll of parchments.

"I'd prefer you not to do this, Sol-Lios… yet seeing you thus determined, I own I wish I were coming too. 'Tis a fair view from Fang-tip by day, and I've never seen it myself by night."

"Then come along, Sir, and welcome!" cried Jehan, a sentiment privately echoed by Hakon.

"Nay, my climbing days are long passed. In any event, *someone* of sound mind must remain below, to see to your funeral arrangements!

'It'll take - what, Thoralson, two hours to the Tip? At midnight we'll repair to the North Tower and watch for your signal light. Then we'll all seek repose – God knows, we'll need it – and you may descend safer in the morning."

Ragnar nodded. "And I dare say we'll pass a cosy night – if we get there! For it's just occurred to me – I took the safety lines down, so we must climb roped together."

"By no means," said Nikos. "We share hazard fairly, Friend Ragnar. I'm twice as heavy as you, Sir - how could you hold me if I fell? No, we must climb untethered, not risk pulling each other to a shared doom. We'd not expected the route to be roped, so are none the worse off for this intelligence."

"O, are you not?" said the King sarcastically, "Perhaps then you'd have the Ladder greased, to make it greater sport? Or take along more of your comrades to enjoy the view? Only break it to me now, pray, that I might know what my nerves must endure!"

To general laughter, Thesis replied, "No more, Sir – it's the duty of Electhood and Kalaia to undertake dangers on behalf of the rest. *We* are more than content to enjoy your hospitality here in the warm, and let our representatives carry the glory."

Berthe and Fran, their fun curtailed, bobbed disconsolately in Elinor's wake as she raged through the corridors, her father's rebuke still resounding in her ears.

"Madam, has the Wolf devoured your senses?" Thorund had said. "To risk a foreign head of state dying under our roof... come morning, we could be at war thanks to your monumental stupidity! Ach, how little you've profited from Lord Sigismund's correction – I was wrong to think it had taught you self-control!

'I'm sick of the sight of you, Princess. Go, beseech Almighty Fafnir for their safe delivery - for I promise, if either falls or if you play such a trick again, I'll see you clapped back in that device and the key thrown away. Then I'll wed you to any Angorian willing to take on such a witless vixen, considering myself well rid. Do I make myself plain? Good - say your farewells, and begone."

Trembling, Elinor did as he bade, receiving in return a hatefully knowing bow from Jehan.

"Good night, sweet Princess - I'll send down a love-token from the Fang to greet you on your waking!"

His remark did nothing to improve Elinor's temper. At her suite she flung wide the doors and stamped into her bedchamber, discarding diamonds as she went.

"Get me out of this damned pagan rig, Fran, and put those gewgaws from my sight! You, Bea, fetch a mead posset, extra strong. Aiee! Would I were male – I'd climb Fang myself, for the pleasure of pushing that bastard out of the Tip! Wolf rend them - and my Father! He's humiliated me, *ruined* my night even more than accursed Sol-Lios - I *spit* on their names! Sent to bed like a naughty child – O, the shame, I'll miss all the watching and wagers - even the *servants* will know the outcome before me!

'And if one of them falls, what will befall *me*? Or if they do *not*... how Jehan will preen, proved beyond question and before all as my husband - and by mine own command! I should *never* have listened to Hakon's villainous suggestion!

'Where's my robe? Is that posset ready? Then leave me in

peace, I can manage – you're both clumsy enough tonight, I might as well shift for myself. Ach, I don't know what's got into everyone since those thrice-damned pagans befouled our shores."

Fran and Berthe curtsied low and made good their escape. The Princess tore off her new silken stockings, careless of holes and ladders; the gossamer-thin chemise and drawers she rent asunder, standing briefly naked to screw the ruined undergarments into a ball and hurl them into a corner. Still cursing, she thrust herself into respectable nightwear and downed her posset in a single draught, grimacing at its powerful herbal taste. Then she cast herself onto the bed and pummelled her pillows fiercely, imagining all the while they were the faces of her father, the Warlord and Jehan.

Meanwhile her women repaired to their own room, not daring to return to the Hall lest Elinor should hear of it and deem them disloyal. Happily, Berthe kept in her workbox a little flask of *aquavit* for medical emergencies, and had loaded her kerchief with sugarplums and dainties from the tables. So they stoked up the fire, turned the lamps low and divested themselves of their best dresses, by now rather limp with sweat and emotion. In nightgowns and fleecy bed-jackets, they clambered giggling into bed to embark upon a private feast of their own, Fran regaling Berthe with the full tale of her new love as they braided one another's hair, their mistress's self-inflicted woes forgotten quite.

Jehan rolled up the charts with an air of resolution. "Are you fit, then, Brother?"

"As I'll ever be."

"Come, then, let's to it! Adieu, comrades – save us some *mocha*, we'll be back for fast-break."

"May the Power of the Wolf uphold you, Sirs," said King Thorund, "and keep your grip firm. I'll watch for your signal with the utmost anxiety."

Iris too prepared to depart. "I mustn't miss this – Kaa and I will keep watch."

Hel rose with her, his flushed pate wrinkled with concern. "The Shelf is no place for a lady, Madam. Even at midday it's dark and perilous, and black as pitch by night – you'll not see a thing."

"Trust me, we'll See quite enough! King Thorund, pray excuse me – and may I take Lord Hel to be my guide?"

Thorund nodded, and the Torturer snatched up his cloak. Blushing furiously at knowing looks and muffled sniggers from certain quarters, he threw the garment across his shoulders and followed Iris from the Hall.

Halting by the courtyard door he exclaimed, "Wait, My Lady! You can't go outside in such a poor thin gown. Let me send for furs – you'll perish, else."

Iris made no reply save to slip her hand into his. Notwithstanding the chilly corridors through which they had walked, and the icy draught from the open portal, her small fingers were pulsing with warmth. She led Hel out into the bailey, threw back her head and gazed open-mouthed at the indigo sky illuminated by its great frosty orb and unfamiliar constellations.

"Holy Luna – Angorian nights seem soft as velvet cushions compared to this! Lucky Elect, to climb among those stars... by the Goddess, I swear one day I'll do the same myself."

Thoralson locked the Baileyside door, lit a dark lantern, and unfastened Shelfside.

"Remember, My Lords: we climb ten rungs apart. Never relinquish a hold till the next is secure, and never touch bare flesh against iron, or it'll stick! When we reach the overhang I'll make my own speed for the Stair, to light a lamp and be ready to help you up. Now, brace yourselves..." He stepped through the door, admitting a rush of frigid air and a sense of yawning space.

The Angorians exchanged glances, and then followed Ragnar out. Beyond the curtain wall, the Thorsgard's bedrock terminated in a narrow shelf, separated from Mount Fang by the deep abyss known as the Lung. Thoralson walked steadily out onto the iron bridge spanning the gulf; and at the opposite platform, hooked his lantern to a ring in the cliff face and began his ascent.

Jehan and Nikos crossed the bridge and tensed, listening. At Ragnar's call of "Twenty, set," the Elect said,

"Climb safe, Brother," and vanished into the dark. A dozen seconds later, Nikos heard, "Ten, set."

With a whispered prayer, the Speaker took up his hold. "One, ready!" he bellowed.

Hel unlocked Baileyside with his skeleton key. The climbing party had not long departed, for the gatehouse still held a faint aroma of testosterone and old oiled sealskin. Ushering Iris within, he kindled the lamp and hunted for a dark lantern.

The Seer reached for a pinch of dried herbs and chewed till her mouth filled with tingling, earthy saliva, watching Hel prepare the lantern with surprising delicacy in his powerful fingers. When it was lit, he looked at Iris questioningly; she merely gestured to the door. Hel shrugged, put up his hood and unlatched it.

"As you command, but be careful! We're close to the edge, so stay by the wall if you value your life."

Outside she breathed, "I can See them - all three, praise Kali! They're making good time, look, yonder, about the height of the battlements... they climb... they pause... and they climb again - they've found the rhythm. Let's keep watch, My Lord, till they get to the Shaft."

Hel wadded up the hem of his cloak and sat down upon it, his back against the curtain wall. Iris nestled within the crook of his arm, hooking her legs across his thighs, and the Torturer pulled his cape snugly around them both. With Kaa perched on her shoulder, Iris again directed her face upwards, and Hel followed their gaze. Shreds of cloud raced across the moon, and he could not descry any climbers amongst the riot of shifting shadows on the icy cliff.

"*Nightblend*," Iris said, in answer to his unspoken question. "It heightens vision and perception both." Reaching for her pouch she fed some to Kaa without averting her eyes from the ascent. "Here, try some. Chew it into a ball, but don't swallow. Hold it in your cheek, or under your tongue. In a few minutes, look once more to the Ladder, and see what you can See."

Grimacing at the gritty taste and texture, Hel masticated the leaves into a comfortable slimy wad and lost himself again in contemplation of her upturned profile. The Seer's skin was pale in the moonlight, her pupils expanded as black and bottomless as the chasm by their feet, and she looked so lovely that Hel's arm tightened involuntarily, pulling her closer into the embrace of his manhide suit. In response she laid her hand upon his breast, offering up a silent prayer on behalf of its previous wearer.

"When you swore to climb Fang, Madam, could you truly do it?" he asked, more for the pleasure of her voice than a desire for information.

"Indeed – it's a Competency of Seerhood. If I couldn't climb, there are many sacred sites I couldn't reach. And whereas mine own preference is for *down*, what goes down must perforce come back up. So yes, I could scale the Fang as well as I could make attempt on this mighty gulf at our feet- O, behold, one – surely Thoralson – climbs on apace. They've reached the overhang, Goddess preserve them!"

Hel tore his eyes from her face, following her pointing finger. The crisp air seemed to boil and squinting, he found he *could* now discern three distant, crawling figures where the rock face bulged outwards.

"It's well they're fit, though I'll wager their shoulders will pain them by morn. Aiee, what a pull – I hope that great lump Nikos won't heave your Ladder from its moorings!"

"They're bold, your companions," Hel remarked. "I wouldn't have expected noblemen to undertake such a feat."

Iris shrugged. "Our *Kali't'aia* and Elect are trained to survive wilderness, to assail fortifications, to make peace where they can, and where not, to wage war on peak or plain. They devote their lives to perfecting the craft- ah, but look! Thoralson's reached the shaft. We'll lose view of the others soon, too."

"Then by the Wolf's Mane, let us go in," exclaimed Hel. "My arse is freezing off!"

"What, are you so keen to relinquish my private company?" Iris softened her words with a chuckle even as she disengaged herself from the armchair of his body. "Their hardest test is yet to come. Pray, indulge me a few minutes longer."

Taking up the lantern she made for the bridge. Stiff and benumbed, Hel struggled to his feet in an effort to detain her, too late; Iris had stepped lightly out onto the suspension.

"Come back!" he implored, not daring to follow.

Iris paid him no heed, but projected her Sight. Her mind's eye filled with iron, slippery with fresh frost; cold black rock, frigid moonlight and steaming breath. She *was* Sol-Lios in that instant, a climbing machine, fighting fire in shoulders and lightness in head, with no thought beyond the next hold, then the next. She could almost feel his heart thunder, the labour of his lungs in the thin high air, and willed him on, a sensation of dread growing in her breast.

"Steady, Jehan, have a care," she whispered. Next moment her stomach dropped with such a sickening plunge she thought the span had given way beneath her.

Thoralson had given fair truth, Jehan mused while he still had the luxury of conscious thought. The Ladder followed the Fang's contours, being in its early stages more or less perpendicular and having much in common with climbing into the *Breath* from a rowing boat on a lively sea: sometimes leaning in, sometimes swinging out, to the constant accompanying tug of the wind.

They settled into the steady, careful beat, hand, foot, left, right, moving up around fifteen feet at a time, then pausing to call in their checks. Straightforward though the stage was, they did not treat it lightly; this canyon between Fang's inner face and the curtain wall was a vortex of unpredictable gusts, the rungs slippery with hoar-frost that constantly melted and re-froze. They proceeded with due caution and the first dozen sets, taking them to the height of the topmost battlements, passed without incident.

Thoralson paused, hooked an arm through the rungs and clapped his shagreen palms to rid them of frost.

"Stage Two, My Lords! Clear your gloves and boots here, and 'ware winds when you climb on!"

At the stopping point Jehan cleaned his palms and soles as instructed, then steadied himself for the section that would carry him clear of the castle walls. Within a few feet the air temperature dropped noticeably, accompanied by a steadier, frigid blow from the north east. The Elect adjusted his grip accordingly, pausing while Nikos made ready to follow; and the three continued as before, on and up to the overhang's black ceiling.

When the familiar pull began in Thoralson's shoulders he grimaced, offering a short prayer on his companions' behalf. They were a hundred yards above Castle Thorsgard's highest tower, only a few stages from the relative safety of the Stair - but this last section was harder and more dangerous than anything they had encountered so far. He called down between his feet,

"Stage Three – this is where I must leave you! Is all well?"

"Aye, well," replied Jehan.

"Well as it can be," came more faintly from Nikos below.

"Then Gods willing, I'll see you at Stairfoot!" Ragnar set off at a pace bespeaking long practice; Jehan, craning back his head, could just make out his dark figure disappearing across the almost horizontal overhang like a spider on a ceiling.

The Ladder was now bulging at an ever-increasing angle from the vertical, carrying them out over the Thorsgard's lamp-lit ramparts. Luckily, they soon had respite from the grievous strain it imposed on their hands and arms: a step in the rock-face where it ran almost vertical for a good ten rungs. Jehan waited there for Nikos, leaning into the lee of the rock, flexing fingers and toes.

"How goes it, Brother?"

"Well enough – but I'll be glad to get out of this wind!"

"Me too – thank Naume it's not much further to the shaft."

Chafing his palms and soles free of slush, the Elect drew a deep breath and set out on the last horizontal stage. Concentrating grimly Nikos followed, and they climbed on in a silence broken only by grunts of exertion and the rasp of shagreen on the Ladder.

At the overhang's abrupt termination Jehan braced his feet, clung tight with his left hand and groped over the rocky lip with his right. Finding the next hold, he pulled himself up to look. Some fifteen feet above his head shone a patch of golden light – it was the shaft! All that now separated him from Stairfoot, where Thoralson stood ready to assist, was an easy stretch of well-nigh vertical rungs.

"We've done it, Niki!" In his excitement, Jehan grabbed the next rung not centrally but by the inner upright, where a sheath of ice had gathered. As he heaved up round the overhang, the transfer of his full weight proved too much for it. It splintered and fell away, along with his hand-hold; the sudden jolt caused him to lose his footing, too.

Glancing up at the involuntary cry, Nikos saw to his horror the Elect dangling by one hand, facing imminent death if his grip or nerve faltered.

"Hang on!" he yelled, climbing as quickly as he dared. But Sol-Lios had no intention of falling, or of dragging Nikos with him in a futile rescue attempt. Stretching to the utmost he snagged the nearest rung, easing the hideous drag in his shoulder and the cramp in his fingers. With every atom of strength and concentration he drew up his leg and groped for a foothold. His left toes struck something solid: Nikos's outstretched hand, guiding them to a rung.

With three holds secured it was a simple enough matter for Jehan to regain the fourth, and thereby a little equilibrium. Mouth dry, muscles squirting adrenalin, he dragged his body around the ledge, careful this time to avoid the remnant of the icy sheath that had so nearly proved his downfall. Safe on the vertical section, he stamped down to make the rest of it shatter and tinkle away.

"Thanks, dross-head, that went right in my face," grunted Nikos. "*And* you nearly made my heart fail back there – what were you playing at?"

"I lost my grip on an icy rung - then cleared it so *you* wouldn't slip, you bloody ingrate. And I'm quite safe and well after my travail, thank'ee kindly for asking."

Iris whooped in relief, setting weird echoes ringing. Then she grasped the iron rail and hung precariously over; Hel's *nightblend-*heightened senses registered the faint hiss of steam as her flesh touched

93

the metal.

"*Aléia, Maia Kali!*" she cried into the abyss.

The Torturer stiffened. Far beneath his feet, he detected a response…

"Beware, Lady Iris!" he yelled, pressing back against the curtain wall. "For God's sake, get off the bridge!"

The Seer ignored him, raising her arms in salutation. There came a deep rumble in the chasm's bowels, presaging the first wisps of vapour. They were followed by a great steaming gale which rushed up with a thunderous roar, fluttering her feather cape and making her unbound hair writhe like a nest of snakes; Iris roared with it, the wild ululation snatched from her lips by the up-draught.

Hel trembled, half in dread lest she fall, half in awe. His lady had spoken to the void, and it had answered – what kind of sorceress *was* she? His loins twinged with anticipation, an erection growing with perverse eroticism inside his second skin as Iris returned to the Shelf and coolly hung up her lantern. Wordlessly he opened his cape, and she stepped into the warmth of his encircling arms. Almost of a height they embraced, the steam of their breath intermingling; he pressed Iris ever closer, not troubling to conceal his burgeoning excitement.

Inhaling tanned Druid alongside Hel's own alien, carnivorous scent, the Seer groaned inwardly. Great Mother, she thought, I had not Looked for this! With his shaven pate hooded Hel appeared less sinister, more like any other Northron male - and a comely one, at that. His thick-lashed dark eyes were especially fine, and as she ran her hands over his bull neck, massive shoulders and the slab-like muscles of his arms, the serpent fire, *kundalini*, ignited in her own belly. Thrusting her pelvis against him she kissed Hel passionately, snaking her tongue over his teeth. Aroused beyond endurance, he returned the gesture in kind, the Gondaran in him faintly scandalised. This was not the behaviour he expected of a high noblewoman; indeed, one would be lucky to get it from an expensive whore. But the man in him was swept and beset by waves of desire more intense than he had ever felt or imagined.

"Come lie with me," he said hoarsely into her ear when she broke the kiss at last, nuzzling her neck and raising more gooseflesh than the night winds had achieved. "Thou art a wonder - I must have thee! Come to my chambers - none will ever know, I swear it. Come now and lie with me."

She looked into his lust-filled pleading face, breathing hard and deep. Tendrils of black fire crackled through her veins. For an instant she succumbed to temptation: saw herself take him right then and there, grunting up against the castle wall, her gown round her waist and the Lung gaping at their feet. The vision's erotic force slammed open a portal in her mind. Iris felt the Goddess don her like a glove, and as power screamed through her body she took Hel's lower lip between her teeth, bit hard enough to draw blood, and sucked at the wound. Startled he reeled back a pace; then they fell on one another again, biting and clawing.

"Let's go to my rooms," he panted when they next broke apart, pulling her towards the Shelfside door. "You must want it as much as I do, or you'd not handle me thus."

The Seer's body followed a step or two before volition caught it up. Hel's darkness attracted her in ways her countrymen seldom did, and she wanted him so violently she could have rent his flesh asunder and worn *him* as a garment, drunk his fluids, consumed his heart to make him part of her forever. She stopped, vibrating with the effort of self-control, and stared up into Luna's tranquil radiance. Not tonight, Mother, she thought, thy Power in me is too strong!

"I do want thee, My Lord," she replied, "but now is not the time or place."

"Then when in the Wolf's Name will it be? O, don't say me nay," groaned Hel. Lust had driven out his former awe; he kissed her again and whispered, in painful frustration, "Don't trifle with me, Madam! I've borne your teasing thus far in good part, but I can bear it no longer. Come with me now, or do I have to make you? You know full well who I am, and what I can do."

Forceful as a bullock, he drove Iris against the wall and caught her by the throat. Gagging her with his tongue, carefully, almost tenderly, he pinched her nostrils tight and cut off her breath. The act almost undid her; she imagined Hel kissing her to death, the pair of them locked, plunging into the abyss to immolate their passion in the planet's molten core.

She went limp. In sudden panic the Torturer slackened his hold lest he had accidentally strangled her, whereupon Iris heaved a deep breath and dragged all the air from his lungs. Gasping, Hel let go. Before he could recover she darted her hand between his legs and deftly caught his testicles in a grip as merciless as his own castrating tongs. Her right fingertips she laid upon his breast, drumming them lightly over the pounding heart she could have stopped with a thought.

"*Make* me, My Lord? What," she squeezed his scrotum in ominous caress, "Take me by force, against my will? Would you, Sir –

dost think you *could*?"

Hel flinched, imagining the Seer spread-eagled on his rack, shrieking as he laid her open with the lash. His expression softened along with the erection that had been pushing insistently against her thighs. He replied with a shudder,

"Nay, Lady, in answer to both. I couldn't hurt thee for the whole of Gondarlan - a grievous predicament for a Torturer to find himself in, to be sure." One hand was still at her throat and he stroked her windpipe gently with his thumb, working his fingers on the nape of her neck. "Woe betide me if His Grace should fathom that an Angorian witch has disarmed his most dreaded instrument!

'Forgive me, Madam – and pray, don't withdraw your favour. For I swear by the Almighty Wolf, I'll never do so again."

Iris kissed his cheek, squeezed his fingers where they lay on her neck and placed his free hand on her bosom. Loosening the fingers at his groin, she cupped him deliciously; and the Torturer, relishing the sensation and the swell of her breast, buried his face in her hair and sighed. They stood quietly for a while, hardly moving, clasping each other's bodies gently and allowing their fires to be quenched by the coolness of reason.

"Believe me, no mere caprice has led to this refusal," Iris murmured at last. "It doesn't take a Seer to recognise that we're a match, Sir - a match deserving of better than casual coupling, no matter how pleasurable or relieving that might be." She laid a hand on her belly. "Under this Moon, my womb quickens... and I'm not free to grow the babe I would surely conceive. Nor would I wish to, far from your side where you couldn't share the joy of it.

"Alas... duty bids us lay desire aside. For I would know thee fully... which I can't do till you understand our Ways and consent in all volition to accept them."

Hel sighed. "You speak good sense, Madam - which is well, for plainly mine own wits have deserted me!" He shivered. "By the Claw, only think on it... to have ravished a noble ambassadress on her first night on the 'Birg... not to suggest I could have succeeded," he added hastily, in the face of her expression. "I speak but hypothetically! And to have got her with child, to boot," he continued, musing aloud. "Little remains secret from His Grace, and the punishment... well, I shall travel no further down *that* road of speculation.

'But it's cruel hard – your mere presence fills me with such pleasure, I tremble to think what it would be to look upon your body, to couple with you and have you entire... and you refuse me, heartless

96

witch! What irony – when I've never wanted a woman as I want you, never before looked into eyes that returned my desire, nor once felt a Lady's caress freely given."

Had Hel but known it, he was closer to securing the Seer's capitulation through sympathy than he had lately been by force.

"What, never?" she exclaimed, genuinely shocked. "What kind of place is this? O, poor man - what a sad loveless existence!"

The Torturer barked with mirthless laughter. "Aye, never!" he snorted. "I'm shunned by all - save my little pal Loki, who knows no better - and to be sure, they have reason enough."

"Well, you're fine in *my* sight," Iris said emphatically, "So puissant in your dark craft. O, to be in Angor... what would take a lifetime in the telling would need but a day in the showing, of how we would value you there."

"Then you're truly an alien folk, an' you esteem such as me." He shook his head slowly. "I fear you mock me, Lady. Only yestere'en at this time we'd never clapped eyes on each other, yet now you stand here in my arms, talking blithely of bearing my bairn... Is that it, some foreign foolery I don't understand – or do you punish me by raising false hopes?"

"Nay, love. Angor doesn't breed men like you - nor, come to that, many women like me! You're every bit as wonderful and strange in my eyes as I am in yours. I neither mock nor lie."

This was a territory as unknown to Hel as Angor itself. Closing his eyes he let *nightblend* conjure scenes inside his lids: Iris gravid with his seed, or feeding a chubby dark babe at her breast while he dandled a stocky toddler on his leathery knees. He could not help but smile at the thought.

"Very well, Lady Soothsayer, you've whet my appetite for things I never looked to have – is it doomed to go forever unsatisfied? How long must I wait to have you? Shall these fancies ever come to pass?"

"Aiee!" cried Iris, clapping her hands to her eyes. "Don't ask - could we stand the knowledge of what I might See? Sight is a curse as much as a blessing... look too hard and I may be drawn to meddle in events, either for selfish advantage or to protect others from hurts it's their *karma* to bear.

'So we must wait patiently... but at least we may do so in comfort! Come, Sir – let's to the gatehouse for a smoke and a sup."

"In you come, Sir!" said Thoralson, catching the Speaker's

collar and hauling him into the lamplight. "Well done - that was a doughty climb! How did you rate it – did I see you have trouble there at the last?"

Nikos and Jehan exchanged glances. "I wouldn't say *trouble*," laughed Nikos, "He had matters well *in hand*, and his *grasp* of the situation never faltered – even as I followed, his faithful *footman*-"

"Enough!" Jehan snapped in mock exasperation. "What my comrade wishes to say is that I slipped, and *he* happened to set my foot to a rung - afore I'd chance to do it myself, might I add."

"Huh - then you can watch your *own* step on the Stair! Seriously, Thoralson, I've ne'er met the like of your Fang. And I'd welcome a break from this ungrateful sod's antics – let's have a rest before we climb on."

They squatted on the small rock-hewn platform of Stairfoot to take a fortifying pull from their flasks. The flickering torchlight illuminated the first dozen or so slick, perilous steps carved into the inner wall of Mount Fang's perforated cone; beyond, the steep spiral was lost in the blackness where a tiny cold pinprick emanated from the moonlit Tip.

"You'd see the place better in broad day, when light trickles in through the sides and the Stair's lit at all the tunnel mouths," said Ragnar. "But tonight we climb in darkness - not that torches make a deal of difference except as reference points – and we'll rest at the tunnels. The Stairs themselves are no place to stop, but go too far or too fast and you risk dizziness or cramp.

'I'll lead and direct you to hazards – remember the risers vary greatly in height so you can't settle into a rhythm. Take off your gloves, go on all fours and use your hands for guidance. We'll leave the lantern to burn out along with the torches – then we're in pitch dark till we near the top.

'So go steady and don't follow too near, lest you take a foot in the face! Stay close by the wall, and brace yourselves for an hundred and fourteen steps to our first stop."

In its way, the Stair was as challenging as the Ladder. While it provided merciful respite from the wind, the Fang's interior was in a lesser state of tumult as mild, often malodorous draughts drifted up from the Lung. Its steps were cut to take advantage of natural irregularities, varying between twelve inches and over two feet in height. The width also varied considerably, the broadest steps a comfortable yard and the narrowest mere inches where they were obliged to edge along with their faces pressed to the wall, clinging to iron rings driven into the rock.

Reaching the first tunnel in short order Ragnar called, "Here it is, Sirs. Watch your heads, though, 'tis sitting room only in this one." He felt for Jehan's questing fingers and drew him within, repeating the operation with Nikos a moment later. There was just room for the tall Angorians to sit side by side, heads brushing the ceiling and long legs dangling in space.

"How much farther is it?" asked Jehan. "We've come a long way, yet yon little star seems as distant as ever."

"Another four hundred odd steps, much the same as we've just mounted. Pray don't be overconfident, My Lords, but we're well past the hardest."

A painstaking hour elapsed before Sol-Lios began to descry the steps ahead outlined in chill luminescence. The Tip was no longer a pinprick but a shining disc broad as a fresh silver penny, illuminating in stark monochrome the narrowing throat where Thoralson crawled towards the final ladder like an animated shadow.

The contrasting play of light and dark on this bizarre geography was beguilingly seductive, and Jehan stopped to admire in the face of protests from his legs and an almost overwhelming desire to move freely in safety. Seeing at last the apex of this dizzying spiral he could better comprehend the true nature of their ascent, the gigantic screw-thread of stairs they had mounted, and his mind reeled under the impact. Drawing a steadying breath he focussed on the riser straight ahead, then the next, one by one, not daring to look up lest deadly giddiness assail him. These few dozen stairs seemed the hardest of all, and it was with considerable relief he heard Thoralson halloo,

"Bravo, Sirs – almost there!"

Chapter 10: Awakenings

The final short stretch of rungs rose vertically up a tubular shaft, in diameter little wider than Jehan's shoulders. Beneath his feet the rocky gullet up which they had climbed with such labour yawned in a continuous lethal drop. Now a scant few yards above shone the proverbial light at the end of the tunnel, Thoralson's sweat-bristled head silhouetted black against the luminescence.

"Sir, would you do me the favour of keeping your eyes shut for a moment? Fear not, I'll guide you in safely."

"Heard you that, Niki? The price of sanctuary is to be denied the very view we came to see! Ah, very well – I obey."

Ragnar helped Jehan in and sat him down on a bench. Stretching his legs with a sigh of relief he took off his hood, trying to gain a sense of the place through his closed eyelids while their proud host prepared to show off his eyrie.

Dragging a round wooden cover over the shaft for safety, Thoralson cast his eyes round the immaculate tidiness. Aye, he thought, it'll do - and they've a fair night to see it! He raised the pair to their feet and turned them to face north.

"Now, My Lords – open your eyes and behold!"

"Aiee!" cried Nikos, falling to his knees. Jehan's jaw dropped then he too sank down giddy with wonder, for they seemed to be floating in space, tiny specks of organic consciousness among the twinkling stars. The glass chamber was flooded with radiance from a moon riding high and bright in a sky of darkest sapphire, trailing wisps of cloud across her fullness like a temple dancer's veils. Hundreds of feet below, *Fafnirsee* flung tall sprays of glittering spume over the rocks at Thorshaven mouth; and beyond swelled the broad sweep of Ocean, its silvery crests stretching uninterrupted to the horizon and the unearthly corona burning over the ice-land of Uttermost North.

"Holy Gaia!" gasped the Elect. "Ragnar, this is incredible!"

"I'm glad you like it, Sir," said Thoralson, mightily gratified, "And you've not seen the half of it yet! Pray turn around."

The south presented another ravishing vista: the Arkengarth foothills and central massif baring their fangs at the moon, the texture of their distant ice-capped peaks etched in infinite, ever-changing shades of azure. It quite took the Angorians' breath and Thoralson, who never wearied of the spectacle, admired silently with them.

"Almighty Naume," said Jehan at length, "This land of yours is beyond fair, Master Mountaineer. And this…" he revolved slowly, marvelling at the Tip's twelve massive stone mullions, its windows and twelve-sided roof all made of a stout double layer of diamond lattice. "I've never seen aught like it in my life."

Ragnar shuffled his feet. "I had a hand in its building," he confessed, "in my younger days. Not the Stair, of course," he added hastily, "that's an ancient thing, hewn over generations. There was just an open look-out platform here before King Thorund ordered this built to mark his accession – the jewel of his crown, he called it. Aye, every block, pane and came hauled up by hand – it took us a full spring and summer, but His Majesty was well pleased."

"No wonder!" exclaimed Nikos. "A prodigious undertaking – surely the most marvellous watch-tower ever-" A sudden sharp rap on the glass cut him off short. Thoralson started violently.

"Don't be alarmed," Jehan laughed, "It's only Kaa - the Seer will have despatched him to fetch news of our condition."

Ragnar opened a window and the Constable hopped in. "That reminds me," he said, "I should send news to His Majesty too. Pray excuse me while I prepare the signal lamp."

"Of course," Jehan's eyes glinted. "And we should do likewise – for I promised to send the Princess a token, and a capital plan has occurred..."

At the turn of twelfth, Thorund mustered his guests and headed for the Tower. His departure effectively ended the feast; the court was dismissed, and porters lugged sundry unconscious revellers back to their quarters with the same practised efficiency as Gentlemen cleared the tables and cleansed the Hall for morning.

It being overly cold for tramping the battlements, certain lesser courtiers found themselves unaccountably popular amongst their still-ambulant fellows, and propelled amidst small unsteady groups to their unfashionable lodgings farthest from the Keep. Coincidentally these afforded the best view of the Fang, and in them wagers were laid and more ale quaffed as the Thorsgard awaited sight of Thoralson's signal-fire. And so it came to pass that, one after another and despite their best intentions, the drunken courtiers passed out, piled before the windows in boneless snoring heaps.

Meanwhile Thorund had bounded up the spiral steps to his observatory two at a time, reaching the topmost chamber well ahead of the rest. On the threshold, he caught a whiff of fragrance seeping from under the door, flung it wide and grinned – Loric had done him proud! The octagonal room glowed with candlelight, striking rich colours from the carpets and astrological tapestries on the walls; its eight windows were shuttered and curtained to keep in the warmth of the braziers, save those facing the Fang, where couches had been drawn up for the watchers' convenience. Its delicious aroma emanated from an unfamiliar vessel steaming over its own little spirit lamp, procured from the High's baggage train along with a nest of Angorian travelling cups and a bowl of cane sugar crystals.

"*Maia Kali*, someone's made a brew!" cried Perikleia, hard on his heels. "Ten thousand thanks, O Thorund – I've been suffering the lack since yester forenoon!" She busied herself about the pot as the others came in, sniffing appreciatively. Handing a cup first to Thorund, she then served a cluster of Warriors who, by some unspoken command, had separated off from their fellows. As the Counsel helped themselves to dainties from the sideboard, Peri raised a cup to her comrades.

"To wakefulness, Brothers and Sisters, with this little taste of Home! Behold, Sir Host: when we would fend off sleep, this is how we take our *mocha*!"

Popping a sugar crystal into her cheek Peri sipped, rolled the hot liquid around her mouth to relish its flavour then downed the remainder in one gulp. Washing it down with a draught of water, she drew a second cup.

"Save some for us, you hog," grumbled Nery.

"Fear not, Oratoria," said Dimitri, "There's *cafe* a-plenty! Come, Loric, let's brew another pot."

"Aye, and keep 'em coming, an' ye love me," she replied, "If Sol-Lios doesn't bestir himself we're in for a long night."

Peri's companions gathered around the table tossing off cup after tiny cup of *mocha* and noisily munching cane sugar. Thorund looked dubiously at his own steaming cup, wherein a gritty pale froth lay atop a liquid almost black in hue. Despite its unpromising appearance, its aroma was rich, warmed with spicy hints of ginger, cinnamon and nutmeg. Juices flowed to his mouth, and when he sipped, a concentrated shot of caffeine, theobromine, sucrose and stimulating spices crashed into his forebrain.

"How do you like our *mocha*, Sir," Peri enquired, "Or *Kick*, to give its colloquial name?"

"By Fafnir, 'tis *well* named!" gasped Thorund.

The Next clapped his shoulder. "Aye, thy Gondaran water brews a *mocha* so noble I feel fit to wrestle a wolf pack! So come, comrades - leave the soft pillows to these luxurious bastards. *We* shall watch from the battlements, as befits true hardy Warriors!"

"Get on with it, then," retorted Jenia, stoking her pipe. "And shove thy vainglory where Sol shineth not - for if you're fool enough to go out in this chill, Peri, I cede you *true and hardy* without contest!"

Atop of all she had imbibed during the evening, Elinor's heavily laced nightcap dragged her abruptly into slumber. She collapsed face down in a tangled heap of bedding, her rump sticking up at an undignified angle and feathers from a burst pillow settling lightly on her hair. The candles guttered out, the untended fire burned low, the chamber grew icily cold; and slumped uncovered on top of her bed, her nightgown-clad body chilled slowly to the bone.

The first volley of taps to rattle her window entirely failed to penetrate her stupor. The second caused her consciousness to reluctantly re-assume its fleshly garment, and her mounded form stirred slightly on the bed. Rat-tat-tat, came the sound a third time. At last, awareness thrust through her sluggish brain. What? Where am I? Is it morning, she thought dimly; then jolted fully awake, her heart pounding, as a perfect fusillade of raps shook the casement. Attempting to rise, she discovered with nightmarish horror that she could not move a muscle.

"Berthe!" she tried to call, panic stricken, but her muffled voice made scarcely a sound, and all her limbs seemed paralysed. Frozen and blind she cried inwardly, O God, is this death? Has Jehan sent an incubus to suck me dry in my sleep?

Another hail of taps hit the glass. This time she heard the tiny splintering as a pane cracked, and her heart leapt to her mouth. There was no tree outside her high window, no way to climb to it... who could be knocking without, save some foul fiend of the night?

The ensuing pulse of adrenalin imparted a little strength to her benumbed limbs. Pushing with her arms, Elinor lurched sideways out of her awkward position, promptly tumbled off the edge of the bed and landed on the floor with a bruising thump. Shocked, disorientated and whimpering she struggled painfully onto all fours, trembling and casting about like an aged hound; then guided by a faint red glow from the last smouldering embers, crawled slowly to the hearth.

The tapping came again, gently, as if whatever sought ingress heard Elinor stirring and wished merely to remind her of its presence. Shivering, she fumbled for a pair of bellows to blow some life back into the coals. A flame flickered tentatively then rose a little higher, shedding a fitful illumination over her immediate environs. Spotting a furred dressing-robe discarded in her earlier tantrum, Elinor gratefully pulled it around her shoulders while she fed the fire with sticks. After a few more puffs with the bellows a confident yellow flame began licking the wood. Kindling from it a taper, she lit a new candle and located her scattered slippers.

Returning light and warmth imbued her with fresh courage. Candle aloft, she hobbled stiffly to the window and drew aside the curtain in search of her mysterious caller. Chilly white moonlight flooded in, softened by a mass of frost-etched flowers that rendered her diamond lattice quite opaque. Elinor cursed quietly, clambered on a stool and blew on the glass to thaw it, rubbing off a blossom or two with her fingertip. Gods damn it - outside all was blackness and she *still* could not see!

Next moment, she gave a little shriek and almost jumped from her skin - a renewed outbreak of taps had hit the pane directly in front of her face. Clearly, she had no option but to open the window, lest her unwelcome visitor's next blow shattered it completely.

"S-stop, in the Name of F-f-fafnir!" she chattered, struggling with the freezing catch, "I'm h-here!" She struck the window frame impatiently with the heel of her hand to break its seal of ice. The casement swung open a crack and immediately, a sharp black beak thrust in through the aperture. It dropped something long and dark onto the sill, and as quickly withdrew.

"Ugh!" Elinor recoiled in distaste. "The Witch-lady's familiar! And what vile thing is this – a worm? Or- O, God, say 'tis not a bunch of mouse entrails!" Steeled for nastiness, she set her dip on the sill and squinted, then heedless of the frosty blast, thrust her window wide. Kaa, waiting patiently to see if she had any return message, hopped in and hailed her with a friendly cluck.

"Bloody raptor – how dare you bring me this? Would that I could see you plucked and roasted alive!" she screeched.

Mightily offended, Kaa turned his back, committed a nuisance on the windowsill and dived off into the night with a derisive caw before the outraged Princess could do more than grab at his tail feathers. She slammed the window shut and ran shaking to the hearth, flung more wood on the fire and blew it into a fine blaze. Lamps and a dozen more candles suffused her chamber with a cheering glow; then with trembling hand, she poured out a goodly measure from the flask of *aquavit* she kept in her nightstand and huddled by the fire.

Sipping the powerful spirit, she looked glumly at Kaa's offering: a plait of hair derived from two different heads, nut-brown and gold, interspersed with tufts of shorter, wiry grey strands. A hot flush rose to her cheek.

"That *bloody* Jehan! 'A love-token', he says – ugh! And Thoralson – how dare he connive to soil my fingers with his chin-whiskers, the *ceorl*! I'll have words with my Father on this, come the morning." Her heart sank into her sheepskin slippers. "At least, if he'll receive me… O, I had forgot how displeased he is with me – and 'tis all on Sol-Lios' account!

'Why couldn't that *stupid* pagan have declined - none of this would have happened!" She poured another shot of spirit. "And what means this latest idiocy? Why in God's sacred Name couldn't he send down a note – unless he's illiterate! For I assume that *this*," she cast the plait onto the fire and watched it writhe and dwindle in a puff of acrid smoke, "means they've reached the Tip intact. Pah! Well, I suppose I should be thankful – now all they have to do is get down again." Heaving a heavy sigh, she gulped down the rest of her *aquavit*. "Regarding the which, I'll hear no more till morning… so I may as well go back to bed."

Rising somewhat unsteadily and supporting herself on the furniture, she went around the chamber extinguishing candles and all but one lamp, which she placed on the nightstand alongside her flask and cup. Moonlight gleamed accusingly on the insult Kaa had deposited on her windowsill, and Elinor pulled the curtain shut with a grimace. Addressing herself next to the maelstrom of vanquished bedding, she brushed aside stray feathers, smoothed it to comfort then kicking off her slippers, at last toppled thankfully back into bed. Despite her agitation, a fresh wave of sleep overwhelmed her. Thinking better of a nightcap, she trimmed the lamp wick to a narrow golden line, burrowed under the covers and curled up in a foetal ball. The chilly sheets warmed around her and her eyelids drooped drowsily…

A moment later they snapped open as the bed lurched and spun in a sickening swoop. Elinor groaned. Her mind and body cried out for slumber, but with eyes closed, pinpoints of coloured light danced inside her lids and swirled her into nausea. She could only alleviate the symptom by fixing her gaze on some still point, and almost weeping, forced herself to focus on the bedside lamp. By degrees her chamber ceased to revolve and Elinor sat up, shakily taking a draught from the ewer to purge the *aquavit* from her mouth.

"O God," she moaned, "What an ill day, to see me end so sotted! Great Wolf, I vow I'll never touch another drop, if Thou wilt only grant me the mercy of repose – for I'll need all my strength to face the morrow."

Sipping *mocha*, Thorund listened attentively to Nerya's discourse on these products of the Centralian forest and their cherished place in Southron culture. Enlivened by the potent brew he packed his pipe with the Speaker's weed and smoked with great enjoyment.

"O Thorund, 'tis late," remarked Zafia. "Why not rest your neck? Surely it pains you, wearing that great heavy crown these long hours."

"Hah – I'd quite forgotten it, so accustomed am I to the burden. But there seems so little notion of majesty amongst you, I suppose I can remove it." He lifted off the spiked crown and set it down on the table. "Ah... aye, by God, that's better!"

The pressure on his cranium relieved and Fang in his sights, Thorund relaxed. By now the climbers must have reached the Stair; Hel and Iris had not reappeared with tidings of any mishap; and since even his good telescope could not see through rock, there would be nothing to look for until a light flared in Fang-tip.

He leant back in his chair with a sigh. All around, candlelight shone on hawkish faces, sculpting long muscular limbs in bas-relief, reflecting from Warriors' weapons and the dagger that Nerya, sitting bare inches away, wore in her belt... Uneasy paranoia took him hold. What if his genial guests were not all that they seemed? What if Perikleia's platoon were not watching innocently from the battlements, but creeping through Thorsgard slitting the throats of its inebriated garrison one by one? He was attended only by the unarmed Loric, their egress blocked by a brace of Kalaia, one monitoring the stairwell, the other watching her comrades who had abstained from stimulants and, in the manner of off-duty soldiers everywhere, had fallen asleep where they sat - albeit with their hands resting on their sword-hilts.

Thorund stiffened, knuckles whitening as he gripped the chair arms. Had he just unwittingly surrendered the kingdom, held hostage in his own tower and uncrowned by his own volition? Nerya, noticing his glassy stare, leant close with a look of concern.

"What ails you, Sir?"

"You might well ask, General Nerya! Congratulations: take King and Castle, and all else must follow! No wonder you didn't dissuade Sol-Lios from hazard when the enterprise afforded such distraction... a night assault while my Household lies sotted, leaving me alone and undefended – hah, my Daughter's challenge must have seemed like God's gift! Mayhap I'm grown dotard and unfit to rule, falling prey so easily to your subtle snares. Well, now you have me… so tell me, what's your next move?"

"Aye, a bloodless coup - 'tis ever the Angorian Way," said Nerya reflectively, "And is it not sweet, bearding the Northron Wolf in his lair on our very first night, with nary a blow struck in anger - *Kali-Maia*, what a triumph!" She drew her dagger and twirled it in the candlelight, piercing Thorund with a look as steely as its pattern-welded blade. Then her stern face collapsed and she grew pink.

"Oho, alas that such a stratagem never occurred! I'm sorry, Sir, I shouldn't tease - let go your misgivings, 'tis only the *pipeweed* opening your senses! Though it's true you're under guard – or protection, at least, if you'll have it. Your friendship to us seems unpopular in certain quarters… and we wish no harm to befall you on our account." She flipped her dagger, caught it by the point and proffered it to Thorund hilt first. "Take her, Sir; she's called Aula, after my dam, and I give her as a pledge of good faith."

It was a beautiful weapon: a wicked steel blade with a turquoise grip the colour of Nerya's eyes, its pommel enriched with a sapphire and diamond Fusion.

The King reddened. "I accept - together with the rebuke you're too polite to utter for doubting your integrity. All I can say in defence is that it's a trick my own barons would play, had they the wit to conceive it." He reached for his telescope. "'Tis *I* should be offering gifts and apology for my *ceorlish* insult. Let me present you with this in recompense for Aula, who henceforth I shall carry always, as a caution against unfounded suspicion."

"A far-seer!" exclaimed Nerya, cradling it admiringly, "What a beauty! Look, friends - Thorund has bestowed a noble gift for us to spy upon Jehan!" Leaping over a tangle of legs she ran to the window and clapped the glass to her eye. "But I can't see a thing! Sir, pray show me how to use him."

The King took Nerya's hands, guiding them into position on the brass tube. Gently, he elevated the angle at which she held the telescope, directing it towards a large clear pane in the roof.

"This way: turn the milled ring back or forth till the image comes clear."

Nerya squinted. "Ah! I have it! Nay, I do not. Oops, too far… *Kali-Maia*!" She reeled back an involuntary pace. "By Naume, what a lens; why, I vow I could reach out and touch that very Tip! What clarity - your glassworkers far outstrip even our best. How can I thank you enough? Ah, I know." Mischievously she grasped the King's beard and pulled his face close.

Thorund had not received such a kiss for many a long dry year. He found it extraordinary; whereas in stature and build Nerya might have been male, in taste and scent she was powerfully female; and when the tip of her tongue collided briefly with his, a bolt of desire struck his groin. Half a dozen exquisite seconds elapsed before she drew back and looked full in his face. His eyes were gleaming obsidian as if The Fafnir was upon him; her own darkened in response to lusty jade.

Watching his master as ever, Loric observed both the kiss and the look. He heaved an envious sigh and nudged Iactus.

"Look - not content with setting young Fran all a-flutter, the Kalaia turns her licentious attentions to *my* love!"

"Hoi, Oratoria!" cried the Highest, following Loric's pointing finger, "Put him down - he's a monarch, not one of your Warrior playmates!"

Sigismund's temples throbbed furiously as he paced in his chamber, lips working, hands clasped in an attitude of prayer. From time to time he scurried to his desk and made notations on sheets of parchment. To a casual observer, he might have been composing a sermon; in fact, his meditations had a more sinister purpose. Everything he could recall about the Angorians was recorded on the appropriate page: physical appearance and age, as far as he could judge it; such details as they had vouchsafed regarding occupation and status; the soldiers' names and armaments; and his own caustic observations upon their speech, morals and conduct. His last sheet held an ominous list: names of all those courtiers and servants who had evinced greater friendliness to the barbarians than he deemed meet, chief among whom was Loric, Thorund's bondsman... Sigismund tapped his teeth, musingly. Loric Sorenssen, that mealy-mouthed Grunewalder deputed to serve them... an idea, an obscure connection, flashed through his mind. He snatched at it as it fluttered by, but was distracted by sounds of commotion without. Cursing, the Archbishop reached for a quill - too late, his train of thought was lost.

Someone was shouting, "Lord Sigismund! Lord Sigismund! Stand aside, Holy Brothers, in the Wolf's Name – I *must* see His Grace!" A moment later Baron Ulfar burst in, puce and panting, threw himself to his knees and wrung Sigismund's hand.

"God save us, Your Grace, from this plague on the Thorsgard! I must take my family away before the infection takes hold, as I fear it has done already in that corruptible fool Thorssen!"

The Archbishop composed his features into an expression of pious shock. Ulfar was a rare treasure, a true zealot converted to the Cult of Fafnir during Sigismund's early evangelical days, a staunch supporter of the Brethren through faith rather than fear.

"Arise, my son - what evil thing has happened to make you speak so intemperately?"

"Dreadful, outrageous heresies!" replied the Baron, getting to his feet. "I can't speak long on it, for I can't bide - I came only to tell you we're leaving. They're too vile to be borne, these perverted Southron! I must warn my kinfolk against them and close the gates of Arkengarth till Gondarlan be purged…"

When Ulfar had apprised him of events, Sigismund patted his hand sympathetically.

"Aye, my faithful Cub - go and preserve the purity of thy heart, and keep a stout watch over thy vassals, all those poor folk susceptible to foreign blandishments. Fafnir will reward thee for cleaving to His straight track!"

"Thank'ee, Your Grace," said Ulfar, humbly. "Would you grant us safe conduct, lest the Gard try to detain us?"

"Of course, my son – I place thee under wardship of the Brethren." Sigismund dashed off a few lines on a scrap of parchment, dropped on a gobbet of sealing wax and impressed it with the holy ring. "Show this pass at the gates, and even Warlord Hakon would not stay thee!

'Now, dear Baron: accept this counsel. Bide quiet in voluntary exile and do naught to bring thee to His Majesty's further notice. Nay, hear me out!" he went on, as Ulfar's face fell, "Now's not the time to be hasty. I share thy sentiments – as do all true Children of Fafnir - and by the Power of the Claw, I shall strive to convince King Thorund of his error in encouraging the heathens. Be assured that he will then praise, not punish thee, for these actions to defend faith and family." He clapped Ulfar's shoulder. "Wolfspeed thy journey; I'll pray for thee, good Cub, and miss thy presence in my congregation! Remember thine old friend the Archbishop, and send him word how that ye do."

The Baron kissed Sigismund's hand and bowed out. Directly Ulfar had gone, the Archbishop countermanded his previous orders to be left undisturbed, bidding the Brethren instead to report immediately on any fresh incident of note, quivering betimes with an arousal almost sexual in intensity. At last! At last, events were unfolding to shake Thorund off the political fence he had occupied these many years, and destabilise Gondarlan's uneasy triumvirate of power. He began logging all the new information Ulfar had imparted, snorting,

"Hah! A 'Warlady', forsooth! Most scandalously indecent," he compressed his lips prudishly as he amended Nerya's entry. "Well, Man or Woman, none are so brawny as can't be laid low. We'll need more archers and spearmen. Hakon must step up recruitment, increase practice at the butts…" His eyes sparkled. "And meanwhile, if any of Thorund's folk be fool enough to lean towards these witchy Southron… then by Fafnir, 'twill be like the old Grunewald days - what a great burning I'll make!"

A scratching at his chamber door, as if someone sought ingress yet was too timid to knock, interrupted these pleasant conjectures.

"Come in, Brother Derik."

The door opened a crack and a small ferret-faced monk sidled in, bowing and wringing his hands.

"What news, my son? Come, Brother, speak up!"

Derik knelt at the Archbishop's feet, his eyes darting nervously. "Er…O, forgive me, Holy Father, there are ill tidings… 'Tis the barbarian Lords, Your Grace: they are gone to climb Fang!"

"*What?*" screeched Sigismund, "What do you mean, 'climb Fang' – and which 'barbarian Lords' – how many of 'em?" He seized the cringing monk and shook him hard. "What in God's sacred Name are you talking about?"

"'Twas Her Highness, Your Grace - she challenged Sol-Lios to scale the peak, and he agreed, with the Lord Nikos besides! King Thorund has given Ragnar Thoralson as guide, and they make the attempt this very night."

Sigismund fell back in his chair. "What madness is this?" he murmured, brain working feverishly, "Why would Her Highness do such a thing, Brother Derik?"

"Um… er, well, Your Grace, 'tis thought… 'tis thought she was prompted. A little beforehand the Princess was seen talking privily to… er… to Lord Hakon…"

"Hakon!" Sigismund shrieked, "*Hakon* put her up to this?"

"I'm sorry, Reverend Father, we don't know for certain!" quavered Derik, "They talked too low to be heard - but after the challenge was issued, His Lordship was smirking mightily."

"Well stop them - they mustn't go up there!"

"I fear 'tis too late, Holiness-"

Sigismund struck the monk a stinging blow across the face. "Dolt, you should have come to me sooner! I must speak with the

110

Warlord *tonight* - bring him here the minute he leaves the Hall, irrespective of his condition... Is that clear, Brother Derik? Then see to it, you blundering fool."

Shortly after midnight and a hurried, whispered consultation, the monks relieved two panting Gentlemen of their burden and deposited it in the Archbishop's suite. Sigismund regarded the malodorous heap with disgust, and dashed a cup of water into its witless face.

Lolling in his seat, Hakon spluttered, "Wassis? Ale? Aye, sirrah, bring it on, I'll take another horn!"

Nothing loath to oblige, Sigismund upended his ewer over the disordered head. Hakon gasped and coughed, displaying an expanse of distended gut as he struggled to sit upright. At the sight of him, like a vomit-stained bullfrog, the remnant of Sigismund's self-control fled. All his rage at the royal family, the Angorians, his own incompetent agents and Hakon in particular became concentrated in the punch he directed towards the Warlord's belly. Stepping back fastidiously as Hakon folded, once again emptying the contents of his stomach onto the floor, he called to the Brethren,

"Fetch towels and fresh water, his Lordship is sick. Hurry now - bring bowls and an emetic, and get this mess cleared up!"

Ire somewhat relieved, Sigismund looked on as the Brethren dosed Hakon with a foul decoction to make him spew his stomach clean, removed the products and cleansed the floor, divested him of his soiled garments, scrubbed him down and dressed him in an old patched habit. Although still reeling drunk, this at least ensured Hakon would become no drunker. His belly hurt strangely, but lightened of debauch and refreshed by the dousing and clean clothes, his spirits began to rise and he to recall the masterstroke he had lately played.

"Good Your Grace," he exclaimed, focussing bleary eyes, "I'm glad to see you, Siggi old lad – I thought ye'd gone to bed! Bring on the Water of Life and les' have a drink, for by the Prong of the Wolf, I've a tale to tell!"

"Later, My Lord," said the Archbishop, wincing privately at 'Siggi'. "Here, take this instead," giving Hakon a beaker of heavily-watered wine, "and speak on! Does this tale perchance concern the attempt certain foreign gentlemen are at this moment making on our Fang?"

"Ha! Aye, that it does," Hakon chuckled. He looked so pleased with himself Sigismund itched to punch him again. "I set 'em a trap, neat as ye please, and into it they fell – or rather, off it they *will* fall, for the Fang is fell, oho ho!" He roared with laughter at the weak witticism, slapping his thighs in enjoyment. "Ho, the only good barbarian is a *dead* barbarian, eh, Your Grace? And I may have slain one, nay *two* of them this night, and them the greatest, without even soiling my blade! I should get a medal of honour for this, what say ye, Siggi?"

"For *what*, exactly, My Lord?" asked Sigismund, icily. "For enabling Sol-Lios to act the hero and win the Princess on terms the dimmest *ceorl* could understand - *by her own command?*" His voice rose in fresh fury. "For letting the barbarians penetrate our innermost secrets? For laying Castle Thorsgard, the Wolfenbirg, the very heart of Arkengarth, bare to their lustful eyes?" He grabbed Hakon, shaking the Warlord until his teeth chattered, and screamed into his face, "A medal! To have our Master Mountaineer teach Outlanders to climb Fang so they might spy on our geography and defences? Ye bladder-headed fool! 'Twas not cunning, 'twas catastrophe – *a total bloody calamity* - I can hardly believe you've done it, let alone look so smug on it."

"Unhand me, holy man, ye go too far," snapped Hakon, thrusting the Archbishop away. "The pagan's my rival for Her Highness – if any man alive is entitled to challenge him, 'tis I! He dared not fight me, but hid behind womenfolk till I goaded him out wi' that prick to his pretty-boy pride. Yet pride goes before a fall, as young Garssen could attest! And these are but nesh Southron, clueless as to their undertaking.

'Ha! I'll be fifty shilling the richer come morn if one falls, an hundred if both - and My Lady and me freed from an irksome gadfly, to boot."

"And think ye their comrades would then sit by idle? When they have warships in dock, a garrison holding the quay, a squadron of cavalry in the Thorsgard, and King Thorund in the palm of their hands? Nay, My Lord, I think not – 'twould be war!"

"Good – my blade thirsts for blood! They're outnumbered here – scuttle the ships and maroon 'em, then we can slay 'em at our leisure! 'Twould strike Angor a mortal wound, cutting off its head of state with one blow."

"And what d'ye suppose would happen if Faal got wind their degenerate allies were killed in Gondarlan?"

"Pah! Let it be given out they were lost in a storm. Who could prove the lie of it when 'tis winter and our shoals so treacherous?"

"Nay - it shall *not* be so, even though I own the thought tempting! I don't disagree with you, Warlord - but to break the accursed Law of Hospitality would bring down the odium of Urth upon our heads. And what then? I'd lay my life His Majesty would call the Gard to arms on Angor's behalf, and the fools would like as not flock to his banner! And our loyal barons yet lack the strength to prevail against a monarch with the unknown might of the South at his back...

'But when they've sailed and taken their pernicious influence with them... aye, we must be patient, Warlord! Affect contrition before His Majesty, and pray Fang delivers the heretics alive, for 'twill better suit our purpose." The Archbishop paused, ruminating. "Princess Elinor won't be best pleased with your plotting if Sol-Lios returns intact. In fact it's hard to see how this enterprise favours your suit."

"Well, if the Jehan gets back alive, he's no better than a Centrali ape-man!" retorted Hakon sulkily. "Poor Lady, to be wed to such a thing." His tone grew maudlin. "Thorund's eye is dazzled. I trow he'll send her South whether she – and we - will it or no. At least *my* plan offered some chance of salvation from yon arrogant prat. She'll remember that, one day."

"Hmm," murmured Sigismund, dawn breaking across his features, "And mayhap that day will come sooner than we think! The Princess sailing to Angor, sore and resentful in her self-endorsed betrothal... why, my dear Hakon, perchance I've misjudged you - there may yet be a way to twist this to our advantage..."

"...beyond Schwartzwald lie the foothills of Arkengarth and the Baron's stronghold, all hemmed about by that ridge we call Wolfsback. Yon tall hooked peak, the Talon, carries a high trail through to Silberthal and onward south towards Grunewald..." Encouraged by his guests' attention Ragnar talked on, extolling his beloved Tip and homeland until he quite lost track of time. When he eventually looked to the moon, he was amazed to see how far it had traversed the sky, though a good while remained before daybreak. Then he glanced northward.

"Shit!" he jumped up. "Sirs, stow your gear – pray make haste!" Cracking open the north window, he snuffed the wind. "Look!"

They followed his pointing finger. On the northern horizon, a vast barrelling mass of dark cloud was approaching, moving with great speed in the strong high-altitude wind.

"Snow storm! 'Twill be on us by dawn - if we don't leave straightway we're stuck till it blows out!"

He began rolling furs, tossing them into cupboards, hauling out harness and lines. "Here, put these on. Nay," he continued, as Jehan made to demur, "No time to argue. You'll do as I say, for we take the quick road down – can you abseil?"

"Aye, if it's what we term 'drop-walk'," replied Jehan, stepping into the straps and pulling them snug round hips and thighs.

All urgency, the Mountaineer rapped out terse instructions as they tidied the little chamber, slung their pouches and donned hoods and gloves. When all was ready, he pulled back the round trapdoor, grasped the ladder firmly, stepped off the rung and disappeared. Nikos and Jehan descended more cautiously lest their arrival at the Thorsgard be rather more precipitate than they intended. By the time they reached the top stair Thoralson had secured lines, clipped on and hung waiting, braced against the Fang's inner wall.

"On you come, Sirs, quick as you like!" he said. "I'll fix the ropes and meet you at Stairfoot."

Chapter 11: Morning

Luminosity limned Elinor's curtains, penetrating her stupor with unwelcome consciousness. She listened, hardly daring to stir for the throb of her head on the pillow. Apparently none were abroad to attend her, so she unglued her cheek from a patch of cold drool and sat up painfully, fumbling on her nightstand for water.

"God's Teeth, what happened to leave such a foul taste in my mouth?" She recoiled from a sticky cup whose odour evoked private debauch. "O, no, I'd best not think on that now!"

She gulped a hasty mouthful from the ewer, grimacing as the stale water hit her stomach like a snowball. Her rudely-awoken belly responded with grumbling complaint regarding its recent surfeit of alcohol and rich dainties; then, with a foul exhalation and sudden horrid sensation of looseness, announced a pressing need.

The dull impact of her feet on the floor made Elinor's head pound. Groaning, clutching her abdomen, she shuffled to her privy closet and sank weakly on its polished seat. Not a moment too soon - the sputtering torrent that promptly exploded was so vile she dry-heaved, grateful, for once, for the whistling draughts in the shaft that diluted its stink. Shivering wretchedly, she prayed her convulsions to end so she could dare a return to bed. Alas, even when the gassy flood was expelled her belly remained tender and swollen, a familiar weight dragging in her pelvis.

"O, no," she lamented, "Great Wolf, what a miserable morning!"

She put herself to rights as best she could, chill-stiffened fingers fumbling the hateful paraphernalia. Where could her ladies be, the slovenly minxes, it must surely be nigh on eighth hour... Clambering onto her window seat, she drew aside the curtain and rubbed frost from the lattice. A false moonshine dawn reflected from new-fallen snow, illuminating the pregnant underbelly of a massive storm-front rolling in from Uttermost North. It was but sixth glass at latest, on what should have been her first untroubled lie-abed since Sigismund's Device was inflicted; Berthe and Fran would not dare to disturb her for an hour yet at least.

Leaning her brow against the cold cracked pane, Elinor glimpsed Kaa's mess still glistening on the sill. Her guts churned anew, waking unpleasant recall of her night visitation and its ill portents for the day ahead.

"O, Gods, I can't think on that either," she muttered, averting

115

bloodshot eyes, then stiffened in sudden interest at a sound in the courtyard below. Her heart lurched disagreeably. Three shadows had marched into view; the barbarians, Wolf rend them, still lived! So she needn't fear the King's wrath, or any further punishment - save the one to which she had condemned herself. For she'd be subjected to all manner of celebrations once the hand-fasting was proclaimed... she could imagine too well how he'd gloat, that self-satisfied bastard, now the *ceorls* would be singing his saga even as they waved him back to Angor with his fair-won prize!

A spasm of cramp gripped her womb, wet heat pulsing in her clumsily wadded crotch. Bent double under her burden of woes, Elinor yanked the bell-pull for her ladies and resumed her chilly bed. Curling into a miserable frozen foetus she thought,

"O, to be a man and spared such degradation! How lightly I'd bear a thousand Devices, if 'twould only make it so."

Not every awakening that snowy morn was so ungentle. In Thorund's observatory, Iris surveyed the blunt profile beside her, the blueing heavy jowl and the sensuous Eros-bow mouth she had devoured with such pleasure the night before, now slumbering so peacefully... Tracing Hel's youth in his lineaments, she mused on what paths an innocent child must have trodden to bring him to this present maturity. How could the blacksmith hands holding her so tenderly be the same ones that fashioned the terrible suit against which she nestled... ah, to tease out the strands of this paradox! And how perilously easy it would be to slide in unnoticed, slip beneath his dark curve of lashes to See what he'd seen through those eyes... Mentally Iris shook herself, dispelling the tendrils of Vision that crawled on Hel's skull seeking ingress.

"Good morrow, beloved," she whispered instead, kissing him, nuzzling his lips apart, abrading her tongue on his sharpened incisors. Hel sighed, stirred, smiled; and rolling onto his side, tightened his arms around her and returned the kiss with passionate interest. Iris pressed against his instant erection deliquescent with desire, luxuriating in his embrace till she realised that the excitement infusing her blood was not solely due to her lover.

She signalled Dimitri, who had passed the small hours chewing coca-leaf and tending the fires. Extricating herself from a tangle of impromptu bedding and Hel's questing fingers the Seer arose, tiptoed stealthily through knots of sleepers and beckoned him to follow. Reluctantly, rolling his eyes in frustration, he adjusted his breeches and

116

obeyed.

Iris gazed out of the window, her mouth a perfect 'O' of delight. "Behold, My Lord, snowfall! Is it not fair?"

"Fair enough," replied Hel, wrapping his cloak round her sleep-warm shoulders. "But you'll glut your eyes on such views in this season – could you not wait till daybreak to see it?"

"O, but I have, Sir – Sol's already conquered the night!"

Confused, Hel sipped the fresh *Kick* Dimitri had silently passed him, raising eyebrow stubble over its steaming intensity. "Surely not for an hour yet, Lady… Come back to bed."

"Nay, trust me, love – 'tis time for our comrades to rise." With a feathery rustle, Kaa alighted upon her outstretched wrist. "They'll thank me for this, by and by."

Spooned cosily between Loric and Nerya, Thorund had sunk into deep, secure sleep. The same cry that jerked him awake sent his Kalaia bodyguard springing to her feet, blade raised as instinctively as her eyelids. All around Warriors reached for weapons, while delegates struggled into complaining consciousness.

Repeating his alarm call Kaa flapped aloft to avoid a well-aimed cushion, landing smugly unruffled on the Seer's shoulder to enjoy the consequences of his announcement.

"Kaa, for the love of Gaia, stop that cursed racket!"

"What hour is it? What occurs?"

"For pity's sake, Raven, 'tis still night without!"

Hel looked admiringly at Iris. "And they call *me* Torturer!"

Observing no more cause for concern than the Seer's heartless laughter, Nerya lowered her sword.

"Blasted witch! Why d'ye rouse us so rudely?"

"And good morrow to thee, Oratoria," Iris chuckled. "Because it's a glorious morning and you'd be woke soon enough anyhow. So have some *café* - perchance it'll sweeten your temper - and hark! More are coming to take early fast-break."

No sooner had the words left her mouth than someone pelted up the steps shouting, "*Aléia*, Sol-Lios, Oratore!" Perikleia burst in. "Our comrades are back, safe and sound!"

Forgiving Iris in an instant the Angorians scrambled for garments, hopping round in stocking feet searching for their boots midst the disarray of bedding. The King laid a hand on his racing heart, breathed a prayer of gratitude and exchanged a relieved look with Loric. Then a grin like sunrise broke over his face, and heedless of his crownless, dishevelled mane, he flung back the rugs to lead a celebratory exodus.

Berthe and Fran scurried down the corridor whispering and giggling, craning their necks at every courtyard window. Slipping into Elinor's suite in a state of high excitement they were greeted by Loki, yawning, stretching and wagging his tail.

Kindling a light, Berthe pushed open the inner door. "Good morrow, My Lady, glad tid-" The exclamation died abruptly in her throat. "O, Highness, what ails you?"

"Hush, for the love of all gods!" Wincing, Elinor put a hand to her brow. "And dim that bloody lamp! I am... unwell. Put a stone on to heat, and bring Tiny here."

She set Loki down, stroking his ears until he submitted to this familiar duty, curling like a live hot-stone on her womb. Her wan face brightened.

"Ah... that's better. Now, stoke the fire and fetch me Sorenssen – I've need of his painkilling craft."

Claiming the latter errand Berthe murmured, mock innocent, "Shall I tell Loric of your monthly ailment, Highness?"

"Of course not!" Elinor said testily, and groaned again. "No, just say my head aches most sorely and my belly is sick, which is true enough - poisoned by unclean foreign food, like as not."

The debris on her nightstand told a different story. Not daring to meet each other's eyes the girls curtsied demurely, compressing their lips.

The Princess sank back on her pillows. "Be off, then, make haste – but no clattering or chattering, an' ye love me!"

Balked of a chance to go forth and perchance glimpse Nerya, Fran placed a hot-stone in the embers and plied the bellows with sulky vigour. Meanwhile Berthe hurried back down. Pushing the bailey door open a crack, she found snow falling thickly again, stifling wind, moon and coming dawn alike; and shivering, tightened her shawl as she peered out in quest of her love. It was hopeless - she could not distinguish Loric among the tall shadows making sport in the luminous gloaming, and dared not step outside for fear of ruining her light indoor slippers. Fortunately, at that moment the Healer whirled by, her head flung back, catching snowflakes on her tongue.

"My Lady! Lady Zafia!" Bea called desperately.

"Who? What?" Zafi spun to a halt. "O, Mistress Berthe, good morrow - hast heard our news? Our comrades are back, so we're much

118

leavened in heart!"

"Praise Fafnir! We suspected as much when we saw the commotion – I'll tell Her Highness directly, mayhap 'twill improve her condition! For alas, she is… sore indisposed."

The Healer's eyes kindled. "Really - how indisposed?"

"She has pain, here and here," Berthe replied with appropriate gesture. After a moment's hesitation she beckoned Zafia close to whisper, then finished aloud, "So we've urgent need of Loric's succour – pray, Madam, d'ye know where he is?"

"Indeed – he's engaged on High service in the privy bath-house, with your King and our companions."

"O, no!" wailed Berthe, "I can't send for him there! What shall I do? Her Highness will bite off my head if I go back alone."

Zafia laughed, "Then perforce you must make do with me! I'll gladly tend to your mistress."

With the comforting weight of Loki on her abdomen, a hot-stone at her feet and the reassuring hum of housewifery in the background, Elinor relapsed into fitful dozing. She was startled back to wakefulness by a cheerful voice from the outer chamber and seconds later the Healer blew in like mid-winter, ice-tang clinging to her outdoor garb, all ruddy cheeks, sparkling eyes and hair prettily curling with snow-melt.

"What's this?" Befuddled, Elinor drew up the coverlet and praying she looked better than she felt, endeavoured to inject some royalty into her tone. "What do ye here at this hour, Lady Zafia? I'm expecting Gentleman Loric."

"He's not presently free to attend you, so I've come in his stead." The Healer took a bag from her shoulder and unloaded sundry items. "In any event, I comprehend this particular malady better than he, and know well how to relieve it." She slipped a hand under Elinor's head and raised it gently. "So first, let us deal with your pain – come, Madam, try this."

Too taken aback to protest, Elinor swallowed from the tiny cup Zafia held to her lips. Sweet syrup flowed over her coated tongue like nectar, replacing the foulness in her mouth with fruity warmth and a curious, bitter aftertaste.

"Now a little water to wash it down and your hurts will soon ebb."

In spite of herself, Elinor smacked her lips. "More, pray – I've a sickening thirst."

Zafia filled a fresh glass from the ice-clinking ewer and set it on the nightstand, then busied herself by the hearth. With the Healer thus occupied Elinor hastily chafed her face, rubbed sleep from her eyes and yanked the coverlet smooth, dislodging Loki with an indignant yip. Adjusting her neckline more modestly, she gingerly finger-combed her tangled hair back, revealing a scene of charming domesticity: Fran pattering back and forth helping Zafia, while Berthe, striving to look unobtrusive, tidied the nightstand.

She hissed at the latter, "Where by Hel is Sorenssen? And how dare you admit this – this *foreign person*, when I'm in my nightgown!"

Berthe's fair skin reddened. Dropping a resentful curtsey, she whispered explanation.

"Huh!" Elinor snorted, unwilling to be mollified; but luckily for Berthe, any further tirade was thwarted by the return of Zafia with a fragrant steaming cup

"It's good to see you sitting, Madam – the cordial must be taking effect. And this brew will complement its action – breathe the vapours, then drink when it's cooled."

Elinor took the greenish-gold cupful and sniffed dubiously. "What a strange odour - it cuts through my head like a knife. Whatever is it, Lady Zafia?"

"*Clear-sage* – is it not aptly named? It's a *euphoriant*, a brain tonic also termed '*wombwell*', being a panacea for female complaints."

The Princess took a cautious sip of the essence floating in a thin oily layer atop a tea of camomile and peppermint sweetened with honey. It was bitterly aromatic, not altogether pleasant yet not disagreeable enough to prevent her taking a deeper draught. Atop the powerful analgesic of *passionata* berry, ginger and willow bark she had just swallowed, a soothing glow ignited in her stomach and she drank the rest willingly enough.

Next Zafi gently pressed her into a recumbent position and shook out a few drops from a little golden vial, releasing the sharp cleansing fragrance of lavender. This she massaged into Elinor's temples, smoothing the tense brow under the heels of her hands, and kneading the skull with surprising strength in her slender fingers.

"Ah – ah," the Princess gasped, head lolling in boneless ecstasy. Zafia's touch was every bit as skilled as Loric's, if not more so, and she yielded utterly as the knots were cleverly teased from her tresses and scalp. Next the Healer fished ice-sherds from the ewer, rolled them in a cloth and laid the compress on Elinor's forehead.

"Now, how goes the pain?"

"It goes, from my head and stomach - I feel better already."

"Excellent!" Zafi turned to Berthe and Fran, who were watching curiously. "Pray, would you leave us while I consult with your mistress in private?" When the girls had gone she took Elinor's hand. "Madam, I gather it's not customary here to discuss such matters freely - yet we must, if I'm to help you. But first let me say I'm a *floria*-Healer – among other things a midwife, as I think your tongue has it. I've birthed more babes than you've had new dresses - no bodily function of Woman is secret to me, nor a cause for disdain. So unlock your tongue as to a physician and answer me squarely: how now goes the pain of your Moon-time?"

Elinor cast down her eyes, blushing furiously, and strove to withdraw her hand. The Healer held on, gently insistent.

"Just nod, yea or nay – is it still griping? Does the flow often pain in this way, with tenderness at your breast and belly?"

Elinor shook off her ice-pack with an involuntary nod. "Aye, to all you say and more!" she said bitterly. "O, how I dread and detest it... every month, cramps and bloody mess reminding me I'm but a chattel of my gender – it's well named the Curse!"

"Ah well, it needn't be thus - your woes can be alleviated." She released Elinor's hand, which she had been manipulating with her thumbs while she spoke.

The Princess raised it to her face, wonderingly, flexing her fingers. "What have you done? It feels like a new hand!"

"So let me practise my craft on your body – you'll feel you've a new womb besides."

The lure of relief overcame scruple and Elinor lay back, albeit in some trepidation. Zafia moved to the foot of the bed and slid her hands beneath the coverlet.

"First I must make diagnos- blessed Gaia, your feet are cold as a corpse!" She flung back the covers. "By the Naume, Madam, I wonder you can walk - no wonder your flows are impeded. Look at these poor, pinched toes and a chilblain, forsooth - permit me to prescribe a less punitive shoemaker!

'I must rectify this before aught else... blockage and poor circulation..." the Healer continued half to herself, rotating Elinor's ankles. "Hmm... I'll need woody essence for grounding... tea-tree and sandal for antisepsis, camphor and pepper for stimulation..."

She poured oil into a small bowl, added drops from a series of vials and lubricated her hands with the fragrant mixture. "This may pain to begin with, but trust me – 'twill pass."

Rubbing the tingling oil over Elinor's soles she worked all the joints of her feet, pressing hard between the small bones and tense, crackling tendons. The Princess groaned and dug her nails into the mattress, for it was indeed excruciatingly painful. Jerking when Zafia dug into a particularly tender spot she cried aloud,

"Argh! Pray stop, it makes my back hurt!"

"Good – that means it's working! Bear with it a moment longer, I'm all but done." Changing the pressure and rhythm of her movements, Zafia drew her hands firmly up, applying mild traction, stretching Elinor's toes into alignment.

"Now, here's my rede," she concluded a few minutes later, "Forgive me if it loses somewhat in translation-"

"No," said Elinor, with a stirring of interest, "Do try me in Angorian, Lady Zafia!"

The Healer bowed. "Thank you – I confess, 'tis a relief to speak my own tongue. In short, you've an imbalance of *Nône* energy, blocking your natural flows as a log dams a stream. *Aum* energy must therefore be strengthened to bring the powers into equilibrium, which I can effect with a draining massage and the Rite of Hag-Moon."

Zafia's speech was lilting, melodious, her accent pure Aumaian. The sound of native Angorian from female lips was a novelty, and Elinor listened with pleasure, if scant comprehension.

"I understand most of your words but not their collective meaning, Lady Zafia. These concepts are too unfamiliar."

"No matter - your flesh will understand. So pray recall your body-High. I need assistance, and 'tis well they should learn how to treat you in Moon-times to come."

Berthe and Fran came readily to her call. "Sisters, we've a High task to share this fine morning! I'll teach you the Hag Rites for Moon-time – then you can heal one another when need arises.

'Meanwhile pray remove your night-shift," she went on to Elinor, "I must examine your body direct."

Shamefacedly the Princess complied. Eyes shut tight she huddled under the sheet, flinching a little when Zafi reached beneath to explore her midriff, probed down to her abdomen then stopped abruptly.

"Good grief – what's this?"

"It's the *Necessary*, My Lady," whispered Berthe, "As we all wear at curse times, though we speak not its name."

"Well, 'tis *necessary* it comes off – I can't heal through such a contraption." She laughed at Elinor's expression. "But I can offer an alternative." She rummaged in her bag. "Insert this little sponge into your conduit – 'twill sop up the flow nearer its source, rendering this altogether *Unnecessary*." Mistaking her patient's expression she went on, "Don't worry, I have plenty more."

"Lady Zafia!" gasped Elinor, "I'll have you know I am *virgo intacta* – what you propose is out of the question!'"

Zafia shrugged. "Then mayhap this Hag-Moon shawl will be more to your taste." She produced a length of soft red flannel, and packed a handful of dried sphagnum moss into a small gauze tube. "The moss-pad sits betwixt these little loops, the whole bound in place with the sash that wraps around... *thus,* and then ties in the front," she went on, demonstrating on herself. "Pray try it – you may find it more comfortable."

"It pains me to speak on such indelicacies, but this can only be an improvement on my present circumstances. Ladies, attend me – we'll make experiment."

While Zafia returned to mixing oils and essences, the Princess repaired to her privy closet. Fumbling under her shift she untied the waist and thigh drawstrings of her bulky canvas bloomers, withdrawing with distaste a wad of bloody rag she thrust into the laundress basket Berthe held ready for the purpose. Then after a hasty toilette, she stepped into the shawl and made a fair fist of emulating the Angorian method of wrapping and tying. The fabric felt warm on her skin, the padded gusset nestling snugly between her thighs as she drew the sash tight round her belly, supporting her womb and swaddling her nether regions in chaste yet lightweight security. Elinor almost gambolled like an infant newly released from napkins as she emerged into her chamber, now fragrant with heady steam from the Healer's incense burner. Zafi herself waited, reclining in a chair smoking her pipe, four cups of *passionata* cordial set ready to hand.

"Thank you, Lady Zafia – this is a most soothing device."

"You're welcome, my dear – though might you not just call me 'Zafi', or Floria, which serves quite as well?

'But now let's take a pipe and sup together, and I'll tell you the *Weird of Hag-Moon.*"

They clustered around, sipping cordial and passing the pipe as the Healer, translating furiously as she went, began to speak.

"In aeons long past when the planets were birthing, Naume called into being the Orders that make up and furnish our world. And as in all else, Naume made balance and Fusion: the Goddesses Gaia and Kali, Birth and Death in terrestrial realms; their mates Sol-Invictus and

Siva, to rule light and dark in celestial vaults; and belov'd of them all, the fair Luna, playing her heavenly peep-bo by day and by night.

'Luna is sacred to Woman, stirring our blood to the universe pulse, our life's almanac by month and by year and by season. At fingernail virgin, her pale slender crescent is a girl's concave belly, her waxing the thickening womb as it ripens for seed. At fullness she's Woman in glory mature, the fertilised ovum; Motherhood gravid and fecund, golden as harvest and promise of plenty.

'But then she falls weary and wanes into Hag-Moon, as we wane each month and in evening of life; fertility passed into barren and after, our months of Moon-Dark even unto the long night when none shall bleed more.

'And so we revere her, Luna Eternally Changing, the Ever Reborn, the Female Reflection; and unlike our poor brethren, *our* bodies pay homage at each ebb and flow. Maid, Mother or Hag, she visits all Daughters alike, in each lunar month and due season.

'Thus goes the *Weird* of Hag-Moon: Woman is mutable like to the Goddess, not changeless like Sol or the phallus in season from budding till nightfall. Our blood-week is holy, renewing and cleansing; life in death, death in life, the cycle of Fusion.

'Aye, Sisters: once there was a time and place, and this a story true; I learnt it at my dam's knee, and now I tell it you. For even in the here and now, the truth of it endures. And now you've heard the *Weird*, you shall see it in action – I'll show you the Dance of Hag-Moon."

Chapter 12: Highness

The climbing party, after regaling themselves with *café* and the rest with a summary of their adventures, were grudgingly released to cleanse off the sweat of exertion. At this, Thorund considerately made offer of his private bath-suite, whereupon a great general hubbub broke forth.

"A bath-house, praise Gaia!"

"At last, to shed the skin of our journey - a thousand thanks, O Thorund, I hope you've hot water a-plenty!"

Disappointment ensued when Thorund revealed that the Thorsgard held only one such bathing facility, his own, which could not accommodate their entire number even in single-sex sittings. It was agreed that the honour of first bath must go to the climbers, with Loric, Dimitri and Dario of the High to attend. Perikleia and her comrades who had stood night watch would take the suite next, while the less deserving drew lots for later turns.

Although it was not the King's custom to bathe in company, he acceded readily enough to Jehan's invitation to join them. With his guests back intact, he was loath to let them out of his sight again lest some other peculiar contingency overtake them; and having been in a muck-sweat more than once the previous evening, the notion of scrubbing off its residues seemed suddenly agreeable.

Despatching a contingent of Gentlemen to stoke the fires and ply the pumps, he conducted his party via their quarters to collect fresh raiment, and thence to his bath suite. This was constructed around the vast chimneys of the Great Hall and Keep kitchens, using heat from their constant fires to warm cisterns of water built into its walls and feed a hypocaust serving the hot rooms. The first of these was clad out with pine boards and heated to searing dry heat by a charcoal brazier; adjoining it was a cell flagged from floor to ceiling in polished granite, a prison for the clouds that seethed from a big copper vessel hissing in its hearth. The next chamber, tessellated with maritime scenes in colourful marble, was comfortably warm and furnished with couches, mirrors, and toiletry implements. All three *Heissraumen* and the unheated *Kaltraumen* lying beyond could be entered from a central tepid washroom with a tank on the ceiling, which at the pull of a chain released a refreshing douche of water through a perforated pipe.

These appointments were so similar to an Angorian *ablutorium* that Thorund's guests felt instantly at home, and stripped readily while the King discreetly disrobed under his mantle and swathed his loins in a fresh cloth. Loric likewise retained his loin-clout in deference to his master's sensibilities, though for his own part he would have foregone it willingly enough. Ragnar Thoralson on the other hand, overawed by the splendour of the bath-suite and unprecedented intimate company of his monarch, undressed reluctantly. He dawdled shyly behind the rest, clutching a towel to his privates as he hunched into the steam chamber where his blushes were obscured by scalding fog.

The party sat on stone benches and dripped a while in silence, breathing in cautious sips until they were red as broiled lobsters and could bear it no longer, whereupon they repaired to the adjacent *Feuerraum*. While Loric attended to King Thorund, the two High tied cloths round their waists apron-fashion and commenced vigorously towelling the scummy condensation from Jehan and Nikos, next rubbing them down with scented oils till they gleamed from head to toe. Then using bronze strigils they scraped over the glistening bodies in long, sweeping strokes, wiping off the soiled residues on their aprons before administering a final rub-down with a rough hempen glove.

Thoralson, wholly unfamiliar with such sybaritic habits, watched in fascination that turned to horror when the High, ignoring his protests, began subjecting himself and Loric to the same ministrations. It came as no shock to Sorenssen, well versed in Angorian ways. He was merely embarrassed to sit in idle indulgence before his lord; but Thorund raised no comment or objection, so Loric permitted himself the rare luxury with a grunt of long-deprived satisfaction. Thoralson too submitted, after a brief internal struggle at the breach of etiquette in the royal presence and the strangeness of another man's touch - surely one of Jehan's own highly-trained Gentlemen, if he was any judge. Dimitri's hands greased him expertly, sliding therapeutically over his stiffened muscles, neither coldly dispassionate nor lewdly suggestive. So good did it feel that Ragnar's objections had melted entirely by the time the High bade him rise and face the wall; and standing considerately behind to shield him from sight of the rest, removed his towel and matter-of-factly oiled his thighs, calves and buttocks.

Breathing deep, the Mountaineer relaxed into enjoyment of the firm scrape of the strigil and stimulating friction of towel and glove. Afterwards he sat next to Loric, both of them grinning and pinkly aglow, while the High finally addressed one another, taking it turn and turn about to service the parts they could not reach for themselves.

Meanwhile Sol-Lios cocked an eyebrow at the King. "I perceive you're an athlete, Sir. Pray, what sports d'ye favour?"

Thorund looked down at his grizzled chest and belly, still flat and lean, with a trace of pride, then shook his head. "None, nowadays; though I was once accounted a fair climber, and rode much to the chase."

"Aye, and to battle too, I'll wager," said Nikos, "For isn't that an old arrow scrape on your ribs?"

"You've a sharp eye, Sir Speaker! It is - and not the only memento I wear from that day," replied Thorund, a far-away look on his face.

With that the martial members of the group commenced a general display of their limbs, exchanging scars and war stories. Rolling their eyes, Dimitri and Dario left to rinse themselves off and garner refreshments. Presently they returned bearing trays of iced sherbet and *passionata* cordial, on which the dehydrated party fell with gladsome cries; and immediate duties fulfilled, sat down to take their ease.

"But enough of this wound talk," observed Thorund at last. "I would ask, Sirs, if you'll forgive the impertinence – on top of all else, why d'ye mortify your skins with these self-inflicted scars?"

"What, the quarter marks? They're mandatory for Warrior castes – lest we're dismembered in battle," replied Nikos. "Then, as long as flesh endures, our parts can be identified and reunited, our kindred informed and our last rites performed. A requirement for us; recommended for any with hazardous Competencies; and permitted to any that wish to wear them."

"They have significance, then – pray, elucidate."

Nikos rose. "A lesson in the tongue of body-Art - very well! Here, as you'll recall," touching his brow, "the Leap gives my gender, the Spray - which is added to yearly - spells my age, while this sleeve," he clapped his left bicep, "shows profession and history, the deeds of my *Lay*. Name, titles and lineage are here, on my thigh, and the whole rendered in brief by this anklet of glyphs.

'Certain of these motifs are permitted only to Kalaia, and only Oratores may wear *this* one - Nerya carries it too, if you look close at her shoulder. But I alone, Nikos Aul'ios del'Aumaia, bear this configuration as a whole – it's mine own, uniquely the tale of my days. So here we stand," he yanked Jehan to his feet and gave his buttock a slap, "as recorded in the School of Art's rolls: the Kalaios, Quartered with bare upper right, and Sol-Lios Elect, Marked in the arm and the arse. Thus alive, dead or insensible – our bodies shall not be mistaken."

"A form of heraldic notation - remarkable!" said Thorund. "Here we blaze our devices on shields, or grave them on badges, rather than into the flesh." For the most part, he amended privately, thinking of his Torturer's suit.

"Shields can be painted out or badges lost, O Thorund – but our Marks can't be erased as long as skin remains. Speaking of which, I perceive mine's somewhat fried - yours too, Jehan, methinks we've cooked long enough. Let's douche and dress - I'm surprised Peri hasn't stove the doors in by now."

The King grinned. "But you're not finished yet - pray accompany me to the *Kaltraumen*. Come, Loric."

Mustering gear and limp towels, they followed Thorund into the intermediate *Warmwasserraum* and availed themselves liberally of its facilities. Standing modestly aside with eyes squeezed tight shut, Ragnar Thoralson rubbed soapwort lather through his hair then started in blind shock when a voice spoke low in his ear,

"Here, my friend - let me assist." A hand reached round, drew his head back, and a gentle cascade of tepid water poured over his brow. Gasping and spluttering, Thoralson yielded lest he drown, finding the combination of rinsing stream and strong fingers massaging suds from his hair and beard disturbingly sensuous. Clutching his towel desperately, Ragnar groped for a washcloth and hastily wiped his face.

"You should come join me in this *Kaltraum*, Mountaineer – methinks you need to cool off a trifle!" grinned Nikos, eyes dancing blue mischief, bulging arms akimbo above the rippling corrugations of his belly.

Striving to look him in the face, Thoralson shook his head.

"My Liege," he said unsteadily, "Pardon me for over-indulging in your Bath when my betters are waiting without – I should leave now, and send in the next."

Thorund replied pleasantly, "Certainly, Thoralson, and berate yourself not; 'tis but scant reward for your service last night."

Relieved, Ragnar bowed out. The King continued to his visitors in the same blandly agreeable tone, "Now, follow me, Sirs, I'll warrant this will interest you – it's an old custom hereabouts, and an invigorating conclusion to bath-time."

He led them into a marble tiled chamber warmed only by residual heat leaking through vents in the floor. It contained a shallow pool of water and was otherwise unfurnished save for a heavy leather-backed hanging on one wall, and a scrubbed pine sideboard whereon reposed bunches of greenery.

Thorund walked down the steps, squatted in the hip-deep water and sculled across in a couple of easy strokes. Emerging at the other end, he crossed to where Sorenssen stood with an evergreen switch at the ready. To the Angorians' collective astonishment, Loric began to beat his back and thighs, forehand and backhand, releasing a fresh cypress tang with every swipe.

"Harder, man – lay on!" exclaimed the King, turning and lifting his arms for Loric to thrash his belly. "Come, Sirs, why d'ye tarry on the threshold?"

"Why indeed," retorted Nikos, "With legitimate chance to give this wretch a beating! Let's to it, Elect!"

Dragging Sol-Lios behind him, he waded into the water which, slightly cool of tepid, compared to the *Heissraumen* seemed as chilly as the sea. A degree of splashing and wincing hilarity ensued before they clambered out, dripping, to lay about one another with the switches. This provoked further mirth, for though the whippy fronds swished alarmingly through the air and made a fearful sound when they struck, even the full force of the Kalaiaos' arm could produce no more painful effect than a stinging tingle.

Soon the air was filled with evergreen scent and the whole group smarting red. Struggling to maintain composure Thorund pulled the wall-hanging aside, revealing a glazed door through which could be seen a leaden sky whirling with snow.

"Excuse me while I take to my *Eisgarten*, Sirs – for I wouldn't expect nesh, lily-livered Southron to partake of its rigour." Bowing as graciously as naught but bare feet and a plaster of wet loincloth permitted, he opened the door and stepped out.

The Angorians raced to the window. Outside, on a flat roof terrace surrounded by a balustrade of stone interlace, stood a round, well-like structure with a close-fitting lid. Nearer to view, King Thorund was poised on the brink of a less mysterious and altogether grimmer prospect, a pool not dissimilar to the one they had just quitted. Earlier on, Gentlemen had smashed its icy surface using the mallet that lay conveniently to hand; but the floating bergs had begun to coalesce again, forming a thin cataract dotted with fresh fallen snowflakes to dim the water's glassy green eye.

Saluting his huddled audience with a nonchalant wave, Thorund stepped through the frozen skin and disappeared from sight. A handful of seconds later he broke surface at the opposite end like a breaching whale, forcing himself by main strength of will to remain submerged to his waist while he squeezed the water from his hair. Then he hauled out of the pool roaring and plunged bodily into a deep snowdrift, rolling around and rubbing handfuls over his limbs. Finally, scarlet, clots of snow clinging to his stiffening breech-clout, Thorund hastened to the tub, pulled off the cover and sank gratefully into its steaming contents. Grinning, he beckoned challenge to his audience.

Dimitri nudged Jehan. "Look, our venerable host mocks you, Elect – that will not do."

"Nay indeed - go defend Angor's honour, Sol-Lios."

"I wouldn't dream of it, my dear Kalaios – after you."

"By no means – I cede the right gladly."

"You're too kind, but I couldn't allow it. Pray, go ahead."

"Well, for fuck-sake, will one of you go," said Dario, "My balls are freezing off while you procrastinate."

"Very well; 'nesh', did he call us? So be it: we must give him the lie. Come, Niki – we'll step forth together."

"Huh!" snorted Nikos, and flinging wide the door bellowed, "Last one in's a lily-livered Southron! *Kali-mara!*" He leapt across the duckboards leading to the pool, allowing momentum to plunge him in before nerve could fail.

Jehan hung back, waiting for the results to subside before climbing onto the edge. As the Speaker's torso erupted whooping for breath he laughed,

"And first one in's entertainment - whoa-argh!"

Nikos's fist had closed about his ankle, hauling him unceremoniously from his perch. Sol-Lios had barely time to catch his breath before hitting the gelid surface full-length, scattering spray and ice sherds abroad and shattering vocabulary into incoherence. He could muster no word to describe the sensation as the pool closed over his head; any variant on 'cold' or even 'pain' felt pitifully inadequate.

Cramped and convulsing he flailed, broke surface wheezing and gasping, and floundered to the poolside. Nikos, wallowing in the drift, greeted him with a snowball Jehan was amazed to find warm compared with the water. He flung in alongside and grappled briefly with the Kalaios, stuffing a vengeful handful of snow into his helplessly laughing mouth. Then they dashed shivering for the hot tub wherein Thorund awaited, his frost-crowned head resting on the rim and arms stretched along the sides, snowflakes melting as they settled on his skin.

Jehan submerged briefly, reappearing with a long bubbling exhalation and shaking water from his hair. "Ah… by the gods, Ice-Wolf – 'tis a noble bath you have here!"

"Thanks, Sol-Lios," replied the King, laugh-lines cracking round his eyes, "Feel free to use it whenever you will – and to demonstrate my *Eisbad* to your colleagues, as you like it so well."

130

"Hah - that we will, never fear!" interjected Nikos, *"Maia-Kali*, I'd give much to watch the Oratoria attempt it!"

At that moment Sorenssen appeared, hair damply tousled, fresh liveried and carrying a tray.

"Good man, Loric!" said Thorund, "My Lords, here comes reward for baring your flesh to the teeth of my pool! You must try this *Pfefferwein*," he passed two fine lidded goblets of niello-inlaid silver, "To enjoy the benefits of the plunge to its utmost."

Jehan choked as a mouthful of hot *aquavit* sweetened with mead and enlivened with ginger and pepper grasped his throat, then an expression of pleased if pained surprise spread over his features.

Nikos tossed down his cup in three gulps. His face flushed scarlet in a heartbeat, an instant dew of perspiration breaking out upon his brow.

Thorund cried, "Quaffed like a Warlord, Kalaios! Well done!"

Springing to his feet, Nikos slapped the King wetly on the shoulder and himself on the belly. "Ten thousand blessings, O Thorund," he coughed, "Your bath rites make me feel like a new man! Or, by the Goddess, a woman - for egad, it hath heated my root... What's your counsel, Sol-Lios? Should I go seek out Nery, or Scylla? Forsooth, I know not which I'd rather be mounting!"

"Nay, go exercise your blade instead – can't you hear our comrades at drill down below?"

King Thorund's heart leapt to his mouth even as Nikos leapt from the tub and onto the broad parapet alongside. Streaming and steaming, he stood poised perilously over the sheer drop to the cobbles of the Inner Bailey, raised his arms in salutation and roared,

"Ave, Kali't'aia!"

Receiving in response a faint hail of whistles, to Thorund's great relief he jumped nimbly back to safety before a freak gust of wind could blow him to destruction.

"*Aléia*, they're making good sport down there! I shall join them, for I must run or explode – are you coming, Elect?"

Sol-Lios grinned, stretching luxuriously. "Nay... by your leave, Thorund, I'll continue my research into Northron bath rituals - aided by another *Pfefferwein* and a stiff pipe of weed, if you'd be so kind, Loric. Don't let us detain you, Kalaios."

"Very well, stew in your own juice, you lazy sod." He padded away, jeering at the High shivering towel-swathed within, "Go take the ice-bath, you soft brace of shite-hawks!"

"Alas, I've no clean garb here - I must hie back to the ship," said Dario, "You perforce must excuse me."

"Me too - I need to ready the *ablutorium* for our fellows," added Dimitri, "Loric can aid me – 'tis overly cold to tarry outside!"

Watching them go Thorund observed, "He hath a great... vigour, your Speaker."

"Aye – too great for his own good at times," chuckled Jehan, "'Tis meet he should go blow off steam - no orifice in the Thorsgard would be safe from him else!"

Reclining in quiet comfort they sipped the fresh drinks Loric presently served, passing Jehan's pipe back and forth, the combined effects of alcohol and smoke expanding their thoughts pleasantly. The Elect extended his tongue and caught a snowflake.

"Hah! Perfect Fusion of heat and frost... this would be impossible at home. A bath-house *caldarium* – now there's linguistic confusion with your *Kaltraum* – has heat a-plenty, but never has a *frigidarium* such bone-biting chill. Aye, Thorund, this is truly a land of extremes – and a privilege for us to be here."

The King smiled. "As it is to have you, Sol-Lios... I'm pleased you can claim my daughter fair and square, and to entrust her to your keeping. Methinks 'twill do her good."

"I'm honoured by your confidence, Sir – would it were shared by the Princess! Still, she may find me more appealing by the light of a new day... so I should bestir myself from this water, or I'll be wrinkled as a prune when I go to pay my respects."

In his fart-redolent chamber the Warlord jerked and snorted. "Hnn - wha'? Wassat?" he grunted into his pillow; then aloud, "Wha's going on? Shut that bloody row, ye poxy buggers!"

Outside, the hubbub continued unabated. Foolhardy sleep-murderers – who could they be? Bent on discovery, Hakon thrust from the bed and promptly pitched to the floor with a thud, feet entangled in the hem of an unfamiliar monkish habit. A bolt of agony jolted his forebrain and cursing, clutching his skull and strangely painful belly, the Warlord knee-walked to the window. Hauling upright with the aid of the curtain, he kicked his legs free of bondage, irritably yanked aside the drape and peered out.

His jaw dropped, bleary eyes starting from their sockets. On the battlements snow-blurred silhouettes ran back and forth, dodging behind the crenellations, while martial cries in two tongues rang from the courtyard below.

"I knew it – I fucking *knew* this would happen!" Straining his hoarse, vomit-seared throat, he bellowed, "Gards!" then hitching the robe to his knees, stumbled round the room, stamping barefoot into boots, buckling on his belt and casting about for his sword. Not finding it, he snatched up a throwing axe instead and croaked at the door-guards who anxiously entered,

"I'll see you both flayed, you cloth-eared sods! Why didn't you wake me?"

"B-but My Lord-" stammered one.

Hakon brandished his axe. "But me no buts – can't you hear? We're under attack - sound the thrice-damned alarum!"

Making such haste as his skirts permitted, he fled from the suite barking orders, accumulating a trail of confused soldiery as he pounded downstairs. The bailey door he flung wide, plunged headlong out then froze dead in his tracks. A scant few yards off, the wild-faced Kalaios was pelting straight at him with blade raised aloft, a trio of Gondarans giving hot chase.

Seeing Hakon, Nikos swerved and tried to stop, but skidding on the packed snow flailed helplessly past until he thumped to a sword-clanging halt beside the doorway. Alas, one of the luckless pursuers had just launched a missile at his back, and deprived of its intended target, it sailed directly at the Warlord.

Registering its trajectory Hakon lurched sideways just in time, whereupon the sentry behind took it full in the face. Meanwhile Skala and Karl, misinterpreting frantic yells and signals, unleashed from the battlements the teetering ambush towards which their comrades had driven the enemy.

Flattened against the castle wall, Nikos watched aghast as a miniature avalanche crumped onto the spot where he should have been standing, burying Hakon from boots to crown. For a moment the white heap stood in shocked stillness. Then the Warlord exploded in a thrashing of arms, spitting icy rage as he shook snow from his eyes.

All around, battle cries and shrieks of merriment died away. One by one, Ingard stiffened into petrified realisation and a chill silence descended, punctuated only by Hakon's irate spluttering and faint, snow-muffled taunts from their Ausgard adversaries triumphantly oblivious to the turn of events.

"*Kali-maia!*" whispered the Speaker, wiping and sheathing a blade lately employed to no deadlier purpose than slicing snowballs from the air, and hastened to his aid. Heaving his boots clear, Hakon shrugged off the barbarian hand brushing snow from his shoulder, pushed Nikos rudely aside and stamped to the centre of the courtyard.

"Who did that? Who the *fuck* did that? Get down here *now*, you bastard sons of bitches!" To the Ingard he raged on, "You sorry bunch of snivelling shit-arsed curs – what are ye playing at? Where's the Captain? I'll have him gutted and fed to the hounds for this! Well? Answer me, dammit! *Where is he?*"

Sergeant Elf stepped forward, miserably conscious of the incriminating spatters of frosty shrapnel on his breastplate. Sinking to one knee he stuttered,

"S-sir, Captain Ha-haral hangs in the Pit... upon thy c-command, Sir."

"Hah! Lucky for Haral... well, you shall hang alongside for this morning's work! But first, get the fucking ranks fell in, and- oho, here come the jokers!" Hakon interrupted himself as Skala and Karl slunk wretchedly down the steps. When the pair had been dragged on their knees to his snow-clotted boots he snarled,

"Now matey boys, let's see how you like *my* sense of humour – twenty five lashes apiece! O, that's wiped your smiles off - not funny enough? Then let's make it fifty!

'Elf! Summon Hel. He can give you a score too, for good measure."

Relaxed, radiating cleanly wellbeing, King Thorund and his guest strolled back to the annexe. Dimitri was there, laying out their garments as he chatted to Iactus and two Warriors new come to bathe, Loric having been despatched to fetch fresh evergreens.

As they variously dressed and undressed, a figure sauntered in from the *Warmwasserraum*, nude save a silver *ankh* necklace and a towel slung over one shoulder.

"Hail, O Thorund - my compliments on your fine *ablutorium*!"

The King's eyes dropped involuntarily from the forehead Mark to the contradiction of flat loins and a perky little bosom.

"Ma-Madam!" he protested, averting them in confusion, "You should not be in here, along with the men!"

"But Sir, Master Thoralson said, 'send in the next'," replied Perikleia sweetly, "And so in we came! But fear not for your High Gentlemen's sensibilities, I arrived in disguise - see?" The Kalaia wiped her brow, letting her Blood-drop blush crimson through a smear of white cosmetic.

While her compatriots guffawed, Jehan slapped her back. "A cunning device, my dear Peri - and no harm done, eh, Thorund? After all, you gave leave we could follow the customs of Angor, where male and female commonly bathe altogether."

"Aye," Perikleia agreed. "So come, Iactus, render me High service – I'm dirty, and need oiling down..." Tipping a wink to Thorund, she undulated from the room.

"At your command, Kalaia!" cried the Highest, catching up his strigil and flasks with alacrity. "Pray excuse me, comrades."

Thorund shook his head. "Angorians! Men and women alike, th'art undoubtedly the most brazen, the... the nakedest folk I've ever encountered!"

"Our climate makes us so," Jehan said lightly, donning his jacket, "Just as yours makes all Northron high-necked and tight buttoned!"

They were on the point of departure when the door burst open and Loric dashed in.

"Majesty, Lord Jehan!" he panted. "Pray, Sirs, come quickly – the Warlord's gone berserk!"

Chapter 13: Scourge

Knots of the ghoulishly curious had gathered at windows overlooking the inner bailey where ranks of flushed, snow-speckled Gards stood to rigid attention. Karl, Skala and Elf knelt bound in the snow, stripped to the waist, shivering with cold and terror. Behind them Hel waited stolidly, his shaven head protected by a ghastly man-hide balaclava, a brutal barbed whip hanging over one arm.

Mustered opposite, the Angorians were remonstrating with Hakon's retinue. The Warlord himself was obliged to hear them out in glaring silence, having shouted his voice away quite.

Striding out into their midst, the King held up his hand. "Peace!" he roared. "What means this commotion?"

Purple-faced, Hakon gesticulated violently to his henchmen. Before they could intervene, Nikos bowed politely.

"It seems the force of your argument has worn out your voice – permit me to speak for you, Sir." Hakon fumed impotently as with a sly sidelong wink, the Kalaios turned to Thorund. "My apologies for the uproar, O King - and for an inadvertent assault upon your Warlord, the which fault I regret lies with me-"

"And with me," cut in Nerya, taking advantage of the lull to sling her cloak around the frozen huddle of prisoners.

"It lies with me," Nikos contradicted, "As I shall relate - if the Oratoria permits!"

It had started in all innocence, Nikos explained. He had found his comrades, ever wont to leaven duty with pleasure, studying the properties of snow, testing balance and footing thereon, and assessing the effects on their fighting abilities. The exercise having proved mightily instructive, they progressed to experiments regarding the stopping power and ballistic capacity of this unfamiliar substance. They sculpted white targets on the castle's dark stones; threw up dummy assailants; fashioned quantities of projectiles of varying size and weight; and taking out their slingshots, commenced investigations.

Inevitably, folk soon wished to try out their skills on moving targets. So inevitably followed errors and 'accidents' whenever volunteers ran the gauntlet, sparking retaliatory feuds among the rest. By the time Nikos arrived a spirited general affray had broken out in which he immediately spotted the potential for additional entertainment, and mustered the *Kali't'aia* into platoons under the generalship of himself and Nerya. Dividing the courtyard into opposing territories, they constructed a few snowy ramparts and dugout defences, supplied themselves plentifully with ammunition and unleashed war-game in earnest.

And so things might have continued – were it not for Skala and Karl. Bored and chilly as they patrolled the battlements, soon they could bear it no longer. Scraping up a soft handful Skala let fly a neat snowball at the back of Nerya's head as she ran underneath, then ducked sniggering back behind a turret.

"Got 'im!"

"Nice one, matey!" said Karl. Following Skala's example, he caught Captain Iamis square between the shoulders.

Peeping over the wall they were delighted to see Iamis glance sharply about for the source and shout incomprehensible abuse at the likeliest culprit. The falsely accused Kalaia responded with an indignant snowball to his face and Nikos, seizing the opportunity afforded by this break in their ranks, yelled to his troops and launched a ferocious counter-attack.

Gradually more and more Ingard joined their covert offensive, even Sergeant Elf rallying to the cause. Having overlooked any possibility of aerial interference, much internecine strife was fomented among the warring factions by these strategically placed missiles, greatly increasing the ferocity of the skirmish and the enjoyment of the concealed spectators.

At last, a particularly audacious shot drew the Speaker's attention. Extrapolating its trajectory, he glimpsed Skala dodging behind a watchtower.

"Pax, Oratoria! Hold, *Kali't'aia*!" he bellowed, "We have a new foe – Gondarlan! *Kali-mara*!"

Instantly the troops put aside their differences and swung into united action, Nerya leading a daring assault on the battlements to flush their assailants into clear view. This duly attracted the notice and involvement of the Ausgard, whereupon a full-scale civil war broke out within and between both baileys. Acts of terrible treachery and retribution were committed on all sides, strange alliances melting and re-crystallising as unpredictably as thaw in a Gondaran spring. Even the servants became embroiled, with a passing stable-lad held ransom for Florian who, innocently minding his business in the stables, had been kidnapped by the Ausgard. This fostered an unlikely coalition betwixt Angor and Ingard to effect his rescue - which Florian promptly repaid by recruiting mercenaries of both nations to punish the Speakers for his ordeal.

Betrayed by their comrades, beset all around, they had run

hither and yon fending off missiles, driven inexorably towards the snowy downfall that would spell instead doom for Skala, Karl and their Sergeant.

"… and so you see," Nikos concluded, "these soldiers were but entertaining us. Pray spare them, Sir. It's all on our account, so if punishment is meted out then I'm the one-"

"*We* are the ones that should bear it," Nerya finished.

Thorund raised his eyebrows. "Sol-Lios, I'm confounded – what's your word on the matter?"

"Well… plainly my companions have provoked and encouraged this, and the affront suffered by Lord Hakon was but a consequence thereof, a most unfortunate accident. So I'm with the Oratores. If the offence is deemed punishable and they wish to step in as whipping-boys, I'll not gainsay it."

King Thorund shook his head. "Hmm… I like it not," he said unhappily, dashing faint hopes in the prisoners' breasts. "It would be unprecedented irregular to treat state visitors in such wise! Anyway, tell me, Torturer, exactly what *is* this sentence my guests volunteer to undergo?"

"Altogether, an hundred and twenty lashes, Sire."

Thorund's eyes widened. "Not with *that*?"

Iris interposed herself between Hel and the intended victims. "Not while I live!" Taking the Claw from his hand, she drew its hooked iron barbs thoughtfully between her fingers. "May I ask, My Lord, what precisely is this instrument's purpose?"

Hel felt the Seer's gaze boring into him through her impenetrable cowl, and shuffled his feet.

"Er… its purpose is corrective, Madam, to… er… to teach a lesson that won't be forgotten."

"And what lesson, *precisely*, might that be?" she demanded, "How to maim a trained warrior and render him useless for his purpose?" Rounding on King, lover, Warlord and cronies alike she spat out the Gondaran gutturals in a voice that rang round the bailey, "Ach - it must work most wondrous well! Yet for how long is the 'lesson' remembered afore its students bleed to death, eh, My Lords? But if under thy Law and by thy command 'tis the only redress for our heinous offence, I offer myself to its kisses – all six-score.

'There now - does that suffice?"

Inside his second skin Hel drenched in cold sweat, blessing the balaclava that hid his expression as Thorund hesitated, surprise rendering him momentarily as mute as Hakon.

"Aye!" the latter was mouthing, punching the air and nodding frantically to his followers. Mighty Wolf, he was thinking, while his coterie of soldiers and Brethren stamped and yelled proxy approval, what a turn-up – this'll put me high in old Siggi's favour, having their *Wyrd*-woman Clawed unto death!

Directing her cowl towards his howling pack, Iris forced her will upon them and stepped smoothly into the silence that suddenly fell.

"There is an alternative I would happily cede to the Speakers." From the folds of her cloak she pulled a whip of seven broad, supple leather thongs and passed it to Hel. "The Meditation Scourge – it concentrates the mind most wonderfully yet breaks not the skin, nor scars or mars the body for its function."

"Aye – spare your back, Seer! Let the Oratores be Scourged - they deserve it, bringing this trouble upon us!" shouted Florian. His call was taken up by the rest until the bailey resounded with chants of, "Scourge 'em! Scourge 'em!"

Sol-Lios looked expectantly at the King, "Well, Sir – will you accept this pain-offering in lieu of Lord Hakon's sentence?"

Thorund considered a moment. "Attend us well, all of you. Gard, you deserted your posts, neglected your duties and caused His Lordship to suffer assault - aided, we regret to say, by a Sergeant who should have known better. The Warlord has cause to be wroth! So have we; and we deem a measure of punishment meet."

Heads bowed in numb terror, the luckless trio waited trembling for the blow of his next words to fall; as did Hel, though for different reasons.

"However, since you three were far from the only ones involved," Thorund looked sternly round the sheepish Ingard, "you should not bear the whole punishment. So, having heard the mitigating circumstances and our guests' compelling pleas, we're minded to grant their request.

'To satisfy martial law, the Speakers will take responsibility for this escapade. And to satisfy Angorian law, the chastisement will be administered with their native instrument."

"No!" Hakon soundlessly screeched. Amid disgruntled muttering from his troop he beckoned his lieutenant and wheezed urgent orders into the man's ear.

"Sire, His Lordship says a tickle with yon child's plaything is no fit redress for the wrong done unto him!" said Lieutenant Rodgar, nervously. "He demands the full weight of the Claw be borne by the Lady."

Emboldened by the groundswell of bloodlust around him, Brother Maris stepped out from among Hakon's men-at-arms.

"Quite so, My Lord King - and with all due respect, may I add on behalf of my Holy Father: 'tis no fit redress for the wrong done unto the dignity of Almighty Fafnir and his Wolf-pack. In the Name of the Wolf and His Grace the Archbishop, my Brethren and I agree with Lord Hakon – let the Lady be Clawed."

Contrary to appearances, the Torturer was not a man much given to anger, nor were his atrocities motivated by hatred or malice towards his victims. Hel simply carried out his allotted quota of murder and mutilation to the best of his considerable ability, completely indifferent regarding matters of innocence or guilt and impervious to pleas for mercy. His was an important job, one he took pride in; and it was largely this dispassionate sadism that made him so esteemed by his masters and feared by everyone else.

Today, for the first time in his career he had waited on a verdict in agony, and on hearing Thorund's judgement sagged within his manhide weak with relief. But as Hakon's faction called for the Seer's blood, new emotion swept through him. He had been pensively caressing the Scourge's thongs, appraising their weight, contemplating their effect. Now without warning he barrelled violently across the court, drew back his beefy arm and released the full power of freshly lost temper on Maris.

The monk shrieked and fell to his knees, clutching a splatter of scarlet welts across his left cheek and eye. Raising the Scourge again the Torturer rounded on Hakon, dark fury blazing through his eyeholes, the sharpened incisors he was not averse to deploying on Pit victims champing at his mouth-slit. Irresistibly reminded of a great *Rottweiler* hound the Warlord recoiled an involuntary step.

"This *will* suffice, when 'tis my hand that wields it!" Hel snarled. "What say ye, My Lord - aye or nay?" Without waiting for answer he turned on the retinue, cracking it in their stunned faces. "What say ye, Brethren - anyone else deem sixty such stripes insufficient?"

Trapped between Hel's fury and the Seer's hooded stare, the bellicose faction subsided. Hakon, his eyes drawn inexorably into the black depths of her cowl, felt adrenalin leak down his chapped legs and out through the soles of his clammy wet boots. Awareness grew of the soaking, snow-caked habit chafing against his near-naked body; the pains of his throbbing head, seared throat and bruised, nauseous belly, and everywhere, the stiffness of bone-aching cold. An acute need for fire, furs and hot *Pfefferwein* drove all other thought from his mind; he shivered, head juddering, seized by an uncontrollable ague.

"Behold - Lord Hakon still says nay, the Scourge sufficeth not!" exclaimed Sol-Lios. "And for the rude end to our toilette I'm inclined to agree. *I* say, double the sentence – give 'em one-hundred-and-twenty apiece! How's that, My Lord?"

Gritting his teeth against their chatter, Hakon forced his head into vertical tremor – anything to escape - and groping for scant comfort, pulled up his hood. This loosed the remnant of avalanche trapped in its folds; and as it cascaded about his ears, the expressions of Thorund and his guests congealed into tight-lipped solemnity. Frozen beyond further humiliation or courtesy, the Warlord twitched snow from his hair, summoned his coterie with a convulsive jerk and stumped from the court as fast as his numb feet would go. His followers trailed behind, Maris with hand clamped to cheek, casting many a loathing glance at Hel from his one good eye.

Thorund fixed the vibrating ranks with baleful glare.

"A Blood Eagle for the first man to utter a *sound!*" he hissed, continuing dryly to Jehan, "If this is how you treat your friends, Sir, God forbid I should ever become your enemy."

Nerya bowed ironically. "Aye, thanks, Elect – I don't think! I' faith," she unfastened her collar, "For all the benefit I'm deriving therefrom, I know not why I bothered packing winter garb." To the courtyard at large she cried, "Six score lashes apiece for a snow-hurling fight – is that fair?"

"Yes, you war-mongering harpy!" cried Florian. "Stop procrastinating and take your pain-offering!"

Arms akimbo, Nery faced him down. "Very well - come, Brother, let us prepare."

They began with the blue huddle of prisoners, hauling them upright and cutting their bonds so that their bloodless arms fell limp at their sides. Nerya rubbed Karl briskly with her cloak to chafe some life back into him, while her comrades ministered similarly to Skala and Elf. Then heedless of cold and audience alike she stripped off her jacket and singlet and dressed his helpless form like a rag doll in the body-heated garments.

"Warrior, pray keep these warm for me!" she said, kneading the fingers that barely protruded below her cuffs. "Poor man, treated so harshly just for playing our games... truly, we merit a beating for what you've endured." She flexed his arms and Karl moaned as blood was forced back into his constricted veins.

141

"Ah, it pains you... here, sup this." Uncorking a flask, she tipped a measure of cordial into his slackly gaping mouth; took a swig herself, passed it to Nikos, and slapped Karl on the back when he sputtered and coughed. Then wrapping him snugly in her mantle, she took his hand.

"Warrior, pray forgive me for bringing this trouble upon you."

Stunned, Karl quavered, "A-a-ah-ay-aye."

Nery smiled her charming crooked smile. "My thanks - then Nerya Aul'aia stands deep in thy debt."

Every window of the bailey was white with faces; every door oozed spectators into the shelter of archways and eaves. All their attention was glued to the bare-chested Oratores, braced in the centre of the courtyard hand in hand, arms held aloft and legs spread as if tied to invisible cross-trees.

Buried in outsize garments, tingling with pins, needles and *passionata* cordial, the slowly thawing Gards had a ringside view from the Angorian camp. Skala's spirits lifted with each throb of his fortuitously still-beating heart.

"By Fafnir, that was a lucky escape," he whispered to Karl. Getting no response he nudged with his elbow. "Eh, matey? *Very* fucking lucky, I'd say."

Karl sighed, his gaze rapt on Nerya."See how bold she bears a whipping for us... what a woman! Nay, she can't be mortal – she's a Valkyrie made flesh-"

Skala gagged theatrically. "Yon foreign liquor's gone to your head – you sound just like a big fairy Faalian fop!" Clasping his hands he cast his eyes to heaven, murmuring in chivalrous parody, "O beauteous Lady Nerrier, prithee accept the undying love of thy humble swain, Sir Karl the Bloody Useless."

"Mock if you will," Karl said stoutly, "I care not! She saved our backs, you thankless dog, and so shall ever be *my* Lady... I'd be honoured to lay my sword at her feet, give my life in her service-"

"Well, she plainly doesn't want your life, or she'd not have troubled to save it! And I doubt she needs your little sword either," sniggered Skala, "She seems quite apt to take care of herself!"

A tense hush fell. Hel savoured the moment, teasing watchers and condemned alike. No blood, the Torturer was thinking, no blood... what can I give 'em instead? Casting around for inspiration his glance lit upon the Kalaia's comrades-in-arms, and suddenly it came to him.

Grinning nastily behind his mouth-slit he moved to the Angorians' rear, sighted down the whip, took careful aim and laid a full-bodied blow across Nikos's shoulder-blades.

"One!" cried Jehan, as seven perfect scarlet stripes splattered over the tawny skin.

"One!" echoed Florian a second later, when Nerya was decorated in similar fashion by the backhand.

Whish-crack! "Two!" Their comrades joined in with the count, clapping in time to the strokes.

Hel lashed systematically up and down the Oratores' backs, marvelling at their stoicism. Mayhap a fresh target would pry some response from those stubborn lips, he thought, licking his; and stepping round to the front, took aim once more. Exclamations burst from the onlookers as the blow struck Nerya full across the chest, viciously crimsoning her bosom.

"Are the cockles of thy heart warmed, Kalaia?" he jeered, and hit her again, on the same spot; then lower, across her taut belly, working from hipbones to clavicles, willing her in vain to cry out.

Her supporters had counted twenty more strokes before the frustrated Torturer switched his attentions to Nikos. By now the effort of suppressing pain was making both Speakers sweat freely, salt droplets spraying as every lash blazoned their skins afresh. Hel perspired alongside, pleasurably heated by his own exertions; he stripped off balaclava and jacket, relishing the refreshing tickle of snowflakes expiring on his scalp and hirsute torso.

Beneath her cowl Iris exhaled a low whistle. Then she laughed aloud, having perceived in that instant Hel's Design. Their eyes met. Tipping her a wink the Torturer began playing for his Lady's favour, working the crowd, a consummate showman: varying rhythm and target, running up or spinning like a shot-putter to increase the power of his blows, skilfully changing his grip to alternate between horizontal and vertical slashes.

Enlightenment dawned on more Angorian faces and much to the confusion of Gondaran spectators, laughter and scattered applause spread through their number. Frozen in stance, the hapless butts of this mirth exchanged sidelong glances, wondering why their suffering had become the object of such hilarity. Meanwhile the Torturer surveyed his handiwork. Aye, that would do nicely, he thought; now for the finishing touches! Licking his palm he drew the Scourge's thongs together and administered a series of precision blows of tremendous force.

"One hundred and twenty!" roared Jehan as the Kalaios

resolutely bore his last stripe.

Hel almost salivated as he stepped across to deliver the last blows to Nery. With slow, deliberate menace he opened his mouth and ran the Scourge between his teeth, curling his tongue obscenely round its pliable leather. Then he extended a finger to tilt the Oratoria's chin up, simultaneously poking the whip handle into her lumbar spine to force her body into a bow-like arch.

Stepping back he brought his hand down in a great whistling arc that would have cleaved her in twain had it held a sword. As it was, the moistly consolidated straps merely thumped a dull, bruising welt the length of her sternum; and to Hel's gratification this at last won a reaction, forcing out an "Oof!" of breath and making her eyes widen reflexively.

For a second Hel saw green defiance glint under her lashes and smirking, raised his arm to strike again. The Kalaia's scarred lip twitched and she tensed to meet him, drawing back her head and thrusting her hips subtly forward to pull her breeches taut over her pubic mound, transforming her demeanour into that of a woman anticipating strokes of entirely different kind.

Whistles and ribald approbation exploded from the *Kali't'aia*. "Go, Nerya *Tantrissima*!" they cried; and, "Ho there, Lord Torturer - give her a hard one for me!"

Only too happy to oblige, Hel applied the Scourge vigorously from the hollow of Nerya's throat to the waistband of her breeches, avoiding her face with great skill. She held his gaze throughout, now panting softly open-mouthed, now biting at her lower lip, provocatively arching towards the climactic blow.

Hel paused, breathing heavily. For a moment, Torturer and victim stood face to face in a communion of strange equality, stripped half-bare and sweating in their black leathers. The Kalaia grinned. Then all triumphant mockery dropped suddenly from her features and she inclined her head slightly, a salute Hel acknowledged in kind, as one true professional to another.

As the Torturer took final aim Nerya laughed soundlessly at the sky, stretching voluptuously, bowing backwards until her body gave off an almost audible sexual twang. In a kind of ecstasy Hel struck her on the pelvis, straight down the lacing of her breeches.

Shuddering she screamed, "*Kali-Maia*! It's done!"

"A hundred and twenty – the Pain-Offering is complete!" Florian confirmed as the bailey erupted in applause.

The Speakers painfully lowered their arms, flexed cautiously and offered Hel somewhat stiff bows; then, niceties observed, dived headlong into a snowdrift to bury their burning flesh in its merciful embrace.

In due course they emerged blowing and steaming like racehorses, snow clogging their ponytails and streaming in melting miniature glaciers down their torsos. The extremity of smarting thus numbed, the Oratores found leisure to examine the Design Hel had wrought upon them. They saw the joke immediately, pirouetting about in mutual admiring display.

"Bravo, My Lord – an excellent conceit!" laughed Nikos, looking down at himself. "To wear such a badge of pride I can forgive you my beating, Sol-Lios – almost!"

"Aye, clever – 'tis an Angorian pun! Forsooth, we're real Blood-Jackets now!"

Fresh laughter broke out as the *Kali't'aia* flocked around and the Gondarans finally comprehended Hel's mordant humour. Hands and faces unscathed, trunk and arms lashed uniform crimson, from afar it was hard to distinguish the Speakers from their comrades; he had whipped them into a facsimile of their Kalaian red coats, the texture of coarse-woven cloth imprinted on their skins in a criss-cross of fine ridged welts, a cunning *trompe l'oeil* complete to collar, cuffs and front seam embossed in angry purple.

"Well done, Sir," said Jehan, "I've never seen the Scourge better wielded. Should you tire of these Northlands, pray come south – you'd find occupation a-plenty in Angor!"

Hel was unaccustomed to having his efforts received in such good part - especially by the victims. He flushed to the tip of his dome while Nikos and Nerya jogged round so the whole crowd might inspect his work at closer quarters.

Shaking his head at their outlandish foibles Thorund turned to the Elect. "Yon salute they're making – what means it?"

"The Oratores are being offered the *Pax Victoria* by their comrades. In return they give the *Vale Vulgaris*, a gesture of admirable economy whose full translation might be rendered, 'Avaunt, ye venereal-diseased vagabond of uncertain kin-root, afore I lop off thy bow-drawing fingers.'"

"I see," smiled the King. "Well, now their lap of honour's run, I'll make a gesture of mine own." He strode into the centre of the bailey and held up his hand.

"Now hear this! Henceforth, *Schneeball* is totally forbidden in our courts! Any transgressor will not find us again so lenient - and let none of you presume upon the goodwill or pleading of our visitors to spare you the consequences of defiance. Until further notice, and without exception, waging *Schneeballkrieg* shall be an offence punishable by the full weight of *our* martial law!"

A chastened air befell his listeners, Angorian and Gondaran alike.

"So that no man put our word to the test either in ignorance, jest or contumacy, it shall be proclaimed throughout Thorsgard with the following addendum: Let those who would be *Schneeball* warriors hie down to the exercise yard at drill hour. Only then and there is the hurling of snow at any guest foolhardy enough to stray within its precincts entirely licit – by our royal decree-"

Faces brightened and one or two Gards dared a tentative, "Huzzah!"

"-but for now – be about your business!"

Slowly the throng dispersed, the erstwhile prisoners dithering uncertainly after their comrades. A bellow from Thorund snapped them to attention.

"Sergeant Elf!"

"Sire!"

"What are you doing? Resume your uniforms at once, and restore those garments to their rightful owners!"

Glumly the Gards dug out their gear from the snow that had accumulated upon it during their ordeal, while Florian and Dario ministered to the Speakers.

"Verily, O Thorund – oo-ow-aie! – you're a monarch sage and clement," gasped Nerya, as the High gently sponged her mortified flesh with a soothing balm. "And there'll be no breaking of your rule, ni by *Kali't'aia* nor by Counsel – I give my solemn oath on that!"

By this time the Gards had wriggled back into their sealskins and mail, shrinking from its icy wetness on their newly warm bodies. They stood uncomfortably to attention as Thorund addressed them.

"Let's see some gratitude to the whipping-boys who have preserved thine unworthy hides - the correct form of address is 'Oratores'," he added, shooting a green twinkle at Nerya.

Dutiful parrots, they chattered, "Th-thank'ee, Or-a-tor-ays."

"Good! Now, mark us well, Gardsmen," the King continued, "We shall remember your faces. Let them not be brought to our attention again for such reason or we'll clap you in the Pit. Now begone to your beat – quick march!"

The trio squelched off, glad to obey that the heat of exercise might dry out their clothing. Iris put back her hood and smiled sweetly at Thorund.

"I'm greatly curious to visit this Pit you mention, Sir," she said, taking Hel's arm. "Might His Lordship be permitted to conduct us thither?"

Chapter 14: Necromancer

"Stop goggling," growled Hel to Brother Portalgard, "We have visitors! Muster the Brethren and clear out - I give you a holy-day to honour the occasion."

"Aye, Sir - thank'ee, Sir!"

As the monk scuttled off Thorund murmured, "You must entertain our guests - I have business to attend to." With a meaningful nod he withdrew, leaving Hel to shrug on the unfamiliar mantle of host.

"Well Sirs, Ladies... to begin with, this is my privy chamber. Er... well, 'tis what you see, I know not what else to say."

Iris picked up a metal gauntlet from Hel's desk. "Then tell us: what is this curious item?"

"Um... it's a species of tongue-loosening device, Madam, my recent refinement of the traditional thumb-screw. It functions somewhat like a cheese-press."

"Fascinating... your own design, too – truly, you're a man of many parts! Alas, I can't quite grasp its mode of operation - come, Sir, a demonstration, if you please."

Her expression was compelling. Hel sank onto the opposite chair, his eyes drawn to her small, blunt-nailed hands exploring the oiled steel, slipping inside to caress its spiked compression plates.

"Do I put it on it right? Pray show me properly."

Hypnotised by the dancing gold light in her eyes he complied, his fingers drawn into the cold jointed metal until needles pricked the quick of his nails.

Resting her chin on her hands, Iris smiled. "Ah, *now* I See - it goes like this, does it not?"

Slowly and inexorably the Gauntlet tightened on Hel's leaden, immovable hand, compressing its every joint and knuckle, piercing his nail-beds, crushing the bones under knurled bosses...

"M-m-my Lady!" he cried, "Please!"

"What - did pleas avail its late wearer?" she inquired coolly, "Nay? Then 'tis well I'm no Gondaran torturer, eh, My Lord?" She lifted a negligent shoulder. "If it pains you, remove it."

Hel wrenched his eyes down, veins cording his bull-neck, nerved for blood but there was none to be seen. Panting through clenched teeth he strove to extract his hand, heaving till sweat stood out in great beads all over his dome.

Iris played him like a fish on a line till she considered her point well enough made. Rocked back in sudden release, Hel wrung his hand. Recollecting the last wreck to emerge from that dolorous grip, he gritted his teeth and squinted sidelong. Then his eyes sprang wide, his mouth gaped likewise and he lifted up his hand, turning it this way and that and flexing the fingers.

"Not a bloody mark! God's Fur, how- what did you do?"

"Little enough," said Iris demurely, "Save share my newly gained comprehension! The rest you did all by yourself."

Nikos snorted. "See why we deem such toys obsolete – it's a waste of good ironmongery when we have our Kali-Ra!

'Now, Sir, what else d'ye have to show us?"

The climax of their tour was Hel's master-work, deep in the Pit. Floating in his vat of tepid saline, 'Red' Arnor's ghost of a smile faded as the sound of their voices dredged a shred of consciousness from the moribund depths. With it came the familiar horrid shriek of bare nerves proclaiming that, alas, he still lived… the soothing vision of himself re-upholstered fit for Valhalla had again been just a dream. Then sensing a presence nearby, his eyelids fluttered. This time something had accompanied him from the dream-world, blotting out the cell wall with its solid black shadow, a raven of unmistakable vitality perched upon its shoulder.

"Odin!" he whispered faintly.

The figure looked down. Arnor saw into its cowl and gaped - it was not the All-Father, but some fair young Druid priestess! She regarded him with infinite compassion for a moment, drew a deep breath, and brought two fingers down onto the inner corners of his eyebrows gently as a settling moth.

Arnor's dreadful agony stopped in an instant, catapulting him to a state far beyond bliss. He moaned and convulsed, heart pounding, penis throbbing into tumescence as his eyes hungrily sought for her face… a face now stretched rigid on the bone, a grimacing skull whose eyeballs glared blank as amber beads.

The horrible transformation shocked his fragile system into terminal arrhythmia. He heaved like a gaffed fish in mingled throes of orgasm and death and as his life ebbed, so her visage relaxed into its former beauty. Smiling, she squeezed the hand that clutched the tank's rim in a death-grip. The Druid exhaled a last gurgle; his poor maltreated body sank under the brine, and his soul flew rejoicing to the halls of his forefathers.

King Thorund paused on the threshold of the holding cell

where two prisoners, stripped to the waist on a heap of reeking straw, were manacled with their hands above their heads. The position afforded them an excellent perspective of the Torturer's workbench and brazier, whose associated collection of gleaming fire-irons took on hideous meaning in such context.

Having dangled before this prospect since the previous day the occupants were in a sorry state, their garments foul with the combined products of terror and helpless necessity. Breathing shallow through his mouth, Thorund crossed to one unfortunate and unlocked his handcuffs.

Nerveless arms dropping limp to his sides, the man pitched onto his knees. "Thy pardon, Lord King – pray, spare me and I swear by my sword I'll never repeat my offence!"

"Desist, desist," said Thorund, hauling Haral to his feet and chafing his arms. "For now we're better acquainted with our guests' peculiar, shall we say, *persuasions*, we hold you guiltless in the matter of their tardy arrival. Indeed, your humouring his outlandish whims has prompted Lord Jehan to speak loud in your praise!

'Meantime Lord Hakon has fallen indisposed, and we can't afford another officer absent from his post. So you're exonerated - be about your duties."

Haral fell to the floor again, gibbering in gratitude and kissing the royal ring.

"Get up, man, get up," said the King testily, "Go, write up your report - but change your breeks afore you track that stink into our halls, or we'll have you clapped back in irons forthwith."

Hastily retrieving his gear from the foetid straw, Haral bowed out and fled. Thorund turned to his second prisoner, whose countenance had brightened considerably.

"O, wise and mighty King! Pray extend thy mercy to this humble servant who, if he has erred, has done so inadvertently! Truly, Sire, I know not why I'm held in durance – surely some terrible misunderstanding-"

"Silence!"

Radnor Wolfblest cringed as a glittering knife approached his vitals, sagging in relief when it was merely employed to cut away his soiled hose. Then his nether parts were roughly scrubbed with straw, his chains unlocked and the King half-carried, half-dragged him to a chair. While Radnor coaxed blood back into his limbs, Thorund fastidiously rinsed his hands at the water butt, took up Hel's ledger and raised an eyebrow at a long list newly entered in the 'Perquisites' column. Delving into a coffer beneath the bench, he extracted a bundle labelled,

'*Itym: onne Black Cloake & Tunick figured in sylver Wolfys heddes &c*' and thrust it at the merchant.

"Follow me!"

Clutching his effects to his podgy nakedness, Radnor obeyed.

"Hush," Thorund whispered, nodding meaningfully towards Hel's privy chamber. They stole deeper into the horrible recesses of the Pit, at length arriving at a dank little rock-hewn side-chamber far from the inhabited cells. The King ushered Radnor in, locked the door and pocketed the key.

"At last, my good Wolfblest, we can talk privately!" He sank onto a rough wooden seat and pulled out his pouch. "Sit down and take a pipe. I'll say one thing for the Southron – they grow a fine smoke-weed!" Lighting up from the lantern, he took a drag and passed the pipe to Radnor. "I regret putting you to such trouble," the King went on, "but believe me, I had due cause – a cause that grows ever more pressing, the more I learn of the Angorian mind. Aye, 'tis time to speak not as ruler to loyal subject, but as one rational man to another – as I've striven in vain to do with their Lordships.

'Those Centrali gewgaws you supplied for Her Highness – nay, spare me your denials! I know how and whence they came, and they've stirred a hornet's nest among our... *visitors,*" he imbued the word with fine scorn, "with their nice sensibilities!

'Aye, your conniving in the Strait could easily plunge us into war. War for which we are *unready*... war against a nation I suspect to be powerful beyond our worst misgivings. I tell this to their Lordships, and do they heed me? No! Not content with pirating booty on the high seas they've begun meddling in Centralia, goading the heathen and his allies as gadflies goad a bull's arse!

'It's a course set on disaster... for all that Lord Jehan seeks alliance through marriage, war he will make nonetheless if we force his hand. Molest Centralia and Angor will leap to its defence; harry Faal and they will do likewise; assail Angor itself and the Emperor will join forces to repel us. Gondarlan can't win the short game by force - so we must stay in the long one by guile, till our masterstroke's ready to be played.

'Now you're wholly acquainted with the facts and my opinion, I hope you've wit to see that these foolish depredations must stop, at least for the nonce. So – what say you?"

Hungry for physical comfort, Radnor had drawn deep on the pipe while Thorund spoke. Now his senses were reeling, his pulse thrumming fast.

"I-I-I'm so greatly honoured by your confidence, M-Majesty, I hardly know what to say," he began, feverishly calculating the hazard of his next words. "A-and whilst I'm ever an obedient and faithful servant who strives endlessly to enrich his master's coffers, I-I fear there may be certain... er... difficulties..."

"What difficulties?" Thorund leaned back and exhaled a luxurious plume, enjoying the performance immensely.

"Ahem! Well, Sire – may I speak openly and without prejudice?"

"Please do," said the King dryly, "'Tis imperative for the common weal that I know the full truth. Fear not – the Brethren can't overhear or report on your words in this place, so speak on. What difficulties might these be?"

Radnor cleared his throat. "Ahem... O most understanding of Kings, then I must tell you that vessels are already at sea, far from recall, and bound for the Straits... um... orders have been placed, and er, down-payments made on the next Centrali cargoes."

He looked to the King, whose expression remained one of benevolent interest. Confidence grew, and his eyes started to glisten.

"Aye, Majesty – and such cargoes you would not believe! Fine timbers, pelts of bird and beast of hue and richness unprecedented... all there for the taking, the natives being too weak and puny to stop us. Surely, Lord King, we could continue our... explorations," he wheedled, "Why, 'tis such a vast uncharted place the Outlanders would never know-"

Thorund shook his head. "You make a compelling argument – alas, this business must stop, and be *seen* to have stopped, by any that are looking. So tell me: whence came the order for this venture - Lord Hakon? Lord Sigismund? Or was the concept your own?" Radnor's mouth worked soundlessly. "Come, this is no time for modesty! If the stratagem was yours, speak up and receive your reward. But mark me, if 'twere another man's design and I find you've claimed false glory, woe betide you."

"Well, Majesty, 'tis hard to recall exactly... 'twas thought on and discussed for many months... er... but I think the idea was first mooted by, er..."

"By His Grace?"

Radnor nodded gratefully. "Aye, Sire - though Lord Hakon was also hot for the plan when he heard it. And for what my humble opinion's worth, I too thought it a worthy cause, one that would benefit Your Majesty and our great Fatherland alike."

"Hmm… it seems their zealous Lordships can't curb their ambitions in patience! Is anyone else involved in this operation? For the good of the state, I must know."

The pipe passed back and forth and Radnor Wolfblest waxed garrulous. Thorund nodded approvingly and murmured encouragement until at last the merchant had talked himself out.

"Excellent! Then I shall make you my trusted agent in this sensitive affair. Go forth privily from the Fastness and communicate my orders to your network, reporting to me on developments and the Brethren's subsequent actions. You must travel incognito," he went on, taking out Aula, "Here: remove all the monograms, badges and insignia from these effects while I prepare for your departure."

"B-but Majesty!" spluttered Radnor, "Could I not fulfil your commands from Thorshaven and maintain the rest of my business as usual?"

"And what, pray, do you think your life would be worth when their Lordships find out you're working against them? No, you must flee – go as, let me see… go as the lowly trader 'Tor Unsen' and equip yourself appropriately – for judging by the weight of this purse, you can well meet such homespun expense! But be discreet and let none know your true name or purpose, or I'd give not a groat for your chances."

"But my goods, my house - my lady wife," Radnor protested feebly.

"Knowing Endrik, your goods will be tallied to the last, stowed safer in our Treasury than they'd be in your house, and will be restored to you in due course. As to the rest, never fear – I'll take care of everything.

'Now I must leave you a moment. If you love life, do as you're bid – and pardon my locking you in, I'd not have your labours disturbed."

Alone, Radnor passed a hand over his clammy brow and exhaled a long sigh. His mind whirled with information, implication, his thoughts seeming too big for his skull to contain – what was he to do, caught betwixt devil and deeps? Compliance seemed his only immediate option. Grimacing at the desecration, he reached reluctantly for his costly apparel, but on the way his hand paused. A second later, it snatched up Aula and began severing silver buttons with alacrity. Of course! He could surely turn the situation to advantage… and whatever course the future took, the security of Wolfblest House would be guaranteed! He sighed at the prospect of flight and its discomforts; smirked, as he thought of the potential illustrious outcome; and hastily re-arranged his expression into one of sober industry as Thorund re-entered.

"Good work, Wolfblest!" said the King, glancing at the glittering pile at Radnor's elbow. "Now we must cover your tracks, so your direction remains undiscovered till the scent has grown cold. Hand me the knife." He withdrew a leaf of parchment from his sleeve and slit it in half. "Pray scribe me two notes, I've brought pen and ink.

'The first to His Grace shall say, *My Lord, to protect our mutual interests I am departed abroad. I shall send further tidings under the alias 'Tor Unsen' and return in person as soon as I may.*

'The second, for the private eye of your good lady, shall say, *My dear* – or however you style her familiar – *Affairs call me away on a long voyage. Ward the house well till the day of my homecoming, be a good servant unto His Majesty, and guard thy tongue – I would not have rivals get wind of my movements and usurp my interests! Adieu* et cetera.

'Sign your signature for the last time, ratify with your seal and give it over. Hereafter, Radnor Wolfblest is dead – though he lives on in the King's agent Tor Unsen!"

Bending low to hide a crafty glint in his eye Radnor obeyed, pressing his seal into the blobs of wax under his name then striving mightily and vainly to withdraw his ring.

"It won't come off, My Liege – otherwise Master Torturer would have relieved me of it yestere'en."

"Pity – it's a dangerous trinket," said Thorund. "Well, hide it under a glove and use it at your peril. We can but hope you lose some flesh on your journey, that it'll slip off the easier! But now, good Wolf-cub," he stepped behind Radnor's chair and laid an affectionate hand on his shoulder, "Are you ready to go?"

Light flashed in the corner of Wolfblest's eye, signalling, too late for him to evade it, the smooth arc of Aula in Thorund's right hand. The bright point jabbed him deftly in the throat, neatly sliced his trachea and as neatly withdrew.

Coughing blood, eyes bulging, Radnor clawed at his hissing, bubbling neck while the King spun Aula appreciatively in the lantern-light.

"One cannot but admire Angorian smith-craft, eh, my dear Wolfblest? Ah, me – we've certainly learnt much these past twenty-four hours. And since your wound is not imminently fatal, there's time to share our learning with you. We know that the Brethren are corrupt, that their Lordships are not to be trusted – and that you're a black-hearted, double-dyed traitor. First you betray *our* best interests and imperil the Kingdom through your pirate operations, then betray the rest of your cohort... why, Radnor, we can read your face plain as a blood-writ vellum! Who would profit by the War of the Red Weskit you'd doubtless engineer? Only the purveyors of goods, the breakers of siege and suppliers of arms... men like you and your mercenary sea-dogs - and your ultimate pay-master. Trust you to act as *our* agent – huh! We'll take no such risk! So reap your reward – the treacherous end you deserve."

Fixing his petrified prey with empty black eyes, Thorund thrust Aula under the doughy mound of Radnor's belly and jerked viciously upwards, parting skin and fat in a ghastly vertical grin. Wolfblest flailed and overturned his chair, toppling sideways into the steaming bowels blubbering onto the floor.

Jumping back from the mess, Thorund flung open the door. "Time to go, merchant – collect up thy baggage and begone."

Reeking of pain-sweat and terror Radnor scrabbled on the dirty flagstones, retching as his own hot tubes slid between his fingers. Holding his belly together as best he could, dragging a glistening purplish train, he crawled in slow agony to the corridor. There he collapsed at Thorund's feet, gaping fishlike in a draught of chill noisome air blowing ominously along the passage floor.

"Journey's end, you faithless son of a bitch," said the King, planting a boot on an ample buttock. He braced against the wall and shoved, rolling the hapless man towards a patch of deeper blackness.

Radnor, divining his intent, felt a last surge of survival instinct and clutched desperately at Thorund's sleeve. His wrist was promptly seized in an iron grip, Aula flashed again and he reeled back in fresh woe, blood squirting from his suddenly three-fingered hand. Grinning wolfishly, the King pocketed his signet ring and tossed the severed digit down the yawning oubliette.

"Hah! Now we have thine identity, Wolfblest – and no further need of thy carcass. So we'll bid thee farewell, 'Tor Unsen'" he gave a mighty heave, calling after, "Not 'till we meet again', for 'tis a long climb back up!"

The remains of Radnor slithered after him into the dark. Poised on the brink, Thorund listened to the diminishing thumps as the body ricocheted off the shaft, counting the seconds until they could be heard no longer. Then swiftly retracing the trail he swabbed the floors with Radnor's cloak; wiped and rearranged the chamber's furnishings; cleaned the residue from his hands, boots and blade with a silk kerchief;

bundled up the late merchant's possessions, and dropped the whole bloody lot down the oubliette. The notes and clinking pile of Wolfblest insignia he secreted in his pouch; and finally, with a questing glance round and a smile of pure satisfaction, King Thorund hastened to rejoin his long-neglected guests.

Finding them on the point of departure, he suggested to the now sober party that they should join him for midday repast, it being well after noon.

"Willingly, Sir," replied Jehan. "We should raise a valedictory glass to the one who passed in our presence."

Thorund glanced at Sol-Lios. Ah, but which one – nay, he could not possibly know! He cast a quizzical eyebrow at Hel.

"Aye – Red- ahem, Druid Arnor has succumbed at last."

"Really? I'll lay His Grace will mourn! I'm only surprised that he lasted so long. Indeed, let us drink to his rest – and to your skill, My Lord, in denying it these many long weeks."

They repaired to the Hall and once formalities were over, the conversation turned to business.

Nikos said, "Someone should go to Thorshaven and see how our comrades are faring. I had determined to go this very afternoon – but between your Pit and this snowstorm, I find my ardour for the journey somewhat cooled! Does the road remain passable in such conditions, Sir?"

"Aye, the main ways are always kept clear."

"Very well… then by your leave, tomorrow I'll hazard the ride, be the weather what it may."

Sergeant Elf, holding Skala and Karl entirely to blame for his recent brush with death, took malicious pleasure in announcing,

"Yon groom-fellow Florian – the one whose work was interrupted by this morning's folly – requests help to make up lost time." Elf grinned evilly. "And since *you* started the whole bloody mess, I can think of no fitter assistants! Leave your weapons here and get off to the stables - go on, jump to it!"

The glum Gards found their new taskmaster standing by a strange contraption, and looked askance from it to the heaps of dung and fouled straw waiting suggestively to hand.

"*Ave*, helpers!" The Angorian bowed. "I'm *Eque'la* Florian, and you are- Skala and Karl? Right, then – Skala, two goodly forkfuls of straw in here, if you please," he gestured to a broad-mouthed hopper, "Then a spade of pure dung. You, Karl, pray crank this handle."

156

They obeyed, mystified. A grinding, chopping sound came from within and the hopper's contents sank down.

"Keep turning till it's all run through." Florian stooped with his ear to the macerator. "More... a little more... stop now." He pulled on a lever, releasing some inner mechanism and a dull, semi-solid plop, slid out an oblong wooden box, and slotted it into a new position under a correspondingly shaped plate.

"This part works like a wine-press," he plied its handle, "See?" The plate inched down into the box, compressing the contents and squeezing dark fluid into a cistern below. When every last drip was collected Florian undid the press, pushed up the bottom of the mould and popped out a yellow-brown brick.

"Well done, lads! First-class dross-cake - or as some rudely call it," he searched for a suitable translation, "Bum-coal."

"B-B-Bum-coal?" spluttered Karl; then, as comprehension dawned, "You mean it's for firing?"

"Of course - bum-coal, dross-cake, soddy, call it what you will." Florian flourished the brick under their noses. "See, 'tis already inoffensive, and when it's full dry it kindles fast and burns without stink. So come, Masters, the next load if you please. Here's the first of our stack," he set the dross-cake neatly in a corner, "And we must press a good few hundred more for the ships – and the big warehouse your King's loaned us for a shore-base."

"Begging your pardon, Sir - why bother?" asked Skala, forking in dung while Karl cranked the macerator. "You could get firewood easy enough, or charcoal – real coal, come to that."

Florian shrugged. "Why burn such treasure? True, soddy doesn't burn as long or hot as earth-coal, but it's self-renewing! And 'waste not, want not' is ever our motto. All our stable dross is pressed into fuel and the ichor goes to our service-ship, *Quintessence – her* press can turn these out ten at a time - for brewing into tonics for the soil." He decanted a mould-full, set it under the plate and inserted a fresh box. "Stoke it up, Skala!" He worked the screw, whistling cheerily.

"You seem happy in your work, Master," observed Karl.

"Aye, I like serving all three Orders at once." Seeing their blank looks he added, "The Orders of Being, I mean: us *la-Galaia*, the creatures; the plants, *na-Galaia*; and *su-Galaia* the rocks, soils and waters – animal, vegetable and mineral, you might say. Bum-coal feeds the *la-Galaia's* stoves, thereby feeding us. Its ashes and essence feed the *su,* which feeds the *na-*, which feed us all, and then we make more bum-coal – perfect!

'Phew - but it's warm work," he added presently, and putting back his hood, swabbed his glistening pate with a kerchief. The Gards winced, trying not to stare, but in the end Skala broke.

"No disrespect, Sir, but I've never seen a head like yours before!" He grimaced. "Leastways, the Torturer shaves his as smooth, but he has no marks like that. I hear they're put on with needles… it must have bloody hurt."

"It did! But it was worth it – look." Florian turned slowly to display the herd of inky horses galloping across his thin tender head-skin. "And when I get home I'll have a Gondaran pony added in honour of my visit. I care not for the sting – it's a pain-offering in thanks for my communion with the *Eques*."

"Pain-offering," said Karl slowly, recognising the term. "Is that what your Ora-torays did for us this morning?"

The High nodded. "Aye, took responsibility, offered redress for affront… akin to a custom you have here – 'blood-money', is it called?"

"*Were-gild*… aye, 'tis similar, though your way is cheaper!" quipped Skala.

"And less bloody!" grinned Florian. "Indeed, they'll be none the worse for it tomorrow… or maybe the day after! But they deserved a leathering for starting that foolish snow-battle… it inconvenienced the *Eques*, for I'd not done freshening their water when I was seized.

'Anyhow, we pain-offer for many reasons: as a sacrifice or thanksgiving to the gods – when in ancient time we offered life-blood, now we offer harmless ordeal, and a continued life of service. Or to atone for an offence, or demonstrate self-control. Some folk even use it for meditation – they find their nirvana in a beating, if you can credit such a thing.

'Aye, when I was a lad I often chose Scourging to pay for some folly – like the time I broke my father's greenhouse with a slingshot, after he'd told me not to shoot in the garden." He chuckled. "I'd rather get a quick beating over than exchange a week's riding time for High-service round the house – another of *Patri's* favourites to teach me good manners." He added a brick to the stack. "Talk of which, hark at me running on! Pray excuse me – I'm so seldom able to exercise my Gondaran on native speakers."

The Gards brushed his reservations aside. Naturally nosy, they had been all agog. Gossip was great currency in the barracks, and they could lord it for weeks on the strength of this encounter.

"You speak it very well," Skala ventured, "How did you learn?"

"Thank you kindly! O, the usual way... from a linguist, who got it from merchants and mariners – isn't that ever how languages spread? And I like your tongue so well, I volunteered for this expedition that I might practice it."

They chatted on, taking turns to load the hopper, press the cakes and garner fresh ingredients. As the stack slowly grew, Karl returned to the subject ever-gnawing at his mind.

"Pain-offering... I can still hardly believe Kal-ayer Nerrier did that for us. And she was so kindly-"

"Hah – kindly!" snorted Florian, "No, I dare say our famous adventuress was but notching up another exploit for the song-smiths to make lays upon."

"*Another* exploit – what, you mean the Ora-toray has had a song made on her already? And she so young!" Karl exclaimed. "If you know it, Master Florian, pray sing it for us."

"I'll try – if I can keep to the verse in translation and work the press at the same time. Let's see..." he sang a line under his breath, shook his head, and then amended loud enough to hear:

> *'Twas in the dark of Hag-moon time that Breath of Gaia came,*
> *And brought Kalaia Nerya to deeds that won dread fame..."*

Chapter 15: Hag-Moon

Elinor sighed and set down her handiwork. To give her eyes respite she lifted them to her bedchamber, whose immaculate tidiness, warm candlelight and crackling, resinous fire lulled her into pleasant reverie. After such an unpropitious waking the day had turned surprisingly agreeable, she reflected, the onset of Curse having conferred an unlooked-for boon: reason to stay closeted with her women, thus sparing herself the Angorian's triumph and the court's vulgar interest alike. She took another sip of Zafia's cordial, savouring her freedom from pain. Next moment she heard a commotion in the anteroom and Fran's voice protesting,

"Nay, My Lord, you can't go in! We're under strictest instruction - Her Highness must not be disturbed!"

"Tish – she'll suffer *this* disturbance, I'll warrant!" With that came a perfunctory tap on her door, heralding the appearance of a mildly flushed Sol-Lios.

He paused in the doorway, disarmed by the fragrant apartment with its pretty rosewood furnishings, bright rugs and tapestries, and elegantly recumbent on a couch by the fire, the Princess herself. She was dressed for private comfort in a loose red tunic belted with cabochon garnets, her cape of unbound sable ringlets providing a pleasing contrast to the creamy-pale face whose previously tranquil expression was curdling by the moment into a frown of discontent.

She waved impatiently at Fran and Berthe, flurrying uselessly behind. "Resume your sewing, ladies – I'll deal with His Lordship! What mean you by this barbarous incursion, sirrah?" she went on, as the door closed behind them. "I suppose you're come to preen and crow-"

Jehan cut into her gathering tirade with a deep bow, proffering a silver salver whereon reposed a covered dish.

"No, Madam – only to bring Zafia's compliments and a gift that will not wait on etiquette." He whipped off the cover.

Elinor gasped, indignation forgotten. In a shallow crystal bowl dewy with condensation lay a Fusion of brown and amber-gold, encircled by a rim of pale cream. Her appetite woke in an instant, her stomach responding with a wolfish growl.

"O, an iced cream - this is kindness, indeed!" Her tapestry slid forgotten to the floor as she reached eagerly for the dish, snatched up the spoon and dug in, too avid to care for propriety.

Her face lit up. "Mm!"

"You like it?"

"Mm! Aye, delicious," she replied indistinctly.

Smiling, the Elect inclined his head. "Then I'll go and inform Zafi of her success. Good evening, Madam. My apologies for the disturbance – I'll leave you in peace to enjoy." He bowed once more and turned to leave.

"You'll do no such thing! Since you're here, you might as well bide - at least till I'm done, so you can take back the bowl!" She softened her ungracious demand with a beguiling dimple, and the pace of her spoon slowed a trifle. "Besides, I wish to know more – what's this dish called, and what's it made of?"

Jehan drew up a stool. "The pudding has no name yet. Zafi seeks to call it in your honour; 'Princess Delight' has been proposed, or 'Wintermoon Bliss'." (He forbore to mention his colleagues' less flattering suggestions, 'Frigid Maiden' among the most decent). "The brown half is cream mixed with *cacao*-bean liquor, roasted *café* and crumb of dark *staycake*. The gold is metheglin sorbet with honey-cake crumb, and the whole circled with plain almond cream. But only Zafi knows the exact recipe, and hugs it close as a state secret - you're the first person to taste it."

Elinor ate on, flattered and confounded. Jehan's demeanour seemed subtly altered tonight - why, he was being almost civilised! His hateful air of finding her amusing had gone, replaced by a thoughtful courtesy... could she possibly have misjudged him? To her discomfiture Jehan picked that moment to glance up, caught her eye upon him, and smiled.

"I rejoice to find you restored to good health and humour this evening, Madam. And, if I may say so, such beauty – for the colour of your raiment is most apt, and enhances your complexion excellently well."

She accepted the compliment with a gracious nod, her dignity slightly undermined by the ring of cream round her mouth.

"I'm touched by your concern, Sir. In truth I hardly merit it after my behaviour yestere'en - for the which my most dread Lord and Father has rightly rebuked me."

"Berate yourself not, Madam. The resulting experience will dwell long in my memory. Indeed, fain would I do it again - and take you with me, for I trow you've not seen the view from Fang-tip. Saving your face alone it is matchless, and well worth the climb! Meanwhile, dare I hope you're not too displeased by my return?"

Recalling her father's dire promise Elinor replied, "Nay, Sir, I should have regretted it most sorely if any harm had come to you. So, taste the reward of success – I've saved you the last bite."

She held forth the spoon. Instead of taking it from her hand, Jehan leant forward and received the melting morsel directly into his mouth. For a second their eyes met, before Elinor hastily dropped hers, an annoying flush rising to her cheeks.

Jehan sat back, rolling the mouthful slowly around his tongue. "Hmm… The Healer surpasses herself - I should deem this her masterwork, a perfect fusion of the cuisine of our lands. Which nicely turns me to the subject, Madam. For I fear that in recompense for hazarding my life in such cavalier fashion, I must now set you some comparable endeavour."

Inwardly, Elinor quivered. Was he about to dare her for a kiss? Eyes downcast she murmured, "'An ye must, so be it."

To her surprise and faint chagrin, the Elect sprang to his feet and gestured around the room.

"First answer me this: are you content to dwell immured, even within such delightful walls?" He strode to her desk and bookshelves. "I perceive you're a scholar – but are you satisfied to learn from books alone? Because notwithstanding the brevity of our acquaintance, I don't believe it! So hear *my* Challenge, Princess: come to Angor not as an unwilling bride forced to an uncongenial groom. Come instead as an ambassador, a student, an adventurer… come however you will, only come in good heart."

Stung, Elinor retorted, "'Dwell immured' - I do no such thing! Why, I oft-times go down to services at the Cathedral, and in summer we go hunting on the Arkengarth Plains. Indeed, for my sixteenth birthday I went as far as the Pass itself, where Baron Ulfar feted me in his noble Gatehouse! So don't talk as if I were some poor prisoner upon whom you confer a great favour."

"Forgive me, Madam! I'm glad you're such a well seasoned traveller – it'll stand you in good stead, should you pick up my gauntlet. As I hope you will, for there are sights I yearn to share with you… so, My Lady, come with us as a travelling companion if no more – and gratify your innermost heart, which surely craves to escape from this Fastness."

"Aye – to go to Faal!" she blurted.

"Ah, *la bel'Empire*, the fabled Isles of Romance... well, I'll escort you thence with great pleasure, as soon as affairs permit. It's over long since I broke a lance with the Princes."

"The Princes of Faal!" gasped Elinor. "What - then you know

162

him, the Crown Prince Eduard?"

"That I do," said Jehan, "And his brother Ricard. We've known one another since boyhood – our parents are old friends."

She clapped her hands involuntarily. "Then pray, Sir," she picked up her tapestry rendition of a knight riding a white horse through a flower-strewn meadow, "Do tell me: is this a fair semblance? I've never met anyone else I could ask."

Jehan gave a low whistle. "But this is exquisite! Exquisite! It is all your own work and design? Then I salute you – this Faalian *mille-fleur* style is very fine indeed. Aye, and the face most skilfully rendered; I'd have known it for Eduard e'en without his devices."

"Is it even so?" she beamed. "You're too kind, Sir. And what of his bearing – is he truly so noble a sight?"

Inwardly rolling his eyes, Sol-Lios indulged her. "A most practised exponent of the *Arts Chivalriques*, as gallant on the dance-floor as he's courageous in the lists. A skilled huntsman, relentless in pursuit of his quarry, he's famed too as a maker and player of love-songs... In short, a man of such charm and excellent parts I could hate him, quite, were he not our stout comrade and ally."

"Ah me... he sounds perfect," she sighed, then had the grace to blush at her want of discretion. "Um... of course," she floundered, with more haste than truth, "the King my Father had once thought to marry us, you see, so... er... naturally, I'm curious whether 'twould have been a good match."

"No more than that?" teased Jehan. "Well, I pledge that one day you *shall* meet him - and if you find mutual love, I'll be the first to dance at your nuptials."

"What? You'd have me marry Prince Eduard? But I thought – I thought you wanted to wed me yourself!"

"Not if you truly loved another and he loved you back! No, never in life – where would be the profit in such a dismal situation? For now I simply hope that as acquaintance deepens you might grow in affection for Angor, and remain with us more for pleasure than political advantage. Though I believe there are other reasons you should quit these shores without delay." His expression grew grave, and he reached out and took both her hands.

"Candidly, Princess, I fear your distaste for me may not abate, compelling me in honour to abandon our compact and leave you behind – which I should fear even more, for I trust not your Father's Lords. And whilst Angor will strive to the utmost to hold peace, war may come whether we like it or no. Hence I would remove you far beyond their grasp, at least till events are resolved." He gestured to the tapestry. "Can't you see me as a shining knight come to your rescue - or am I too ill-favoured to play such a part?"

Elinor pulled back her hands, unnerved. War! That dread word again – it made her stomach churn. She was gratified by Jehan's confiding, if shocked to hear the position outlined so plainly. That he might rather sail without her than take her unwilling had not previously occurred; it simultaneously mollified and piqued her pride, and jolted her with quite unexpected panic. Her wish to be left unmolested suddenly seemed less attractive, now she apparently had the power to make it come true by a simple refusal. For the first time, her Angorian prospects seemed more inviting than the weary constraints of home, where even if she stayed it would be impossible to recover the tenor of former existence – and God alone knew what her father would say…

She took a steadying pull from Zafia's flask. "I appreciate your sentiments, Sir. And I can't fault your logic or judgement, for neither do I trust Their Lordships. Therefore I accept, and will go with you not by the King's command, or because I'm won by Challenge, but of mine own inclination."

Jehan kissed her hand. "Princess, you both absolve my worries and do me great honour. Mayhap in a few days I can repay it, by presenting the last of the gifts we've brought you."

"Another gift - how lovely!" Grasping at this welcome diversion from serious business, she pouted prettily, "But what is it? May I not have it now?"

He smiled at her frank childish greed. "Better to wait a few days – you'll enjoy it much more once your Hag-Moon is passed."

Elinor blanched. "*What* did you say? How did- O, Zafia must have- Great God, this is outrageous! How dare she prattle of her patient's complaints? Why, you bloody traitors – discussing my unspeakables!" She snatched up a cushion and swung it at Jehan. "Get out, you disgusting, foul-mouthed infidel!"

Jehan evaded her blow, darting behind the couch as she commenced pelting cotton reels and hard words with equal ferocity. It served only to intensify her fury when he ducked, dodged or batted her missiles harmlessly aside until her workbox arsenal was empty, laughing helplessly the while.

"How dare you laugh at me? Get out! Get out of my sight!" she screeched.

"I dare laugh but at this foolish misunderstanding," he retorted, "And shall bide till you've suffered correction! Kindly refrain from

164

maligning Zafi, who has said naught of your condition - nor needed to, for I know too well the scent that clung to her raiment and spoke in her stead. Indeed, I've known it from boyhood, for we have a rhyme which goes:

> *Woe betide Man*
> *When his lover or dam,*
> *His sister or aunt*
> *Calls for clear-sage:*
> *It presages ire*
> *And tongue-lashings dire –*
> *Best comply then flee*
> *Off to the fields, Man!*

'There are twelve more verses, one for each Moon of the year, which I'll spare you – but in short, I'm no stranger to your plight. Forsooth, its precursor accounts perfectly for your conduct since our meeting - hence my continuing forbearance of your peevish ill-temper, which otherwise, Madam, I should frankly have found insupportable."

"Why, you patronising- get out of my bedroom," she yelled, "Get out!"

Groping for the nearest available weapon, she hurled it with full force. The crystal bowl almost grazed Jehan's nose before crashing on the door-frame in a glittering explosion. A red line arose on his cheekbone, drawn by a flying glass shard; he dabbed at his face, raised an eyebrow at his blood-stained fingertips, then the hateful light of mockery danced afresh in his eyes.

He swept an obsequious bow. "I' faith, I'd sooner risk the Fang than thy chamber again – there's better chance of returning unscathed! Pray excuse me, lest I bleed on thy carpet."

Stung into new voice the Princess shrieked, "Aye – go, and don't dare to come back!"

All of the Healer's good work was undone in a trice. Too mortified for confidences, Elinor summarily dismissed her women and passed the night in a storming frenzy, fulminating, weeping and raging, nigh as angry with herself as she was with Sol-Lios.

"I was starting like him," she sobbed, "I thought him gentle and kindly, while he knew all along what was happening in my most intimate being... Great Wolf, the humiliation! He was but humouring 'my condition' and laughing up his sleeve. O, the bastard, the bastard – how dare he?"

Next morning Berthe and Fran found their mistress tossing scarlet in a swamp of drenched linen, having whipped herself into an hysterical delirium. They looked at each other alarmed.

"Great Wolf," exclaimed Berthe, "Whatever's happened? Quickly, Fran, pass me Lady Zafi's cordial - then run and get her!"

Mention of the name roused Elinor to instant lucidity. "No!" she cried, "Keep that witches' brew from me! I'll have none of her poison - take it away, and let naught Angorian near me again, on pain of a flogging!"

She sank back on her pillows, exhausted. Nervously they packed up the Healer's accoutrements, and while they swept up the mess of shattered glass Fran whispered,

"Go fetch Loric – surely she'll suffer his aid."

Berthe squeezed her arm gratefully. "Madam," she enquired, "Shall I take these things back to Lady Zafia?"

"Aye, get it hence," murmured the Princess, without opening her eyes. "'Twas them made me ill, with their meddling... I'll have no more of their devices!"

Elinor lay confined to her bed for the whole of that day, and the next. Loric would fain have given her *clear-sage* but the patient was obdurate, demanding the cures of her homeland. So they dosed her fever with bitter infusions of willow-bark, and sponged her down with honest Grunewald lavender cologne; but for the sake of quietude, Loric guiltily doctored her posset with ground *passionata*, reasoning that what she didn't know wouldn't hurt her.

As she recovered her ladies were avid to learn what had transpired with Jehan. To them she dissembled, protesting convenient amnesia, and they dared not press her; but to Loki she lamented privately,

"O, I'm caught now – every which way! Commanded by Father, won by Challenge, bound by agreement – and constrained by necessity! So much for volition – what choice is there, really? *And* I must go in the semblance of gladness, or they'll leave me behind. God's Fur... I'd end up wed to Hakon, sure as eggs!

'Whereas if I *do* go - with a brute who cares so little for me that he'd stand by and watch me wed another – if I *do* go, what then..." Her eyes narrowed, calculating. "What if Jehan *does* take me to Faal... why, I could refuse to leave, with no Father or Lords to gainsay me! I could throw myself on the Emperor's mercy, beg sanctuary at his court… and God willing, procure my own marriage. Perchance I could even enlist Sol-Lios' help, given his milksop prating on 'consent'!

'Hah, Silkie – 'twould be ironic if I set out to become Queen of Angor, but returned instead Empress of Faal! That'd confound these bloody men… mayhap… just mayhap it'll turn out alright, if I can but keep up the sham."

A plan born of expediency and low cunning hatched in her mind. After careful thought she penned a brief note in a feeble, palsied hand:

My Lord Elect, I regret that indisposition curtailed our last meeting and has since kept me from thy company. I hope that th'art not too sorely hurt, and look forward to resuming our discourse as soon as may be - E.

She waited tensely until Loric relayed his prompt reply:

Madam, I appreciate thy pains in writing from thy sick-bed, and on thy concern for my well-being. I survive - albeit in darkness unrelieved by thy luminous presence. So Godspeed thy recovery, for I await our next encounter with anticipation equal to thine own. Warm regards, JS-L.

Sarcastic pig! But her plan had cleared the first hurdle. Jehan had responded in kind, the hints of their recent altercation too oblique for prying eyes to comprehend; and since no storm of recrimination had broken over her head, Elinor could only suppose he had made no report to her father. Satisfied, she relaxed on her pillows but did not lie quiet for long. Her rage had bled out along with the receding symptoms of moon-time, and she felt bored, restive, inclined to conversation and gentle female pastime – but what to do? Pondering thus, a happy thought struck; she sat up and called for her women.

"Why, My Lady, 'tis good to see some roses back in your cheeks!" cried Berthe.

"Aye, now I'm only sick of idleness – and there's work to be done. I must think about packing – doubtless the journey will be on us soon enough."

Berthe gaped. "Packing! Why, then all is well with the Lord Elect, Madam?"

"Aye – why would it not be?"

"Er… O, no reason, Highness! So it's all settled, and we really *are* going to Angor?"

"Of course – you've known it these several weeks past."

"Aye, but… well, it's just that…" she sought desperately for tactful expression, "You seem less averse to the prospect than when His

Lordship left the other night, Madam."

Elinor smiled. "Having reconsidered Lord Jehan's proposals, I find my wishes accord with his, and those of my royal Father. This will be an adventure - I even begin to relish the thought! So no shilly-shallying, ladies - my Wardrobe's long overdue for reviewing."

Her Highness's Wardrobe was not an item of furniture but an adjoining apartment, of equivalent size to the one Elinor herself inhabited. At its centre was a large dressing chamber furnished with mirrors of Faalian glass, costume racks, mannequins and sewing benches; and radiating from it, a communicating suite of smaller rooms dedicated to different types of apparel. One held nothing but accessories: gloves, purses, sleeves, belts, fans, kerchiefs and shoes, chiefly delicate indoor slippers of myriad form and hue. Others contained headgear and outdoor garb; the linen room was full of night-shifts and caps, petticoats, drawers, stays, stockings and the like. A freezing closet was set into the north wall, the scent of basil and woodruff sachets vying with draughts from an adjacent garderobe shaft to keep moths from the furs and feathers hung therein; and there were a half-dozen more rooms besides, each containing rack upon rack of apparel. This profusion was not entirely the product of Elinor's extravagance. Royal garments were too valuable to be discarded, and those outgrown or outmoded were routinely let out and refashioned before being stripped of embellishments and the scraps consigned to the ragbag.

"O, what a lot," she cried, "Wherever shall we begin?"

"Why not discount what you need least, Madam?" suggested Fran. "I doubt you'll need to pack aught from this one."

Elinor looked nostalgically round the Thorssen Cabinet whose cedar-wood coffers contained, literally, the fabric of her family history. Within lay her antique white samite christening robe, heirloom of Queen Gudrun's house, and the shawl worked by her mother's own hands with Elinor's emblem, a white wolf-cub in a silver crown. There were the cloth-of-silver drapes from her cradle and the rose-pink velvet hangings of her first four-poster bed; exquisitely embroidered caps, bibs and bootees, gifts from ladies of the court which it was politic to retain; and several miniature court gowns worn on important occasions throughout her childhood, including the plain black taffeta made for her mother's funeral.

She turned quickly from that one; and twitching aside another calico cover, cried, "O, look – my investiture robes... and all my birthday dresses – goodness, how many there are! Here's the gold brocade I wore at the masque for my sixteenth…" There came a silvery jingling as she riffled through the rack. "And the lovely blue dance frock with ribbons and bells in the seams that I got the year after… I'd forgot I had it, quite!" Fingering the cloth, she heaved a heavy sigh. "Ah me – my life, in garments… without them, who shall I be? How will I know who I am? Will I still be myself, d'ye think?" She laughed a touch hysterically. "Nay, ignore me – the Curse has made me fey! Yet I'm sad to leave the part of me that once had a mother and siblings…"

Dashing a tear from her eye, she sighed anew. "Alas, poor Queen - what would she make of me now, I wonder? Would it have come to this pass had she lived, and my brothers and sisters?

'Hey ho… of course my baby things must stay here - but the dance dress is too pretty to leave! Put it on the list, Fran.

'There, now! We've made a start, and only one thing to go from this room. How very practical I'm being – Lord Jehan should be well pleased!"

Chapter 16: Nikos Rides Out

The horizon over eastern *Fafnirsee* was suffused with radiance, gilding the underside of a low band of mackerel cloud in the otherwise icy-clear sky. To the west all was still sapphire darkness, with a frosty moon and hard, bright stars glinting on yesterday's snowfall.

Flaring his nostrils, Nikos snuffed deeply. The air flayed his sinuses with the tang of salt and snow, and his heart soared as high as the far-off summits. He felt keenly alive to the beauty of the moment: the mewing seabirds above, the goodly aromas of horseflesh and leather, the vitality of his body, warm within his clothes; master of his own private universe, yet dwarfed to insignificance by the celestial pageant unfurling all round.

Now Sol's glowing fingernail groped over the sea, setting it aflame and flooding the eastern sky with crimson, the distant peaks blushing delicate rose in response. Gathering the reins, Nikos urged Scylla to a trot. As Thorund had predicted the going was safe, the roadway so impregnated with salt and trodden by patrolling guards that ice could get no lasting grip on its surface. Besides, he wished to hurry past the next gatehouse, whose looming bulk sorely impeded his contemplation of the view.

The night shift had but recently retired and the newly wakeful day sentries had watched his approach curiously; there tended to be little traffic at this hour, and it was especially rare to see a lordly rider abroad. They waited in a hum of speculation until Nikos drew rein at the gate, whereupon one challenged him according to form.

"Halt! Who goes there?"

"Hail, Warriors! Nikos Aul'ios del'Aumaia goes here, on your King's business." He dug in his bag. "Behold, I've brought an edict regarding the comings and goings of my countrymen, which King Thorund desires posted in your guardroom. His Majesty also wishes me to take copies to Thorshaven, to be nailed up in the market and cried about the place. So, lads - as acting royal courier, will you let me through?"

"Indeed, My Lord." The heads disappeared; he heard the thud of boots on stone steps, followed by clinks and muted swearing as they fumbled with the frozen iron fastenings. Then the mighty doors groaned apart and the guards took their positions either side, saluting respectfully as Nikos rode into the dark arched vault and handed over Thorund's instructions.

"And now I must attend to my other deliveries – after which,

I'm minded to sample the delights of your fair city. Thinking on one in particular, pray, can you tell me where I might find…?"

The soldiers seemed only too happy to supply the required information. Nikos went on his way, contemplating the mountains Ragnar Thoralson had named, tracing their outlines on his memory. Under the growing sunrise, the shadows about their roots were now resolving into the far pine forests of King's Chase and delineating the mainland highway leading to Ulfar's lands. Through the crystalline air, Nikos thought he could even discern a dark bulk squatting in the mouth of the central pass which must surely be the exiled Baron's stronghold at Arkengarth Gate.

Ahead the road arced, the panorama of Thorshaven's roofscape and harbour drawing his eyes with ever-increasing frequency to the nearer perspective. As the spit of land they were traversing widened, Scylla snorted, scenting the open pasture where two days previously, he and his equine companions had enjoyed their first gallop in weeks. Nikos looked round. There was no-one in sight to permit or deny him passage, and in truth, he felt as restive as his mount. He slapped the horse's neck.

"So ho, lad, you've talked me into it – let's run!"

Scylla neighed, half-rearing in his eagerness to comply. Nikos bent low, baring his teeth ecstatically into the wind as the grey satin muscles beneath him flexed and extended. United in fierce male joy they sped over *Thegn* Pavel's land, leaping hedges and ditches in their path until the Kalaios adjudged it prudent to reduce their rate of progress, for they were coming up fast on the point where they should rejoin the highway.

"*Ho*, Scylla," he panted, tightening the reins, his face ruddy and flecked with snow from the flying hooves. "*Ho* there, boy!"

Snorting rueful protest, the stallion slowed to a canter. Nikos put him to the field gate and he jumped it tidily, landing back on the roadway in an iron-shod clatter. They now stood but a half-mile from the city, their cross-country run having brought them directly among the straggle of outlying hostelries, shops, manors and homesteads of Thorshaven's suburbs. Here, between the efforts of lamplighters, servants of house-proud *thegn's* wives, and tradesmen anxious to entice passers-by into their establishments, the road and pathways had been dug clear of snow and scattered with salt and cinders to prevent them from freezing. Despite these endeavours Nikos could see no sign of present industry, even though the time was close on seventh glass; the buildings were still darkly shuttered, and scanty wisps of smoke from the chimneys attested that their fires had not yet been stoked for the day.

It was so quiet that the noise of Scylla's shoes on the cobbles made Nikos wince. He was glad enough to move through the streets without curious crowds, and luckily had no need of persons from whom to ask directions; finding his way was a simple matter of retracing their original journey along this main thoroughfare, *Burgstrasse*, until it opened out into *Marktplatz*.

There, locating the town crier was also simple. Ferdi Mickelsprech sat in a mean little hut behind the market cross, toasting a piece of stale rye bread over his brazier and watching the last grains of sixth glass trickle out. He glanced instinctively towards the sound as Scylla clopped into the square, started to his feet at the unexpected sight of an armed, helmed Angorian and dropped his toast onto the charcoal.

Promptly recovering his aplomb if not the smoking remains of his fast-break, (he was after all the Voice of Thorshaven, ever eager for news to impart), he hastily upended the empty hourglass, seized the alarum bell from his belt-hook and rushed forth.

Swinging the bell widely, Ferdi proclaimed, "*Morgen sieben-glaß, und alle ist schön!*" He was a burly man with a full chestnut beard curling onto his massive pouter-pigeon chest, and his huge resonant cry rolled impressively round the vacant stalls and silent market halls. Tipping Nikos a wink he continued,

"Thorshaven, hark to my tidings! *Wolftag's* weather stays fair, the sea remains calm – and a stranger's abroad in our town!"

Nikos rode across and saluted him. "You've a rare pair of lungs, Sir Crier! Yet I could wish you'd forborne to announce me – I'd hoped to conclude my business here unmolested."

Slyly, Mickelsprech twinkled, "What, Lordship? Skimp my duty when your noble presence is of such interest?" He chuckled. "But fear not for your privacy. No-one would heed me this early on *Wolftag-morgen* unless I ran through the streets screaming fire, rape or invasion - none of which, I trust, will be necessary in this case!"

"No, indeed! I'm only come to bring these, with King Thorund's compliments, then to visit my colleagues in dock."

Mickelsprech received the documents with a bow, raising an eyebrow as he scanned quickly through the neat clerkish script; by the end, he was happily smiling.

"So, then, there will be much to and fro betwixt harbour and 'Gard in these coming weeks," he mused, "Hmm, high society doings... hah! The blessings of Fafnir upon you, My Lord. For once, I'll have more to cry than the day's price for herring and who has lost their purse! Pray, Sir: if you've aught to tell the townsfolk, say it through me. Remember my name, Ferdi Mickelsprech – you can always find me hereabouts, ringing my bell on the hour."

"My thanks, Ferdi – I'll bear that in mind," Nikos grinned.

Leaving Mickelsprech gleefully nailing up Thorund's proclamation, he rode into Wharfgate where the masts of the *Breath* and *Quintessence* were visible, towering over the thatch-roofed dockside buildings. They trotted down between the deserted boat chandleries, rope and net-making workshops and maritime clothing emporia; and at *Harborplatz*, Nikos followed his nose to the warehouse that locals had already dubbed 'Little Angor'. There at last he found other folk up and about. Fighting through cheery salutations and a welter of curious questions, he gave Scylla into the tender care of the *Eque'la*, and delivered sundry notes from the contingent up at Thorsgard.

Next he repaired to their High House for a steaming shot of *Kick* and tossed it down in one gulp. Soon attracting a knot of comrades with leisure to pause from their labours, he regaled them with an account of events at the castle. So swiftly passed the pleasant hour that Nikos was astonished to hear a hand-bell pealing without and familiar tones crying,

"*Morgen acht-glaß und alle ist schön!*" The voice continued in declamatory style; Mickelsprech had obligingly come into *Harborplatz* to proclaim Thorund's ordnance for the benefit of his shipmates. Reluctantly, the Kalaios drained his cup.

"Alas, I must go – I've messages yet to deliver, then I plan to conduct a little, um, shall we say, reconnaissance mission before I leave town! If anyone desires communication with our kinsmen, let their words be written down. I'll return by-and-by to collect."

With that he hastened to *Breath of Gaia*, where Next-Captain Marinus received him, and the letter he carried from Iamis, alike with great warmth. Together they rousted out *Quintessence's* Captain, to whom Nikos gave an urgent missive from Iris, and then both officers mustered their crews on the *Breath's* main deck so he could distribute such mail as was left.

Mission accomplished he treated the assembled mariners to an update on matters at court, concluding a quarter-glass later,

"…all granted full liberty of the Wolfenbirg, by King Thorund's command. Therefore make the most of your shore leave, sisters and brothers! I certainly intend to – if you'll excuse me."

To collective chagrin, Nikos withdrew to his cabin, made a few quick preparations and furnished himself with essential supplies; sneaked like an assassin back to the deck; bade a shouted farewell to his shipmates; fled down the gangplank, and sprinted from the seafront before they or the roving Mickelsprech could waylay him with further enquiries.

Dodging into an alley, he leant against the wall to recover his breath and his thoughts. "Let's see, what said those Gate-guard?" he muttered, looking about to orientate himself, and being possessed of a well-honed warrior's sense of direction, set off with purposeful stride. "Back of *Harbourplatz*, aye... past the *Fisch-halle*, which to judge by the smell should be *this*." He passed the large building painted with a writhing interlace of netted fish, and creaking above its door a signboard carved in the shape of a cod.

"Now cross Gutters Lane – faugh! – and go left at *Springstrasse...*" Carefully skirting the congealed splashes around the public well-pump, he turned into an unprepossessing street of dingy ice-houses, timber yards and fish-smoking sheds. "Follow along directly to the inn with the double bay... and if I'm not mistaken that's it up ahead, yon side of the road..."

As the soldiers had told him, the house *was* distinctive. It seemed at first glance to be much more genteel than its neighbours: a two-storey, half-timbered hall whose ground floor façade boasted a costly pair of glazed bays, furnished inside with drapes and upholstered banquettes. In between was a door painted matching deep red under a stone lintel engraved with a frieze of maritime motifs. Its centrepiece was a grotesque mermaid endowed with fat pouting lips, protuberant breasts, and what looked suspiciously like a swollen vulva peeping from her scaly crotch.

Alas, The Mermaid did not stand up well to closer inspection. Although Nikos was no expert on Gondaran vernacular architecture, he did not believe a thatched roof should look so dishevelled, nor the plaster-work of an upper storey so cracked and stained. Neither, he observed, crossing the well-trodden street, was this shabbiness confined to the outside. The drawn curtains and love-seat cushions were threadbare and faded behind window frames criss-crossed by fungal decay, with sundry chips missing from their diamond lattice; and the beige daub of the lower walls was thickly scored with indecipherable runic graffiti (and some all too decipherable sketches).

A noisome whiff grew stronger the nearer he approached; now he comprehended the purpose of a barrel that squatted by the entrance, seeping yellow stains into the snow. Nikos paused on the threshold and listened. Faint sounds within suggested that at least one other person in Thorshaven was abroad, so he unsheathed his sword and rapped on the door with its pommel.

Nothing happened. He rapped again a little harder, bringing a patter of footsteps and an exasperated young voice hissing,

"Stop it, ye'll wake the whole house – d'ye not know it's *Wolftag*?"

"Then open up, Blossom," said Nikos gently, "Lest you prefer that I knock again louder."

Even through inch-thick pine he felt the vibration of shock at his accent and tone. She replied in a hurried, tremulous whisper,

"O, no – please, Sir, don't! I'll unlock if you bide for a moment but prithee, make no more noise."

"You've my word on it, Madam; or rather, my silence," he chuckled.

Sheathing his weapon to avoid further alarm, Nikos waited. There was a shooting of bolts, a rattle of chain and the click of a key in the lock. Then the door squeaked ajar on its salt-rusty hinges, and a pair of wide, frightened gentians peeped out.

The Speaker bowed. "Good morrow, Mistress," he said quietly. "Nikos Aul'ios at your service."

Her eyes rounded in wonderment. Involuntarily she pulled the door wider, a small, slender, pale-faced girl who appeared to have but recently arisen; she was wearing felt slippers, an apron tied over a white linen night-shift, a heavy woollen shawl round her shoulders and an unbecoming bed-cap to confine her flaxen tresses. The apron was soiled, and there were smuts on her cheek redolent of fire-making duties. Aha, thought Nikos, this maiden must be *la-Hai*!

"May I enter," he continued, "Or must I compound the disturbance by crying my business out here in the street?"

"B-but My Lord, w-we're closed," she stammered, "And-and they're all still abed-"

"Splendid! Come, sweetheart, admit me. Hear me out and if it transpires I'm not wanted, on my oath I shall leave."

Utterly disconcerted by his obvious rank, his courtesy, the foreign lilt of his tongue and the flirtatious glint in his eye, she stepped aside. Nikos ducked in, momentarily eclipsing the clear morning sun with his shoulders, doffed his helmet and smiled kindly down. Instinctively she adjusted her shawl and half-raised a hand to smooth her hair; then recollecting the ugly bed-cap, abandoned the motion as

175

fruitless and dropped him a curtsey instead.

"Pray, Lord, forgive me... When you first knocked, I thought you were just a- I mean... um... I thought you were somebody else..." she trailed off.

"Not at all, Highness!" Taken aback, she searched his expression for sarcasm but found none. Disregarding her blank stare, he went on, "Pray forgive *me* for intruding on your work - and for my ignorance respecting the customs of your 'Wolf-day'. So, to before I impose any further: I'm told to enquire here for a certain Madam Freya. Have I come to the right place?"

"Aye, My Lor-"

"Nay, not your Lord, love," he interrupted good-naturedly, "By Naume, I've ne'er met such a folk as yours for the Lording! 'Nikos' will suffice, by your leave."

"Aye, My- Master Nikos, this is Freya's house."

"Then I should very much like to see the lady. Pray, would you ask her to receive me?"

"O, but Sir - 'tis her rest-day, she'll be fast asleep, and I'll be sorely chided if I wake her afore-noon."

Nikos grinned. "I lay she'll chide you the sorer if you send me away, for she has, so to speak, invited me."

"She has?" Assessing him with a quick flick of her eyes, the lass dared a tiny smile back. "Aye... I dare say she has!" Repenting her pertness she continued in more fitting style, "Very well, Sir; if you'd care to step into the parlour, I'll go and tell her you're here." She beckoned him in. "Please to wait, Sir – I'll be back soon as may be." Bobbing another curtsey, she scurried away and disappeared up a flight of stairs in the corner.

He traced her path across the upper storey by the pit-pat of her slippers over the flaky plaster ceiling, and the presumable location of Freya's room by the place her footfall stopped. Looking more generally around, he saw a substantial chamber of rectangular shape; more he could not easily discern by the dim light filtering through two dirty horn windows in the back wall. Restraining the impulse to fling wide the curtains lest this attract more unwelcome visitors, he compromised by teasing open a chink at the top of the west bay. The eastern drapes he pulled further apart and peeped into the alcove: a deep pentagonal bay lined with cushioned seats, and a wall-bracket either side holding a candle in a red glass shade. It might have been a cosy little nook were it not for the draught whistling through the cracked panes and round their age-twisted leads; yet someone had patently spent time there, for her ragbag and work-box still lay on the floor.

Nikos turned away, and when his eyes had adjusted to the thinner gloom, gazed about in fascination. The parlour had a tri-partite layout vaguely suggestive of Thorund's Great Hall, albeit more modest in scale and appointments. At the east end, its rush-strewn floor was raised somewhat like the King's dais, although in place of a High Table, a sideboard stood against the wall beneath a species of serving hatch. On this basis he guessed that service quarters lay beyond, whence his hostess had originally emerged via the door propped ajar in the corner. The central portion was plainly but adequately furnished with pine tables and benches, bearing witness to recent carousing by their litter of overturned candlesticks, stale-smelling tankards and sticky ale splashes. The west end was delineated by an arcade of eight massive, square-cut columns in line with the foot of the stairs; continuing the newel posts' design, they were richly carved on all four sides with a marine interlace. Nikos surmised them to be decorative structural timbers, but could not fathom why such a fine feature should be marred and partly obscured by the lengths of cheap, coarse fabric stretched from floor-to-ceiling and nailed unsympathetically to one face.

Between the two central columns the material hung loose, forming an entrance curtain; curiously, he drew it aside. Within was a squalid dormitory crowded with half a dozen narrow, mean pallets, devoid of bedding bar a few matted grey fleeces serving as pillows. Was it a regular Gondaran habit, he wondered, for a hostelry's patrons to get so pissed they preferred such minimal provision to their own beds - and if so, why was there no-one snoring off the last night's debauch?

The recess stank, fusty and animal; Nikos thankfully withdrew. He detected no sound suggestive of the girl's imminent reappearance, and having exhausted the interest of his immediate environs, set out in search of further diversion. A moment later he had proved himself right. There was a kitchen behind the dais, with a stack of dirty dishes waiting to be washed, and a hearth with last night's embers raked into a neat glowing pile. He about-faced, his options now shrunk to waiting in the dank semi-darkness, or...

"Freya, wake up!"

Freya grunted, rolled over and tried to ignore the voice hissing low in her ear. Her shoulder was shaken.

"Uh? Wha-?"

"Come, waken! There's a gentleman asking for you - a Master Nikos! Do get up - you *must* see to him."

Freya sat up blinking blearily and shrugged her ample shoulders; the name meant nothing to her. Long-ingrained habit kept her grumbled reply to a murmur.

"Nick who? I don't know any Nicks! For God's sake, Freyling, tell him to come back tomorrow. We did well enow yester-night, I've no cause to be working today."

"But you'll want to with this one, I warrant – he's come from the ships!"

"So? He can wait like the rest. I'm going back to sleep."

"No – he's a Lord from the *big* ships, the foreigners!"

"*What* - an *Angorian*? You silly goose, why'd ye not tell me straightway! Which- who- what does he look like?"

"Tall and big, and right bonny," sighed Freyling, "Wi' long hair, and nice-spoken."

"Why, that could be any of 'em!"

"Well, you must know this one – he says you invited him."

"Nonsense - when could I have- O, great *God*!" Freya's hand fluttered to her throat. "Can it be- O my God, Freyling, I know who it is! Mighty Wolf, what shall we do?"

"I'll bid him begone, as you've no wish to see him."

"You bloody won't! Nay, lass, give him a drop o' the best stuff while I get dressed, then I'll come and- O, no, how can I bring him in here… I know! Show him into the Great Chamber."

Freyling gasped. "O, Freya - what if Ecbert finds out?"

"Bugger old Egg-head! He won't show his face till tomorrow night – 'twill all be cleaned up by then, and no-one will tell... will they, Freylina?"

"Tell what, Mistress Freya?" she rejoined innocently; then making to leave, froze with her hand on the latch. The stairs were creaking. Freyling turned a panic-stricken mask towards the bed.

"He's coming up!"

"God's Hooks, Freyling! Get out there and stop him!" squeaked Freya. "Stall him, at least – he mustn't see me like this!"

Freyling slipped out just as Nikos arrived on the landing. She put a finger to her lips, raising her other hand in the universal gesture for 'Stop'; but Nikos had done so already, stunned by the prospect ahead. Originally, The Mermaid's first floor must have been a gracious space, open to the hammer-beam roof and flanked by separate chambers at the east and west ends; but now, like the parlour, it was sadly defaced by gimcrack additions. The plastered wall of the room to his left was extended with a shoddy plank partition, punctuated by five flimsy doors daubed each a different colour and bearing a runic nameplate. A bare eight feet high, the ramshackle construction stopped far short of the pitched ceiling and the shared air above was alive with slumberous noises.

Freyling crept towards Nikos, hastily closing the whitewashed door nearest to him as she passed. "Master Nikos, pray go back downstairs!" she whispered. "You'll waken the girls – and Freya's not dressed yet!"

"She needn't fear," he whispered back, "I've seen women in *dishabille* afore now! Come, let me pass."

The heat of his breath raised gooseflesh upon Freyling's neck; her hair crawled. "But Sir – Freya won't like it..." she protested weakly.

Nikos laid his hands on her shoulders and looked deep in her eyes. "Tush, little one; she *will* like it! You may trust me on that." To prove it, he pressed a gentle kiss on her lips. "Stand aside - I have business with Madam, whatever her present condition."

All of a flutter, she obeyed, wistfully watching his back until he reached Freya's threshold, then tip-toed downstairs to resume her interrupted housework.

By the time the latch snicked behind Freyling, Freya's slippers were on. Wrenching off her nightcap with trembling fingers, she thrust it under the mattress, plumped up the pillows, tugged the covers straight, and with commendable presence of mind pushed her urinal out of sight under the bed. She clawed out the seeds from her eyes, flung a robe over her shift and snatched up her most prized possession, a fine lambs-wool shawl, winding it becomingly round her head to hide her uncombed hair. This perforce completed her emergency toilette; Freyling had evidently proved an ineffectual barrier because she could hear a cautious masculine tread approaching her door.

Chapter 17: *Tantrissima*

Anticipation kindling his loins, the Kalaios tapped lightly upon Freya's door. A latch clicked in instant response. Slowly the door cracked ajar, then with sudden resolution swung wide.

Helmet tucked in the crook of his arm, Nikos made a mute bow; as mutely Freya curtseyed, and beckoned him in.

She bolted the door. He set his helmet on the dresser. Still wordless they stood face-to-face. Freya, heart throbbing fit to burst her corsets, (had she worn any), could scarcely credit her fortune. Was she really to lay with this man, she wondered, her innards on the point of liquefaction; next second her stomach plummeted horribly. Surely, 'twas likelier he'd come with no more carnal purpose in mind than to negotiate the hiring of whores for his men...

No sooner had this unwelcome notion occurred than Nikos broke the silence.

"Madam Freya?"

Dumbly, she nodded.

"Well, you take some arousing, My Lady! And fearing yon maiden not up to the task, I came to render assistance: Nikos Aul'ios at your service. Before you say aught, I'm not your Lord or Master, just Nikos - even Niki, if you will. Pray forgive me if I intrude. I'll depart without protest, if not without reluctance, if my presence is irksome. Or will you grant leave I remain?"

She nodded, a broad grin lighting her face. "Why- I've never seen that on a man before!"

Nikos grinned back, creasing blue eyes enhanced with a sooty ring of kohl on rims and lashes. "Really - well, 'tis our custom to be so adorned afore embarking on a quest of this nature."

"And what sort of quest might that be, Sir?" she whispered archly. Hope rose in her considerable bosom, yet still she was braced for a let-down.

"Why, to know thee, Madam," he replied, stepping closer. "To conjoin in the Fusion of Tantra; to which end, I sought to make myself pleasing in thy sight." He fluttered his eyelids. "Tell me, have I succeeded?"

Freya did not altogether understand his words, but their tone was unequivocal. "Aye... aye, it suits you! Only," she spluttered, mirth overtaking her, "For God's sake, let not our docker-men see it – or 'twixt that and your hair, they'll not know whether to fight you or fuck you!"

"Perchance I had rather the latter," he rejoined unabashed, "For 'tis ever our Way to make love and not war!"

He was outrageous; Freya's heart was won quite. "Well, my fair Sir, if true Sir you be -"

"O, you'll have the proof on that directly," he cut in with significant look.

"-you sound like a bigger tart than me, so I'll be honoured to have you! Only first 'tis *my* custom to be clean of a morning - I must heat up some wash-water, if you'll allow."

"By all means."

"Thank'ee kindly, Sir! O, but where are my manners? Pray make yourself at home while I make *myself* fit to attend you."

He divested himself of sword and cloak, pulled off his boots and set them neatly at the foot of the bed, upon which, for lack of suitable alternative, he reclined.

"Do you mind if I smoke?"

"Please do," she replied. To provide him with warmth in the meanwhile she lit a whale-oil lamp and a couple of candles, then commenced bustling at the hearth.

"Thank'ee, Madam. Who's the young maid, by the way?"

"What, Freyling? She's a good lass... we call her that, 'Little Freja', because her name sounds like mine, though 'tis spelt different."

"It suits her," he said, recalling the fragile shoulders under his hands. "Is she kindred of yours, to be similar named?"

"Nay," Freya sighed as she raked up the embers, "No kin of mine - or anyone else's, poor child! She's an orphan, which is how she fetched up in this place." She broke off as a blue fragrant coil reached her nose. "That's not Faalian leaf! Or Grunewald Gold... what're you smoking?"

"A blend of our smoke-weeds called 'Passion.' Would you care to imbibe?"

"Aye, once this fire's caught," she said, plying the bellows.

Nikos exhaled a long smoky breath in her direction. "I can hardly wait – pray pump with all vigour, Madam."

To distract his eyes from her too-tempting person he cast them about the room. It was long and narrow with a sloping ceiling, its plaster stained and flaking in the southeast corner where the thatch above had leaked. The fireplace in the gable wall could have held a blaze large enough to roast the tenant alive; to circumvent this unfortunate possibility a small cast-iron stove sat in the inglenook, wherein Freya had kindled a more modest fire. The window, curtain still drawn to keep out the draught, looked similarly oversize and uncomfortably asymmetrical, thanks to a dividing partition of thin rough planks, the cracks and knotholes meticulously filled with daub and generously whitewashed by a more careful hand than the joiner's. Luckily this rude screen reached the ceiling; nonetheless, if he concentrated, Nikos could faintly hear the sleeping woman next door. Forsooth, no wonder they acted like mice! Myriad questions clotted his tongue; eventually he marshalled sufficient Gondaran to ask the most obvious.

"Tell me, what *was* The Mermaid, when first it was built? Its present condition seems strangely at odds with its design."

"I can tell you somewhat. So move up, Sir, if you please! Fill me a pipe o' yon fine foreign leaf, and I'll give you the tale."

Willingly, Nikos obeyed. Semi-reclining beside him, Freya began, "Well... its old name was *Seehalle*. Solvig Seablest the merchant-venturer had it built, nigh a hundred years ago. He left it, and his business, to his son Sedwig – a wastrel who drank and gambled all away, and ended up hanged for stabbing a bailiff. So it was auctioned to pay off his creditors, which is how our landlord came by it. 'Twas Burgher Ecbertsson who made it like this – huh, poor old Seablest would spin in his grave to see the place now."

Before he could question her further, the kettle began singing and Freya excused herself, withdrawing behind a screen in the corner. There followed the watery tinkle of a bowl being filled then her garments appeared, one by one, slung over the screen as she shed them. Sounds of splashing and rinsing ensued.

Resisting the impulse to spy, Nikos adjusted his breeches and re-appraised his surroundings. The occupant of this degraded chamber was plainly no slattern; everything, from the floorboards to the furniture of cheap knotty pine was as clean as its shabby condition permitted, and brightened by a bed quilt, composed, like the curtain, of a patchwork in washed-out red and purple with diamonds of rusty black velvet.

"I like your soft furnishings, Madam."

"Thank you – they're all my own work," the screen whispered back, "Made from old scraps and off-cuts from Ecci's shop – he wouldn't waste good gelt buying such fancies for the likes of *us*!" She let out a satisfied breath. "Ah... that's better – all done!"

To his disappointment, the shift and robe slid back over the screen. A few moments later his hostess emerged duly clad, her face scrubbed and shining, a bone comb in her hand.

"Just my hair to do now- O, but what's this?"

"Sundries from the ship. Would you care to break fast?"

Nikos had laid out on a kerchief a small picnic of travel cakes, nuts and dried fruits. Freya's stomach gurgled.

"I would indeed," she grinned, "And have the very thing to go with it!" From the bedside cabinet she extracted a bottle and two wooden beakers. "This'll warm the cockles of your heart!"

Pouring a goodly measure, she thrust a poker into the cup till its contents were hissing hot. This she handed to Nikos, prepared another for herself and sat down beside him.

"Your health, Sir."

"And yours, Madam." He sipped warily. "Whew - as you say, very warming – what is it?"

"Nettle ale, with honey and mustard."

He drank again, deeper. "A potent brew for morning! Still, 'tis a feast-day, is it not, so let us indulge."

When they had breakfasted, Nikos wiped his hands and picked up Freya's comb. "Might I dress your hair, Lady?"

"Why yes, if you want to," said Freya, amazed – though in truth, she'd heard stranger requests. "'Twould be a rare treat."

"Thou art gracious." He sat cross-legged behind her on the bed and smoothed back her abundant tresses. His touch made Freya's spine thrill; acutely aware of his body-heat through her thin night-clothes, she abandoned herself to the luxury.

"What a crowning glory... like molten copper... I've seen some rufous heads among your countrymen, Madam, but none as rich as this. What d'ye call this colour? We know it only through the artifice of henna."

"Kind folk call it auburn; the less kindly, Carrot or Rusty."

"Au-burn... I like that. Aye, auburn is the word that best describes you." He fell silent, teasing out the tangles, combing from the crown to the tips of her ringlets with long, sensuous strokes. Freya's shoulders slumped and her lips parted in bliss, the slow, hypnotic rhythm lulling them both into a sort of ecstatic trance.

"You're truly a man of surprises, Master Nikos," she sighed at last, "I would ne'er have expected a lordship to be such a dab hand wi' the comb."

"Well, we all are, more or less; 'tis needful when so many wear the hair long. My half-sister and I have busked for each other since childhood – for we were both called early to the Blades, and soon learnt to keep our tails tidy. I enjoy it, too... feeling the living silk, knowing the pleasure it imparts, or receiving such ministrations myself.

183

Even to watch the grooming of others soothes me almost unto sleep. Forsooth, had I not become *Kali't'aia*, methinks I should have turned body-High full-time!

'There, you're finished." He pressed her gently round towards him, stroked back her fringe and ran his fingertip lightly across her plump round cheek. "My Auburn of the changeling jewel eyes... on the harbour-front I thought they were emerald, but I was mistaken. Close up they're topaz stars, gleaming in a smoky-quartz heaven." Freya's heart hammered; their faces were almost touching, the hot breath between them electric. "And closer still, the stars are eclipsed by jet moons till all now is lapis-blue twilight... hmm... dare I believe 'tis desire I see, reflected in their darkness?"

Pleased, embarrassed, she retorted, "Tish - you've a pretty tongue for the flannel! Tell me - is it as apt to other purpose?"

Nikos chuckled. "Thou shalt be the judge – for now our breath has ceased congealing on the air, the time has come!" Sliding off the bed, he unlaced the points of his doublet.

Eyes glistening with fun she replied haughtily, "High time indeed – and make haste, you've kept me waiting long enough! Ah yes... a prime piece of man-flesh," she went on as he shed his upper garments. "O, but why are you stopping?"

The Kalaios had paused bare of torso, hand at his breech-thong. "I' faith, I'm afraid you might mock me. My privy member falls so far short of a spear's length you'll deem it sadly wanting."

She beckoned imperiously. Nikos clenched his jaw and rolled his eyes to the ceiling while Freya squeezed his black leather crotch in professional appraisal.

"Nay, it seems satisfactory," she concluded with ill-suppressed glee, "Pray, continue."

Nikos unbound his ponytail and shook loose his sun-streaked mane, unfastened his breeches, turned his back, wriggled them provocatively to the floor and stepped out. He was naked underneath, having foreseen this contingency aboard the *Breath* and left his braies behind. Slowly he revolved to present a full-frontal view and struck a pose, raising a quizzical eyebrow.

"Smaller than my spear but greater than my finger – will I do, Madam?"

He was the most beautiful man Freya had ever seen - and by far the barest, his tawny skin naturally smooth, his blond pubic thatch cropped to close stubble. As excited by the burlesque as he plainly was, she said breathlessly,

"O yes – you'll do very well."

His eyes travelled deliberately to the ample snowy cleavage swelling from the V of her gown.

"Come then, reciprocate." He drew Freya to him, unbound her sash and slipped her gown down to pool at their feet. His towering bear-hug made her feel tiny, as dainty as Freyling - a delightfully novel sensation. She reached up and fondled his hair, sensuously caressing the nape of his neck.

Eyes half-closed in pleasure, Nikos pushed against her yielding belly. She trembled as his mouth grazed lightly over her jaw and cheeks then gently, fleetingly, his teeth closed round her upper lip. Freya gasped as a flick of his tongue pierced her vitals with shivers.

"O God! Stop! Stop, please, My Lord," she moaned, "I can't stand it... you'll make me waken the girls."

"Not if I gag you – as you deserve, for have I not vetoed that title?"

Prolonging the agony till she was on the point of screaming, his smiling mouth slowly descended. Then their lips met, full and warm, and her stomach gave a great lazy roll like a wallowing whale. She floundered in the embrace, clinging as a shipwrecked soul might cling to a rock while the kiss, soft at first, grew to a passionate tempest. Sucking hard on his probing tongue, she rejoiced to feel him groan and clasp her tighter in response. Straining together they fought mouth-to-mouth, devouring each other with lip-bruising hunger. At last, flushed and panting, they surfaced for air.

"Now, Madam - methinks 'tis only fair that you shed this last veil," breathed Nikos heavily. His hand lingeringly traversed her bosom, loosened the neck of her shift and pulled it down from her shoulders. It hung momentarily suspended from her nipples then fell, with a small delicious friction, to settle snugly on her mounds of hips and belly.

Nikos's jaw dropped along with it. "Great Gaia - those are astounding!" Awe-struck, he gathered her up in overflowing handfuls. "Truly, thy breasts are a banquet – I must feast upon them!"

Freya dug her fingers into his hair, biting her lip to keep in the moans as he sipped at her bosom with butterfly kisses, then stooped lower and lower till he was squatting at her feet, tugging at the folds of her shift.

When it gave way and fell to the floor, he remained for a moment in boggling, absolute silence. Then to her unutterable mortification he collapsed, sides heaving, both hands clamped over his mouth while sooty tears squeezed from his eyes.

"O-Orange!" he spluttered, "Your fleece is bright orange – verily could I dub you Tangerina!" A glimpse of her expression soused his mirth with ice-water. Instantly contrite, he rose to his knees. "O Madam, thy pardon - but I was taken by surprise, not knowing such colour could grow upon humans. In fact, I refuse to believe it," he went on adroitly, "which confirms my suspicion - for if fox-fur grows not upon mortals, thou art plainly a goddess!"

His voice was sincere, his upturned eyes irresistibly appealing, blue as rain-washed cornflowers dancing in a coal-field. Suddenly, the bizarre nude tableau they must present struck her as ludicrous. Her lips twitched helplessly as she wiped the teary kohl-smudges from under his lashes with the ball of her thumb.

"Hum! You're so silver-tongued, Master Nikos, I wonder you've need of a sword when you can talk your way so readily out of trouble."

"Can I? Then I am forgiven? Ten thousand thanks, My Lady - I kiss the shell-like nail of thy pretty white foot! Yet that seems insufficient… I kiss too thy fair dimpled ankle… and thy sweet rounded knees… and the sumptuous sweep of thy thighs…" Nikos slowly ascended, tracing the words on her skin with his tongue, prickling all of the hairs on her body erect.

"And think not I distain this." Freya shivered as he gently teased out the curly tendrils with his fingertips. "Nay, this is rare; bright as a spark compared to the embers of thy head." He laid his cheek against her pubis. "Aye, thou art lovely, boundless Freya; I would not pain thee for worlds."

Their position no longer seemed risible, and a warm flood of feeling washed through her; the nearness of his face to her private parts, coupled with his affectionate tone, set her knees shaking. Reflexively she clutched at his shoulders, his hair; Nikos's head turned and she felt the kiss of his breath, the slick hot dart of his tongue…

"Stop!" she gasped, pushing him weakly away.

"Why – don't you like it?"

"Not like this! Please, I can't stand it – my legs tremble so, I shall fall."

"Then you shall lie!" Rising, the Kalaios hooked an arm behind the said tremulous limbs and without apparent struggle, hoisted Freya off her feet and deposited her gently on the bed before she had time to say, "Don't, I'm too heavy."

Nor had she leisure to marvel at his strength; Nikos was on

her, parting her thighs to plunge in between and resume his interrupted explorations. Freya convulsed, clawing the quilt, chewing her fist to stop herself crying out as she squirmed against the exquisite lap of his tongue. He moved along with her, intuitive, modifying the caress to suit her response, incredibly skilful. Abandoned completely to rapture, an image rose unbidden in her mind, an obscure echo of the sensations thrumming through her: herself floating in a warm blissful sea, breasting over the waves, riding their swell like a seal. She found the vision strangely erotic, and rolling with it in sensuous rhythm, felt herself merging, becoming the ocean itself, with Nikos the ship borne upon her; vast, fathomless, a goddess indeed, and gathering like a tsunami.

A rosy flush burst out upon her, and glancing involuntarily down at its source, she caught Nikos's eye and could not look away. The intense stimulation of body and mind made her cry out, thrusting and surging into his face as within, the tidal wave crested and broke. Bucking in uncontrollable spasms she grasped Nikos's head, pressing him to her till the crescendo subsided; then covered her face with her hands and burst into tears.

"What is it? Have I hurt you?" He knelt over her, full of concern.

"Nay," she sobbed, "Nay, sweet Niki!" She had been weeping and laughing together; now the latter prevailed. "You just took me by surprise – which doesn't often happen in my line! And I'm embarrassed, having done naught for your pleasure – *and* made you all wet, to boot."

"Tush, 'twas my pleasure too; but you can, at the least, wipe my mouth."

Employing fingers and tongue Freya did so, and they fell once more to kissing. Nikos subsided upon her, his erection hard between her thighs, sliding minutely, ecstatically over her sensitive parts where desire had brought on a deep hollow ache. She wriggled artfully, manoeuvring into position and slowly, slowly, Nikos inched inside.

"O! O, my God!"

He stopped. "What? Not too far, already? Nay, Madam - surely you can take a little more! Like this? Or further, even…" Suiting actions to words, he edged deeper.

She gasped as her elastic inner walls blossomed to receive him; still he hovered on the brink, teasing them both with superhuman restraint. Freya could bear it no longer. Grabbing his buttocks, she wrapped cushiony thighs round his hips, ground her pelvis against him and hauled Nikos in to the hilt.

He held the thrust, skewering her to the bed while she writhed in immediate climax, sinking her teeth into his patterned shoulder to stifle her cries. After this, he felt entitled to pursue his own long-delayed satisfaction, and began moving slowly at first, then quick and urgent as lust overtook him. Freya rocked with him, stroking and scoring his back, kissing his face and neck, sucking at his chin. Nikos was whispering what crudities or compliments she knew not, for he was far beyond speaking any tongue but his own, and soon even that deserted him. All subsequent discourse was conducted in the wordless language of passion until at last, aroused beyond further endurance by the abundance of pliable flesh heaving and moaning beneath him, Nikos felt his own orgasm mounting. The rough speed of his breathing, the feel of his hardness pulsing and breaking inside her undid Freya a third time and they came together, her climax so forceful it arched her back like a bow, lifting her lover bodily off the bed for all his muscular bulk.

Panting, they collapsed in a welter of sweat.

"O… O my… O, great Wolf… you're a bloody good fuck, Master Nikos – I feel like 'tis me should pay *thee*!"

He rolled off and stretched, consciously magnificent, outrageously immodest. "Aye, so 'tis said. And so I should be - I served long enough in the Temple of Tantra when I was a lad! Which reminds me," he reached for his kerchief, "Here, Madam: let me attend you." Gently he mopped the stickiness from her thighs then wiped himself down, afterwards considerately tucking the cloth under her bottom lest residues stain her fine quilt.

"Why, you've not the air of a monk – what's this temple you served in?"

"Ah, the Temple," he smiled in fond reminiscence, "Domain of the Tantric priesthood; a university of recreational arts, a school of the senses, a house of entertainment – akin somewhat to this, only larger and better appointed."

"Like a big Mermaid? What… you can't mean… you never whored in a brothel!" She cocked her head reflectively. "Nay, on second thought - I can believe it, quite! But how could a gentleman come to such pass?" Trailing her bosom provocatively across his chest, she delved in the bedside cabinet for her pouch. "Let's have a smoke while you tell me."

"Hold hard," said Nikos, "What weed is that?"

Freya giggled. "'Tis Faali Fine Shag."

"Hah – that'll go well with Angorian Passion!" He combined a pinch of each in Freya's pretty little meerschaum pipe shaped like a mermaid, her tail-fins forming the mouth-piece. Nikos loaded his mixture into the open bowl of her head, and lit up. "Ah... a fine blend, heady yet mellow." He passed it to Freya.

She drew deep. "Mm.... and now a goodly tale, if you please, to go with it."

"Very well – but let it be under the covers, lest another goodly tail freeze!"

They cuddled together, passing the pipe back and forth.

"Well, to put it in short: when I attained manhood, I chose for my rite of First Fusion the one who was love of my life, and I of hers. Our season of bliss was all the sweeter because we knew it would be brief - she was pursuing our Calling so vigorously she had little time left for love. But I was a lusty youth, and she woke such appetites in me that I took leave from my own training and entered the Temple as a novice.

'I served there six months, learning the arts of pleasing others even as they consoled me for the one I couldn't unite with completely and forever. Then I resumed my military studies - became Adept, a blooded Warrior, and in due course Kalaios and member of the Elect's Counsel. And so, eventually, I fetched up at Thorshaven – and the rest you know, more or less."

"And that's it? O, typical man! Forsooth, Master Nikos: whatever you learnt in that temple, it wasn't story-telling! For a start, who *is* this woman that set you a-whoring? And why can't you have her – doesn't she love you?"

"Who is she? Why, you've seen her! You spoke on the wharf... she is Nerya."

"Nerya?" said Freya, puzzled, "Nay, I spoke to no ladies, only your companion- O! She was never that handsome young soldier who rode at your side!"

Nikos laughed. "That she was! Kalaia Nerya, First of our host - the finest blade I've ever crossed swords with! And she does indeed love me... we're as one, bound by ties that are stronger than common - ties that inasmuch as they strengthen our love, render impossible its ultimate expression."

"But how? Why? O, do tell it better!"

"Alright, I'll try for a history: because once on a time lived two Warrior lovers, Orestis and Hefaiston, who greatly desired to be fathers. So Orestis asked his comrade Aula to be their Vessel and she agreed, having enjoyed her first bearing - and I'm the result. Together,

189

my fathers and Aula reared me in Aumaia, my city of birth, to the age of six months. Then we went on our travels abroad, and I didn't see my dam or my birthplace again till I was seven.

'It was then that I first beheld Nery, tall and strong, graceful as an antelope, her hair already grown into a Kalaian tail... We grew inseparable - eating, playing, training, competing, sleeping - we did everything together, all through our late child-years and into our teens. She won my heart; she's my comrade-in-arms; I respect her more than any being alive. But one day I should like myself to have a child, and with her I can't.

'Nay, we're too close in blood. Nery is firstborn of Aula - she's my half-sister. Thus our love has been ever a bittersweet thing, as it is to this day... Now, if my narrative be still too sketchy for your liking, here's the detail."

Freya traced his tattoo with her finger. "What, in this pattern? Isn't it just decoration?"

"More than that – it's my life wrought in symbol. Look: here's Nery; our Fusing; the Temple; my Warrior path, and so on."

Fascinated, she peered close. "Every bit has a meaning? What's this one?"

"My birthplace: triple-hilled Aumaia."

"The long marks?"

"Flames and blades - battles I've fought in."

"And these little circles?"

Nikos grimaced. "A headcount of my slain; these glyphs are their names, where I knew them. I'll save you the trouble of counting: my tally is an hundred and eighteen, four less than Nery's.

'There, Madam, now you have me summarised – does *that* rate as a story?"

Freya was open-mouthed. "I'll say! But- 'tis lots to take in... I mean, is it normal in Angor to lie with your sister?"

"It seemed so to us... we were as strangers, and lacked the natural antipathy of siblings raised together. And consanguinity is indeed licit among us, subject to certain restrictions."

"And for men to lie with men - that too is allowed?"

"Certainly, and women with women. Some, like my fathers, prefer one or the other; most, like myself, lie with both – which doubles one's chance of a shag!"

"It sounds like a rare land, indeed - but be careful who you say such things to... and whose holes you poke your prick at! These matters are life and death here, and I'd hate to see you gelded."

"I'll smoke to that!" He sat up and re-loaded her pipe. "What a cunning thing this is – I like its workmanship."

"You do? Then take it, from one tart to another - a Thorshaven keepsake, for sharing your tragic romance."

"I'm honoured – I'll treasure my little Northron mermaid, and remember you whenever I suck on her tail!" He felt for his pouch. "But now you're pipe-less – you must have mine in return."

Freya gasped. "I can't take this! One like mine you could buy on the market for pence, but this…" it was chased silver-gilt, inset with a yin-yang in ruby and jet, "must be worth a month's wage or more, without the jewels. It's too much."

"Nay, that's your pipe, and this mine; it's a fair gift exchange. Besides, I'm a guest in your house, and your country. Take it in hospitality – and think on me when you smoke it."

"O, Niki! Are you really sure? O… well then, thank'ee! 'Tis beautiful, the loveliest thing… the kindest thing anyone…" She broke off, choking a little.

"Tush, sweetheart," he stroked her hair, "if you think it too much, level the balance – tell me your tale in return. Truly, I'm baffled to know how a woman so fine can dwell (begging your pardon) in these sordid surroundings, where you shine like a pearl on a dung-heap. How came you here, Freya, and why d'ye stay?"

She wiped her eye and nestled against him, idly stroking his corrugated belly. "Now that's a long story! Load a fresh smoke in my handsome new pipe, and I'll tell… only *I* shall begin at the beginning, pass through the middle and end at the end, with all proper detail in place – unlike Master Back-and-Forth here!

'It all began in Arkengarth, in the hamlet of Ulfheim where my parents lived. They're pious, respectable folk, a seamstress and a craftsman-carpenter, both servants of Baron Ulfar-"

"Ulfar? I know of him."

"Don't butt in, I'll lose my thread! Aye, Ulfar… 'twas for his estate they worked. Their first decade of wedlock was barren, but they prayed and sacrificed, and at last I was born. And two years later Gerda, my sister – I hear she followed Mamma as a seamstress, and made a fair marriage after all.

'Anyhow, I was raised to serve in the Baron's household. I wasn't a naughty girl then, though you mayn't believe it! I liked sewing, and chapel-school, and learning to housekeep - I wanted to be a good maid and make my family proud.

'When I turned thirteen I went to work at the Garth. I was very innocent, a virgin, and hadn't yet started my blood-months. All went well at first, once I got over my homesickness and nerves at being in the big fine house - the other servants were kindly enough, and work no harder than it had been at home.

'But everything changed at fourteen when these," she gestured, "ripened, and suddenly all the lads were about me. I was still a child and thought them tiresome and rude - all but one. He was handsome and gentle, and wooed me so sweetly… we used to creep off in secret whenever we could, and walk in the woods, and eventually – well, you can imagine.

'O, but I loved him, and what we did together! I never dreamt to feel such bliss… I wondered why Mamma hadn't told me what joy love could be. He said we'd marry, and gave me a ring – I still have it, somewhere – and I longed for the day we'd announce our hand-fast. Yet even then I worried how he'd bring it about - I knew his parents would be wroth that he'd chosen a dowerless girl. For he was Ulfred, the Baron's son, and expected to make a rich match – still, I was young and in love, and I hoped...

'I didn't realise I'd fallen in trouble… I didn't even know what we did was how babies were got! But the laundress noticed my moon-blood had stopped… and she watched me, and made report to the Baron. And so we were caught; 'twas Ulfar himself followed and discovered us, shagging in his hay-loft.

'He did naught at the time – I didn't know we'd been seen till the evening, when he bundled me into a wagon and drove me back to Ulfheim. Nor did I know I should never see Ulfred again, or I think I'd have died there and then from very grief!

'When we got home he bade me wait while he fetched my father without, and talked to him very low and long; I heard money change hands. Then after a word to Mamma, they muffled up in big hooded cloaks and we drove off again. It was terrible - Pappa scolded and preached all the way to Thorshaven. I'd have been excited, else – 'twas the longest journey I'd ever been on. But I was so miserable and frightened, and he wouldn't tell me what was going to happen, only how I'd brought on him shame and dishonour and like as not spoiled my sister's prospects into the bargain.

'They took me to an old midwife who made me swallow some stuff, and put something inside me, that brought on my blood… thus Ulfar lost his first grandchild, to my great pain and woe. After, we went to my uncle's inn where Pappa left me, with a little money, to the care of my aunt. When I got well, I could work in the bar for my keep, or go straight to Hel – they wouldn't have me back, I was ruined, disowned, I'd looked above my station, betrayed our lord and disgraced both our houses...

'I recovered soon enough, in body at least; started helping round their quarters, and then in the bar... where all the men liked a buxom lassie! Too popular for my own good, that was ever my problem - and since swallowing that horrible potion, I seemed to plump up more than ever. Auntie grew jealous, and when she saw uncle's eyes stray to my bum once too often, 'twas the end of my job, through no fault of my own.

'I'd only been there three months, and scarce left the inn - I hardly knew a soul, or my way round the city. Yet they sent me out, with no help but an address near the docks where they needed live-in staff. I lasted two days, the landlord was a pig – he'd have raped me for sure, if I'd stayed any longer.

'So then I was out on the streets. My box was stolen straightway, by a man who told me he would deliver it to some nice lodgings. My small coin was soon spent or tricked off me, and all I had left was my work-bag and what I stood up in. I found my way to the harbour, so footsore and desperate I was going to put an end to myself in the sea... and was screwing up courage to jump when Ecbert found me. He saved my life, as I thought - fed me, clad me and gave me shelter and employment under this roof. By then I was nigh on sixteen... fully eight years ago. Ah, me, how time passes!

'And that's how I came to The Mermaid. As to why-"

"Wait - you've not said what befell your young man."

She sighed. "He also left, for the far south of Grunewald – as far off as could be. 'Twas said he'd been called away to manage his father's estates, but *I* know he was banished... I hear he's since married a nice dull heiress, which must somewhat redeem him in Ulfar's eyes. I wonder if they have bairns... or if he ever guessed that he might have had another."

"You call mine a tragic romance - it seems comedy, put next to thine... So why do you stay and endure this?"

"*If* you recall, I was coming to that! Because I'm bound in contract, like the rest - I can't afford to leave. But I hope to afore six years are up, or I'll be out on my arse will-I nil-I. He likes young fresh girls, and will keep none of us once we pass thirty."

"I begin to see... Pray, Madam, if your voice isn't wore out: tell me more of this Ecbert, and how he runs his house."

"Ah, Master Ecbertsson - I liked him well enough, to begin.

And I was grateful – truly, he'd rescued me from worse…

'Folk think him a pillar of society... his family are prosperous mercers, he has a shop on High Street, and lives in a mansion up on Thorsgard road. He's very wealthy but has no heir, only six spoilt girls to find rich husbands for. Hah - the thought of emptying his coffers on a half-dozen dowries makes him like to piss his britches, the grasping old tight-purse!

'When Sedwig went bankrupt he bought this place cheap, split up the rooms and tried it as a seamen's hostel. But that didn't fetch enough gelt, so he lit on the plan of bringing in girls. God knows there are enough on these streets who'll do aught for a bed and a crust - and Ecci's good at spotting them.

'Aye, he keeps six of us. We each pay six shillings a week, all but Freyling who can't earn yet. We do all the shopping and cleaning, cooking and serving - and shagging. In return we get room, firing and raiment, and our meals from the table he has us keep for clients. We must open at noon, dressed plain for daytime, and wear the face of an ordinary inn. Then at twilight we change into fine, and if 'tis quiet we sit in the windows to tempt passing trade, every weekday till midnight. Saving *Wolftag*, when respectable folk go to worship and we of ill-fame are not welcome, nor does Ecbert like us showing our faces abroad on holy-day. So we stay indoors – 'tis our one blessed rest!"

"Your companions: who are they? Are their histories as doleful as yours?"

Freya nodded. "All brought low by men, one way or another. Gretel," she jerked her thumb at the wall, "is twenty-eight, and has been here longest bar me. She was shunned by her kin for leaving her drunken pig of a husband, who beat her.

'Ingrit's father gambled away their house, and more besides. She only just escaped when the *thegn* took her family for bond-slaves, and is working her back off to buy them out of debt.

'Else was raped by her stepfather when she was thirteen. Her mother walked in on them, believed her husband's excuses, and cast Else out as a trollop while Anna, poor girl, fell in love… with a rascal who promised her marriage to get her in bed, then got her with child. Then he told her he'd a wife already in Faal, put to sea in his boat and was ne'er seen again. Her son was born early and dead, the same week she came here.

'And last there's Freyling, our baby. She fled Grunewald three years ago, when her kindred were scattered or slain in the purges. Up to now she only does housework, but Ecci's licking his lips for the day she's grown up. Once he's had his fill, she'll start whoring with the rest of us. Then he'll find some other little lass to put behind the white door, and throw Gretel out to make room - as he did to poor Agathe after I came...

'Aye, I soon found out the measure of his charity! Though I realised straightway how the girls got their money, in my first weeks I had but to help in the kitchen, and I slept in the Great Chamber. Then one evening he joined me and explained, ever so patient and kindly, that with a ten-shilling bond against theft and damage, and my rent and whatnot for a month, I owed him nearly two pounds! He showed me what he'd laid out on my behalf, all written down itemised. Poor old Ecci could no longer afford to support me, 'twas time I began paying back - and as I had no such funds, well, there was another way...

'Thus began my new career... ach, I'll not tell you how long it took to cancel that debt and earn my weekly dues so it got no larger – but at a penny a squirt for a quickie, you might imagine!"

"Not altogether - pardon my ignorance, but I know not how this money-system works."

"Well... Your basic shag's a penny downstairs in the cots, tuppence up here in private, with a penny extra either way to go without a cundum – and each day we must earn twelve pence for Ecbert afore we keep a farthing for ourselves-"

"But that's outrageous!"

"Nay, 'tis a fair enough price! Though it *can* be had for less - a ha'penny for a knee-trembler from the sad clapped-out sluts round the docks... a fate poor Agathe was reduced to... ah me. So things could be worse. The Mermaid only gets decent types who won't carp at the cost or make a ruck – soldiers, sea captains, merchants - regulars, mostly, and nice fellows in the main, not rough filthy drunks who'd knock us about. O, don't look like that, bonny Nikos – it's not such a bad life."

"It seems so, to me," he said thoughtfully. "And speaking of money-"

She flushed. "There's no charge today! 'Tis my holy-day, I can entertain who I like. Besides," she laughed, embarrassed, "By my reckoning, 'tis me owes you sixpence!"

Nikos kissed her tenderly. "Generous in every respect – have thy virtues no end? But that's not what I meant..." He took a purse from his pouch and tipped out a soft clinking handful. "Look: this is Angorian coin. We have *stels*, ten to the *lune* - of which thirteen make up a *sol*. How would they equate to your currency?"

"How pretty! Well, we have twelve copper pennies to a silver shilling, twenty shillings to a pound, and twenty-one pounds to a gold crown." She weighed one of each appraisingly in her practised palm. "Judging by weight, these with the star feel like shillings... which makes the moons worth a pound, more or less."

"Ah... so this *sol*," he dug in the purse, "Equals one of your crowns?"

Freya's eyes opened wide. "O," she breathed, extending a tentative finger to the beaming sunburst of its face, "It's *beautiful* – like solid sunshine! May I hold it? I've never seen a golden coin before." He dropped it into her palm. "God's Fur, 'tis heavy!" She cradled it for a moment, then handed it back. "Aye, 'twould be same as a crown – not that I'd know for certain, of course!"

"So what could you buy with it?"

"Much!"

"How much?"

"Hmm... well, if 'twere mine, I'm not sure I should spend it at all... it seems too shiny and lovely to part with. I'd wear it on a chain next my heart, to remind me of its giver."

"Now who's got a flannelling tongue? But seriously – what could you buy?"

She pondered. Twenty-one pounds! "Let's see... added to what I have salted away, I could pay off my bond, buy Sk- um, buy someone out from the army... and with the leftover I could rent a little house, and keep us till I was set up as a dressmaker."

Nikos shook his head in wonderment. "Your life could be changed that much, by one simple *sol*? Then you'd best keep it." He folded her fingers around it. "There now, Madam Freya – get ye gone from this hell-hole forthwith!"

Chapter 18: To the Rescue!

Freya's fist clenched, the *sol's* milled rim biting deep into her palm. Right there, warming in her grasp, a whole ounce of freedom... instant salvation from six more years' grind followed by a lifetime of-who knew what? But now - today, tomorrow, as soon as she'd packed - she could go! Find decent lodgings, petition for Skala to tramp his last duty, and then... mayhap they could wed! She was not utterly dowerless now...

Nikos saw her face begin working, and tears ooze from the corners of her eyes. She lifted the coin to her lips and kissed it then with a regretful shake of the head, handed it back.

"Nay, I can't take it - I can't leave."

"Why? Isn't it enough?"

"It'd be plenty for me - but not for the rest. And I can't desert them, especially Freyling – not now! They've all done so much for me. We help one another out, you know, when one's had a bad day and can't meet her rent... aye, this could buy me much – but never a day's peace or happiness, knowing what I'd left them to. So take it back; 'twas the kindest of thoughts, but I can't."

Reflectively Nikos weighed the coin in his palm. "This isn't a *sol*, it's a life... so, my *Tantrissima* – keep it. Stay if you will - only keep it. Keep it because you see the value of beauty. Keep it to recall our first glorious Fusion." Punctuating words with kisses he went on, "Keep it because, by the Goddess, you've earned it! Keep it for the fine loving between us... pray keep it for me next thy heart, bonny Freya."

Her tears flowed freely, wetting his lips with warm salt.

"That's different - that I *can* do, and gladly!" On a sudden her spirits were soaring. "It shall be my treasure, my nest-egg for us all against disaster!" Now she was laughing as she wept. "Not that 'twill take any coin to remind me of you..." A fresh gush of passion surged through her; she seized Nikos and kissed him enthusiastically. For a moment or two he responded, then broke free.

She floundered in his eyes. "Come, Niki, I would thank you properly! Let's- how d'ye say it? Let's do Fusion again!"

Nikos sat up, excitement on his face. He tapped his teeth, considering. "Hmm..." She quivered in anticipation. "Tell me: if I procured a *sol* for each of your friends, what would happen?"

Freya blinked. "Why... I suppose we'd all go. First Ecbert would screw from us all the gelt he could, to spend on his little princesses, laugh us for fools as he waved us goodbye, then fill up the house with new girls and start over. I dare say 'twould do wonders for trade! But let's not talk of old Egg-head…" She bent for a kiss but Nikos restrained her, his cheeks flushed by a quite different excitement.

"Hmm…" To Freya's surprise and dismay, he sprang up and began dressing as if he had just heard the call to arms sound.

"What- where- O no, you're not leaving already?"

"Alas yes – I'm heartily sorry, Madam, but matters of the utmost urgency tear me from your side!"

He did not look regretful, though; indeed, Nikos looked almost indecently pleased as he mustered his gear and made haste to be gone. Typical man – shag and run! Tears pricked anew at the back of Freya's eyes, born of disappointment, anti-climax and the fear she had somehow offended him with that palaver over money.

Nikos gave her no time to fret on the subject. "Come," he beckoned, "Show me where I can empty my bladder - and while we're about it, pray show me the rest of your Mermaid. Tantric Houses interest me and I'm minded to see her entire."

He was all soldierly now: brisk, matter-of-fact, bristling with energetic purpose. Reluctantly, Freya slipped on her shift and work-day kirtle. At least I'll have his company a little while longer, she thought, and must content myself with that!

They stole past the row of closed doors, a belatedly futile precaution; a knowing circle of grins and raised eyebrows waited below in the parlour, her companions having quietly arisen and helped Freyling set things to rights. A merry fire blazed in the hearth, where a kettle of hot mead was standing ready; curtains were drawn, and lamps lit; and at the table, the five lingered over their nuncheon of last night's supper remnants.

Eight frankly appraising eyes, and two that were wistful, fixed on them. In unison, the women rose and curtseyed, singing out in mock demure chorus,

"*Guten Wolftag*, Sir! *Guten Wolftag*, Mistress Freya!"

"*Ave, pulchrae Tantr'aia!*" returned Nikos amiably, sweeping an inclusive bow. "I'm honoured to meet thee – Nikos Aul'ios at thy service."

Claiming the right of first acquaintance, Freyling stepped forward. "Would you care for some refreshment, Master Nikos? The fare's only plain, but our spiced mead is good."

"Thank'ee, Freyling. Alas, I can't tarry – duty calls!"

"O, but Sir," cried an attractive brunette with saucy dark eyes, "Stay at least for introductions – I'm Else!"

Nikos bowed politely to each one in turn. "*Tantr'aia*, would I had time to deepen our acquaintance – but other affairs command my attention!" He flirted his eyebrows suggestively. "Moreover I'm bursting for a piss, if you'll excuse me.

'Ye Gods, what a lowly High Place," he exclaimed a minute later, as Freya led him through the squalid back yard to an encrusted pit, partially screened by a rude wattle hurdle. "Phew! Good job it's cold – I'll lay this stinks to high heaven in summer."

He made his own hasty contribution then thankfully withdrew. Ten minutes later, having seen all he wished to see, he was standing on the threshold with Freya.

"Farewell, ladies!" he saluted the rest; and to his hostess murmured, "Trust me – I leave only that I might come back the sooner."

"I'll see you again, then?" she dimpled.

Nikos kissed her fondly. "Aye, sweetheart, you will – as soon as may be! But now I must fly; anon, well-beloved."

As Freya bolted the door behind him, the parlour erupted.

"Gods, what a giant - did he split you in two?"

"What was he like? Was he good?"

"He *sounded* good, from what I could hear!" slyly interposed Gretel.

"Did he make you do strange for'n things?"

"O come, Freya, tell us about it!"

She sank dreamily into a chair, and tossed off the cup they had poured her.

"Now then, confess," demanded Else, "What have you been up to these past hours, with all that squeaking and humping?"

Cupping her chin in her hands Freya leaned on the table, more intoxicated by recollection than by the half-pint of mead. She heaved a great sigh.

"I think I've been making love."

Mickelsprech had just cried *Moon-tag* eighth glass. Lost in daydream Freyling leant by the range, absently stirring a cauldron of snow-melt for their morning water.

Next second she started violently and dropped her ladle. Her hand flew to her mouth, her heart pumping so fiercely that an instant rose bloomed on her face. Wiping her hands on her hessian apron, she scurried to the door before anyone else could respond.

"Who's there?" she inquired hopefully of the wood.

199

"*Ave*, Mistress Freyling - may I come in?"

"Aye, Master Nikos!" She shot the bolts with alacrity.

He stooped under the lintel and to Freyling's delight, saluted both cheeks with a kiss.

"We meet again – good morrow, Blossom! Are your housemates up? I must speak with all of you together."

"Aye, Gretel's out back emptying the chambers, the rest are bed-making."

"Pray fetch them – I'll wait here, if I may."

In due course Gretel, a strained-looking strawberry blonde, entered via the kitchen while the others, led by an overjoyed Freya, flurried downstairs.

Nikos came straight to the point. "Pardon my brusqueness and early intrusion – but I've a proposition to put, and must do so succinctly. If you can agree without detailed exposition," he winked at Freya, "I'll tell you what's required. Meanwhile I've a companion without – may he come in?"

"By all means!" said Freya.

In answer to his piercing whistle a gawky youth appeared, red-faced with shyness and cold.

"Allow me to present Master Rupert, my capable assistant, who shares my interest in The Mermaid." The young man shuffled his feet, nodding his downcast head. "So while we talk, d'ye mind if he looks about the place?" He slapped Rupert's back. "For I whetted his appetite yestere'en with my descriptions - did I not, my friend?"

"Aye, Sir – you did!"

"Of course, Master Rupert," said Freya, puzzled, "Look anywhere you please. The Great Chamber's already unlocked – I was dusting in there just this minute."

"Now, to business!" said Nikos, as with a bashful smile and a nod to the company, Rupert withdrew. He tipped a gleaming pile onto the table. "Here are six shillings, or their close equivalent, one each for your wage in advance - I wish you to shut up shop and keep your time clear for my purpose. Will you do that, *Tantr'aia*?"

Agog, they all nodded.

"Splendid! Now tell me, when will your landlord next appear?"

"Well, he stays away *Wolftag*, so has two day's takings to collect tonight - which makes him eager and early! He dines at his shop, and comes here straight after... sometimes by seventh, not later than eighth," Freya said.

"That's well..." Nikos mused. "Till that hour, consider yourselves engaged by me. Here's my charge: prepare a repast, deck yourselves fine, and await our return in good cheer." He laid another *stel* on the table. "Will this cover expenses?"

"More than cover," Else, an inveterate market haggler, cried in delight. "Thank'ee, Sir – by Fafnir, we'll sup well tonight!"

Freya's face fell. "O, but Nikos – what shall we do when our customers pound at the door? What if one goes complaining to the shop – Ecci doesn't come here in daylight, but news that we're shut might just fetch him."

Nikos grinned. "Fear not – 'twill all be taken care of!"

Ecbert Ecbertsson proceeded to his inn with all the speed that pompous dignity allowed. He was pondering who should be his evening's consort... Freya was always good for a tumble, or Else – ah, but would little Freyling were ready! He indulged in his familiar fantasy of ploughing her tight virgin furrow... 'twas a piquant idea, she being of an age with his younger daughters, only *this* nicely ripening bud would soon be his completely... might it even be tonight? Licking his lips Ecbert quickened his step, savouring the rub of the semi-tumescent member in his codpiece.

Spring Street seemed unnaturally quiet as he turned its corner and groped down the ill-lit road with his staff, straining his eyes for the familiar lamps. He blinked and shook his head, wafted at imaginary mist, and peered again. Why - he was not befogged; no lights shone ahead to be seen. How could this be - it was closed!

Instant panic jumped in his throat. What had happened? Not a fire, he'd have heard... O God, surely, his lady wife couldn't- nay, 'twas inconceivable she had aught to do with it! He mended his pace. The Mermaid was indeed shut, her bay windows blank and bereft - but not empty, Ecbert realised. Nay, he could distinctly make out a buzz of conviviality behind her closed drapes.

"What are those skiving tarts up to?" he said furiously then pulled up with a jerk. The noisome piss-barrel had gone from the doorway, and in its place lounged a brace of tall figures he could barely descry through the night.

One cracked a lantern and held it aloft. The glow revealed two soldiers, conspicuously armed in the fashion of Angor.

"Who goes - is it Master Ecbertsson?"

"Ah... I... aye," he sputtered, "But who are you, Sir?"

"Our names are irrelevant," smiled Kalaia Heraklita, "Our

201

function is guarding the party within! But you're expected – pray walk in, Master Ecbert." She and her companion politely made way.

"Walk in, indeed," he muttered, peevishly shoving the door, "Into my own house – who do these bloody Southron think they are?"

Indignation died on his lips. The parlour before him was spotless, cheerfully heated by an extravagant log-fire. One table held the remnant of a generous buffet: ham, soused herrings, oysters, bread, cheese and pickles of various kinds, and a pot redolent of Freya's renowned fish chowder. Another was robed in embroidered linen from his very own bed, lit by the handsome pewter candelabra purloined from his chamber, and set with his own private stock of lead-crystal glasses. And if his eyes were not deceived, in the latter foamed his best Faali champagne... which those thieving whores were quaffing like small ale, disporting themselves shamelessly in their flashiest frocks, impudently defiant, secure in their masculine escort.

Rising to his feet, Nikos unconsciously assumed a combat stance and made a brief bow, pinning Ecbert's boggling eyes with a steely blue stare.

"Ah... the honourable Ecbert Ecbertsson, I presume! I'm Nikos, Kalaios of Angor. And this," he gestured to the younger man beside him, "is Rupert Endriksson."

Ecbert blinked. The surname seemed familiar, though in his shocked state, he could not immediately place it.

"We've keenly awaited this meeting," went on Nikos, with a smile that failed to thaw his eyes, "Your reputation precedes you! Here, Sir," he lifted a glass, "Come drink with us. We've matters of importance to discuss."

Ecbertsson wobbled gratefully into a chair. What in Fafnir's Name was going on, he wondered, as Nikos resumed his own seat and courteously poured out some wine.

"To The Mermaid!" the Angorian exclaimed, "The blessings of Tantra be on her, and on all those who serve under her venerable thatch!"

"Er- to The Mermaid," said Ecbert, his weak rejoinder lost in a rousing echo from Rupert and the girls.

"Aye, you see, 'tis like this," said Nikos, relaxing into an air of bonhomie, "I'm so impressed by the service I've received in this House that I'd like to enjoy it on a more permanent basis... In short, Master Ecbertsson: on behalf of the Counsel of Angor, I wish to purchase The Mermaid."

All mouths but Rupert's dropped open.

"Buy The Mermaid?" Ecbert gasped. His avaricious mind galloped swiftly ahead. "Impossible, my dear Sir! Why... why, this house is precious to me, and my staff are as daughters! I couldn't part with it for any sum."

"O, but surely you could – for the right one!" said Nikos, silkily. "You're a man of affairs... and I've taken a fancy to your Mermaid. Forgive my ignorance of market values, Sir – I hesitate to insult you with an inappropriate bid - and pray name a figure, based on her worth as a going concern."

The burgher's heart beat faster, a greasy film of sweat breaking out on his smooth barbered jowls. What unexpected fortune – a stupid, rich barbarian, ruled by his decadent bollocks - Ecbert would fleece him, and his darling Villemina would get, after all, the wedding of her dreams to Cedric Pavelson! Calculating furiously, he drained his glass; Nikos poured him another.

"Thank'ee, good Sir! Hey ho, I had rather not sell," he sighed, "But since you force me to put price on the priceless... 'tis said The Mermaid cost over an hundred crowns to be built, and is nigh on a century old - endowing her with a certain quaint charm of historical merit. And, given her many superb original features, and close association with one of Thorshaven's late luminaries, I estimate her value should have appreciated to... O, let's say one hundred-and-fifty gold crowns...

'Then when you've added in stock... and furnishings... and goodwill, naturally, this being a long-established inn of vibrant custom, well-famed for its simple home comforts... I reckon two hundred, maybe two-fifty crowns, is realistic. I'm sorry if that be too dear for your purse."

Nikos raised his eyebrows. "Is that really the going rate? Did you mark that, friend Rupert?"

Inwardly, Ecbert sneered. What could that long streak of piss know about it?

Endriksson cleared his throat. "I marked it well, Sir." For the first time, Ecbert observed a wax tablet and stylus lying by his elbow. "And with respect, Master Ecbertsson, I deem your valuation somewhat high..." He retrieved a sheaf of parchments from the satchel at his feet. "First one must consider the building fabric; within and without, 'tis in parlous condition. Thatch, drains, gutters, plaster and paint, woodwork and windows – all stand in need of repair-"

"Ah- well, the sea-gales wreak ruinous havoc... And you can't get good workmen these days-"

"Also the, shall we say, 'quaint' facilities leave much to be desired. The site lacks fresh water; the well-spring is choked so it seeps under the scullery floor causing much mould and fetor, and thereafter puddles to waste in the yard where it makes a foul mud. The abominable privy ..." Inexorably, he enumerated, "...inadequate laundry... leaking roof... rotten woodwork... obscene graffiti in public view..." and many other failings. His audience regarded the spectacle with immense enjoyment, Rupert's stock rising with every second that Ecbertsson writhed on the pin of his critical assessment.

"...lock stock and barrel, I'd rate her present worth no higher than twenty-five crowns."

Ecbert's mouth worked like a landed haddock while Rupert paused to wet his throat with a draught of champagne.

"Ah, Master Burgher, I see you're amazed!" Nikos said. "Forgive me, I should have explained. My able young friend is the son of your Treasurer, Endrik, and Chief Clerk of Accounts to King Thorund. Hence his eye for appraisal and keen head for figures – regarding which we shall hear more anon, eh, Rupert?"

The young man drained his glass, grinning a grin that turned the burgher's knees to water.

"O, yes – that ye shall! Aye, Master Ecbertsson – we've not turned yet to other deductibles."

Ecbert blenched; Great Wolf, what was coming?

"Chiefly, the matter of taxation - for though I ransacked our archive, I could find no record of The Mermaid as a lodging-house. Nay, 'tis listed as a 'non-profit-making benevolent concern for the succour of fallen women', and sundry claims for charitable exemption made in this regard. Yet I'm given to understand that said unfortunates pay a rent – an extortionate rent, might I add – from which no tithe has been given." He riffled his parchments. "According to my earlier calculation, let me see, where is it? Ah, yes: five paying tenants at six shillings a week each, for fifty-two weeks – that's seventy-eight pound a year... for the past twelve years... a grand total of eight hundred-forty pounds undeclared income, of which His Majesty's Treasury has seen nary a groat!"

"B-b-but," blabbered Ecbert, "M-my expenses, Master Endriksson, my overheads-"

Rupert frowned. "Negligible, from what I can judge! But I'm glad you reminded me," he rustled again through his sheets, "Aye, here we are, under sundry expenses: extensive claims for maintenance and repairs, yet I fail see the evidence thereof; a generous hospitality allowance for 'clients', who must surely be frequent and greedy visitors; plus 'furnishings, raiment, victuals &c for staff' consistent with an army that dwells in a palace, dresses in velvet and feasts upon dainties!"

"Well, I... er... but-"

"And speaking of staff, something else puzzles me, Sir; you've not claimed the allowable expense of their wages! Could it possibly have slipped your mind to pay them? You should have had bills of... er... yes, six shillings a week or thereabouts, for six live-in housekeepers. Thus I estimate you owe them fifty-two shillings apiece, less legitimate deductions; say two pounds each, for every full year they have worked here.

'Alas, Master Ecbert – it doesn't add up! But rest assured, with the help of my fellow clerks, I shall scrutinise your records most inquisitively. Then might this grievous misunderstanding be speedily resolved, and a fair tithe of your earnings submitted to His Majesty.

'For the nonce, some contribution is plainly overdue." Dipping once more into his satchel, Rupert produced a fine vellum scroll. "According to my appraisal, The Mermaid's entire present value barely suffices to pay the back wages owing her staff, let alone make a drip in the ocean of what's due to King Thorund! Which at a tenth, I estimate conservatively to be eighty-four pound – excluding, of course, annual non-payment fines and punitive interest thereon.

"So I'm authorised in His Majesty's Name to ensure that the process of recovering your debt commences forthwith. Therefore I must inform you that, by King Thorund's express command, this inn is forfeit to the Crown with immediate effect – I have the requisite document here." He rolled it across to the pallid, sweaty Ecbert then turned with a small bow to Nikos.

"Sir: mindful of your partiality respecting The Mermaid, My Lord King wishes to offer it in gift to his esteemed guests, the Counsel of Angor. Alas, His Majesty feels he can't yet in good honour do so, given her condition; hence he further commands that all costs claimed by Master Ecbertsson towards maintenance and repair should, belatedly, be spent!" A gasp broke from the burgher's white lips. "I'm charged to dispatch tax-gatherers to his properties, to seize cash or goods commensurate exactly with the expenses falsely submitted. His Majesty then most earnestly implores you to superintend refurbishments here, that the place be brought into fitting state to be gifted to Angor and thereafter managed as the Counsel sees fit.

'So you see, Master Nikos: from your own pocket, you've no

205

need to pay a penny."

"Ha! Great Gaia, heard you that, Master Ecbert?" Nikos cheerfully addressed the broken wreck sagging low in its chair. "Now there's an Accounter for you! Ho, from two-fifty in gold, he has wrangled your price down to nothing!"

"Finally there's the question of criminal charges," went on Rupert. "I'm no lawyer, Sir, but even I can see wrongdoing here – why, I myself have just witnessed you try to cheat a visiting ambassador!

'Altogether, Master Ecbertsson, you've a lot to answer for. To such degree His Majesty bade me invite you to Thorsgard, where suitable lodgings have been prepared for your convenience whilst you assist us in," his lips twisted grimly, "Our... investigations. Meanwhile your family will be held under house arrest, and your business and effects impounded, until our assessment's complete."

By now, the sound of cartwheels and hooves on the road outside had become generally audible. Nikos arose.

"Ten thousand thanks, friend Rupert, both for your masterly exposition and the timeliness of its ending!

'Hist, Master Ecbert – your sins have caught up! Truly, I can't pity you; had your heart matched your face and your words your deeds, you'd not be in such dire straits now.

'Leastways, you needn't worry about getting home tonight." Seizing the dumb, nerveless burgher under his terror-drenched armpits, Nikos hoisted Ecbert to his feet and walked him bodily to the door. "Come, Sir – thy carriage awaits!"

Chapter 19: Orgy of Celebration

The women sat stunned, hardly daring to believe the implications of what had transpired; Rupert, drained pale by his performance, was in no fit condition to enlighten them further.

"Wh-what does this mean?" quavered Freya, "With Ecbert gone, are *you* now our landlord, dear Niki?"

"Yea and nay," he chuckled, "We have no such concept, precisely! I'm to be more of an agent; a care-taker appointed by King Thorund and my Counsel, and charged with overseeing works here till such time as we leave."

"O, how did you bring this about – and wh-what does it mean?" she faltered, "Are we- are we free women?"

"Absolutely!" He laughed as a rosy flush overspread Freya's face, her mouth and eyes opening wide.

"D'ye hear that? Old Eggy is done for – we're free!"

A tumult of hugs, tears, kissing, jubilant whoops and transports of unrestrained joy ensued. Freyling, white to the lips, ran over to Nikos and cast herself down on her knees.

"D-does that mean - I don't have to lie with Ecbert?"

"Aye, Blossom – you'll never lie with *any* man you don't choose, any one of you, ever again. I'll see to that."

"O, My Lord - you've saved my very life! Belov'd Master Nikos, I lack words to thank thee enough."

Nikos gently raised her. Tears stood in his eyes too, as he smoothed back Freyling's hair and dropped a light kiss on her brow.

"Nay, sweetheart, be not premature in your thanks – you've not heard the best of it yet! Come, let's to table; and crack another bottle of Ecbert's champagne to revive Master Rupert, for we've more intelligence to share."

When excitement had cooled to a simmer, Freya raised her glass. "A toast to our saviour, our patron, our truly esteemed benefactor: to Nikos Aul'ios – long life and good health!"

"And to Rupert Endriksson, without whose acumen this enterprise could never have succeeded!" cried Nikos.

"To Rupert!" they chorused heartily, as the clever accountant blushed and ducked his head.

More toasts followed: to King Thorund; to Jehan and his Counsellors; to the energetic Treasurer, who had briefed his son so well; last, more soberly, to Aggi and other absent friends.

In due time, Nikos recalled them to matters in hand.

"*Tantr'aia*: in anticipation of receiving monies owed by your former landlord, King Thorund has made arrangements for your most pressing needs. Mayhap friend Rupert can explain?"

"Willingly!" said Rupert. Fully restored, flushed with triumph, awash with female attention, he was having the night of his life. "My Liege has justly decreed that your back wage as house-staff, at two pounds per annum rounded up to the nearest full year of service, shall be held in the Treasury, with compensation of two pounds apiece for its lamentably overdue payment-" Unheeding their collective sharp intake of breath he concluded, "-the sums payable range from eight pounds on Mistress Freyling's account up to eighteen for Madam Freya, to be available as and when needful by application to me."

"Wolfblest," cried Gretel, instantaneous heiress to sixteen pounds, "We're rich, as well as free!"

There were more tears, gasps, and blessings called on His Majesty's generous head as the women computed their worth.

"A further ten pounds shall be set aside for continuing repairs, replacing worn-out linen and the like," interposed Nikos. "And The Mermaid needs staff, so if you're willing, the King and our Counsel desire to retain you – all of you, for howsoever long you wish to bide. The daily running would be left in your hands entire, since you know the place best. Run her as a boarding inn; sell your foodstuffs, your craftworks. So long as there's ever a warm welcome here for Angorian folk, the Counsel will be well content."

Ingrit looked pensive. "O… then… what about Master Thom? He's such a sweet old chap… One of my reg'lars, Sir, been coming to me since his wife died. He's so lonely, poor fellow; sometimes he just wants to cuddle and talk, or for me to comb his beard like she used to… Poor old Thomi - if I'm not to be a-whoring, who will he go to instead?"

"Aye," exclaimed Anna, "And there's my Cap'n Roti… I'd be sad not to bounce *him* again."

Nikos grinned. "Fear not! 'Tis not Angor's concern, or your King's, how you privately entertain your favourites, nor what gifts or perquisites they might bestow in return! Join with whom you will, when you will, now you can freely enjoy without having to turn a living from't."

"Then I'll work for you, Sir!" cried Ingrit.

"Me too!" responded the rest enthusiastically, Freya meantime thinking of Skala with a curious pang in her heart.

"'Twill be my pleasure to report this to His Majesty," smiled

Rupert. "My Lord King was hoping you'd agree! For there's a final issue to be raised of great import to us all, and with which King Thorund requires your assistance.

'Aye… when first His Majesty learned he'd been gulled and deprived of his rightful tithe, he waxed exceeding wroth. But next My Lord King waxed exceeding interested… and his royal attention turned most keenly to wondering how many of Ecbertsson's ilk dwell in his city, profiting by the sweat of women's thighs, defrauding his Treasury, preying on his least fortunate subjects and depriving them of freedom and livelihood. So My Liege commanded a Commission of Inquiry into this noxious trade be established, and entrusted its superintendence to me. My first charge is to locate your predecessors, Ecbert's earlier victims-"

"O, Agathe!" Freya burst into noisy, joyful tears. "May the Wolf bless King Thorund! Aye, aye, Master Rupert, we shall help you find all! Ah me, if they live – 'tis a year since last I saw Aggi, and she was looking very… worn, the poor thing…" she trailed off.

"We'll search diligently," he reassured, "and when your friends are found they too shall find succour at The Mermaid. They'll also be recompensed for past servitude to give them wherewithal to set up as maidservants, shop-keepers or what-they-will, and a dowry should they wish to wed.

'And - where any of you know or hear of other such cases, other vice-ridden parasites who suck lifeblood from the bodies of women and State alike," his voice trembled with unwonted rage, "then make report to my Commission – and in His Majesty's Name, I vow to prosecute the offenders to the utmost!

'By these means, our King strikes his first blow 'gainst this loathsome flesh-trade, and transforms Ecbert's charade to the truth. Henceforth this shall be an embassy of sorts, a hostelry for the folk of Angor - and a permanent living for Ecbertsson girls, past and present. Your board will be all above board, so to speak – and 'twill be my special privilege to help keep accounts straight."

"O, this is wondrous! More wondrous than I could ever have dreamt," laughed Freya. "A thousand thanks, Master Rupert, for all you've done on our behalf– pray, tell our Lord King 'twill be our pleasure to accomplish his noble designs!"

"Certainly, Madam – then let this be the first step." Extracting the last clean sheet of parchment from his bag, he inscribed in his neat clerkish capitals, 'CLOSED FOR REFURBISHMENT UNTIL FURTHER NOTICE: BY ORDER OF HIS MAJESTY', sealed them with the Treasury seal and added his name and titles. This Nikos nailed on the door, prominent in the light of a lantern he slung overhead.

Thus secured against potential interruption, the now-superfluous Kalaia were called in to quaff a celebratory cup before they returned to 'Little Angor'. By now it was well past tenth glass. Ecbert's Faalian crate was nigh empty, and the evening's joyous effusions had settled into a high yet mellow happiness as the truth of their marvellously altered situation sank home.

Freya drew on a 'Fine Passionate Shag', as their smoke-weed concoction had been dubbed. "Now, Master Back n' Forth: we know the beginning and end of your tale, and some parts of the middle – but what happened between-times? What did you do while you were gone, that has wrought such a miracle for us?"

Accepting the pipe, Nikos smoked for a minute in silence to collect his thoughts then recounted the following adventures:

Emerging from The Mermaid he had jogged through Thorshaven's dockland, using his ears to guide him. Although it was early afternoon all the businesses were closed and the streets deserted. Believers and unbelievers alike had all gone to worship, the pious for fear of spending eternity being devoured by packs of celestial Wolves, the impious for fear of more immediately painful retribution at the hands of Sigismund's Brethren. It was therefore easy for Nikos to pinpoint his quarry, and he caught up with Ferdi Mickelsprech at the corner of Wharfgate.

"Ho, Sir Nikos - *Schöne Wolftag*! What's the hurry?"

"Phew! Fair Wolf-day to you too, Master Crier!" Nikos panted. "Why- why're you not at the shrines, wi' your fellows?"

"O, I've special dispensation," Mickelsprech twinkled, "After all someone must still cry the hour – for Time does not wait on devotions!"

"Indeed… well, friend, could you spare a half-hour of this fleeting time for me?"

"Aye, Sir – there's none hear me anyhow save those few souls that lie low on holy-day."

They repaired to Little Angor's High House where, over *mocha* and smoke, Nikos mined Ferdi's rich seam of civic knowledge till the crier's nose twitched, scenting a story.

"Tell me, Sir: are your folk looking to settle in our city?"

"I hope some will, in due course," Nikos smiled, "And your people in my homeland, too! So if you please, instruct me in matters pecuniary: what, for instance, would you pay in Gondaran coin for these drinks and sweetmeats…?"

Ferdi's emptying hourglass brought their enlightening conversation to a close. When the crier had set off on his beat, Nikos made a brief round of his colleagues on land and sea to collect their messages, and arrived back at Thorsgard just as twilight was thickening. The news he related caused Thorund to transform, before his startled eyes, into The Fafnir. By Naume, thought the Kalaios, I should not like this man to call *me* foe!

"We'll send him to Hel," snarled the King. "The treacherous cur, the whore-mongering hypocrite – he'll pay sorely for cheating us!"

"Wait, Sire," Loric had urged, "With all due respect to Lord Nikos, we don't have the full facts – mayhap Master Endrik can shed more light on these affairs."

An hour later Endrik Treasurer burst in, red-faced and apoplectic, trailed by his hand-wringing son.

"Sire, 'tis true – you're royally swindled! How dare he, the po-faced, thieving, devious bastard – begging thy pardon, Lord King – how dare he withhold the full tithe! His records-" Endrik broke off, emotion choking him quite. "H-his records present this Mermaid as an inn, a benevolent concern… yet nowhere on his household rolls are there listed six staff, nor either six tenants!

'Ach, My Liege, 'tis my fault - taking the Honourable," he imbued the word with heavy scorn, "Ecbert's accounts at face value, I didn't interrogate his claim. Alas, Sire - now I know, to thy woeful cost, how the fraudulent hound affords his pretensions of nobility."

"Never fear, Endrik – we shall have our redress! First we need an unimpeachable witness to Master Ecbert's conniving, a role I deem apt to a certain Chief Clerk… What say ye, young Rupert?"

On the Mermaids' part, the men's next visit had left them in a hum of excitement. Else and Gretel promptly sallied forth to market; Anna chopped firewood and rendered cauldron upon cauldron of snow for Ingrit's swabbing and mopping, while Freyling sat in the Great Chamber gleefully picking locks on the cupboards and chests wherein lay Ecbert's private luxury hoard.

Meanwhile, engrossed in erotic daydreams while she tidied and dusted the parlour, Freya had lost track of time. Mickelsprech's noon-cry came as an unwelcome shock, and despite Nikos's earlier assurance, she braced herself for a tide of hammering and protest. Steeled for the first knock she drifted again into reverie, broken by the sound of Gretel and Else's chattering passage outside the curtained bay. Their footsteps were light and they sounded in mighty high spirits for a couple of weary laden shoppers; O God, Freya thought, the silly tarts have only fetched men back! When the door opened she was waiting for them, hands on considerable hips.

"Now who've you dragged in off the str- O!"

The girls had preceded indoors two Angorian soldiers who had intercepted them on the corner of Spring Street and carried their baskets home. Suddenly Freya understood why there had been no customers this last half-glass – a second pair had stationed themselves quietly outside the porch to ward off incomers. Now they too ducked under the lintel and politely doffed their helms.

"See, you're not the only one, Madam – we've found some bonny soldiers of our own! *And* there's plenty more on the ships, 'Klita says!" chirped Else, reclaiming her basket and smacking a hearty thank-you on its former bearer's lips.

The warrior thus saluted swept a bow. "Ho, Madam – Freya, is it? I'm Kalaia Heraklita; these are my comrades, Philos, Akiles and Dora." The trio bowed one by one as she named them. "The Kalaios has sent us to protect the house from disturbance so he may go about his business unimpeded."

Something in the light, musical voice made Freya look sharply at the speaker, whose brow, like Dora's, was marked with a crimson teardrop; the counterparts borne by their companions were white, same as Nikos... Does his sword-woman Nery wear a red drop or white, Freya wondered; forsooth, is this how you tell 'em apart when they're dressed? O dear, should I tell Els- nay, she can find out for herself!

"Aye, I'm Freya!" she replied, dimpling mischievously; and recalling her manners, offered the Angorians refreshment. After courteous refusal they withdrew to resume their guard duties, leaving the women to coo over the rare cornucopia of dainties that had been got by Else and Gretel with their shilling.

Mid-afternoon, Nikos himself had popped his head round the door, but to general disappointment, after a quick check on proceedings and a word to his comrades, he hurried straight back to the High House. Rupert, stoked high on nervous energy and strong coffee, was driving away furiously with his quill, flicking the beads of his pocket abacus back and forth, scribbling calculations on his wax tablet and erasing them with his thumb, cross-referencing between parchments that lay round the table in untidy but meaningful heaps.

"'Tis pleasant to see one so enamoured of their toil," Nikos remarked.

"O! O, Master Nikos – you've made me do a blot!" exclaimed Endriksson. "But I'm nearly done here – well, I say 'done', but in truth I'm only just starting! I can't wait to look deeper into this… Still," his tongue was running at the speed of his pen, "I'm almost ready to write up my fair copy. O, this Ecbert's a double-dyed villain – my father will have a dozen fits when he sees how His Majesty's been skinned!"

Nikos left Endriksson to it, and the accounts were all done by fifth glass; plenty of time to freshen up, take a leisurely stroll to The Mermaid and digest a hearty meal before Ecbert appeared.

"…and the rest you know – more or less."

"Aye – and mighty mysterious you were, my fine Sirs!" Freya snapped tartly, "Making chitty-chat talk, and all the time sliding away from aught of importance! How could you keep it from us so long, cruel beasts?" The words were directed at both, but it was Nikos she thumped with a cushion.

"Ouch! Mercy, sweet Freya – forgive me!" he laughed. "Well, we didn't wish to raise false hope in advance. Nor to spoil the surprise – for truthfully, we didn't know exactly how the scene would play out. But 'twas a rare treat to behold Master Rupert's expert demolition. You've a ruthless streak, my young friend – I ne'er hoped to see the man broken so quickly!"

"Um… the credit rightly belongs to Endrik my father, for training me so well," mumbled Rupert, pleased and red.

Nikos clapped his shoulder affectionately. "Ah, but not for the cool head and intellect which are thine alone."

And so the happy evening continued. When the question of re-naming the new establishment arose, the debate waxed ribald. The Stickitt Inn was proposed, also The Angorian's Head and The Rosy Cock, rudely conjoined to The Rosy Angorian Cock-Head. Then The Seamen's End held sway for a while before The Jolly Roger emerged as firm favourite; but as night wore on, they agreed to defer a final decision until they were in more sensible condition.

Presently, a glint of green mischief in her eye, Freya observed, "You must be tired, Freyling – go to bed, lass, 'tis past midnight."

Freyling gestured at the party detritus. "But what about-"

"Nay, Freylina! Leave the rest, there's no rush. We can do 'em tomorrow – no more early rising, remember?"

The girl hovered, reluctant. "O… alright… only first," she came forward hesitantly. "I would speak with Master Nikos." She knelt at his feet, clasped his hand and kissed it fervently.

"Good My Lord, you've made me so happy – I can sleep easy knowing old Egg-head won't be fumbling at my latch! You've gi'en me my life back – even if I thanked you an hundred thousand times, 'twould not be enough."

"Ah, Freyling - to know you're safe is all the thanks I could wish. Your joy is my joy - may it sweeten your dreams with delight."

She rose, dithered briefly, then with sudden resolution bent and kissed him on the mouth. "Good-night, Master Nikos."

"Good-night, pretty Blossom - sleep well." Softly she kissed him again, for a few seconds longer this time; Nikos willingly returned it in kind. With a faint sigh Freyling straightened up, bestowed a tiny smile and a nod on the company, and withdrew.

Freya turned to the rest with a wicked expression. "Now, girls – I think our noble Kalaios should get a proper thanking for his heroic endeavours." She treated him to a passionate, open-mouthed kiss before standing aside for the rest. "Come along, ladies!"

Anna cried, "Aye – let's thank Master Nikos!"

"Yes, we should kiss him! We should all of us kiss him!" giggled Else, "'Tis only fair after what he's done for us."

"Aye," Ingrit agreed, "Lest he think us ungrateful! O, get off him, Anna – you've had long enough, it's my turn."

Amid laughter and squealing scuffles, Nikos was comprehensively thanked.

"So…" went on Freya, smiling archly, "Freylina thanked him afore she went to bed; then I did, and Anna, and Ingrit, and Else; then Gretel - and Else again, greedy tart! Is anyone left out- O! Master Rupert – come, you must kiss Niki too!"

"Nay, Madam – Master Nikos wouldn't want that!"

"Oho, don't you believe it," Freya gave a dirty chuckle. "Anyhow, does he not deserve one teeny-weeny kiss for his pains? Why, your new commission's down to Niki – you'd have known naught about Ecbert else. Some pledge of gratitude is called for, sirrah!" Freya was circling while she teased; suddenly she pounced, and hauled Rupert from his seat. "Come, Anna, help me! Gretel, Ingrit, both of you – grab t'other!"

Together they woman-handled the hapless clerk, weak with terrified champagne giggles, across to the chair where Gretel and Ingrit held Nikos, arms pinioned. The men exchanged glances of rueful predicament; then bashful, Rupert pecked Nikos's cheek.

Freya cuffed his head, playfully. "Come on, boy, get on wi' it–

give him a real kiss, for God's sake!"

Resigned, Rupert screwed up his eyes, pursed his lips and leaned forward. The moment lengthened... and lengthened. Nikos wrenched free of his captors and embraced Rupert back, gripping the nape of his neck. The kiss continued to mount, along with the heat in the room. Both men were breathing hard, biting, fencing with their tongues... and Freya, who had got considerably more than she bargained for, was not altogether sorry when Rupert sprang to his feet flushed and dishevelled.

"Well, well, Master Rupert," she gasped, "Most edifying - we'll make a tart of you, yet! So, was your first man-kiss good?"

"Truth be told, I've no standard against which to judge -'twas my first such either from crested or cloven," he confessed, somewhat shamefaced.

"O, poor boy!" cried Anna, "We must remedy that! Come, girls – we must all kiss Rupi now!"

"He seems to have picked up the knack fast enough," muttered Freya, faintly chagrined.

"Ah, but a little more practise won't hurt!" returned Anna, "Will it, young master?"

"Aye – then you can tell us which you like best, boys or girls," said Else cheekily, tugging down her bodice till a rosy sliver dawned on the horizon of her neckline. "I lay you'll plump for cloven in the end!"

As her friends clustered around, brushing suggestively against Rupert's stifled, half-hearted protestations and fumbling for the laces of his garments, Freya turned her attention to Nikos.

"Ah well, Sir," she sighed, when their lips parted, "I suppose these kisses must mean our good-night."

"Must they? Why so?"

"Well, 'tis late, and you've a fair way to ride-"

"What – would you throw me out of mine own house, then? Nay," he smiled, "We're not expected back, your King having shrewdly adduced we would wish to pass our night here making... ahem... merry."

Freya beamed. "O, I quite love King Thorund!" she said, radiant. "Pray tell our gracious Lord that we're bound unto him with our lives." She twinkled. "And if it should ever be His Majesty's royal pleasure to visit The Mermaid, I shall personally see to it that he receives the most royal service!"

"Indeed, I'll pass on the message – I'm sure the King will be flattered – and with my heartiest recommendation."

"Meanwhile, my love, pray excuse me," Freya slid off his lap, "As you're staying, I'll ready the Chamber – 'tis the only fit room in the house, as well as the biggest of beds!"

She pattered softly upstairs, lit the lamps and pumped up the embers in their late landlord's private sex-palace. This was the sole chamber furnished as it might have been in the old *Seehalle* days; rich tapestries, costly rugs on the floor, sumptuously carved and upholstered furnishings, and heavy velvet curtains to the glazed window and monstrously looming four-poster bed. Freya gazed round, seeing it as if for the first time, exulting in the power of possession – O, how she would pay Ecbert back for the nights she had spent here, unwilling! A wicked idea flowered in her mind...

By the time she got downstairs to share it with the rest she found Rupert, his doublet long gone, shirt hanging to his waist, standing in imminent peril of losing his hose. Ingrit and Anna had betimes stripped Nikos to his breeches the better to admire his torso.

Freya interrupted their bacchanal with the announcement, "My Lords and Ladies, thy chamber awaits!"

Glad to continue their sport in greater comfort, they crept giggling aloft clutching their clothing. Else and Rupert subsided without delay onto a Faalian *chaise-longue* while Freya embraced Nikos on the four-poster, gesturing surreptitiously over his shoulder with nods and winks while she inched him to the centre.

Next he knew she was kneeling on his right arm, pinning it immovably. Gretel, the next most substantial, followed suit on the left while Anna and Ingrit bound his wrists with the straps on the bed-posts. When his wrists were secured Freya unlaced his breeches, eased them, along with his braies, over the swell of his buttocks then whipped them off together in a smooth, practised movement. Plainly, Nikos was not altogether displeased by such ungentle handling; nor when Ingrit and Anna likewise bound his ankles, laying him helpless and spread-eagled to their view.

Freya grinned broadly as she stood frankly admiring. "Right then, my Rosy Angorian Cock - lest you can't hold up to pleasuring us all: Gretel, the love-ring, if you please!"

Sniggering, Gretel procured from the bedside table Ecbert's device to sustain flagging ardour. Nikos gasped, his eyes starting wide as Freya slipped the twisted penannular ring of walrus-ivory onto him, rolling it several times the length of his erection before settling it tightly round the root.

"There – that'll keep it up," she giggled, "While we all do our business!"

Yanking at laces, wriggling out of frocks, the women flocked round like crows descending on a carcass. There were hands and mouths everywhere; Freya, devouring him, was joined soon by Gretel, their disorder of entwined ruddy tresses tickling his belly as Nikos groaned and thrashed in ecstatic torment. Then the quartet took turns to straddle his face and penis, the spectators meanwhile fondling whichever part they could reach while urging their sisters on. He had fallen among *Tantr'aia* indeed; he dimly wondered whether they would desist of free will before the extreme titilation made his testicles explode.

Mercifully, this unhappy circumstance did not occur. After due time they withdrew, temporarily sated, leaving Nikos thoroughly slimed, empurpled and panting.

"Please..." he gasped, "Please take this off... I throb for release – and haven't I earned it?"

"Ha! Not yet, a-ways," Freya cackled, billowing majestically across the room.

"O no!" Else squeaked as she was plucked from Rupert's lap, where matters had not quite proceeded to their logical conclusion. "Why d'ye- O, I *see* - very well!"

She scampered to the four-poster to avail herself of Nikos while Rupert fell back gasping, thwarted on the brink.

"Come on, young master – we're playing share-and-share-alike!" Pitiless, Freya pulled him to his feet and thrust him towards the bed. "Look, there's room for you both!"

Now the others were on him, pinning his arms while they stroked, kissed, and impelled Rupert ever nearer the bed-head. There on the pillows Nikos's eyes were closed in excruciating bliss as Else bounced him vigorously.

Freya announced, "Aye, you must try us all – and there's *six* whores in this room! Is it not true, Master Nikos – that you've 'entertained' for a living, like us?"

"Uh?" His lids fluttered. "Ah... uh... ah... aye, in a way-hey... I had the... uh-honour... to serve... ah! in a... in a Temple of Luh-huh... of Love... as a lah-... as a lad!"

"Then show us how you learnt to honour *this*!" Grasping Rupert by a convenient projection she drew him forward.

Rupert squirmed in her grip. "Nay, My Lord, heed her not, 'tis forbidden – moreover, for you, most unseemly."

"Hah! Wha- what is... ah... seemly... in this ha- house

217

tonight?" Nikos laughed breathlessly. He looked deep in Freya's eyes. "I defy thee, Ma-madam - do thy worst!"

"Then suffer the consequence!" Cupping her palm behind his head, Freya simultaneously tugged Endriksson forward.

"Ah!" Rupert cried, "O, Great Wolf!"

The unseemly act lasted but a minute. Rupert convulsed, collapsing at the knees. Ingrit and Gretel lowered his limp weight gently to the floor while Else, aroused beyond containment by what she had witnessed, ground herself to climactic spasm and rolled off with a satisfied grunt.

Rupert leant forward and kissed Nikos deep, tasting himself on the Angorian's mouth. "O, My Lord... truly, this has been a night of firsts!" he managed at length.

"Aye – and 'tis not ended yet!" Freya strolled to the foot of the bed. To Nikos's unutterable relief, she slid off the ivory ring. "There, my boy – as he has for thee, so do for he; finish him off!"

By now nothing loath, Rupert moved to comply.

"Stop!"

They all nigh on jumped from their skins.

"Stop, I say! You shan't do it – *I* want to!" Freyling burst into the circle of lamplight and frozen nude figures.

"Freyling - God's Fur, girl, you gave us a fright!" cried Freya, as abashed, everyone (bar Nikos, of course) scrabbled for cover. "We thought you were sleeping!"

"Sleep, through such row – you must be joking!" she snapped. "Nay, first I watched from the stair, then through Eggy's spy-hole to my room. Then I crept in, and have sat in the corner, in the shadows. You were all much too occupied to pay *me* any heed!"

Weakly, Freya whispered, "You saw everything, then?"

"Everything – though not all close enough to suit!" Approaching the foot of the bed, her youthful scrutiny wrought upon Nikos a blush that none of the evening's previous frolics had accomplished. "O, but this view is most pleasing – and since you've all had *more* than enough, I'd now like to enjoy it for myself – privately. So good-night, everyone – and please to take this mess of garments when you go."

Such was the authority of Freyling's tone her elders began instantly, shamefacedly, to comply. Then Freya stopped short, her shift half over her head.

"Wait on a minute! We're going nowhere! Don't be silly, Freyling – you're too young for this, by a good way."

"Well, that's where you're wrong, Mistress Know-All! I had my first blood-week three months ago - only the one, mind, but quite clear. And now I have the belly-ache," she stroked herself, complacent, "So I think it'll soon come again."

"O, your Curse has begun! Freyling, why didn't you tell us?" cried Ingrit. "We could have helped – a maid shouldn't be alone, her first time."

"I dared not, lest anyone gave it away. I've been very careful of my laundry this year past, just in case – I planned to keep it secret as long as ever I could."

Freya embraced her. "Poor child - twelve years... it's an early burden you bear, love."

Freyling laughed. "In that, too, I fear you're deceived! I've ever looked young of my age, and lied about it when it suited... 'specially to keep men away - or when I wanted folk to feel sorry for me." She struck a pose, twiddling her hair and winding one foot round the other; twelve seemed a wholly believable claim. "Really, I was that when I came here! Now I'm fifteen, rising sixteen - same age as you, Madam, when you first lay with Ulfred.

'So you can stop calling me Freyling! I'm Freja; I'm a woman, and I want *this* man for my first." She stamped lightly on the rug for emphasis. "I claim him for my right – and you cannot forbid me, or in fairness deny."

Freya nodded pensively. "You're right, chick – we can't!" She kissed Freyling's cheek. "Go to it, girl, and enjoy – it's a rare thing, losing your maidenhead to someone you love.... Come, ladies, Master Rupi – let's to my room."

They mustered their scattered raiment and departed.

Nikos lifted his head from the pillows. "Freyling, are you sure? I mean... you're so very tiny, and I, well," he glanced down at himself helplessly, "I wouldn't want to hurt you."

"I hurt already – I have, since the second I saw you." She gestured with painful expression. "How it twinges and aches! So I care not for pain; the act could be no worse than this. And *don't* call me Freyling – I'm not as little as you think. Look."

Throwing off her shawl, Freyling took hold of her threadbare old nightshift, rent it from neck to hem and dropped it on the floor – she could afford new linen, now. Nikos caught his breath; she was not frail but slender, firm with housemaid's muscle, and pale as a wand of peeled willow. Her small breasts were demure and virginal, yet riper by far than mere buds, a strange contradiction to the hairless cleft of her

219

pubis. Seeing his look, she tittered.

"That's a lie, too! I've shaved and plucked these two years since, lest Ecbert surprise me at my toilet!"

Nikos guffawed. "You're a caution, to be sure! But what would you have done when the stratagem was finally penetrated - or did you hope to maintain the pretence into your dotage?"

Freyling sat beside him on the bed. "Ah…" she said, gravely, "Then would I have got him drunk and thrust my eating-knife into his eye… and stolen his money to run back to Grunewald… and *then* the Brethren would have hunted me down, and I'd have been dragged in chains to the Pit as a thief and a murderess." She shuddered. "Or submitted and lived safe enough, with a 'pothecary to treat my pox, and a midwife to hook it out if I got pregnant, hoping betimes old Ecci would peg out afore I turned thirty… Nay, I'd rather have taken my chance with Dread Hel!"

"Hah - so a Kalaia heart beats in that perfect tender bosom! I'm honoured that you choose me for your First, and will gladly oblige your desire… come, untie these bonds."

"Not yet awhile… I've ne'er been so close to a naked man before, let alone touched one - I would savour the moment…" Her slim fingers, somewhat pink and rough from housework, slid over his flank and down to his thigh with shivering lightness; then lips and tongue followed.

Swathed in gooseflesh, turgidly throbbing, Nikos groaned, desperate to embrace and caress her in return.

"O, you're cold," Freyling giggled, pinching the hard bud of his nipple, "I'd better warm you up." She wriggled into position.

He gasped, "Ah! Freyling… untie me, for all love."

Lightly, she tapped his cheek. "I… told you… do not call me that," she gasped in return, rotating and twisting her hips, then a minute later, frustrated, "O, why can't I do it? Why won't it go in?"

"'Twill be the seal of your hymen, sweetheart – it can cause an obstruction, in some."

"Humph! It shall not obstruct *me*." Freyling gritted her teeth, tensed momentarily then bore down with all her meagre weight. "Aiee!"

Nikos cried out too as she fell forward, her bosom pressing sweetly on his chest, her weight so slight he could barely tell she was there but for the wet heat clamping him with such exquisite tightness. It was deeply erotic; he ached to touch her.

"Ah! Ah! Is't in now - am I doing it right?" She kissed him

tremulously, her little pink tongue flicking over his lips and darting between, moving her pelvis in cautious tiny thrusts. "O, O *God...*"

"Aye, you're a quick learner, Mistress! And not overmuch pained, I trust?"

"Nay... aye... I don't know... partly... partly it makes t'other pain go." She stretched to unfasten his restraints. "O no... I can't undo it, you've pulled the knots tight – I'll have to take my teeth to 'em!" Dismounting, she worried at the bonds. When his right hand was free, Nikos helped unfasten the rest and at last, gathered her into his arms.

"I should spank thee for keeping me so long in bondage," he whispered in her ear, making her giggle and writhe. "But instead, I'll pleasure thee even as I have been pleasured..."

When it eventually came the climax, his first and her fourth, was stupendous. Afterwards, bearing his weight on his elbows as he wilted agreeably, Nikos kissed Freyling's eyelids, her cheeks pink as musk-roses, the wet red bloom of her mouth.

"We're bonded now, Freja my beauty," he murmured, "Thee to me, and I to thee. Bonded for life by First Fusion – the first virginity I've taken since I surrendered my own, close to your age. Ten thousand thanks, sweet rose unfurled! Never did I dream tonight would end this way – 'twill dwell forever in my memory."

"Mine too! And thank'ee for having me," giggled Freyling, minding her manners, "'Twas... wonderful! O, but," she struggled, "Get off me – I must look..."

Obediently Nikos disengaged, watching bemused while Freyling leapt from the bed and swiped between her legs with the torn shift. It came away bloody.

"My maidenhead's gone – I'm truly a woman!" She danced round, waving the raddled tatter like a victory flag. "I'm woman! I'm grown up, at last – O, I must show the others!"

Laughing, Nikos pulled her back on the bed. "In the morning, My Lady – there'll be time enough for that in the morning..."

Chapter 20: Morning After

By ninth glass Rupert Endriksson was in the parlour, making a hearty breakfast on last night's supper remnants. Washing down a mouthful of ham and rye bread with small ale, he burped in huge satisfaction - by the Wolf, he'd been ready for that!

He had woken soon after first light, forced by hunger to disentangle from an unresponsive Else, muddle into his clothes and tiptoe downstairs, his mouth juicing at the prospect of the still-laden board. Now, leaning back contented, he loaded a leisurely pipe. Rupert normally broke fast in the Great Hall surrounded by scores of others and Gentlemen rushing in attendance, so this early-morning solitude came as a rare pleasure even though he'd had to serve for himself. Having spent so little time in abodes other than Thorsgard, it gave him a curious feeling to gaze round the parlour, musing on the sights these old walls had seen... He flushed, recalling the most recent and his own role therein.

"God's Hooks – what a night," he said under his breath, "What a *fucking* incredible night!" He savoured the vulgar adjective, it being the first time he could legitimately apply it to his own activities, next mentally declining the verb: I fuck, I have fucked, I will fuck... I'm a fucker. He could almost hear his old tutor Ranulf's scandalised 'Master Endriksson - really!' It pleased him enormously. Images flashed through his mind – had he *really* done that, let alone *that...* he, the object of so much derision for his lanky limbs and the rash of adolescent spots that clung stubbornly to his twenty-year old cheeks; had he *really* done *all that*?

Aye – the memories were clear and zesty as Ecbert's champagne. He shifted in his hose, pleasantly uncomfortable, lit up his pipe and drew deep. Today he would return to Thorsgard a man, more sexually sophisticated in certain respects than either his peers or his very own father. Rupert felt buoyant, cocksure (aye, he could truly claim that word too, thanks to Else!). His outrageous secret made him swagger within, envisaging how he would smile in silent superiority when his more comely fellows boasted (habitually, with gross exaggeration) of their conquests among the court fillies.

Then there was the promotion, the trust of his King and his father, the new role itself... he felt he could live with the jealousy 'twould surely provoke! It would bring him often to town, to The Mermaid, doing work precisely suited to his talents and taste - a thrilling liberation from Castle routine and the simultaneous indulgence of his passion for figures (including those of more corporeal nature) and every thwarted romantic instinct his soul possessed… ideal for a chivalrous heart without a knightly physique to contain it. Rupert had not previously known that the like of Ecbert existed; now, he was zealously aflame to see more such unmasked and wiped out. Bethinking on the girls, all of whom he liked immensely, finding them… well, refreshing, in their humour and frank sexuality, and attractive in their different ways, especially… Bethinking on them engendered a sense of injustice so monstrous he could have rent Ecbert's flesh with his bare hands and teeth, the way Hel was rumoured to do. But in lieu of that he could be content with rending the burgher's accounts: his manor, his shop, affairs great and small – all would be scrutinised so that not the least minim escaped attention. He hoped that once he'd recovered every farthing to which the King was entitled, His Majesty would punish Ecbert's transgressions to the utmost… and by God, though customarily lacking the stomach for such spectacles, he vowed he would be there to witness.

Besides all of which stood his new… friendship, and what it portended. He surveyed the fledgling embassy, visualising how it would look, all restored… and what might happen there in future with their exotic allies - if and when the latter came back, as they presumably intended to do. Perhaps when the Princess was crowned Queen of Angor…?

He puffed out a cloud of 'Passionate Shag' and grinned, guiltily. King Thorund could have their balls off for last night, if he knew… but would he? The Kalaios, the Counsel in general, were riding so high in favour – especially at the Treasury, and even with Lord Hel, if such a thing could be credited – Rupert believed His Majesty might forgive the Angorians anything. Including the seduction of his Clerk of Accounts, he prayed most devoutly, if word of these adventures ever spreads! Endriksson shook his head, amazed at himself, then pricked up his ears. The floorboards above creaked, and slow, cautious footsteps began creeping downstairs; then Nikos emerged gingerly from the stairwell and groped his painful way along the wall.

"Good morrow, Master Nikos," he piped up, bright as the chinks of sunlight streaming in at the top of the curtains.

"Uh? Uh… Rupert! Didn't see ye, lad-" The footsteps took on a new urgency. "Sorry, can't stop, I must- I'll be-" Nikos stumbled towards the kitchen; the back door slammed. Grinning, Endriksson poured out more ale, stoked a second pipe and waited.

"Great Gods," Nikos whispered hoarsely, a quarter-glass later,

"I need healing… My piss – you should see it! All dark and *thick* and evil-smelling… and I've been grievously sick… such volume of stuff… and as to what came out behind, faugh! I wonder, d'ye think those oysters were quite fresh?"

"Ah," said Rupert wisely, "I'm acquainted with this malady – 'tis naught to do with oysters, fresh or otherwise."

Nikos croaked piteously, "Has it a cure?"

"O, aye-"

"Pray could you – could you speak a little softer?"

"Sorry! Aye, there's a cure," Rupert murmured, "But I must examine you better afore I prescribe." Mischievously, he flung open a curtain. Nikos flung his arms up in front of his eyes.

"Aiee! For the love of Gaia, Rupert! Argh… O, my head," he subsided onto the table, groaning.

"Aha, sensitive to daylight…" Relenting, he shut out the sunshine and lit a candle. Its merciful glow conferred an illusion of warmth on the Angorian's unwontedly sallow face, knocking off a few of the years that last night's debauch had etched there.

Nikos regarded him with bloodshot, pouchy eyes. "What ails me?" he implored, "I've ne'er felt like this in my life! Everything aches, above all my head… and my gut's a veritable acid-pit… *Kali'maia*, I feel like to die."

"Well, you won't – it's only Brewer's Revenge - a common complaint hereabouts, particularly of a morning."

"And are you immune, then, to be so… chipper?"

Rupert chuckled. "Not entirely – albeit more so than you, to judge from your state! You've but overindulged in champagne, but never fear, I know the remedy well. First, the Hair of the Wolf, a big shot of plum-brandy-"

"No! O, ouch… no, thanks, I'd rather suffer the sickness than the cure. I vow on my sword I'll ne'er take liquors again without they're well watered - ever, if this be the consequence."

"Very well – then instead you must eat, to re-line your stomach. Can I bring you some pickled herring and a slice or two of this goodly fat ham? I found they went down a treat."

"N-no." Hand to mouth, Nikos blenched. "Speak not of food – quick, change the subject!"

"What to?" queried Rupert, heading for the table; sensing he was unlikely to have the Kalaios at such physical disadvantage again, he was having great fun. "O, I know," he poured a beaker of water from the jug, "Guess how much we put away last night: a crate-full, twelve whole bottles! Two apiece, more or less... and you probably had more." A happy idea occurred: he squeezed in the juice of a Faalian lemon, an expensive delicacy Else had proudly served to garnish the oysters, and which were widely rumoured to have curative properties.

Nikos shot him a baleful glare. "Neither does that topic please me... d'ye torment me on purpose, sirrah?"

Rupert rounded his eyes. "Never in life; I do but make conversation and helpful suggestions for your recovery - which you then rudely dismiss! But disregard *this* to your woe," he handed Nikos the lemony water. "E'en if it makes you sick again – keep trying till you can stomach it."

"Ah!" Nikos took a sip, then a gulp, then drained the remainder in a single draught. "Ah... aye, this I can take."

"Good." Rupert poured him another. "Now, sip this one slow while I see what else I can find to physick you."

Leaving Nikos morosely rehydrating, he went into the kitchen and rummaged through the old-fashioned food presses. Thanks to the girls all was neat, logically arranged, and Rupert soon found what he wanted: Bane-ease, the ubiquitous hangover tea compounded of liquorice, peppermint and ginger, with a generous proportion of willow bark. Usefully there was also a full honey-pot and a crock of milk – he'd soon put Nikos to rights!

Back in the parlour he poured hot water onto a measure of Bane-ease, and set it to steep. Tearing a leftover white manchet roll into a basin, he soused it with mead, poured milk overall and put it to warm by the fire; then strained dark, bitter tea into a cup, added a generous dollop of honey and stirred it well.

At first taste Nikos grimaced, but as it flowed hot and soothing over his seared inner membranes, he began to sup greedily.

"Quite palatable - I think this is doing me good."

"This will, too - sit back and shut your eyes." Gently, Rupert swabbed the swollen eyelids with a damp napkin.

Nikos breathed a long sigh. "Aye, you're right, it does that." Taking the cloth, he dunked it in his water and laid it on his forehead. "Ah... I revive!"

"Good – maybe now you can manage this milk-sop." Rupert fetched the warmed basin from the hearth. "It's quite apt to one in your state, being commonly served to babes, invalids and toothless dotards."

"Huh - you shouldn't mock your patients, Healer." Nikos took a hesitant spoonful of the soft sweet pap, then another; before long the basin was empty and colour was returning to his cheeks.

"Why, I'm restored… almost. Aye, you've the makings of a fine Healer, if you could but rid yourself of certain sadistic tendencies! Might I trouble you for more water, and another cup of that refreshing tea? I think I've rallied enough for a pipe."

When Nikos could focus again, he looked at Rupert searchingly. "And how do you fare this morning, my friend?"

"Exceeding well, thanks, if a little tired. But that's to be expected, as we went to bed so late."

"Would I could say the same! You must have the constitution of an aurochs, Master Rupert. But that wasn't altogether what I meant, as I suspect you very well know. Come, reassure me: you're not dismayed or disturbed by yester-night's events?"

Rupert glanced down. "But I am - and no wonder! I sat by and watched a visiting peace envoy subjected to physical assault and gross indignities… then compounded my offence by taking part.

'Being guilty of such outrage, only one path remains for me, in honour. I shall make full confession to King Thorund, and then willingly submit to Hel's knife. Ah me – I'll end my days a eunuch… at least I had the one chance to exercise my member afore it's fed to the crows." His bent shoulders began shaking, and tears to splash upon the table-top.

With stricken expression Nikos knelt at his side. "O no, I should've thought, I should've stopped- O gods, what have I done?"

"O, oho, disturbed me, that's what ye've done!" Rupert wept, helpless. "I'm so-ho much disturbed… by how easily I broke our laws… and how-how much enjoyed and how little care that I've done so. O, I'm a miscreant wretch, to be sure!"

"You *bloody* blackguard, Endriksson!" Nikos exploded as Rupert fell back, weak with hysterics. "I wonder you don't work for Lord Hel! Huh, I must truly be addled this morn… God knows, I've had lesson enough in your poker-face not to be so taken in."

Rupert wiped his eyes. "I'm sorry, I couldn't resist! True, I'm disturbed - but in agreeable ways, and not dismayed in the slightest. Except for fear I've affronted you… when you were hardly in a position to refuse."

"Why should I refuse to be your First in that way? Ah, not being raised to the Tantra, you don't understand… even as I don't understand the Way here… why does Fusion give rise to such punishment and woe?"

"You should ask My Lord Archbishop! Meanwhile," Rupert drew Nikos to his feet, "It joys me to know you're not… offended. For

226

whilst I shouldn't care to repeat the experiment with any or all men, 'tis somehow different with you... I think I can honestly say that I love you, Sir – that's to say," he hastily backtracked, lest this seemed over-effusive, "I respect and esteem you a great deal more than is common for me. Moreover," he added with a cheeky grin, "As a noble guest of my King, I'm bound to obey for your pleasure... and if Freyling hadn't stepped in I should have gone on to do so last night, to the fullest of my ability."

They kissed, Rupert's heart full on his lips, standing locked a long minute.

"Provocative youth – I'll have thee Angorian yet!" whispered Nikos throatily, "Alas, we'll have to wait awhile..." Rupert gasped as the ram-rod fresh risen in his hose was squeezed mischievously. "For those witches have me worn me quite down to a nub, so I cannot oblige thee this morning."

"Pity - then perforce I must go and rouse Else!" With a valedictory swat to Nikos' backside, Rupert darted giggling upstairs.

Else was not the only one to be rudely awoken by the newly fledged cockerel. Below, scratching a hasty, 'Back anon – N' into Rupert's wax tablet, Nikos grinned; a rising hubbub of curses and imprecations was being flung at the noisy lovers while footsteps, no longer tentative, rapped through the boards as the resentful quintet went about their ablutions.

Propping the tablet where it would be seen, Nikos slipped quietly out to visit the ships. When he returned a half-glass later, head wondrously cleared by the sea air, all save Rupert and Else were up and about, variously sipping Bane-ease, nibbling breakfast and ruefully comparing notes on their self-inflicted maladies. A short time later the couple themselves emerged, somewhat pink and sheepish, into a round of ironic applause; and by first glass after noon, the men had bidden their last fond adieus.

As they set off to attend to their business they left The Mermaid swarming: one squad of *Breaths* already dismantling the gimcrack partitions upstairs and sorting the timber for re-use or firewood, and a quintet of *Quintessences* addressing themselves to the foetid privy pit. Freya was buzzing like a queen bee with refurbishment plans; the rest, led by Freja, were tearing down the parlour screen, piling up the cheap, stained bedding for disposal and breaking the hated cots down to be burnt.

Stealing a sidelong glance at Endriksson, Nikos smiled. The

lad – nay, the young man – looked three inches taller, his slim shoulders squared, his head held erect, a confident swing in his walk… overnight he seemed to have shed an awkward load of knuckles and knobs; even his pimples were lost against the healthy, if slightly hectic, flush of his cheek.

"A good night's work - and but one task outstanding, afore we ride back and report," he remarked. "Tell me, does your tight-buttoned Way of the Wolf permit male friends to walk arm-in-arm?"

"Aye, Sir – it's a mark of high favour, especially at Court. A hand on the shoulder, or arms linked thus," Rupert demonstrated, "is naught to complain of, whereas hand-in-hand is only for children and lovers, and would be much remarked upon."

Nikos patted the hand lying in the crook of his elbow. "Good – for you ride high in my favour, right trusty and well-beloved friend."

Rupert flushed. "Thank'ee, Sir – and 'twill do His Majesty's new Commissioner 'gainst Iniquitous Affronts no harm to be seen in such close company with the Kalaios of Angor."

They walked companionably on and in due course encountered Ferdi Mickelsprech in the thronging marketplace.

"Hail, Master Ferdi," cried Nikos, "We've news to impart!"

They crowded into the crier's little shack. Mickelsprech's ears, eyes and mouth opened wider and wider as Nikos recounted the tidings; by the end, he was beaming.

"So the greasy old bastard has got his come-uppance - well done, Sirs! The mighty Ecbert Ecbertsson, 'assisting with Treasury enquiries'! Serves the bugger right… I can't say I'm sorry for him."

"Me neither," said Rupert grimly. "So Master Crier, pray put out the official line: Ecbert is taken for tithe-evasion and his businesses impounded, and The Mermaid is closed for renovations, under my supervision… another issue of public interest, as we'll be in the market for all manner of craftsmen and supplies.

'As to the full detail of my Commission, I must swear you to secrecy lest similar miscreants should flee forewarned. But pray make wide enquiry for old girls from the inn – we need to trace and rescue any survivors, and hear any testimony relevant to our case."

Mickelsprech bowed. "Master Endriksson, upon this subject my lips are sealed, until you bid me open 'em - on my honour as King's Crier. In any event, I would ne'er imperil your work; 'tis a right worthy cause." His voice dropped, confidentially. "For I've known long enough how the greedy old burgher ran *that* establishment – though he

228

was so well-connected, it wasn't expedient for me to cry aloud what many have murmured for long years past.

"'Twas a sinful disgrace how he treated those girls. They told me all about it... I was a regular there, you see, Sirs, after my good lady wife..." He broke off with a sigh. "Hey ho - 'twas the hours Missus Mickelsprech could not stand, and my zeal for the news... so she left me for Stiv Schiffwright, who works normal days and comes home of an evening – and truly I can't blame her, I wasn't much of a husband to the poor woman! She saw more of me here, in my hut, than she did in our marital bed...

'Anyway, they were kind to me, the girls... even let me nap on the cots after closing, betwixt my midnight and early morn rounds... Ah me, I'll miss that, from now on."

"No you won't," laughed Nikos, "Never fear, Master Ferdi – whilst *any* traveller will henceforth find refreshment and a respectable couch at The Mermaid, the true friends of our esteemed *Tantr'aia* will ever find a warm welcome. Their friends are ours, and thereby of the King – which you may mention, discreetly, to those such as Roti and Thom with whom they share genuine fondness."

"Aye, His Majesty seeks not to interfere in his subjects' private affairs," added Rupert. "His royal pleasure is that all true lovers of the Mermaids should continue meeting in amity – and if conversations should touch on other poor girls in like plight, why then, he'd be most interested to hear of it." He looked meaningfully at Mickelsprech. "And, I dare say, the Treasury would duly reward any... snippets leading to the recovery of more ill-gotten gains belonging to the State."

Ferdi chuckled. "Trust me, Masters – I'll have quiet words in some ears, and loud ones in others... and as ye feed tidings to me, then I shall feed tidings to thee! O, Wolf bless you for this charge, 'tis the best news I've had to cry – or whisper - in years!"

They left him pealing his bell, declaiming, "Hear ye, hear ye, Thorshaven all! Burgher Ecbertsson arrested for withholding his tithe! Mermaid Inn closed for repairs! Hear all about it..."

Chapter 21: Luna

Berthe set down Elinor's breakfast tray. "How fare you today, Highness?"

"Much better - my Curse is departed! In fact I'm so far recovered I'll stew here no longer. Set out my riding garb, Bea – and send to the stables, I want Schneeball ready for tenth. Poor pony, I've neglected him sorely of late.

'O, but what's this you've brought?"

"It's a message from Lord Jehan, Madam."

The Princess rolled her eyes. Great Wolf, she thought, can I not take my fast-break in peace?

Esteemed Princess, she read, *Trusting to find thee restored to good health, I beg the honour of thy company for some equestrian pursuits. Hoping to see thee in the Horse Hall at tenth glass, JS-L*

Elinor's cheeks flamed. "O, this is *too* provoking - I've half a mind not to go… yet why should that bothersome man spoil my day? He shan't – but what can I do? O, I know… first I'll *dress* for company - so make it my best habit, Bea, the new one, and bid the grooms saddle Schneeball straightway. Go on, girl, hurry!

'Hah!" she said as Berthe scurried off, "So I'll have my private hour at least before Sol-Lios arrives... then I'll show him how a Gondaran Princess can ride." She dimpled mischievously. "Hmm… chance to start laying my plans… and for *me* to display some accomplishment, for a change… and to wear my new habit, which is so *very* becoming.

'And didn't he promise me another present, when- when I was well? Mayhap I'll get it today." She checked, hand to mouth; and had the grace to blush, recalling the memento she had bestowed on Jehan at their most recent parting. "Ah, no… I'll get no more gifts, not since I laid his cheek open. O, would he hadn't so provoked me - I never would have hurled that glass else!"

A half hour later, Elinor was dashingly arrayed in midnight blue twill: a jacket that fitted closely to the waistline and flared generously at the hip, accentuated by a spotless white stock at her throat, and a racy ankle-length skirt disclosing shiny black boots armed with silver rowel spurs. A lustrous net of black silk dusted with seed-pearls confined her ringlets, all capped by a fetching little domed riding helm faced in black velvet; a pair of yellow kid gloves and a silver-headed whip completed the ensemble.

Smugly, she beheld her reflection. The colour flattered her complexion as the cut did her figure, its plain severe lines adding height and making her look dignified and mature. Excitement sparkled in her eyes – suddenly she itched to see Jehan, and how could she fail to impress him, looking so-

"Wonderful!" cried Fran. "O, Highness – it suits you marvellously well, your new costume."

"Aye, it *is* very smart." She paced up and down before the mirror in a jingle of spurs, whip tapping impatiently at her boot heel. "Alas, I can't tarry in self-adoration, but must hie me straightway to *Pferdhalle*!"

The *Pferdhalle* was a large rectangular barn with lime-washed plaster walls, a packed earthen floor, and a viewing aisle round its perimeter, delineated by a barrier of poles. Elinor swished in at five minutes to ninth, pleased to find it deserted save for Schneeball, his groom, and the usual attendants. Hugging the pony's neck, she buried her face among the ribbons bedecking his mane.

"Dearest Snow, how I've missed thee," she crooned, stroking his velvety muzzle, "Let's go for a nice ride together!"

Clambering into the saddle she commenced warming up, at first stiffly self-conscious, braced at every moment for Jehan to put in an unscheduled appearance. But she soon relaxed, exercise and concentration driving all else from her mind, and by the time he arrived, prompt on the turn of tenth glass, she was too absorbed even to notice.

Sol-Lios paused in the doorway, enjoying the sight of Elinor circling in a dainty collected canter, planting arrows into a target from a light hunting bow. He watched till she had shot her quiver empty, then while she waited for an attendant to collect her missiles, made discreet advance behind the rail.

By happy chance, he came upon her mightily self-satisfied and consequently, in such high good humour that even her suitor's appearance could not dim the mood. Tossing aside her bow she wheeled Schneeball round, trotted down the hall and met Sol-Lios half-way.

"Good morrow, Sir," she hailed gaily, "Did you see that? An adequate grouping, methinks - two inners, two outers and a bull!"

Her face glowed with exertion and the most agreeable expression he had yet seen her wear; she looked ravishing. Jehan smiled in genuine approbation.

"Indeed, My Lady – good morning, and good shooting!" He

vaulted over the rail, caught her whip hand and kissed her gloved fingers. "And may I say what a joy it is to see you again... the days have seemed long in your absence. But don't let me interrupt - pray, Madam, finish your ride."

Nothing loath, she showed Snowball's paces at the walk, trot and canter, hopped over a trio of low jumps and for a finale, wove deftly through a line of standing poles. Then she rode back to the steps, unhooked herself from the side-saddle and somewhat breathless and heated, called for a cup of small ale.

Jehan was pleased to find her so able a rider – an asset for any putative Electa - and greatly struck by her garb. More formal and voluminous than any Angorian would choose, it was undeniably picturesque and strangely erotic, accentuating her excellent upper figure while decorously concealing her lower; and its hue contrasted richly with the crimson trappings and pale flank of her mount, which he regarded with similar interest.

"Bravo, Madam – well ridden! I marvel at your skill on that contrivance. Indeed, I marvel you manage to stay on at all."

She looked puzzled. "What – mean you my saddle? Why, it's among the finest in Gondarlan! 'Tis perfectly secure."

"Evidently - well, I salute you, Lady. I doubt I could even sit on it, let alone leap a hurdle."

"No matter, Sir - as my instructor would say, just as ladies are not meant to ride astride, men are not meant to ride a-side."

"I'm relieved to hear it." Turning his attention to Schneeball, Jehan stroked the pony's neck. "He's handsome – a native breed, I take it?"

"Aye, a Great Thorsheim, bred at the King's Stud in Arkengarthdale. Mine is Snowball, by Snowfire the Third out of Seafoam. He's among the tallest of his kind, though Wolf, my Father's blue roan, stands two fingers higher."

She chatted on, knowledgeably extolling the points of the breed. Away from the stultifying atmosphere of the royal apartments she seemed freer of spirit than he had hitherto seen, confident mistress of her equestrian milieu. Jehan's heart rose – maybe she *would* be apt to another, greater part. Maybe Hag-Moon aside, *this* was her true nature – a decidedly more amiable being than the murderous harpy of their previous encounter.

As if answering his thought, Elinor broke off with a half-abashed laugh. "I'm sorry, Sir - you didn't come to listen to me prate!" She hesitated, dropping her lashes. "But one thing more I must say...

I'm sorry too I hurt your face. I shouldn't have flung that dish – 'twas unforgivable."

"Not so – it's entirely forgivable, if not yet forgot!" he chuckled, touching the thin scab on his cheekbone. "But if you mention it no more, it'll be forgotten quite."

Elinor smiled and gratefully changed the subject. "Then pray, Lord Jehan, where's your mount - for did you not invite me to *join* you in equestrian pursuits?"

"That I did - and have kept her waiting long enough." He put two fingers to his lips and whistled shrill.

There came a shrill whinnying reply and in trotted the mare who had accompanied Jehan from the *Breath*, trailed by Florian with an armload of tack. She came directly to where they were standing, whickered a brief greeting then addressed her nose to the Elect's pocket.

"How well she knows me!" he laughed. Drawing forth a handful of horse-treats, he let Luna snuffle them up from his palm.

When the mare had finished munching, he spoke a word in her ear. She set forth walking in a circle until Jehan clucked his cheek, whereupon she broke into a trot; next time he clucked, she extended into a canter. After a couple of circuits he cried, "Ho there," and whistled again. Luna promptly turned on her haunches, trotted briskly back to his side and nuzzled at his pocket for reward.

"Well, Madam, you're plainly a judge of fine horses, so tell me: what think you on her?"

"O," breathed Elinor, round-eyed, "She's magnificent, utterly magnificent! And astonishing well trained - pray, My Lord, what's her name?"

"Luna – after her race *Lun'argenta*, for she bears the true Moon-silver colour: mane, tail and legs black as night, a silver-white body, and grey-dappled rump like the Moon's face."

"It's a good name." She called softly, "Luna!" with so much love in her voice the mare turned immediately and nosed at her arm. The Princess ran a hand over the satiny coat. "What a beauty.... and how tall she is! Is she yours, Sir?"

"No, she belongs only unto herself - and I asked you here today but to speak on her behalf. She will render the other gift I lately promised - just as she bore your presents up from the ship, she claims the honour to bear you in our land."

Elinor paled, too overwhelmed to register his curious mode of expression. "You mean she's for me?" she gasped. "A thousand thanks,

233

My Lord! To be sure, I'll need a mount in Angor... and I can't bring Schneeball, I suppose?"

Sol-Lios shook his head. "Alas, we've no room to berth him – even if he'd thrive in our clime which I doubt, being bred to the cold."

"Ah me," Elinor sighed. A shadow crossed her face. "Something else cherished I must shortly bid farewell."

Jehan touched her arm sympathetically. "Take heart, Madam – you'll surely see him again one day. Meantime Luna can console you - would you like to try her now?"

"I'd love to!" exclaimed Elinor; then looking up at Luna's seventeen hands, her stomach twinged nervously. "O, but she's very big... d'ye think my side-saddle will fit?"

"Nay, Lady, nor is she schooled to one," Florian said. "This is hers – she's used to a leg on each side."

Elinor's face fell. "But I can't sit on that! O, Sir," she appealed to Jehan, "Please can we try my own saddle on her?"

The High and Elect exchanged glances. "Very well, Madam – but I can't promise aught," said Florian dubiously.

She bade her groom remove Snowball's saddle then return with the pony to the stables. Florian hefted it on and Luna's head swivelled to inspect it perched ludicrously high on her back, its too-short girth dangling uselessly. She rolled her eyes, shook her mane, and blew out a snort of disgust.

"I doubt you need me to translate, Madam," Jehan chuckled as Florian replaced the offending item with Luna's own. "'Tis far too small, and she won't wear it! So, as we lack time to make one that fits or to teach her side-riding commands, you must instead learn her language - for which you must ride her astride."

Elinor hissed, "I cannot... it's highly improper! Only the lowest class of woman would sit a horse like that."

"I beg to contradict you – the Empress of Faal herself straddles, as do all the ladies of her land. Besides, are you not the arbiter of fashion? Set a new trend, riding *à la mode Faalienne*! I lay the rest will follow, soon enough."

She shifted uncomfortably, torn between longing to ride and revulsion at the manner in which it seemed she must do so.

"Also, permit me to relieve you of whip and spurs," the Elect went on, "Luna won't understand, and they'll only hurt her feelings. Pray, be seated."

Relinquishing her whip, Elinor sat reluctantly on the mounting steps while Sol-Lios knelt to unfasten her spurs. Deprived of these familiar aids, however was she to urge and guide her horse? An irritable spasm twitched in her foot; narrowly, she suppressed the impulse to kick out and send Jehan sprawling on his backside.

"Now, a few words of advice afore you start, Madam. Luna's Angorian, so use our tongue when you bid her walk, trot or canter - or just cluck your cheek, as you lately heard me do. 'Ho' or 'Ho there' will stop her; 'Hup' gets her over a jump; shout 'Hai!' and from any gait, she'll leap to a gallop.

'So much for paces; as for direction, I expect our rein guidance is much the same as yours. As to the rest: 'tis body and legs that do most of the talking, if I may demonstrate."

He swung into the saddle. "Look, I'll tie the reins thus," he knotted them round the pommel then clasped his hands behind his head, "and you'll see how much guidance comes from below."

In response to some imperceptible signal, Luna walked a figure-of-eight round the hall. Next she trotted and cantered in circles, executed a dainty diagonal side-step, and finished by weaving through the standing poles as Schneeball had done.

Elinor watched with grudging admiration and sinking heart. Jehan was an excellent horseman, so subtle his commands that she could not tell how he was communicating them. She swallowed a hard lump of tears. Great Wolf, she thought, this Angorian style is beyond me. I'll never ride my beautiful horse!

She greeted his return with a rueful head-shake. "I hope you don't expect me to emulate that, Sir! For I confess, e'en after you've shown me, I'm none the wiser."

"Fear not – now we've sketched in the background, we'll fill in the detail. Whereas you guided your pony by taps of the whip, we guide the *Eques* by transfer of weight in the stirrups, and pressure of knee, calf and heel at various points.

'Behold: we'll do it again that you might better apprehend. To move off, I apply both heels *here*," he leant forward, squeezing gently behind the girth. "Then to bring her round, I... *imagine* the act and my body follows my intention, swinging with the knees, pushing *here* with the calf. To go in the opposite direction, I do but repeat myself in mirror image, thus..." He carried on commentating while Luna responded in kind to his slow, exaggerated movements, pirouetting and dipping elaborately on her haunches.

"She's dancing," cried the Princess, "Aye, and I see how you're making her do it! I wonder if she'd ever dance so for me?"

"There's but one way to find out." Jehan rode back to the steps and dismounted. "Come Madam, do try."

Elinor hesitated. To… to *straddle*; she winced at the mere ugly word let alone the act. But she ardently wished to ride Luna… and 'twould not be diplomatic to refuse, her inner voice conveniently reminded; her duty was to placate the King and his guests, not risk causing them further offence. Besides, and she brightened somewhat at the thought, if that was *really* the way Faalian empresses rode, one day it might stand her in good stead…

She stepped forward in sudden resolution. "Very well - but I warn you, Sol-Lios: try to look up my skirts and I'll send you forthwith to Hel!"

"Heaven forefend, Madam," he grinned, and with punctiliously averted face, helped her into the saddle. Hastily, Elinor arranged her skirts, discovering with great relief that they were sufficiently ample to conceal her legs and ungainly attitude. Altogether it was not as bad as she had feared. The Angorian saddle was plainly designed for long-distance comfort, supporting her fore and aft with its high sweeping pommel and cantle; still her position felt highly unnatural, not to mention precarious.

Jehan adjusted the stirrups and guided her feet to them. "There – keep your heels down… and imagine a plumb line from the crown of your head down through here," he drew a fingertip line down the side of her body, "which gives the basic posture. Grip with knee and thigh to hold on, and merely lay your fingers on the rein. Then relax - Luna and I will do the rest."

It was quite different to riding Snowball, Elinor found; this big horse made her feel like a child, an outright beginner with untried leg muscles clumsy and weak. And like a beginner, absolved of the need to control her mount she focussed on her position, head and back erect, heels correctly aligned and elbows tucked in.

"Perfect," Sol-Lios cried, after they had twice made the circuit. "Now give your own leg-commands. Bid her move off, as you saw me do – that's right – then to halt her, lean back a trifle and bear down your weight in both heels. Excellent - you did it, with nary a need for rein, whip or whoa! Pray try it again…"

Flushed with success she complied. Before long they were too engrossed to heed Florian's departure, or the noon glass being turned - or the arrival of newcomers, shortly thereafter. For King Thorund had come seeking his daughter, accompanied by the Kalaios and Loric. Forewarned of the gift, he was unsurprised to find her trotting rings round the Elect, rotating her arms like a windmill in an exercise for improving the balance. Nonetheless it was a rare spectacle, a Gondaran Princess bestriding; even rarer that the capricious minx was apparently enjoying her suitor's society as much as her lesson.

Elinor, gaze fixed firmly between her mount's ears, remained oblivious to the trio's approach until Jehan called Luna to stop. The Princess glanced questioningly round and let out a glad exclamation. Wheeling the mare competently, she trotted over to meet them, drew rein by the barrier and offered a cordial greeting, pink with exertion and pride.

"Good morrow, Princess!" Thorund hailed in return, "I'm rejoiced to find you restored to such, ah, rude health! And now I understand what has kept you from luncheon... learning to ride like a Prince, forsooth," his eyes twinkled, "*and* on a right princely steed! My thanks for seeing Her Highness so well mounted, Sol-Lios," he added, as Jehan caught them up.

The Elect laughed. "Rather thank Luna! Apropos of whom: come, Lady, dismount. It's later than I thought, and we all stand in need of refreshment."

Elinor sucked back an involuntary pout; she did not dare wheedle for longer in front of her father. Besides, rebuked conscience, he was right; poor Luna had been working hard these past two hours, without so much as a mouthful of water. Conceding the point, she relinquished the reins and let Jehan lead her back to the steps.

On solid ground, she turned to make obeisance to the King but faltered in her curtsey, clutching the rail with an odd expression. Loric and Jehan started forward, but she waved them away with her free hand.

"Fear not, I'm quite well, 'tis just-" that my thighs quiver like aspic, she thought, suppressing a giggle, and feel as if they still grip a phantom horse – though 'twould be indelicate to admit as much! "'Tis just that I'm unaccustomed to riding *à la mode Faalienne*," she apologised with perfect if incomplete truth.

"Then pray be seated, Daughter," said King Thorund, "If you be not too saddle-sore! And I trust you'll *become* accustomed, so you may fully appreciate this great gift. To which end: by your leave, Sir, Her Highness will ride with you daily until you depart."

"A splendid idea, O Thorund - the more you come to know one another, Madam, the better you'll find you can ride her."

Elinor nodded. This was one command she could happily obey – indeed, she would have begged on her knees for the privilege!

"I recommend your ladies join in," Jehan added, "since they'll be travelling with us. We can lend mounts for them to learn on."

King Thorund clapped him on the back. "Most generous, Sir - then, 'tis fixed – *Pferdhalle* is yours for the mornings, Princess, except when duty requires you elsewhere – as it will do at tenth glass tomorrow.

'Aye, My Lord, I wish to convene a certain meeting we discussed – and 'tis timely that you're back in health, Daughter. By the Elect's specific request you're to attend, since the matters in question concern you so closely."

Elinor nodded, wide-eyed. Required to take part in a State conference - only wait till she told Berthe and Fran! What a pity it was Jehan she had to thank for the honour...

"Tenth glass suits us well," said Jehan. "The sooner matters are resolved, the better I'll like it."

"Good, I'll inform Their Lordships accordingly. Though that can wait till we've seen somewhat more of this Luna - pray, Madam, introduce us."

While they were thus occupied, Nikos nudged Jehan. "She *can* laugh, then - ho, is the Ice-maiden thawing? I lay she'll prove a feisty filly, should you ever come to mount her... did you see that pretty little pout when you bade her get down? Would her disposition were ever as sweet as her looks, eh, Brother?"

"Well, she has one redeeming feature," said Jehan wryly, "E'en if she doesn't love me, she loves our horses... so much that she broke some dire taboo in straddling Luna today. 'Twas bravely done, and I salute her for it; it augurs well, perhaps..."

Chapter 22: Counsel

Next morning the King strolled into his anteroom as the last grains of eighth glass ran out. His Lords were already waiting, Hakon hunched morosely in a chair, his sore throat enwrapped in a red flannel scarf and a powerful odour of goose-grease.

The Archbishop meanwhile paced back and forth, and the moment Thorund entered he cried, "Praise Fafnir - Majesty, Radnor Wolfblest is gone! When I sought him to- to, ah, interrogate him, he was not in the Pit... and neither Hel nor the Brethren could account for his whereabouts! And what about poor Master Ecbert-"

"Aye," rasped the Warlord, "Elf tells me his lads' favourite tavern is shut - I seem to be missing a lot, while I lie sick-abed."

The King raised an eyebrow. "Good morrow to thee too, My Lords. By the Wolf, this must be crisis indeed, to have so banished civil tongues from thy heads!"

Somewhat abashed, they returned his greeting.

"Never fear, we shall address your concerns, albeit concisely. We've a meeting with the Angorian Counsel at tenth, which is why I summoned you - of course, you must attend."

Two mouths simultaneously opened, one to gape and one to expostulate. King Thorund held up his hand.

"Peace, My Lords – permit me to answer your most besetting questions afore haranguing me with more!

'Merchant Radnor I dealt with myself. I questioned him, he satisfied me, and I dispatched him. I wished him gone without attracting undue attention, after his hand in that dangerous farce with Her Highness's waistcoat. So I took him out the Dark Way- O, and he did leave something for you, Sigismund." The King drew from his sleeve Wolfblest's unwitting suicide note. "My apologies for failing to give it you sooner – I've been so occupied with our guests that it slipped my mind quite."

The Archbishop broke open the seal, scanned the few cryptic lines with growing frown and scrutinised the signature.

"How extraordinary - not to mention *highly* inconvenient! I needed- that is, I should have liked to speak with Radnor myself... Alas, according to this he'll be long gone by now."

Thorund waved dismissively. "I dare say you'll hear from him anon - perhaps you should inquire at his house for further news.

'As for the rest: Captain Haral I released back to his duties, he being guilty of naught but humouring our visitors' whims."

Hakon shrugged, too distracted by sundry discomforts to recall his own rage or the misdemeanour for which he'd had the Captain imprisoned.

"Lastly, Ecbert Ecbertsson was arrested for gross tithe evasion, and is even now undergoing inquisition. His assets are correspondingly impounded, and we've claimed that inn called The Mermaid in immediate reparation for his debts. Henceforth, the said Mermaid shall be as he falsely claimed it: a wholesome establishment to keep unfortunates from the streets, run by free-women under Lord Nikos' superintendence – we've gifted it to him, as he's taken such fancy to the place."

Sigismund gasped. "M-Majesty, you cannot cede a prime city centre plot, a thriving business, to an Outlander!"

"Faugh – we've ceded naught but a broken-down whorehouse on an ill-kempt street, to be kept respectable," the King retorted, "With gratefully beholden housekeepers who will pay our proper tithe. Unlike that accursed Master Ecbert… in view of whose crimes, naturally, his daughter's wedding to Cedric Pavelson will not proceed - so squander no time on a sermon, Archbishop!

'Surely you cannot protest, Holy Father? Restoring *Alt-Seehalle* is a seemly undertaking - an act of civic pride entirely consonant with the teachings of the Church, and apt redress for Ecbertsson's manifold sins. Either way, give no 'cannot' to thy King! You'd do well to remember that Thorshaven is *our* royal city; we need no man's consent to dispose our estates therein as we will.

'We'll return presently to the merits of our decision – but for the nonce, let's move on." Thorund spread his hands upon the table. "Our position is this, My Lords: Princess Elinor will soon depart for Angor, and we must make arrangements for her passage." He quelled Hakon's incipient complaint with a penetrating glare. "There's no going back on this! State considerations aside, the Princess is won – and *seen* to be won – on her own terms and by immemorial custom.

'And she must go in safety - therefore *all* naval operations against Outland shipping will cease forthwith. Any vessel of Angor or its allies may henceforth be carrying word from Her Highness, if not the Princess herself – we know not how or whence she might travel, or what messages she might need to send, once she's gone.

'Certes, you'd not wish harm to befall her, nor have our means of communication imperilled. For these paramount reasons, My Lords, the sea lanes must be as safe as we can make them - thus Gondarlan will no more commit, abet or otherwise profit from piracy, either at sea or on land.

'Remember: we – and now the Angorians - have seen undeniable proof of connection between Gondarlan and these Centrali raids, thanks to Wolfblest's thrice-damned red feathers. And should Angor choose to make war against us on that account, we cannot prevail! Mark well, we have *no choice* but to bide time in peace, gather intelligence and offer no further provocations. We therefore decree, with immediate effect, that it is forbidden to acquire, import, transport, trade or otherwise own by whatsoever means, all manner of foreign commodities without they have the proper licence and documents of lading.

'So, Admiral Hakon, recall the fleet. Let them make scrying missions only, and provide escorts for any Angorian or Imperial vessel in our waters. Have others put to patrolling the harbours for illicit cargoes, and assisting the Brethren in a most stringent control of the Custom-houses."

Bowing to present necessity, the Warlord glumly nodded.

"Then it's settled. And should any Angorians chance into port they may berth at an embassy of sorts, their own mission in *Seehalle*... see, My Lords, there's method to my generosity. If Thorshaven is perforce opened to Outlanders, let them be kept where we can see them - under the eyes of our 'Mermaids'!

'We'll brook no disputation at the meeting, but listen to our guests, and co-operate with any reasonable terms they propose, in return for their scrupulous care of our Daughter. For believe me, Sirs – I have all our best interests at heart, in the long run. There, now," the King rose, rubbing his hands, "that resolves our private business, I believe! On to international affairs - and since the hour is advancing, let us straightway to the Presence. I wish to take refreshment ere Counsel convenes."

Flinging open the door, Thorund gestured them out. Punch-drunk they complied, the Archbishop's knees a-tremble like the whole corrupt edifice of his hidden empire. Unwitting or deliberate, the King had struck at its very foundations, imprisoning his disciples or driving them to flight, and he was powerless in their defence. After all, he could hardly preach against upholding the tenets of his own creed, or the laws of the land. O, for private speech with Hakon... and O, how he wished he had donned his wolf-mask, how naked would his face be without it! But the King swept irresistibly on, denying all opportunity to attend his concerns.

More shocks lay in store at the Presence Chamber. Many of

the delegates, including an addition to the Angorian contingent, were already seated therein round a large circular table. The Lords were surprised to see Hel amid their number; all the more so when Thorund sat down beside him, and nonchalantly called out for ale. Next moment they found themselves separately ushered to chairs and furnished with drinks, while the remaining seats filled until only two were left: one, flanked to the rear by a pair of low stools, on Thorund's right hand, and the corresponding opposite place.

At nigh on tenth glass, their designated occupants entered together. Princess Elinor had dressed carefully in garments bespeaking her status and right to attend: a sleeveless purple velvet surcote lined and edged with ermine, open to reveal a cloth-of-silver kirtle belted with antique pearls and rainbow moonstones, heirloom of her mother's house; and on her head, a matching tiara over a kerchief of translucent white tissue.

Sol-Lios handed her into the chair beside Thorund, politely saw Berthe and Fran to their stools and assumed his own seat. Elinor cast down her eyes to hide their glint of triumph. At long last, a place on the Council - now their Lordships would know how impotence felt! Their astonished displeasure was palpable, but they could hardly object, or even remark upon her presence, without exposing themselves in an embarrassing light to the company.

When all were seated and refreshed sundry Gentleman withdrew, leaving Loric to preside alone over the sideboard. King Thorund rapped on the table.

"Tenth glass - is everyone ready? Good - but before we proceed, some introductions are required for the benefit of a guest lately joined us from Thorshaven."

This newcomer was a handsome salt-tanned mariner somewhere around Thorund's age, with creased dark eyes and a long black ponytail greying at the temples.

"Good morrow, O King and Counsel of Gondarlan. Aurelia Maren'aia, Captain of *Quintessence*, at thy service," she announced in flawless Gondaran.

"Greetings and welcome, Captain Aurelia," replied the King, urbanely. "Permit us to introduce our household: here is our well-beloved Daughter and Princess, Elinor - attended by Mistresses Olsen and Fischer, her travel-companions." Berthe and Fran sat stiffly to attention, nervously proud in their matching grey gowns. "Along of Her Highness is Olaf Steward, our Master of Supplies; then His Grace the Archbishop, Sigismund Wolfsbane; and Master Endriksson of the

Treasury, who scribes for us today.

'To our left is Lord Hel, our chief inquisitor; beside him Warlord Hakon, General of our armies and Admiral of our fleet; and lastly," he gestured to the side-board, "Our Head Gentleman, Loric, to attend on our comfort."

"Thank'ee, Sir," replied Jehan. "For the record, Master Rupert, I shall return our names and titles. I'm Jehan Sol-Lios, Elect of Angor. To my left, the Seer Iris," she had positioned herself thus, opposite the Torturer, the better to admire him, "our advisor, with our messenger Constable Kaa; then Oratoria Nerya and the Next, Perikleia, of the Kalaia; finally Captains Iamis and Aurelia.

'On t'other side is Oratore Nikos for the Warriors; High Priest Thesis, for spiritual affairs; and Iactus the Highest for, ah, more material concerns, with Zafia, our minister for health.

'And afore we continue in any misapprehension, may I clarify the point upon which all else hinges: are we formally agreed that Princess Elinor will return with us to Angor?"

Thorund met his gaze. "For our part, it is so agreed."

Sol-Lios looked his question to the Princess. She drew breath. It was a crucial moment: her first voice on Council, her first step from the 'Birg, her first step towards freedom…

She nodded. "I'll come with thee right gladly."

"*Aléia!*" cried Jehan, "We rejoice upon this confirmation! And that we shall so soon gain the pleasure of your company, Madam – for we must make sail when the next moon is full."

"What – less than three weeks!" exclaimed the Archbishop. "Why, it gives barely time for Her Highness's rites of betrothal, let alone to arrange a royal wedding!"

Hakon glowered, hating Sigismund for voicing the obnoxious idea, but his countenance was lifted by the High Priest's reply.

"Indeed, Sir. Which is partly why - meaning no disrespect to your virtues, Princess – we should defer such formalities. For 'Electa' is no empty title, and the art commensurate with it is something peculiar. There's much you should learn of the Angorian Way, Madam, to determine whether you've the taste for it."

"Also," interposed Zafia, "Angor's climate is very different to this – if it proved injurious to your health we would of course return you forthwith."

Hakon snorted. "Then why not wed one of thine own and have done wi' it, instead of inflicting this dubious proposal upon *our* Princess?"

Before a wincing Thorund could reprove, Sol-Lios mildly replied, "A fair enough question – certes, we have plenty worthy-"

"But we wouldn't have you!" grinned Zafi. "Myself, I wouldn't stand as Electa unless the whole weal of Angor hung upon it. I couldn't retain my Vocation as Healer... only be an Electa with some healing skill, which is not the same thing by a long way."

"True – Elects have no calling save Electhood," Jehan agreed. "Kindly, you could term it a broad discipline, wherein we must know a little about a lot, more about some, and a lot about little! Unkindly you could say it makes us jacks-of-all-trades, and masters of none. But like any profession, it's best performed by those who love it, not those who find its idiosyncrasies irksome-"

"Pooh, administration," groaned Nikos. "*Maia Kali*, the endless debates... weighing advantage, benefit against cost – nay," he shook his head, "I care not for process. Just give me result and tell me where to wield my sword!"

"-nor by those who love power for its own sake," went on Jehan. "To me, it's an endless fascination - and one I'd readily share with you, Princess. For you're born of a governing house, as am I; you speak three tongues I know of; you're scholarly and able in the saddle – relevant attributes all. And as you become acquainted with Angor you'll doubtless question and challenge our ways – in short, we'd value your perspective.

'Does this answer you, Sir? Princess Elinor has qualities shared by none of my countrywomen, no matter how richly they may otherwise be gifted; she is Gondaran! So, Madam, if you incline to such path, you'd make an Electa unique in our history."

Iris laughed. "Forget not the *other* reason! That a certain Seer of yore, my ancestral fore-mother, was graced with a Vision she recorded with this foretelling:

> *In the Goddesses' youth, She made all Galaia as One.*
> *Not till Fire and Ice Fuse and the Oak-leaf renews,*
> *Shall they be One again.*"

"Its simplicity is deceptive and its interpretation is still a matter of debate," Thesis added. "But perchance now comes the dawn of her Vision's fulfilment. The old harmonies may be restored through the agencies of our Summer-Son and your Winter-moon... so this present conjunction may prove highly auspicious, not only for our peoples, but for all the wider nations of the Urth."

"So it's no light undertaking," said Jehan, "but a choice you can only make from full and conscious volition. For which reason, Madam, we request that you give us a year, from the day we make land in Angor; one year to learn our culture and habits, afore making any decision regarding your longer term role."

A mere twelve months to endure – then she could ask for release and set sail to Faal! Elinor seized the initiative.

"Your proposal seems reasonable and prudent, Sir."

"Splendid! Then by your leave, O Thorund, when the Princess has passed a twelvemonth in Angor we'll review the situation, and let our subsequent course hang upon the outcome."

The King scratched his beard thoughtfully. "Aye... Her Highness is yet young and untried in such a... such a State capacity. She will no doubt profit from this experience, be the result what it may." He turned to Elinor. "I concur, Daughter. Take this year and apply yourself to studying Angor's ways... together with the advice and guidance we propose to regularly dispatch, if we may turn now to maritime communication..."

"...our pact is concluded. The Gondaran fleet will provide safe conducts for all allied vessels, and rigorously prosecute pirates in our waters. Any miscreants apprehended will be dealt with by Hel. Thus can Angor ensure that a flow of desirable commodities from Centralia will be maintained - is that the way of it, Sol-Lios?"

"Aye – mainly medicines, spices and foodstuffs. Whatever is fairly asked and can be spared without harming the Forest, its custodians give open-handed - but Angor will suffer naught taken from them by force.

'The one favour asked in return you've already pledged: a stand against piracy. And even as we speak, the first gift-tribute should be under way as a gesture of anticipatory thanks. Following consignments must perforce wait till the winter storms have abated. Thereafter we undertake to send a carrier-ship every month, conveying the goods and such mail as we wish to exchange. The duration of this arrangement shall be for the year of your sojourn in Angor, Madam - after which its terms will be likewise reviewed."

"Entirely acceptable," said King Thorund. "Pray convey our gratitude to the Centrali people, Sir. Though we can't let your ships sail back bearing naught but a few scrolls of parchment! Surely we can offer some better cargo," he twinkled, "Perchance casks of mead, or *aquavit*?"

"No, thank you, Sir," replied Iactus. "Much as we've savoured Gondarlan's powerful liquors, there are products we would value even more 'Highly'! Ice, for one - Master Steward gives me to understand it can keep itself well, if properly packed - we'll use it to create Aumaia's first ice-house.

'Also your pure silver sand... and instruction, that we might learn how you deploy it to craft your perfect glassware. Altogether we'd deem that an excellent exchange."

"Steward, did you hear that?" exclaimed Thorund. "Frozen water and sand from our beaches preferred to the pick of our cellars! Well, by all means, an' it please thee. The former can be had readily enough; for the latter, Master Glassman shall set down his method, and muster the ingredients to send.

'So now... given the increase in sea-traffic that will naturally ensue, may we move on to the issue of accommodating such Angorian sailors as might dock at Thorshaven..."

"...to sum up, The Mermaid should be fit to re-open by the time we depart – although the finer points of titivation will continue long after, if I judge Madam Freya aright!" finished the Speaker.

"We're delighted to hear it," said Thorund. "And re-provisioning the vessels, that too is proceeding apace?" There were nods around the table from Steward, the Captains and Iactus.

"Very well - our agenda is complete! There being no further business to transact, we declare the meeting closed at, let's see, half after twelfth – minute that, Master Endriksson." He rubbed his hands briskly. "Come, Councillors, you must be an-hungered by now – let's to the Hall for our nuncheon."

Loric cleared the morning's debris from the table as the Presence Chamber emptied; only the sea-captains dawdled, exchanging ship-board gossip and stoking their pipes. Iamis lounged in the doorway to smoke his, watching the company's retreating backs, and as soon as all the Gondarans were out of earshot he tipped a wink to his companion. She went instantly to Loric and embraced him fervently.

"*Ave*, Loricus Aurel'ios! Well met, *charo-lios*, after all our long separation!"

"*Ave*, *Maia-chara*! Well met indeed, Mother dearest."

Chapter 23: Preparations

The convivial luncheon that followed seemed never-ending to their Lordships; hollow they sat through the pledges of thanks and accord, still dazed by their monarch's sudden outbreak of decision and his overturning of so many cherished customs. Plainly suffering, Hakon was excused from the celebrations once he had supped a bowl of gruel. Sigismund dared not follow lest he appear too obviously conspiratorial; chafing, he was obliged to endure under King Thorund's keen eye till the party dispersed.

Hastening straightway to the Warlord, the Archbishop found him muffled on his couch where he cared naught but for quiet and iced lemonade.

"Ah, Siggi," he yawned, "'Scuse my not rising – come, pull up a seat."

"Huh – at least one thing today is unchanged!" snapped Sigismund. "Drunk again, I see - and at such time-"

"Drunk, on three horns of mead? Never! I'm sick, not besotted. Though I'd felt somewhat better till you disturbed me."

"You *should* be disturbed! We've urgent matters to discuss, as well you must know."

"Discuss?" said Hakon tiredly, "Nay, this cursed ague hath robbed me of strength. But do ye talk; I'll reply best I can."

"Very well – though where to begin, I scarce know… God's Hooks, these new devices of King Thorund will cripple us, Warlord! Just like dear faithful Ecbert – such a generous pillar of the Church… and now behold!" Sigismund snapped his fingers. "Shamefully ruined - and his business, his lodging-house, gi'en over to an *Angorian Mission*, forsooth!

'Bah! We'll be over-run, our sea-lanes and harbours thrown open to these heathens with their *pernicious* influence, their licentious, perverted, ungodly habits- O, and Claw take Radnor Wolfblest, the craven, witless-

'Hmm… and yet is he… what if His Majesty let something slip? Radnor's shrewd - any sniff of these plans might explain why he fled in such haste. Well, now… if that *is* the way of it, what would he do? Where would he go, d'ye think?"

Hakon considered. "Most like Sudheim, if he's seeking to warn off his crews. I'll find out when I relay the King's orders."

"And I'll send to Wolfblest House for more recent tidings… But I must say, My Lord," Sigismund finished acidly, "I'd not expected you to take these grievous setbacks so serenely!"

"No choice," Hakon shrugged. "Her Highness can't be risked. Had the King not decreed it, I'd have recalled the fleet myself on that score – she's a prize surpassing any pirate booty."

"Ah yes, it means renewal of your hopes, does it not – if, as 'twould appear, her Angorian match is no foregone conclusion. They be too oily-tongued to admit it, but I lay they regard Her Highness more as apprentice than ambassadress – hence they wish no immediate betrothal, much less consummation. For if on closer acquaintance the Jehan deems our Princess sub-standard, he's free to reject her, pack her off home and save himself a bride-price."

The Warlord raised his eyebrows. "A sore insult, put like that. Yet I'll not oppose what so well serves my purpose. Indeed, I pray My Lady has wit enough to fail their expectations - they can't ship her back again soon enough for me."

"And she'd be ripe for de-briefing," His Grace smiled slyly. "With a year spent studying the barbarous land and its customs, seeing first-hand its geography, its major roads and cities, its administration-"

"Its population and resources, its defences – its army and navy," the Warlord picked up the thread in sudden animation. "Privy to all the secrets of its strength - and its weakness…"

Sigismund's eyes gleamed. "Twelve months' top-level intelligence in exchange for our Centrali trade ventures … let's hope it'll prove a worthwhile investment! 'Twould behove me to cultivate a correspondence for Her Highness's, ah, spiritual guidance while she's abroad, to complement King Thorund's more worldly instructions." He chuckled. "Aha! I believe I glimpse His Majesty's mind – I trow the Old Wolf's fangs are growing back! He compels us to play his 'long game', hazarding much on his chief playing piece... and then, when the Princess returns-"

"When she returns to arm us with knowledge," Hakon grinned savagely, "then, by Fafnir – we'll make war!"

Now the days gathered momentum as throughout the Castle, indeed the whole 'Birg, folk prepared for the delegation's departure as feverishly as they had lately done for its arrival. The Thorshaven Road had never seen such a volume of traffic as now traversed it daily: carts laden with provisions; messengers with proclamations; hunting parties, shopping parties and business excursions; riders bent on visits or simply exercising their horses; and pedestrians exercising legs of their own. So constant was the stream that the King, much to Hakon's disapproval, ordered all the great gates of Castle and causeway thrown open from dawn until dusk, to save wear on their hinges. The skies too were busy overhead, Kaa and Kia, his partner from *Quintessence*, having established an air-message service that flew regularly betwixt Thorsgard and ships with the more pressing communications.

Thorshaven itself was alive with activity and gossip. Every new dawn brought fresh juicy items for Ferdi Mickelsprech to cry: the Ecbertsson scandal; rehabilitation of The Mermaid; Gondarlan's treaty with Angor; new royal laws and the penalties for breaking them... and a countdown of days till full moon, being the latest date their Princess was expected to depart. Faced with this surfeit of novelty, many citizens began (or affected) to feel *blasé* about foreign affairs; the aliens had grown too ubiquitous, too commonplace as they rode through the streets or gangled like storks round the harbour and markets. Who cared if the lads looked like lasses and the lasses like geldings - they all paid alike in good coin! And business was business, reasoned the chandlers and ropers, the joiners and dealers in lumber, and all others enriched by Angorian custom, now measuring with regret the dwindling parcel of shopping days left to their lucrative cash-cow.

Elinor's days sped likewise apace, so busy she had scant time to register how quickly they passed or how few remained. Her mornings were spent in *Pferdhalle* with Berthe and Fran, all three furnished with riding culottes cut to a design which, Zafi assured, was the last word in Faali high fashion. Loki too shared their lessons, riding in a comfortable pouch of soft leather slung across Elinor's body or from her saddle bow. He took straightway to this thrilling new mode of transport, his nose replete with Luna's scent as his ears flapped to the rhythm of her paces. What all these developments might portend, he knew naught and cared less; but something was clearly afoot, else the Castle would not be in such foment, nor his mistress's suite so disordered...

This chaos in Elinor's chambers was a monster that grew daily between luncheon and feast, the hours she was free to devote to her packing. It was a mammoth undertaking; not only her Wardrobe but every shelf, drawer and coffer she possessed must be ransacked for any long-forgotten treasure she could not leave without. In consequence every flat surface, including the floor, was laden with piles to be sorted, or neat labelled bundles and boxes ready for crating: Hair-dressing Tools & Ornaments; Jewellery (Day), Jewellery (Evening) and Jewellery (State); Perfumes & Essences et cetera, et cetera; and forlorn among these chosen, a sad little heap designated Things For Throwing Away (an ink-stained handkerchief, an odd laddered stocking, a fur collar eaten by moths and an ear-muff divorced from its mate).

On this particular afternoon the Princess was whirling through her stacks, list in hand. "What next – O, we must pack my writing-desk! Fran, be sure 'tis equipped with the necessaries – and order more sealing wax, mine is well-nigh exhausted. As to books... I must have my Faali romances. Boh, and I suppose I must take *these*," she gestured to her Angorian dictionary and grammar, "Though I hate the sight of them, thanks to Brother Maris!

'So... matter for reading and writing, check. As to other pastimes, my sewing-box must come... O, bother – where is it? Where's my work-box? I put it out yesterday, ready!"

The ladies made dutiful search. "I've found it, Madam!" cried Berthe, rummaging, "Buried 'neath Travel Cushions, Shawls (Lightweight) and Cloaks (Winter-heavy)."

"Then exhume it and set it by the door where it won't be forgotten," for I may yet complete my needle-portrait of Prince Eduard from the life, Elinor added silently, dimpling at the prospect.

No sooner had Berthe done her mistress's latest bidding than a rap sounded on the said door. She opened it. Two porters stood on the threshold.

"Delivery for Her Highness," said one, "Compliments of the Angorian Captain. Where d'ye want it, Mistress?"

"O, thank Fafnir," exclaimed Elinor, hastening forward, "The travel crates are here! Bring them in, bring them in - at last, we can start packing proper!"

They hefted in a stout wooden trunk. The Princess glanced at it, then past it. "Where are the others?"

The porters looked blank. "What others, Highness?"

"My other boxes, you dolt," she said impatiently.

They shrugged apologetically. "I know not, Highness," ventured the boldest. "This was all we were given to bring."

"Well, it can't be the only! O, begone, fools," she snapped, "it's no use talking to you!

'Fran, go find Captain Iamis. Tell him I urgently need the rest of my luggage, if he desires us to sail afore the year turns."

Nothing loath to escape the maelstrom, Fran caught on her way out a look of mute envy from Berthe and Elinor's voice, "So, Bea – on to Hosiery and Shoes." Breathing deep relief she set off on her errand, hoping to encounter Nery on the way.

"Captain Iamis said *what*?"

"He said, 'Look in the box', Highness," Fran repeated.

Mystified, Elinor lifted the lid; and still mystified, blinked at the contents. "What in God's Name *is* this?" she cried, hauling forth a long tubular item.

"A seaman's bag, Madam, I think," hazarded Fran, "My father has one very like, for his sea-fishing gear."

"A fisherman's bag – do they jest? O, enough of this tomfoolery! Go back to Captain Iamis. Ask him- nay, *tell* him, he must come at once and explain himself in person."

"But Madam-"

"But me no buts, Fran – be firm, and fetch him directly."

Dutiful, she sallied forth again; and duly returned to find Elinor supervising Berthe's excavations of the shoe-mine at the bottom of a closet.

"Well? Bring him in!"

"I'm sorry, Madam – the Captain wouldn't come."

"Wouldn't come? But – how dare he refuse me? Why - what exactly did he say? Tell me, Fran, his precise words!"

"He said he couldn't – for that you'd regret it, if he did."

"What – does he make a veiled threat?"

Fran's self-control dissolved. "Ha-ha-hardly, Madam. More a naked one- he, he, he's in the *bath*, Highness! And feared you'd find his immediate condition offensive – though some might consider his suit apt for a privy audience, he said!"

Blood rushed to Elinor's cheeks as a picture rose unbidden in her mind. "Vulgar, impertinent man; to be sure, I find his *humour* offensive – do shut up, Mistress Fischer, 'tis no laughing matter! We simply must get on... and since Captain Iamis declines to assist, try instead to find the Lord Jehan-"

"No need, Madam, he's here," Fran broke in, piping a tear from her eye, "My Lord was also at the baths, but had already finished. So he came in lieu of the Captain, and is waiting without."

"Why didn't you say so, you silly goose? Admit him!

'Now, Sir," she went on to Jehan, "Will you tell me – for I can get no sensible answer from your Captain – when I shall get the rest of my packing-crates?" She gestured round the room. "These are my things - most of them, anyway... well three quarters, at least. So I'll need a goodly score more boxes like this one."

"You mean there's more – atop of all this?"

"'All this', he says – hah! I'll have you know I've laboured long and painfully, paring down my wardrobe to so little."

"Then you'll have to keep paring, Madam – or to cram 'all this' in, we'll have to leave half the crew behind! Aye, and surrender our beds for your robes to stretch out on... and heave out our fodder and water to make space in the hold!" he laughed.

"Do not mock me, Sir," she rejoined stiffly. "These garments are entirely necessary to my proper estate."

"Be that as it may, you can only take what fits in the sea-chest and kit-bag allotted – which is equal to my own allowance, and more than a regular Mariner's."

"But you can't expect me to disgrace my homeland with such an inadequate supply of apparel! You're the Elect - countermand his unreasonable ruling!"

"I can't. The Rule of Ocean takes precedence aboard the *Breath*, where the Captain is absolute master. Besides, Madam, trust me: in Angor you'll not want 'all this'."

"Don't be ridiculous! Of course I want my most costly and beautiful outfits, and they'll not fit in one box and bag."

"Well, take naught but what's simple and serviceable. If I'm any judge," he cast an ironic eye round the Wardrobe, "then you'd be packed in a trice - and I wager you'd have room to spare.

'But I'll not argue the toss - the *Breath* is a battleship, not a pleasure-barge. We've nigh two hundred souls on board, and a like number on *Quintessence*. A long voyage across open seas lies ahead; we have three extra persons – and a small canine - to house, with their chattels and rations, in our vessels of finite capacity. It boils down to a stark simple choice: if we lay a month becalmed, would you rather dress fine and starve, or dress plain and dine?

'Nay, cheer up, Madam! On my honour, I promise: if you still desire this grand raiment a week after docking I'll chart a vessel and have it all shipped over, down to the last lace and button. Though I'll lay fifty *sols* you'll not take up the offer... mind, if you do, I'll make certain you wear aught you send for! Betimes, you'll not run to rags; we have our own tailors, you know."

Crushed by his inexorable logic, the Princess hardly noticed this consoling whiff of new clothes.

"Then there's no help for it... all this, all our labour, has all been in vain!" Elinor tossed her lists into the air and gazed vacantly while the sheets drifted down, settling on the dress-racks in autumnal parody. "Pouf! Farewell, all the days of my life." She revolved

252

helplessly, sending leaves wafting from the floor in the draught of her skirts. "One box and one bag... Great God, what should I take- O no, my beautiful things, how can I choose?" Giddy she swayed, and turned white to the lips; Jehan reached out and steadied her arm. "Nay, Sir, release me," she said faintly. "I must go and lie down. My heart can bear no more of this today."

"So she's not packed her bed, yet?" Sol-Lios hissed, as Fran led her away.

Bea clamped back her laughter with one hand and slapped at his wrist with the other. "Fie, Sir, for shame! My poor lady so loves her fine... I trow she'll take more pain parting from her wardrobe than she will from aught else in Gondarlan."

Jehan tapped his teeth. "Aye... I'd no idea 'twould hit her so hard. Berthe, let's spare her further woe and pack for her. Come, I'll tell you what she'll need. For a start, none of these," he waved dismissively round sundry rich-crusted confections of satin and brocade. "But these look ideal."

Berthe giggled. "They're undergarments, Sir! Day and Night Shifts, wool for Winter, linen for Summer and silk for Best."

The Elect considered. "One each of wool... two each of linen and silk - that should suffice. These, too, look suitable."

"Under-kirtles (Plain), Sir, Evening and Day."

He picked out a blue and a grey. "Two wool... four pale linens... And do I take it these are Over-kirtles?"

"That they are, Sir," she dimpled.

"Good – we'll have this one. What else? Riding garb... a warm hood, cloak and shawl... stout footwear, naught high and spindly... a dressing-robe and slippers... changes of body-linen. There," he grinned, "That should cover the essentials."

"I should think so, My Lord," said Berthe, impressed, "It'll take no time to lay these away... with room to spare." Her eyes shone. "O, well done – and thank'ee, Sir! We've been sorely tried of late, she has run us both ragged with this, this," she waved a hand, lost for polite expression. "But now we can finish today."

Chapter 24: Nerya's Lay

"I won't go riding," said the Princess, next morning. "There's too much miserable work to do in my Wardrobe."

"Nay, Madam, we've good news on that score," replied Berthe brightly. "Your bag and box are packed already, and Lord Jehan says your work-box and writing desk count as cabin furnishings, so they may come too."

Elinor said wanly, "That is good news, in its way."

"Wait, Highness, there's more!" Fran exclaimed. "We don't need our full luggage allotment - we can manage with two bags and one chest. So you can have our other box."

"Well – riches indeed! That means I can take my emerald brocade... or should it be the cloth-of-silver? And maybe my purple ermine mantle! No, I won't ride – I must pick out my extra frocks!"

"Shall we put the rest back in their presses, Madam?"

"No... leave them out," she replied thoughtfully, "'Twill save time when the ship comes to fetch them." (So she had heard Jehan, after all). "I wish to ponder my choices... and write some directions for the porters, which I can do best by myself.

"Aye, take the morning off. Why not go for your usual lesson? Luna still needs exercise - you may ride her if you like."

"I will - thank'ee, Madam!" said Bea.

Fran hesitated. "If you wouldn't mind, Highness, I'd rather take Loki for a walk."

"Of course – but don't let him off the leash. He mustn't run off and get lost so close to our leaving!"

Rejoicing in their deliverance, the girls embarked upon on their respective missions of pleasure. In the courtyard, Fran reached into her kirtle and extracted a tiny linen bundle from its home next to her heart.

"Here, boy, sniff – there's a good dog! Now, where's Nery? Go find Nery! Seek, Loki, seek!"

Loki snuffled at the lock of hair, its scent heavily overlain by Fran's own but nonetheless recognisable. His ears cocked; his tail wagged; he let out a yip of excitement. They were going hunting! And a fine morn it was for it, too; crisp, blue and frosty, with scents hanging pungent on the still air. He circled and sniffed, unravelling the criss-crossing trails, tail whipping in a silvery blur. His quarry had been here, and recently... aye, there it was!

With an urgent yip he plunged forward, almost jerking the

leash from Fran's hand. She tripped behind at the full stretch of her arm, and alight with cheerful expectation, broke into song.

At the outer bailey Loki checked abruptly and strained back his head, nostrils a-quiver. Crying to Fran, "There!" he dragged her on to the battlement steps.

Fran glimpsed a flash of silver helmet between the crenellations. "O, clever boy, she's walking the walls - let's surprise her! *Aye calley-hiya, aye calley-hiya, aye calley-hiya-hah*!" Still humming she pattered up the steps, rounded onto the battlements and halted: there stood Nerya, arms akimbo.

"O, I'd hoped to come on you unnoticed - good morrow, Oratoria! Why, what's wrong? You look as if you'd seen a ghost."

"Heard one, more like… just then, you were singing-"

"Aye – and my voice isn't cracked enough to put such a look on your face! Whatever's the matter?"

"I- it's just- Fran, where did you learn that song?"

"The Castellan's sewing-girls were singing it while we were making our new riding culottes-"

"And the words - did they teach you the words?"

"Nay, they knew only the chorus, this *aye calley-*" She broke off at Nerya's wince. "What's *wrong*? 'Tis a pretty little tune – a soldier's song, I think they said."

The Kalaia gave a short, bitter laugh. "Aye, it's a soldier's song. The proper refrain goes *Ai Kali-mara, Ai Kali-mara* - it's a battle cry."

"O, I thought they were just nonsense-words. You know it, then?"

"Hah! I know it, and I wish I did not! For it is mine own, the *Lay of Kalaia Nerya* – and loathly in my ears."

"Your own Lay – what, a song has been made on you, like the heroes in sagas of old? I don't understand… if 'twere me, I should sing it all the livelong day!"

Nerya shook her head. "Alas - truly, you don't understand… 'tis at once my fame and my shame. O, Goddess, I'd hoped to be spared this a while yet… Let's go somewhere quiet, I'd rather you heard its tale from me than at second-hand."

She led Fran to a sunny sheltered corner of the walls and spread out her cloak.

"Here, sit." Nery fumbled out her pipe; Fran was surprised to see her fingers shaking as she loaded and lit it, and fortified herself with a long draw. "Now hark, I shall sing it." She began in a soft, husky contralto, "*'Twas in the dark of Hag-moon time that Breath of Gaia came…*

'…Ai Kali-Mara, Ai Kali-Mara, Ai-Kali-Mara, ah…" she presently ended. "There, did you follow it?"

"Somewhat," replied Fran doubtfully, "Of a voyage, and a battle, and… and of some man that you slew? But there were too many words unfamiliar… can't you sing it in Gondaran?"

"Nay, I can't versify in a foreign tongue. I'll tell the tale instead, although perhaps first I should explain…

'Angor only has one enemy – not through choice, but because they'll have it no other way - the D'Oron of Islay del Oros in the Southern Straits. Their perverse code is never to ask where they can take, never to trade where they can steal… faugh! They're a curse upon honest and peaceable folk! Ordinarily they're too much engaged in their own private wars to trouble the world overmuch. But from time to time they boil forth like a plague of locusts, bent upon wider rapine… as they have been for several years now, thanks to their new Lord of the Isles, one Carlos Sablo.

'Black Charlie killed the other pirate chiefs, united their crews under his own bloody banner, and sent them trawling abroad for slaves and gold. They started preying on the Sealanders who dwell off our south-western coast, and merchant or fishing vessels plying the Straits - and even assayed a raid or two on Lower Angoria, to their great cost! So we tracked their slaving fleet to Shellton on Lesser Sealand, whence they were plundering the islands at leisure. Under cover of a moonless night, we anchored in a neighbouring bay and made our way over land to the township. Their look-outs were easily despatched – we could smell 'em a mile off, so sotted were they on the foul liquor they call 'rhum'. Then while my Sisters took up position I heard certain sounds… and crept to a hut and peeped through the shutter.

'What I saw is graven on my mind's eye to this day - a twelve-year-old girl lashed down on a mean bed, and a D'Oron with an eye-patch, his hands round her throat, rutting upon her… So I kicked in the door and dragged him off by his long greasy pigtail. Faugh! His member still stood all engorged, befouled with shit and virgin's blood, and… and *wagging* at me. So loathsome was the sight that I '*clove it in twain, tip to root*' with my sword… then undid his belly on the upstroke and left him weltering in his spilt guts. His torment didn't end till I'd cut the girl free… she asked for my dagger and drove it through his one eye and into his brain.

'Meantime, down on the beaches, our Brothers had fired the

D'Oron ships with a great explosion. The pirates staggered forth to see what had happened - and we fell upon them. More than ten score we slew on the night of Nerya's Lay, and burnt a dozen ships... and released a stockade of prisoners bound for slavery, and restored them to their homes. Altogether, 'twas a grievous setback for Black Charlie - especially since yon vile rapist turned out to have been his first mate and cousin, one Migel Un'oy!

'So Fran, there's my fame and my shame. What think you of your fine Kalaia now?"

Fran had listened wide-eyed. "Great Wolf - what *should* I think?" She shrugged. "I see the fame, but where's the shame? It was war, wasn't it – and that wicked man deserved to die, surely?"

"Not like that – 'tis not the Warrior's Way. Where we *must* kill, we kill swift and sure. The quick clean dispatch is our only mercy... our Code of Honour, the essence of all our training.

'And I betrayed it! I could have, I *should* have, smote off his head, or run him straight through the heart... but I gave myself up to blood-rage, maimed him deliberate and left him to suffer. It makes me no better than a D'Oron, a traitor to my Sisters, my Goddess, myself... I of all people, the Oratoria, who should have known – *did* know – better!

'*That's* my shame, Fran. And that I've heightened the danger for my comrades by bringing down a great price on my head. Sablo offers a fortune to the man who delivers me alive, that I might be impaled first upon his person, then upon his saw-edged knife."

Fran shuddered. "And your people – do they too blame you so harshly? Is that why they sing on it, to punish you?"

"Almost, I wish they did – it'd be my just dessert. But most don't realise... and the rest can forgive. Even the Counsel, to whom I made full confession, can't help admiring the blow's precision. Nor can some, it appears, refrain from harping upon it! Only another Oratoria could truly comprehend how deep this goes with me; not even Niki fully grasps it.

'Ah, me... anyhow, I've washed myself clean as I can. I saw decently to Un'oy's remains... he and his cohorts were burnt in the wreckage of their boats, and washed out to sea. And I did penance, made my pain-offering before the assembled *Kali't'aia*... and I wear him, as a permanent reminder." She pulled down the neck of her doublet, baring her shoulder. "Here he is, in my Mark – these glyphs are his name, and this his emblem."

Fran scrutinised the tattoo. "What, this red fountain? Why- O,

I see." She swallowed. "Well... I *think* I understand a little now. But Nery... if your countrymen forgive you, mayhap it's time to forgive yourself – or try to, at least."

Nery smiled ruefully. "Mayhap – yet it's hard to forgive when I can't forget... and I can't forget, when I hear the *Lay* sung."

"Then I'll sing it no more," Fran declared stoutly, "Nor suffer it sung in my presence – nor even speak of it again, unless you wish me to."

"Thank'ee – I care not to hear it, and should dearly like to know how it came here so I might quash it at the source!"

Fran nodded. "I'll do what I can, discreetly, to discourage the girls... but if, as they say, 'tis a soldier's song, you might enquire at the barracks.

'But afore we leave the subject, can you tell me what became of that poor girl? What's she called? Did she live?"

Nerya smiled the first genuine smile Fran had seen that morning. "Aye, she lives – and thrives, thanks to Zafi and Iris. Her name's Shana. She's nearly sixteen now, and," touching her forehead, "has just received her Blood of Blossoming. You may meet her in Aumaia - she came to live in our sister-house, and follows the Path of Kalaia with great promise."

"So she'll be a warrior? I'm glad to hear it! Then some good has come of this, surely... besides, I'll lay your shrewd blow still gives those bloody pirates pause for thought!"

Nery kissed her gently. "Ten thousand thanks, my love, for thy sound common sense. To think I'd dreaded this moment, only to find that confiding in thee has soothed my soul."

"Well, I'm glad of that, too," said Fran, kissing her back. "But now I must rise, this cold stone's making my, ah, making me stiff- O! O, no!" She leapt up, brandishing an empty leash. "Loki's slipped his collar! O Great Wolf, where's he gone? I must find him, or Her Highness will skin me!"

Loki at first had sat patient enough, waiting for his walk to resume; but as the women's talk went on... and on... he drooped into boredom. Cocking a hind-leg he scratched listlessly at his ear, then at his collar; then froze, nostrils flaring – he had caught a friendly scent upon the air!

He scratched at his collar again, more deliberate, shooting Fran a quick guilty glance. Her face was still turned from him, all her attention bent upon Nerya's story. Furtively, the Seekhound lay down and worried the collar with his front paws, knowing that if he could but scrabble it over one ear, the rest would follow easily...

...and it did. Slowly, stealthily, he wormed into the shadow at Fran's back. Slowly, stealthily he snuck away, claws pulled in lest they click on the stone; not until he had rounded a corner out of sight did he break into a run, off merrily a-hunting once more.

His quarry was not hard to find. Nerya and Fran were not the only couple taking the air that fine morning; the Torturer and his Lady were abroad too, sharing a pipe on the southern ramparts.

The Seer's eye, when she could tear it from Hel, drifted ever and anon to Thorshaven harbour far below.

"What is it, Madam? Are you looking for something?"

"I Look for many things, Sir," she dimpled enigmatically, "Both near and far away! But for now, I'm bird-watching."

Following her gaze, Hel spotted an object growing steadily bigger, gradually resolving itself into an osprey, a big one, carrying a basket in its claws.

Iris hugged herself in delight. "She comes, at last! I've been waiting on this moment since yestere'en, when Kaa brought me word of their arrival!"

"Of whose arrival?"

"Wait, you'll see in a minute- here, Xanthe, to me, to me!" she waved frantically to the approaching eagle. It hovered over the wall-walk, set its burden gently down then settled on the battlement, greeting Iris with a melancholy peep.

"Well done, dear bird!" She drew from her pouch a strip of dried fish, and fed it to the osprey. "Meet Xanthe, our sea-carrier – all the way to Faal and back she's flown on my errand of mercy! Pray, Sir, open the basket..."

Hot on the trail Loki bounded along, jinking past the odd patrolling Gard. He skittered up a flight of steps, rounded a final corner then stopped dead in his tracks, claws scoring stone. His nose affirmed that his eyes were not deceived, and he advanced as if drawn by a magnet with stiff-legged gait, ears cocked and tail erect, his nostrils wide to savour every delectable atom...

Iris saw him first. "O, behold," she cried, "Here comes a playmate!"

Detaching his love-gift's tongue from his ear, Hel bent and released it carefully from his cupped hands to the floor. It circled; it yipped; it made a beeline for Loki, and almost bowled him over.

It was a Seekhound puppy; a bitch, said his nose, although too young for mating! She butted and bit at him with tiny teeth, snapping at his paws and tail, her own a silver blur of naughtiness as she goaded him to attack. Loki's heart was lost in an instant. Growling, he took her neck in his jaws and shook her; then in similar friendly manner, addressed his nose to her rump. She responded with an indignant high-pitched protest, and clamping her tail down in maidenly fashion, scampered back to her new master.

"Ho, my lad – methinks you play too rough for my poor Lila," the Torturer laughed, as Loki trotted up panting. "You must be kindly, she's only a bairn!

'Now, you two behave, and become better acquainted. Here, boy, stand quiet. And Lila," he held onto her collar, "Greet him politely!"

She strained towards Loki, snuffing excitedly, and licked at his muzzle. He responded in kind. Hel gradually slackened his grip until both dogs were free. They pranced about, striking at each other with their fore-paws; dropped down in cat-like crouches, waggling their behinds; and then began playing in earnest, chasing one another up and down the wall-walk, rolling over and over in a tangled fighting ball.

Hel and Iris were still watching the antics, tears of merriment on their cheeks, when Nerya and Fran came panting up.

"O... O, thank the Wolf, he's here!" Fran gasped. "Nay, he is there- what?" She did a double-take. "Where did the other one come from?"

"From Faal, like your Loki," said Iris. "Her name's Blanche-Liliana the Fourth of Romaine, or Lila, for short. She's my parting gift to Lord Hel."

Chapter 25: Royal Progress

The court's preparations for its Feast of Farewells were dark days for Berthe. Her duties continually balked her of any chance for private conversation with Loric; and when she *did* see him he appeared distracted, less approachable than was his wont. So she dared not venture the question that had preoccupied her own mind as time slid by, although she feared she knew his answer anyway; Loric had not given the least indication by word, deed or languishing look that he wished to come with her. Which he surely would have by now, Berthe lamented... and yet, argued faint hope, with all that extra housekeeping, his Gentlemen to oversee, being in constant attendance upon the King's guests... he'd been so sorely pressed, he'd scarce had a moment to ask her!

"O, what to do?" she agonised. "What if he thinks I don't want him, and so refrains from even hinting... or simply hasn't thought of it, but would like the idea well if he did? Perchance if *I* don't broach the subject, neither will he!"

And if you do, and he plain does not want to, said reality's cold leaden voice, what then? What if he avoids the issue to save you that pain – isn't it better to live in dignified doubt? Mayhap, heart retorted; yet is it not better still to risk living in love, than resign to a dead certain parting?

In the end, heart, hope – and impulse - prevailed. Berthe spotted Loric that noon in the Great Hall, and on the pretext of a forgotten shawl, scurried back to find him after luncheon.

"Good day, dear Berthe," he returned her greeting pleasantly. "How apt - there you are, about to embark upon your great adventure; and here am I, planning the farewell banquet to sweeten your leaving! I'm a mite envious, I admit... it's years since I sailed, or set foot on Angor."

Taking her courage in both hands, Berthe strove for a light tone. "Then why not come with us? I dare say Lord Jehan would gladly have you." She dropped her eyelids. "As- as I would, too."

"As would I, sweetheart - alas," Loric sighed, "I could never ask for release while His Majesty needs me – and he'll need me even more, with Princess Elinor gone."

Berthe willed her voice not to tremble. "Ah, that's a shame. I should have liked you for a guide," she forced a gay laugh, "Aye, and a translator, for when we forget the foreign words!

'O well, I durst not tarry longer," she went on, suddenly

purposeful. "Where's that shawl? I think it slid behind the bench."

Loric was not fooled. Catching her arm he drew her close, and kissed her on the brow.

"I'll miss you, Bea," he said gently. "I'm sorry I can't share your journey. Part of my heart will always belong to Angor... so truly, I'd come if I could! Let me pledge this instead: if I *can* come, I *will*. 'Tis the best I can say, till circumstances change."

Berthe smiled bravely. "Aye – or till Madam decides it's not to her liking, and ships us all back home again!" she said wistfully. "But speaking of my mistress, I must hasten back or she'll scold me. So come, Master Loric: pray help me find my shawl."

Next morning the first feeble glimmer of dawn awoke the Princess, who had barely slept for horrible excitement.

"It's come, then!" she murmured. "My last day... and tonight, the last I shall sleep in this bed..."

Her words sounded ominously like the utterance of a condemned prisoner. Agitated, she sprang up and kindled a lamp, threw on robe and slippers and peered out between the curtains. Shadows bustled in the courtyard below, haloed by the light of torches flaring through the mist: grooms, porters, carters, Gard, all setting about the business of this momentous day.

Elinor watched for a moment; sat back on her bed; jumped up again a second later, and began pacing. There was room to pace now; by dint of supreme effort, her luggage monster had been re-confined to the Wardrobe, whereupon her ladies had tidied the suite to such an unprecedented level of neatness that it had the air of a guest apartment. Everywhere she perceived small absences: of the habitual clutter spilling from work-box and writing desk; of the most precious potions from her decimated dresser; of the favourite books from her bedside cabinet, and the jewel casket from her table. Her familiar surroundings felt impersonal as an hotel, and as pregnant with impending departure.

"O, what to do?" she fretted. "Everything's packed – e'en if I could settle to sew or read, which I doubt! Yet I can't sit here twiddling my thumbs- I know, I'll go and check my Wardrobe."

In the central room they had dubbed 'Transit', the hanging rails and stretcher racks were swathed in dust-sheets. Dozens of linen-wrapped bundles and wickerwork baskets were neatly labelled and stacked; her detailed lading instructions were prominently displayed upon the table; nothing remained to be done.

"Now what?" she said irritably, back in her room. "'Tis too

early for fast-break, e'en had I appetite... though perchance a hot posset would soothe me. I'll send for the girls."

They did not take much chivvying up. Fran had been too excited for sleep which was as well, or Berthe's alternating tears of joy at Loric's pledge and woe for their coming separation would have disturbed her more. Both were grateful for distraction, and seventh glass saw them ensconced before a merry blaze in Elinor's hearth, all somewhat pink about the eyes, supping at Berthe's special restorative posset.

By ninth they were dressed in their new culottes and redingotes, overlooking the courtyard's activity as a procession of servants strained out from the Keep.

"Look Madam, our luggage - there go the sea-chests and bags!" exclaimed Fran, as porters hefted them onto a waiting cart.

Elinor squinted. "Have they got my satchel of books?"

"Aye, Highness – it's in yon crate, with your sewing-box and writing-desk and dressing case and small jewel casket," said Berthe, counting on her fingers. "And see, there's your box of Angorian things. That's everything, is it not?"

The Princess sighed heavily. "Huh - it's hardly *any*thing! O, I wonder how long the journey takes betwixt here and there – and when I can soonest expect the rest of my Wardrobe?"

"Not till Spring, Madam," Fran said, mischievously. "Earlier wouldn't be safe - just think how dreadful 'twould be if your finery were drowned by winter storms! Never mind, you'll get plenty of new clothes in Angor – I can scarcely grasp we're setting off tomorrow," she went on, blithely disregarding Elinor's expression. "Nor can I wait to see our ship – what will it be like, d'ye think?"

"Too small by half," the Princess muttered sourly.

King Thorund rarely graced his city with a personal visit, but he had lately conceived a desire to inspect The Mermaid – and to see how his daughter would be housed for her voyage. At least, that was the excuse Thorund gave himself for his curiosity regarding the Angorian ships.

Not wishing his business impeded by pomp and circumstance, it was only a small group that set out sharp on tenth glass: Thorund and Jehan; Nikos and Rupert Endriksson; Captain Iamis; the Princess with her ladies; and Seer Iris. For escort they had Nery and Jenia, Florian and Dario on the baggage cart, and a pair of Gard deployed to mind its contents.

263

The Princess felt somewhat deflated. There would be no huzzahs ringing through bright frosty air, no cries of approbation on her handsome mount; and being so enveloped by her heavy riding cloak, she might as well be wearing a hessian sack for all the attention her costume would attract. For the early morning mist had congealed into a freezing fog so dense that for safety's sake, the Kalaia rode fore and aft with blazing torches, while Skala and Karl, the cart-guards, were sternly adjured to keep the rear lanterns alight.

The few miles seemed long and irksome as the fog pearled into minute droplets on their hoods and lashes, running into eyes and causing frequent sneezes, blotting out view, conversation and enjoyment alike. At last a tang of pine-smoke spiced the mist, announcing their arrival at Thorshaven's outskirts. As they rode on, more of the city's exhalations became trapped in the smothering blanket, forming a well-nigh solid patchwork of odours ranging from savoury to downright disgusting. Tanners, fullers, cess-pits, brewers, bakers, smoke-houses, all successively announced their unseen presence; but as their destination approached, one pervasive reek intensified to dominate all the rest: the smell of fish, fresh, curing, frying, boiling or decaying as offal in the gutters.

They clopped through the murky streets finding no-one abroad save folk with pressing business who, being so accustomed to the Angorian presence, groped past buried in their cloaks and spared the riders hardly a glance.

Huh - a fine day to come viewing ships, thought Thorund. To Jehan he said, "Here we are, Sir, Harbour-place - where we'll leave you to stow the goods and chattels, and give Her Highness chance to put her berth in order. So if you'll kindly excuse us, we'll pay our respects to *Seehalle*.

'Follow me, Lady Iris. Come, Oratore, Master Endriksson."

The King and his companions wheeled about and vanished into the wreathing whiteness. The rest dismounted on the quayside; Nery and Jenia led the horses to 'Little Angor' for a rub-down, while Captain Iamis crooked a gallant elbow in Elinor's direction.

"May I conduct you aboard, Madam?"

She mounted the gangplank to a piping accompaniment from the mustered crew.

"Mornin' Cap'n," chirped First Mate Portia. "Elect, Ladies – welcome aboard *Breath of Gaia*, not that you could tell her from a fishing smack in this! You must be cold after riding through such a pea-soup - come and have some hot *café*."

To King Thorund's first glance, The Mermaid's parlour seemed little changed from the Old Sea-hall he distantly remembered; only Nikos with his recent familiarity could fully appreciate what a great resurrection the past weeks had wrought. The place was much lighter, to start with; the bay windows shone clean and whole, with fresh glazing substituted for the dim horn panes at the back. The plasterwork was newly whitewashed, the floor rushes replaced by a pale woven matting, and the serving table draped in snowy napery, gleaming with Ecbert's finest glasses. All warmly reflected the brightness of lamps and a crackling fire, and the room was suffused with the grateful aromas of coffee and baking.

Nikos was especially pleased to see the row of interlace columns marching proudly denuded of their tatty, disfiguring screen; and that beyond, a squad of Angorian fitters had almost completed their work.

"Ho there, comrades!"

Freya sprang up from her sewing in the west bay, followed by Freyling, wryly gathering up the pins and threads sprinkled by her hasty exit.

"Niki! *Gut' tag* – and to you, Master Rupert!" she cried, "And this must be the lady doctor." She bobbed Iris a curtsey. "Thank'ee kindly for coming, Ma'am. But who else is this? Tarry not in the porch, Sir – and shut the door, for pity's sake, you're letting the fog-" She broke off; the stranger had put back his hood and shaken out his long silver mane. She dropped to her knees as if pole-axed. "O, my- my, my liege, my most dread Lord and King!"

Freyling sank down at her side, wide eyes fixed on Thorund's face. She had never before seen the King – nor expected to, under this roof!

"P-Pray forgive a foolish girl, Sire, for speaking out of turn. O, and after Your Majesty has been so kind to us and all…" Freya trailed off, overcome.

"Nay, the fault is mine own, for coming upon you unannounced. So arise, Mistress- Freya, is it?"

She obeyed with a trembling curtsey. "Aye, Lord King, I'm thy bondswoman, Freya. And this is Freyling, Sire – another one delivered by thy mercy."

The sound of visitors had fetched in the rest from the kitchen, wiping floury hands on aprons and tidying their hair. One by one their mouths fell open; one by one they sank into obeisance, hardly believing

265

their eyes.

Freya introduced them, concluding, "…all of us thy most humble servants, Majesty. As is the last of our number, Agathe, restored to us but lying sick abed - which is why this good lady," she gestured to Iris, "has come, to attend her."

"Then I wish her a speedy recovery. Do you wish to consult with your patient now, Madam?" Iris nodded. "Very well – and while you're so engaged, perhaps our free-women would show us around."

"Gladly, Sire - pray follow me." As Iris headed upstairs, Freya led them between the carved columns. "Well, to start with: this we are calling 'The Snug'".

It was an apt name for the formerly squalid alcove, completely refitted and the old fusty stink driven out by goodly scents of new pine and wax polish. The walls had been lined with built-in couches upholstered in dark blue velvet from Ecbertsson's impounded stock, interspersed with low chests-of-drawers that doubled as tables; a continuous shelf ran above the couch backs bearing sundry jugs, glasses and lamps. The floor in between was covered in pale rush matting, with another pine chest free-standing in the middle; the upper walls were freshly whitened; and two massive blue velvet curtains hung from a ceiling rail just inside the row of columns, to provide comfort and privacy as required.

"Snug indeed," observed Nikos. "Well done, mates – you've made a fine job of this!"

"And you've not seen the best of it yet," dimpled Freya. "O, it's a cunning thing – behold."

An obliging carpenter stooped and pulled out the base of a couch. Its seat cushion slid forward, the back one slid down and lo, there was a bed, luxurious for one, commodious enough for two if they were friendly.

"We can sleep up to ten folk on these," said their hostess. "And see – the bedding goes in these table-drawers. Of course, 'tis not finished yet; we're still a-sewing of the pillow cushions, and we'd like to work some hangings for the walls… but we could lodge guests straightway, if need be."

"Aye, all we've left to do is put up some hammock hooks," the carpenter added, "Then six more could bunk in here, easy."

King Thorund nodded. "Splendid work - my thanks, Sirs; and to you, ladies, these furnishings are excellent."

Freya curtsied, rosy with gratification. "Thank'ee, Sire, I'm glad it pleases thee - as I trust will the upper rooms." She led the way upstairs. "Here's the Great Chamber," she whispered, pointing to the closed door, "Which I share with poor Aggi; while Anna, Else and Ingrit sleep here, in our new dormitory."

Nikos looked round approvingly. Without the mean partitions this was a handsome space furnished with three half-tester beds hung with matching flowered drapes; at the foot of each was a clothing chest, and at the head, a bedside cabinet scattered with girlish paraphernalia. A substantial dressing-table-cum-washstand stood beneath the middle window with a colourful rag-rug lying before it, and one corner boasted a magnificent Faalian pier-glass confiscated from the Burgher's town-house.

"We can easy fit more beds in, if we find any other Mermaids," said Freya. "And this last room is Freyling and Gretel's. I lay you'll think 'tis improved, Master Nikos!"

"That I do," he grinned. Freya's old cell was restored to a generous chamber with a central window, the fireplace commensurately shrunk to appropriate dimension. It held two delightful four-posters hung with rose-pink brocade, former possessions of Ecbert's spoilt daughters, along with their rosewood bed-chamber suite: bedside tables, chairs upholstered in pink matching the curtains, a clothes-press, and a dainty wash-stand behind a carved screen.

"Well done, indeed," said the King, "*Alt Seehalle* is a proud house once more! We're exceedingly pleased – and trust your compatriots will be too, Sir, when they sojourn here."

"Certes they will," agreed Nikos. "Also they'll be relieved, you might say, to find how we've transformed the other, ah, facilities!"

Approaching the bed, Iris surveyed its occupant's pallid, sweaty features. "Mistress Agathe? I'm Iris Kali-ra, and have come to ease your trouble. Would you care to tell me about it?"

"Good morrow, Madam," Agathe replied weakly. "O, 'tis good of you to come! Well," her eyes filled with tears, "At first my Curse stopped, so I thought I'd got with child. Especially when I started with sickness, and tenderness here," she gestured to her breast. "But then it started paining me, low down in one side... and I've a lump. Mostly it just aches, but there are sharp pangs too, coming more often now... with faintness, and fever."

"May I see?"

Agathe nodded, her tears over-spilling. Gently, Iris drew back the covers and lifted her night-shift, exposing deathly-white skin marked with the fading bruises and healing sores of recent ill-usage; she

267

was still so pathetically thin that the bulge in her right groin could be plainly discerned.

"Breathe easy, and fear not - this won't hurt." The Seer passed her hands back and forth, an inch or two above Agathe's body, feeling at once the angry disturbance in her aura. A few minutes sufficed for diagnosis; pulling up the clothes, she sat down by the bed and took her patient's hand.

"Be of good cheer – 'tis not a tumour."

Aggi's face rose, then fell back. "So I'm having a baby?"

"Not that either, exactly. You're indeed pregnant… but not in your womb. Alas, there can be no live birthing… for if it continues to grow, you will rupture within-"

"Great Wolf," Agathe broke in, white to the lips, "Then cancer or no, I *will* die!"

Iris patted her hand. "Nay, we've caught it in time. I can stop it today – just close your eyes and relax."

She cupped her hands above Agathe's pelvis and shut her own eyes. Filaments of Vision crept from her fingertips, down through the coarse weave of blankets and the finer mesh of linen sheets; through pale skin and subcutaneous fat and dark muscle, down, into the pulsing red tube where a tiny powerhouse twinkled. The Seer tensed, driving toward it a thread of volition infinitely finer than a needle, seeking out its small pulsating core. A heart cell burst, painlessly leaking its minute volume; another followed suit, and another; then more and more, spreading out like ripples on a pond. The vital spark faltered, flickered and dimmed; then quietly and gently, went out.

Iris exhaled a long sigh. "*Maia Kali* be praised, it is done."

Agathe blinked and gulped nervously. "So… are you going to fetch the instruments – will I be cut now?"

"Cut?" the Seer looked blank. "Why would- nay," she laughed as understanding dawned, "Nay, I'm finished! Can't you tell – how does it feel?"

Aggi slid her hand down her belly. "Warm," she said, in a wondering tone, "Sort of… tingly, and melting – and the pain's easing." She sat up amazed, colour already returning to her cheeks. "By the Wolf, I feel better! But how could- what have you done?"

Iris smiled. "You might call it faith-healing… I'm a priestess of the *Nône*, a Necromancer, blessed with the art of stoppage. But I must also call on our *floria*-Healer for a balancing cordial to cleanse out the residues, so that your moon-time will come in due course. You'll bleed heavier than normal, mayhap with cramps, but keep supping the draught and your willow-bark tea. Go steadily for a few weeks, and you'll soon feel back to normal." She squeezed Aggi's arm sympathetically. "Bodily, at least... as to the rest, I do sorrow for you, Mistress, on the loss of your babe."

Agathe had grasped little beyond the salient fact. Her eyes filled anew. "It's really truly gone, then? Ah, God forgive me, but I don't grieve, I can't... I didn't want it, poor little thing! For I know naught of its father save he was one rough man among many, a user of cheap worn-out whores... and I despaired of how I'd cope when I couldn't afford a doctor to root it out.

'Then His Majesty had me brought back here, where 'twould not have been so bad... and the girls would have helped. Yet still," she was sobbing now, "Still, in my heart, I didn't want- I've had enough of men, I want naught of them inside me! Much less to bring a lad into the world, who might grow up just as bad - or a lass doomed to suffer like me. So I thank you, Ma-Madam, a thousand times, for ridding me on it!"

Iris embraced her. "That's right, Aggi," she whispered, "weep out thy woes... all is well... and all will *be* well."

"This is a great boon," said Freya, "Why, these days it hardly feels like housework, with everything so easy and convenient! Dry underfoot and overhead, no more melting snow or hauling water from the street pump; and as for our other 'convenience', 'tis a marvel!"

Certainly, the work teams had effected a wonderful improvement. The miry back-yard had been flattened and resurfaced with hard-packed earth, and a perimeter boardwalk constructed to make a raised path to the outbuildings. These, an old scullery, buttery and cold-room, laundry and wood-shed, had all been renovated, and a continuous front porch erected to shelter the Mermaids as they passed in between. Outside the scullery, the disused well was restored to function; and opposite, in place of the noisome privy-pit, a new crowning glory had risen towards which Nikos was striding with purposeful step.

"Come, see this High-place, O Thorund," he called over his shoulder. "It wouldn't disgrace the Thorsgard - or our palace in Aumaia."

Intrigued, (and in similar need), the King followed. The convenience was a nice fusion of indigenous and foreign lavatory traditions, warmly lit by a large brass lamp wherein scented oil was burning. A comfortable two-seater privy stood along the back wall,

269

with a bin of dried sphagnum moss handily placed at either end. Its other furnishings consisted of a piss-barrel into which the Speaker was draining himself, a rack of clean towels, and a wash-stand equipped with basin and ewer, a cake of olive-oil soap and a curious pottery flask.

"Good, eh?" said the Speaker, laving his hands. "There's one like it next door for womenfolk; and behind, in the alley, access for the dunny-men to dig it out. Aye, all the, ahem, solid waste – kitchen peels, ashes from the fires, soiled mosses, hair combings - all such can go down here, with a sprinkle of Earthseed," he nodded at the flask. "And before long, it rots down to a right goodly mulch for spreading on your fields."

"It *is* good. You're a sterling overseer, Kalaios – I'm deeply obliged."

"Don't mention it," Nikos chuckled. "The Mermaid has occupied our shore leave most enjoyably! Now, shall we rejoin our shipmates? I believe our mission here is well-nigh concluded."

"Aye – I dare say my daughter's luggage is unpacked by now, and I'm keen to see her quarters."

Convening in the parlour, they found Iris waiting and made their thanks and farewells. Young Master Rupert's taking his time bidding Freyling adieu, thought Nikos; hmm, methinks romance is in the air! Indeed, the couple's flushed cheeks and downcast glances, the idle patterns traced by their toes on the mat, seemed to make this supposition likely – as did the way they sprang guiltily apart at his approach.

"I was just, ah, commending Mistress Freja on the excellent order of the house," faltered Rupert, scarlet. Freyling fiddled with her hair.

"A long job indeed, with so much to commend. Alas that I must tear you from it prematurely - my apologies, sweetheart. Never fear, you'll see him again oft enough - eh, Master Endriksson?"

Chapter 26: Aboard

Breath of Gaia loomed ahead through the mist. King Thorund felt a thrill of anticipation – she promised to be a magnificent craft, if her figurehead was aught to go by! Cursing the fog, he squinted at the Earth-Goddess for whom the *Breath* was named. Her bare flesh was painted green as the living forest with diamond stars forming her nipples, her gilded tresses entwined with leaves and flowers of coloured gemstones and crowned with golden sun-rays. Low on her belly, an inverted silver moon poured a rippling cascade over her thighs, shaded from pale aquamarine to the deepest sea-blue, leaping with silver fishes and edged with a froth of tiny cabochon diamonds and moonstones.

Nikos slapped the hull fondly. "Well, Sir, what think you of our Gaia?"

"Glorious – I wish it was a finer day, she must look dazzling in the sunshine. This treatment," his pointing finger traced the lines of hair and waters, "puts me in mind of our animal interlace – you recall that fine example on the columns at *Seehalle* – but your style is more, more…"

"Naturalistic?" offered the Speaker.

Thorund nodded. "Aye," he said thoughtfully, "that's the word… Fascinating! Between two distant nations a unifying artistic concept, but rendered in our individual ways. Interesting, indeed - I look forward to seeing more of this on board."

Iris laughed. "An art connoisseur - alas, you'll find all our opulence has been expended on *Ma'Gaia*, Sir! Elsewhere the *Breath's* beauty derives from pure form and function-"

"Which is an art in itself," interrupted Nikos, chafing his hands, "Well exemplified by Princess Elinor's cabin! Let's go view it – unless you'd rather stay out drenching in this stew."

Thorund found the fore-cabin immaculately constructed, every inch of its space cunningly utilised with fittings of fine varnished wood and polished brass; a seamless effect, beautifully executed but quite without ornamentation, the simple, neutral theme continued in soft furnishings of plain unbleached canvas. The Princess, for her part, recognised the futility of bewailing its size or triangular shape – it was, apparently, the best they could offer, away from the noise and smell of the galley and far superior to the cabin below, which Berthe and Fran would be sharing. The latter had soon folded away her depleted wardrobe into the lockers and drawers lining the walls, packed her toilet articles in its tiny wash-room, and laid her night-things ready on the hanging cot (which to Elinor looked horribly like a suspended coffin). Her sea-chest was slotted neatly into its recess at the prow, where it doubled as a window-seat, with her work-box and other possessions stowed safely inside. And that comprised her miniature realm; at least, she reflected thankfully, she could safely stand in it upright – unlike her father and the Angorians, who were prone to knock heads on the ceiling.

"Excellent... very compact and convenient... you should pass a comfortable voyage in here, Madam! My thanks, Captain, for seeing Her Highness so well housed," said the King at last. "Where shall we go next, Sir?"

"To lunch," replied Iamis, to Elinor's great relief, "Where you may view the stern cabin."

The ship's officers customarily met for meals in this spacious cabin, whose diamond-lattice windows were today so befogged that the lamps had been lit. Their glow reflected from the floor of black and white chequered sailcloth, the polished wood of built-in chart-lockers and cabinets, and the big central table hung round with canvas hammock-chairs. Adjoining it to starboard were the Captain's quarters – a mere closet fitted with a desk, storage lockers with padded lids that doubled as seating, Iamis' sea-chest, a wash-stand and a hammock; and to port, the comparable cell shared by Nikos and Jehan.

The luncheon they ate was as plain as the tableware of square wooden trenchers, but tasty and wholesome: fish soup with juicy shreds of seaweed; fried chickpea balls in spicy sauce; frittered roots and salad; and a compote of fruits steeped in mead, served with ginger iced-cream (for which the Angorians had quickly acquired a passion, along with the knack of its making).

Afterwards, at Thorund's request, they toured the rest of the ship. Iamis took them first to the well-appointed galley, where *la-Hai* were baking ship's biscuit and *staycakes*. Conspicuous among their brown uniforms was one in sober black, with the badge of a skeletal silver tree on his breast and a bloody apron round his waist; *necro'la* Sandros was filleting fish.

Berthe and Fran looked about keenly, but Elinor's interest did not spark till they reached the under-deck where her Luna would be housed. There she was suitably impressed by the horse-stalls with padded walls that slid into crushes for holding the animals gently yet securely in rough weather; then rapidly grew bored as they passed through the lower decks of storage holds and the mess-hall, where the bulk of the crew slept on hammocks.

King Thorund warmly extolled the ship's size and facilities but to Elinor it seemed hideously cramped. Mighty Wolf, she thought, how ever can two hundred great lanky Outlanders *live* in such tiny conditions? What's more, how can I – it's bad enough here in the harbour – what will it be like out at sea? O, I mustn't think of that now, or I'll scream! A panicky claustrophobia seized her; luckily Iamis soon pronounced the tour complete and she made thankfully for the top deck, blessing her Faali culottes as she scrambled up the ladders.

"Well, there you have her," said the Captain. "Our well-beloved *Breath* - and now you've seen her as well you can on such a drear day, we'll send to Little Angor for the horses and you can be away before eventide."

"Hold hard!" said King Thorund, "We haven't yet viewed the *Quintessence*."

O, *no*, the Princess silently lamented as the walk-way was run across and she trailed reluctantly after her father. Oblivious, Thorund pointed out the *'Essence's* figurehead: a golden Tree of Life, its branches bedecked by leaves, flowers, fruits, animals, birds and human figures, all prettily wrought in coloured gems.

"Behold, Daughter – Yggdrasil!" he laughed. "Here's another consonance, Oratore – the Life-Tree is an image from our most ancient myths."

Being herself fond of art, the Princess could have admired this for longer had not the day been so dank. As it was, she shivered under her cloak in a mixture of cold and impatience while Captain Aurelia welcomed them aboard.

"As we're sister-ships, you'll find *Quintessence* similar to the *Breath* – in form, if not in function," she told them. "Also some of our nautical terms are different – this, for instance," she gestured expansively around, "is on High-ships called the sea-deck, not the top. Immediately below is our own top-deck, and underneath, what we call our high, higher and highest decks," she grinned, "for reasons that will soon become apparent!

'So, our highest would be called 'lowest' or 'bottom' on the *Breath* – it's a mite confusing at first, but you'll get used to it. "

She led them down into the warm fug of the top-deck. Milling with goats, geese, and *anima'la* forking straw into stalls, preparing hanging nests and scurrying about with bags of corn, it looked like a veritable farmyard.

"Why, there's a barn-owl," exclaimed the Princess in surprise, "Up there, on the hay-rack!"

"Aye, that's Ooli, our mouser," said the Captain. "His mate Oola hunts for the *Breath*."

Ooli stirred at the sound of his name; peered owlishly at them a moment; shrugged his wings and went back to sleep. The Princess was disappointed; she had hoped he might fly down so she could pet his pretty white feathers.

"What a funny thing – I thought ships kept cats for that."

"Aye, Madam, we used to. But if - Gaia forbid - the vessel should founder, an owl may at least fly to safety. So can our egg-layers – we carry ducks and geese, rather than chickens."

Next they descended to the process decks, Elinor clutching to her nose a bunch of fresh mint Aurelia had considerately supplied. As King Thorund pored over the settling tanks, dung-press and other foul-smelling apparatus, quizzing their operators with interminable technical questions, her face grew nigh-on as green as the leaves she crushed to her nostrils. Even through the mint she found the reek in the low, windowless hold becoming unendurable; forced to plead faintness, she bolted back with her ladies to the comparative freshness of the *Breath's* stern-cabin.

"Whatever's my father thinking of? Do I *look* like a laundress or- or a *dunny-man*?" she demanded indignantly, as Berthe poured out a restorative coffee. Sipping, Elinor shuddered. "Faugh, how could he subject me to that - what care *I* how they do their horrid work? I can still smell it, clinging around us!"

"Leastways we'll stay clean on our journey – just fancy, making all their own soap and suchlike aboard," Berthe consoled.

"Humph – scant recompense for the stink. His Majesty carries politeness too far, methinks, staying down in yon- ugh, no wonder they call it the bowels of the ship! Pray God he won't linger – I want to go home and shed these tainted garments."

At long last, the King's appetite for maritime novelty was sated. By this time it was late afternoon; although the mist had thinned somewhat, the twilight had thickened, and the city was shadowy and quiet enough for them to return incognito as they had come. The Princess rode pensively, oblivious to her ladies' muted chatter. Her mind was filled with images of the day passed, and imaginings of the night ahead... and of the morrow, when she must exchange her luxurious apartments for that tiny floating box. She shivered; however would she bear it, for week upon week, cast away so frail and insecure on the great wide face of Ocean?

"My new home," she sighed under her breath. "Ah, me, 'twill be like living in a doll-house! Would God that my father had betrothed me to Faal..." Her eyes became dreamy. "I could have had a lovely summer passage along the fjords and seen somewhat of my own land... then only a few days' sailing from Sudheim to Linnaise, and the Imperial barge to take me through the Isles...

'But instead I am to Angor, and weeks in that dreadful little bed. I can only pray it won't become my coffin... O, but I mustn't think of it now, or tonight will be ruined! I needn't think till the moment it happens – which isn't yet awhile, not for another score of hours. I *must* think instead on getting cleansed and changed, and the feasting and dancing... tomorrow can take care of itself."

Skala and Karl meanwhile rattled along with no more to guard than the cart's red lanterns. They had had a merry day of it, starting on the quayside bantering with the Angorian sailors, and accepting pulls from pipes and flasks while the wagon was unloaded. Then no sooner were the goods all stowed than King Thorund had returned from The Mermaid, and dismissed them to Little Angor to tend to their cart-horse and bellies.

The warehouse had been largely stripped of personal possessions and the crews' sleeping quarters; only the refectory and makeshift *ablutorium* remained, with horses, goats, geese and ducks wandering freely throughout. Nonetheless the Gards were made welcome and spent a happy interlude of coffee, smoke and gossip until the royal party arrived, whereupon with reluctant farewells they harnessed the horse, refilled the lamps and awaited the order for home.

"So much for 'another shit detail'," sniggered Karl. "Hah - 'sat in the fog all day freezing your balls off'... just think of Elf's face if he'd seen us, stuffing our guts in the warm by His Majesty's order!"

"Well, he didn't see us – nor will we tell him, else the bastard won't let us come tomorrow." Skala's grin faded as he returned to the matter he had fretted on all day. "Who'd have thought it, eh matey... our King in a bawdy-house - The Mermaid, by royal appointment! What if the girls are too grand for the likes of us now – will I ever shag Freya again?" He sighed, glanced at his fellow victim in love, and brightened mischievously. "Still, at least I don't set my cap as high as yours – panting round your Kal-ay-er like a bloody lapdog!"

"Piss off," Karl retorted, "A man can admire – and 'twill be the last time I get chance, mores the pity, so shut your stupid yap." Turning a cold shoulder to his insensitive comrade he leant back against the tail-board and began softly whistling the latest Gardroom hit.

It carried on the breeze to Nerya, riding postern with the torch. For an instant she froze, and then urged Glaive forward.

"Ho, warrior! A word, if you please – tell me, where did you learn that tune?"

The shock of his beloved's appearance, the dangerous edge in her voice, almost pitched Karl headlong from the cart.

"F-f-f," he stammered uselessly, "F-fl-"

"Florian," cut in Skala, panicking lest she lose patience. "'Twas the Horse-High they call Florian, My Lad- er, Mad- um, Kal-ay-er – we learned it off him."

"Confounded fool!" she muttered. "And what of the words, did he sing you them too?"

Dumbly they nodded.

Nerya narrowed her eyes. "Then, bonny lads, you'll know how I served Migel Un'oy... and if you don't want serving the same way – *don't fucking sing it again.*"

Chapter 27: Feast of Farewells

"Singularly appropriate," said King Thorund, "Quite a new departure."

Jehan took another bite of filbert rissole. "Aye... Angorian recipes with Gondaran ingredients, Northron dishes with Southron spice – it works well."

Between them they had devised a uniquely informal farewell feast, attended only by Thorund's immediate household, the Angorian delegation, and their ships' officers - an intimate gathering of no more than two hundred. This was partly in courtesy to the visitors, who having stowed their baggage were left with only their travelling clothes and overnight essentials; and partly to ease the burden on kitchen and waiting staff, that they too might derive some enjoyment from the occasion.

To many younger courtiers, the central buffet table was a risqué innovation; a rare chance to mingle, napkins on shoulders, spearing morsels on their eating knives. It fostered a certain amount of flirtation over the bite-size pastries: the meeting of eyes, the accidental brush of fingertips as titbits were exchanged, the suggestive nibbling of a miniature sausage...

Senior die-hards looked on sourly. After a first course of earthy mushroom soup, only the High Table continued to be served at their places. The rest were obliged to give up their recognised seats, mill about among lesser ranks, serve themselves from a common board – and all for the sake of these mimsy little mouthfuls! What they wanted were vast crackling joints and stuffed moose and roast birds to tear asunder, not tiny meatballs half made of fruit in a sauce that set one's tongue afire...

"The buffet seems popular," observed Jehan, "on the whole! Which is the essence of our Way – melding the best of two worlds, creating new compounds..." he tipped his glass to the Princess, "becoming greater together than the sum of our parts."

Hakon shifted uncomfortably. He felt in strange humour that night: elated to be rid of the Outlanders, despairing at the attendant loss of his Lady, and disgusted by the legacy the barbarians seemed like to bequeath.

"Taking over, more like," he sneered. "Infecting our people with decadent customs – conquering our birthright by stealth!"

"We're not conquerors," Sol-Lios gestured emphatically with a battered parsnip. "Consider the Empire of Faal: is it subjugated,

277

become a colony of Angor? Has Angorian ousted Faali as first tongue? Hardly – while we're close allies they still follow their way and suffer us to follow ours."

Silver mask hiding the scowl on his face, if not from his voice, Sigismund demanded, "And what of our Faith, which has been subverted by thy very presence? Already, seduction of the Pack, erosion of their morals, the seeds of godless anarchy sewn-"

Thesis took advantage of his momentary pause for breath. "The door of faith swings both ways, Sir. If you're offended by our Way, convince us yours is better. Come to Angor and preach your doctrine! You and your Brethren would be feted like princes; the temples would be mobbed, so rare is the opportunity to hear a new theology expounded."

The Archbishop bowed. "I shall certainly bear that in mind."

Around them, the atmosphere thickened and mellowed even among hardy xenophobes as the first courses took their effect: the *passionata* leaves in the tansy-cake, the glimmer of psylocybin in the soup… there was general relaxation, the heartiest eaters were flying high, and the next phase of hunger set in.

"Praise Fafnir – pudding!" Elinor exclaimed, as a fanfare sounded. Sternly warned by the King not to over-dress, in a fit of nostalgic pique she had dug out her old dancing-frock, and it was a little tight around the midriff. So the light grazing had suited her well, and appetite far from sated, she had looked forward keenly to this moment.

"Lord King, Thorsgard all," a herald announced, "The chefs of two lands proudly offer a special creation to honour Her Most Serene Highness: the Crème Bel'Elinor!"

A chorus of appreciation greeted the cartwheel-sized confection, and the bells on Elinor's dress jingled as she bounced in greedy recognition.

"Huzzah!" she cried, as her individual yin-yang arrived in its frosted crystal bowl. "My mouth has watered to try this again!"

While Gentlemen carved the centrepiece into fair portions, others re-filled the buffet with an assortment of *staycakes*, seed-cakes, crystallised fruits, frittered pears and apples, syllabub, and metheglin sorbet with *passionata* syrup. As the peace of concentrated guzzling settled over the Hall, Sol-Lios rose.

"My friends, I trust you're sweetly enough disposed to lend me an ear." A scatter of groans and cries of, "Boo, speech," greeted his words.

"Never fear, I shan't keep it long. But this is our last night, and afore we leave there are two things I must say. The first is simply thanks, from all of us to all of thee." (Cries of 'Hear hear!" from the Angorian benches). "We've been greatly enriched by our stay – not least by this treasure," he bowed to Elinor, "by means of whose gracious person alliance is fostered between us. We now have a trading partnership and a mission at The Mermaid; the foundations of mutual peace and prosperity are laid.

'The second is to issue a general invitation. In like exchange, Angor will found a Gondaran Mission in Aumaia and deed it to your Crown, O Thorund. And as Thorshaven receives us, so shall we receive thee. Come visit your Princess and bide long time or short; come as travellers, story-tellers, teachers of your crafts and tongue; do but come in friendship, and all are welcome."

He raised his glass. "To all Peoples of the Wolf and of the Sun: peace and accord!"

"Peace and accord!" was echoed to rousing applause, tinged with relief as the Elect resumed his seat.

When the sweet dishes, all but licked clean, had been taken away, minstrels struck up. The last course came in, led by a fabulous ice-sculpted cornucopia from whose plentiful horn cascaded silver and gilt sugared almonds, marzipan fruits, peppermint creams, and the roasted, chocolate-dipped beans of *café* and *cacao*. It was accompanied by bowls of roast nuts and fried, thinly-sliced roots; a selection of cheeses and savoury biscuits; and to wash it all down, hot spiced mead or scalding black coffee. Finally the *Hausgard* and servants were summoned and given their customary tot, and the closing toast was quaffed.

"I wish I could unloose my corsets," hissed the Princess. "O, why did I eat so many cake-lets, I've scarcely room left for these lovely crunchy things! Or, well, mayhap I can manage just one more. O dear, they're stuck together - two, then."

"Perhaps a little exercise would help, Madam!" Berthe said. "Why don't you dance? It'd be a shame not to, in that dress."

"I doubt I can walk, let alone dance!" Elinor groaned. "I'll take a cup of *café* – O, and a sniff of *aquavit* - and think about it."

While she pondered, the Oratores and Next stripped off their jackets and took to the floor.

"Angorians," bellowed Nikos, "Time to work off those bellies – let's perform the *Vi-aqua* to entertain our hosts."

"O, folk dancing," Elinor yawned, as Perikleia clapped out a rhythm and crooned a wordless chant. Then she sat up. "Wait a moment… why, I know this! *Vi-aqua*, Way of Water – it's the exercise Loric taught me!" She watched as one by one the Angorians joined in, until the entire contingent was synchronised in flowing, sinuous movement. "O, I never realised what a lovely dance – how well it looks, all doing it together."

"Why don't you join them, Madam?" said Fran.

"Nay," she demurred, "I can't- but then again, why not? You're right, I will! Loric! Master Loric!" she jumped up and grabbed his arm, "Come along, tutor – dance the *Vi-aqua* with me!"

"It wouldn't be fitting," he protested, but the Princess was not to be denied. Like waves, the Angorians parted to make them a place, then flowed back as they picked up the motion. Elinor felt stiff and jerky at first, but her confidence grew as her limbs fell into familiar routine, dipping and whirling, bowing and swaying. And, she was gratified to realise, her dress might have been made for this dance, its gauzy streamers swirling like spume, its silver bells a tinkling brook against the ebb and flow of Perikleia's chant.

Gradually the others dropped back to watch, leaving her in possession of the floor. Closing her eyes, Elinor danced as she had never done before, sensing the meaning in each subtle move, her body *becoming* as water, from rippling stream to roaring tidal surge… She repeated the full cycle alone, ending to a rapturous ovation that left her rosy and sparkling with pleasure. Returning to the High Table triumphant, fanning herself with her hand, she allowed Sol-Lios to pour her an iced cordial.

Sigismund, meanwhile, was thoughtfully tapping his teeth. "Yon sea-captain," he murmured as Aurelia passed on the way to her seat, "Who does she remind me of…?"

"Who – why, any one of 'em," Hakon snorted, "They all look the same, bloody Southron!"

"Nay, this one has a look of- wait, 'tis on the tip of my tongue, I shall have it in a minute… ach, it's gone! Their accursed pipe-smoke hath addled my thoughts – nor does this music help."

"O, my favourite bransle is starting," Elinor cried, "I must dance again! Who will partner me? Nay, Lord Jehan, you don't know the steps."

Hakon rose and offered his arm. "I should be honoured, Highness."

She shrugged, smiled and accepted; the introduction played on as they proceeded to the top of the hall and took up position, the Warlord's eyes never leaving her face, then the bransle proper began.

Bow, curtsey, clap; meet in the middle, clap palms together.

"I'll miss thee." Retire and repeat.

"Thou art Gondarlan's Princess…" Jump, spin and clap; retire and repeat, "…come back to us." Jump, spin, clap stamp; hands raise and clasp; trip down the aisle; change sides and retire.

Moved by an impulse of fairness, she considered. Prince Eduard was a quantity unknown; Jehan apparently regarded her with the same fond amusement as he might a wayward kitten; but the Warlord was here, plainly and painfully serious. Paunch trimmed by recent illness, beard trimmed to a saturnine point by his barber, smartly dressed, surprisingly sober, Hakon was not entirely repellent. Quite personable, even; powerful and rich; he probably *could* rule Gondarlan, after a fashion…

Yet as a suitor… a *husband*… it required a leap too great for her imagination. Besides, he was only her equal in height, shorter in her heeled dancing slippers; at least Sol-Lios made her feel pleasingly petite, and she regretted he knew not the dance. But what answer could she give, in all discretion?

New top couple, repeat from the start. She thought quickly.

"Angor is not my first love." Retire and repeat.

"If I wed any Gondarman, it will be thee." Jump, spin and clap; retire and repeat.

"Then can I hope?" Jump, spin, clap stamp; hands raise and clasp.

"One can always hope, My Lord." Demure downcast eyes; step one-two to the side; old top couple down, new top couple repeat from the start; and so on, a dozen times more till the Princess and Warlord were back where they started.

Hakon stooped to kiss her hand as she curtsied in the final movement. "So, a twelvemonth of biding in hope," he murmured, "Then shall I hold thee to thy pledge, my dear Madam."

The entertainments continued until tenth glass when to the court's surprise, King Thorund ordered them to don outdoor clothes and muster in the inner bailey.

Elinor and the Moon, revealed by a stiff breeze that had blown off the last shreds of fog, regarded each other full-face. Confronted by its implacable clock, her stomach churned; the year was turning to *Mit'winter*, her birth-month, and if *this* weather held, her voyage would indeed start tomorrow. Shivering, she pulled herself back to the moment.

"God's Teeth," she grumbled, her breath smoking on the air. "Why has my Father dragged us out in the freezing cold-"

"What's to do on the battlements?" cut in Fran, speaking her thought. "Look Madam, up there, with the lanterns."

Before Elinor could reply, a drum rolled and a fanfare rang through the darkness. Suddenly, *fizz-whoosh – CRACK*! Folk instinctively ducked; the night lit up crimson; the Princess and her ladies shrieked.

Fizz-whoosh – CRACK! CRACK! More flares shot up and exploded, green, white, red again. There were screams, gasps and shocked exclamations. People clutched their neighbours by the elbow, sleeve, any convenient projection; yet the King watched fearless among his guests, all wearing broad childlike grins that acted as a bulwark against mob hysterics.

Fizz-crump! Crump-crump-crump! Incandescent spheres leapt into the sky, where in rapid succession they burst into stars of Gondaran scarlet and white. As the last sparkle died a second began, in Angorian sapphire and gold; then both together, emblazoning Mount Fang's looming backdrop in patriotic fire.

Swoosh-crackle: amid clouds of smoke, a glittering silver cascade poured down the bailey wall, the sparks sputtering, hopping and dying on the frosty black flags. So far Thorsgard had not tumbled, nor had anyone died. Emboldened, "Ooh!" and "Ah!" cried the crowd till the fire-fall ebbed out.

Then *fizz-whoosh*! A comet of coppery sparks arrowed high and cracked into a giant golden flower; then another, and another, until the night was one gigantic blooming, fading nosegay, ever changing violet-silver-blue.

Whoosh-BANG! Crack-bang-pop-BANG! The cries of awe and delight turned once more to terror as a horrid star-shell skittered through the air, randomly exploding. Dogs barked, frightened ponies whinnied and kicked in their stalls; there was a scuffle on the battlements and a voice floated down,

"Don't light the rest! I *told* you to leave out the bloody bangers!"

After brief hiatus, a smoke cloud puffed forth from the wall and a drum-roll began. A red flame ignited, grew tall as a pillar then emitted a fountain of bright golden sparks, looking every bit like a volcano. Up went a dozen rockets, one for each month of Elinor's promise, and exploded into rainbows. On the left of the wall-walk, a lesser eruption spat glowing balls of red and white into the air; another on the right spat blue and gold.

Finally, *WHOOMPH*! A huge rocket launched itself high, higher, dwindling to a pin-prick among the stars. There was a collective intake of breath. *Boom*! Four subsidiaries trailed down like shooting-stars. *Crack-pop-pop-pop*! A quartet of overlapping fire-flowers burst overhead, red-white-blue-gold, a cascade of petals raining almost into the crowd's upturned faces before dispersing harmlessly in showers of tiny silver sparks.

The volcanoes died down. Momentarily, silence and the smell of salt-peter held sway. Then began a fresh eruption of cheers and applause, whistling, stamping; even a few tears in some quarters. Similar sounds could be heard beyond the wall, from the lesser Thorsgard watching from the outer bailey.

"What sorcery was that?" asked the Archbishop faintly, as the fire-teams descended and bowed to tumultuous acclamation.

"Not sorcery – *pyro-teknia*, if I have the word right," replied Thorund, "I don't pretend to understand its cause; suffice that I'm pleased by its effect!" He chafed his hands. "Brr… but 'tis a chilly spectacle – let's back to the Hall."

Spent with excitement, an awestruck court cupped grateful hands round their mugs of mulled ale, hot *Pfefferwein* or egg-nog and listened to King Thorund's closing address.

"…thanks once again to the Delegation of Angor for providing such a sparkling conclusion to our evening's entertainment! Now, since our travellers need rest, it remains only for us to bid farewell to our memorable Feast of Farewells - and bid all of thee good-night."

It took nigh an hour for the courtiers to file past the royal party, giving thanks and adieus as required. Elinor followed the last out with a sense of reluctant anti-climax. She craved more admiration, more celebrations in her honour, and felt she could dance until dawn… being thus sent to bed seemed a dismally mundane and premature conclusion.

O well, she consoled herself, I can at least talk to the girls… and we might as well stay up late, for all the sleep we're likely to get!

King Thorund also felt loath to relinquish his company. Repairing to his apartment with a select group, he thankfully removed his crown and sank down on the couch.

"Ah," he sighed, "Thank the Wolf, peace at last! Loric, whip us up a night-cap, there's a good fellow.

'Our last night, eh? Truly, I sorrow – the month's passed too quick for my taste. But those fire-works," he chuckled, shaking his head, "A suitable finale, methinks! They're a means of signalling, you say?"

"Aye – *pyro-linga* is a tongue in itself," said Zafi. "For instance, a purple flower summons a *floria*-Healer. Red flares call for help, red rockets call for *Kali't'aia*, and a blue-and-gold one announces the docking of a ship with long-awaited cargo. Of course," she smiled, "They're best for night-calls! For day-time we use *Avian* post."

"A fascinating invention," Thorund said thoughtfully, "And I see why you keep their making a close-guarded secret! But tell me, what mean the green, and the silvery-white ones?"

The conversation continued through a pleasant hour of smoke and hot drinks. Then the King set down his cup, blotted off a chocolate moustache and heaved a regretful sigh.

"Ah well... I suppose I should obey mine own edict and release you to your slumbers." He embraced them one by one, all the Counsel save Iris and Nikos who had excused themselves at the Great Hall, and bade them sleep well.

While Sorenssen conducted them out, Thorund kicked off his shoes, pulled off his stockings and undid his belt.

"O, Loric, fetch in my slippers," he called, hearing the inner latch click. He took the proffered pair without turning round; stooped to don them; and when he straightened up, hands slipped the robe from his shoulders and a low voice said in his ear,

"I'm sorry, Sir," Thorund froze, "But Master Loric has retired. I'm come to serve thee instead." He turned slowly round. "Will I do?"

The King swallowed. "Ah- aye, you'll do finely, but- but I don't understand..."

"Really – I think you do, well enough."

"Mayhap... yet still, I hardly dare hope I construe thee aright."

"Dare."

His robe was laid aside; the neck of his shirt untied; the garment pulled off with a shiver of fingertips over his ribcage; his furred velvet bed-gown drawn gently on.

"Now, My Lord King, I shall follow suit - for it seems, ah, disrespectful, that I remain clad when you're so nearly naked."

Thorund sank weak-kneed on the bed as the Kalaia matter-of-factly stripped off boots and socks, doublet and hose, singlet and braies. It was the unselfconscious disrobing of a soldier, of one man before another; curiously un-erotic, breathtakingly aesthetic. Naked save for the ring-headed cross that swung between the mild swell of her breasts, Nery methodically folded her garments on a chair with a military

284

precision that Thorund found somehow heartbreaking; set her footwear neatly in front, and her weapons to hand by the bed.

Had he fallen asleep? He gazed, fearful this was some fantastic dream that might be dispelled if he blinked. But she seemed solid enough, the firelight gilding her tawny muscles as she squatted down to mend the hearth then padded round the chamber, extinguishing all lamps and candles bar the one at his bedside.

Extending a hand, she drew the King to his feet. They stood toe to toe. Two pairs of green eyes, jade and ocean, met in devouring gaze, their pupils dilated by dim light and passion. Nerya stroked Thorund's cheek, catching a finger in the corner of his mouth, parting his lips.

"Methinks I've another service to perform," she breathed hotly between them after a long, unbearable moment. She dropped slowly to her knees, tracing fingertips through his grizzled chest-hair, down his belly, toying with the lacing of his braies. "For these too should come off, should they not?"

Thorund gasped. In an instinct of fear, modesty, he hardly knew what, he reached out to stop her but she stayed his hand. With her other she untied the knot, slackened the drawstring; the braies sagged inexorably; snagged briefly on his erection; then slipped down to pool at his ankles.

"There, now," she murmured, "Pray Sir, step out."

Trembling, he obeyed, gasping afresh as her hands stroked up the back of his thighs, cupped his buttocks and pulled him gently forward. Then he cried aloud; her tongue was dipping between his legs, sliding hot and wet over his scrotum, teasingly up his full length to the exquisitely sensitive, empurpled tip… He thrust involuntarily, deep in her mouth, feeling the vibration as she answered his ecstatic groans. The unprecedented sensation shook him to the root. A few seconds more and he was panting,

"Stop! Stop, please – else you'd have me spent already!"

She nodded delicious acquiescence and withdrew. Rising sinuously as a great snake she put her arms around him. Thorund returned the embrace, running hands over her lean flanks, up to her powerful shoulders and well-muscled arms, down to her pectorals and the turgid buds of her nipples. It was Nerya's turn to gasp and bite her lip. Then she bit his, darted her tongue in his mouth and at last they kissed deep, deeper, grinding their bodies and faces together.

Thorund marvelled at her stature, her strength, full great as his if not greater in the vigour of her youth. Grappling with a soldier,

285

forsooth – he found it disconcertingly arousing. He fell back on the bed, Nerya atop him, their mouths still passionately locked. She straddled him, rubbing her slick open parts over his, jockeying for position; finding it, she thrust simultaneously up with her arms and down with her pelvis.

"Ah!" the King cried. Grinning, Nerya sat back to unbind her tail and shook loose her corn-gold hair. Then she began riding him, sliding up and down, rotating her hips, varying the pace expertly from gentle trot to moiling gallop.

Thorund moaned. He had never imagined a woman like this, so achingly handsome, so forthright in her desires... she was moving urgently now, clamping her inner muscles tightly, biting back low cries of pleasure. He felt himself gather, pulsating within; Nerya felt it too; and throwing back her head she surrendered to orgasm the same instant Thorund exploded.

When their spasms and cries had subsided she collapsed onto his chest. They rocked together a few minutes longer, kissing and murmuring endearments as their lust ebbed in a crawly trickle.

"Were we in Angor, O Thorund, we could call the *la-Hai* with fresh towels!" Nerya disengaged herself with a moist flaccid plop, clapping a hand to her closely-trimmed crotch. "But here you must High for me. Quick – pass a cloth of some sort."

Thorund fumbled a handkerchief from his bedside drawer. As she applied it to the requisite spot he lay propped on one elbow, shaking his head.

"By the Wolf, I've never encountered thy like... such a body, a face... thou art peerless, Kalaia."

"I'm glad you like it, Sir. *Androgyny*, we call it, the fusion of male and female essence... to please, and be pleased by, both sexes... 'Tis a trait much admired in my country – and with which the Kalaia are abundantly blessed, if less generously endowed in other directions," she laughed, glancing down.

"You do please me – better than I've ever been pleased in my life. And though I never thought to speak such words again, this I must avow: I love thee well, Nerya. Indeed, if you'd have me, there's none I'd rather take unto my Queen."

"Hah – pillow talk," she chuckled. Next moment her eyes snapped wide open. "Is it not? Great Naume, you can't mean it!" An expression almost of panic crossed her face. "*Kali-maia*, can it be - is *this* the prophecy? Not Jehan and Elinor, but Nerya and Thorund! Is this my fate- nay, can you see it?" She shrugged Thorund's dressing robe low on her shoulders, bunched it in one fist beneath her negligible bosom and proceeded to mince back and forth.

"I should trade in my breeches for petticoats, and my sword for a needle – la, Sir, me fight? Why no, I might break a nail! I shall sit at thy foot and embroider, instead." Her mimicry was cruelly accurate; the King smiled guiltily into his beard. "*Can* you see it – seriously, Thorund?" She faced him, suddenly grave.

"No indeed," he smiled, "Not like that! But as a she-wolf, a Warrior Queen by my side, at my right hand... now that I *could* envisage, and like well."

Nerya lay down again. "Hmm... an Angorian Queen would be highly unpopular in some quarters. Their Lordships... Baron Ulfar... you'd need me as a soldier, the realm could be riven in two!

'But is that how it *should* be - is that my *karma*? To leave my Sisters to Peri and 'Klita; leave my homeland and Fr- friends; make trial as your daughter will with us, a species of governor-in-apprentice?

'You'll not take it amiss, I'm sure – but the future of Angor's Oratoria is a weightier matter than she can decide by herself. I must take rede with the Counsel on this, this most unexpected proposal, and give it earnest consideration. Then if it's deemed to be my destiny, my duty... aye, Thorund, if 'twere for our common weal, I'd be your Queen."

He looked rueful. "Duty - not pleasure?"

She smiled. "That too! I can't deny you're fine in my sight, a man I'd be pleased to know deeper. Hmm... to forge a life with you here... maybe to turn children from passing thoughts into flesh... there could be worse fates. Truly, my qualms are more for the office of Queenship than for thy person, My Lord!

'Yet... yet this is so greatly unlooked-for, I don't know what to say – save that I'll keep it in mind, while we wait on present outcome."

Thorund kissed her. "A fair reply – I could scarce have expected more at this juncture." Stroking her neck, his fingers collided with the body-warmed pendant at her throat; instantly her hand clasped his wrist.

"Touch it not."

"Why – what is it? O, begging your pardon – is it sacred?"

"In a way... it is *ankh*, Life Eternal. Shall I explain its arcanum? Aye... well, first 'tis what it somewhat resembles, a key – to universal understanding. The shaft is the path of material existence; the boss, the crossroads betwixt life and death where we all meet – man and woman," she indicated the cross-arms. "While beyond lies the unending circle of soul: life-in-death and rebirth.

'Second it is *Androgyne*: the embodiment of *Kali't'aia*, the Fusion of female and male. This road becomes a phallus, the side-branches testes; the ring all at once ovum, vagina and womb.

'Third it's a *Kali't'aia* joke. Behold: though I caution again, on your life, do not touch." She squeezed the boss, slipped a finger through the loop and drew out a miniature blade.

"Judiciously applied, 'twill slit the great vein in neck or thigh. But its real point," she punned, "rests in the pad of tow here." She tapped the end of the shaft still hanging from her neck-chain. "It's steeped in a virulent toxin; one pinprick and your foe's dead in three heartbeats. Hence its nickname, 'Soldier's Secret' – our covert means of dispatch to Life Eternal – and I have revealed it to thee, O Thorund, as a pledge of our trust." She clicked the deadly little thing back in its sheath. "Apropos of which, d'ye have Aula to hand?"

"Always." Thorund passed it to her.

Nerya jabbed her left index finger, then Thorund's, pinched out two fat ruby drops and pressed them tightly together. Raising Aula to her breast she made a short incision over her heart, and treated him likewise; licked off the blood from his chest and bade him follow suit; then embraced him closely, salt stinging minutely in their cuts as fluids mingled.

"Now, blood of my blood, flesh of my flesh, we're insolubly bonded. Whatsoever transpires, know that I am thy friend – with all the host of Angor at my back."

They fell once more to kissing. Desire rekindled; this time Thorund took the lead. In a less frenzied conjunction he found she could play the maid too, gentle and tender, mewling in bliss like a kitten. Slow but sure, they ascended the peak; and as slowly came down, wallowing in the after-glow.

At length he rolled off her, utterly spent. "Thy pardon, belov'd… no disrespect," he mumbled, "but must close my eyes…"

"Typical! Then sweet dreams, dear heart."

She kissed his cheek and blew out the candle. Thorund fell forthwith to sleep; Nery lay till her eyes were accustomed to the dull light of the smouldering fire, then slid quietly out and got dressed.

Five minutes later she was slipping between the King's door-guard as they nodded on their halberds; sneaking through the shadowy corridors; stealthily unlatching a door.

Within she unlaced and dropped breeches and drawers to her

ankles. Wiping a hand between her thighs, she held out glistening fingers to the occupant of the bed.

"What ho, Loricus - I've fetched thee a gift from thy Lord."

Chapter 28: *Bon Voyage*

Dawn broke fresh and clear, with a high scudding cloud. The Thorsgard was already stirring: an early fast-break being laid in the Hall, grooms grooming, Gards polishing armour and weapons, Angorians packing their overnight traps into saddle-bags. Loki and Lila, happily ignorant of their impending separation, pattered importantly through the guest quarters. They had thus far scented out a kerchief, a comb, an odd sock, three silver *stels* from behind a sofa cushion, a hair-ribbon and a pair of Zafia's drawers balled up under her bed (along with two forgotten *staycakes*, which they hadn't declared).

The Princess and her ladies were also abroad. To prolong the fun, they had slept (if that was the word) all three together in Elinor's bed. Dissection of the guests, the food, the dancing and dance partners, the entertainments and the fabulous finale went on until the early hours. Speculation inevitably followed regarding the morrow (rather, the imminent morning), the voyage, the weather... whence it was but a short step to storms, shipwrecks, sharks and sea-serpents, tidal waves, pirates, the terrible Kraken... every watery horror Fran could dredge up from her family stock of sea-faring lore until all three were frightened beyond thought of repose.

"O, God, will we ever get there alive?" moaned Elinor.

"'Course we will, Madam," said Berthe stoutly, patting her shoulder. "Get away with thy tales, Mistress Fischer! Did not *Breath* and *Quintessence* sail thousands of leagues to Gondarlan, in perfect safety?" she consoled herself as much as her bed-mates. "Remember what Loric has told us, these folk go sailing for *pleasure* – it can't be all that hazardous! We'll get to Angor well enough... and I can't wait to see the Palace of Aumaia. I wonder if it's bigger than Thorsgard - and what will our lodgings be like?"

Her ploy worked; imagining Jehan's home, laying a giggling wager on whose picture should prove closest to the truth, made for an hour's pleasant distraction. By now eyelids were drooping, conversational gaps growing longer; so they snuffed the candle and went on with desultory chat in the dark, while each became progressively enwrapped in her own thoughts and dreams.

Barely forty winks passed, then came a rap at the door. Loric entered, bearing a candle-lit tray; there was a spring in his step and a glint in his eyes, notwithstanding the bags underneath.

"Good morrow, Highness, and Ladies – how convenient to find you together! Here's a pot of whipped *mocha* and cream, for you must rouse yourselves - 'tis nearly sixth glass and Captain Iamis wishes to set off by ninth, to be sure of the tide.

'So, Madam, I'm charged to direct you: pray be dressed and fast-broken by seventh. His Majesty wishes to see you straight afterwards, and Lord Sigismund also requests an audience."

Briskly he kindled the lamps, blew the hearth into life and poured them out three frothy cups. "By the time you're up, breakfast will be ready in the Hall – or I can bring you some in, if you give order at the door," he said cheerfully, and with that departed.

The trio grumbled awake and hunched over their drinks, somewhat bloodshot and green round the gills.

"Break fast," Elinor groaned, "the very idea makes me nauseous!" She took another sip and licked off a foamy moustache. "This will do… at least I can stomach it." She groaned again. "O God – breakfast or last minute lectures, I know not which is worse!"

In the Great Hall, Hel and Iris picked at a platter of boiled eggs, roll-mops and frumenty; neither had much appetite. Too niggardly of each other's presence to squander precious hours in sleep, they too had lain wakeful all night in the Torturer's chamber; the Seekhounds (Loki with compassionate dispensation) lay curled together in Lila's basket at the foot of his bed.

They did not conjoin; indeed, Iris did not even wish to see him fully. So they kept their drawers on and solaced themselves with the rest, savouring minute by minute their kisses and caresses, their gazing and whispers. All too soon, the night trickled by. Calm and resigned they had risen, almost wordlessly dressed, and gone forth with their canine companions. Silent they sat over cup upon cup of strong *café*, passing the pipe back and forth, numbing their desolation with caffeine and smoke. What *could* they say, what topic did not lead inexorably back to their parting, upon which they could hardly bear to reflect?

"Live in faith," said Iris at length, "As shall I, Sir, trusting to the purpose in this! Meanwhile let's make this pact: let's make midnight our time to think on each other, to be united in spirit if not in the flesh. Let us do so especially at Hag-moon, when midnight is darkest – then spend an hour thinking on me, thinking of thee."

Hel grimaced. "Easy enough – I'll be thinking on thee in any event… every minute of day and night like as not, no matter what phase of the moon."

"I too - yet we must try and resist! We must focus our longings upon these nightly meetings, and honour our daily duties with full attention. We'll have all manner of new business to engage us; aye, private, political, our lives can never revert to those we knew... before."

"You're right – 'twill be better than nothing," (indeed, he felt a curious comfort at the prospect). "Besides, I have Lila to console me - the most considerate of gifts, my dear heart."

King Thorund on the other hand had slept very sound. He roused at the first glint of sunrise relaxed and refreshed, suffused with well-being and hungry as a wolf. He yawned and stretched, feeling something wonderful had happened last night- ah, Nerya! His piss-proud groin twitched then his dawning smile faded; his questing fingers had found her pillow cold and empty.

Not empty! Thorund's hand recoiled as if from a serpent. He fumbled for tinder and lit a stub of candle. Where her head had lain, something glinted. Cautiously he picked it up, turning it this way and that. It was a fine piece of silver-smith work, plainly moulded, all the beauty lying in its form, meaning and smooth burnished surface. Carefully, very carefully, he manipulated the boss, probing for the trick of opening. Vainly did he press and squeeze until he remembered to pull at the same time, crooking his finger through the loop. With a tiny click the polished steel drew out, barely more than an inch long or wider than a grass-blade. Thorund approached it to his face with great care; sniffing, he detected a slight acrid whiff, and saw the faintest of yellow-brown smears round the tip. He replaced it in the sheath; withdrew and replaced it twice more; hung the chain around his neck, and practised till he could competently draw it with one hand.

"What a keepsake," he sighed aloud, "Incomparable Nery!" In truth, Thorund reflected, he'd had little enough to compare her with (though he'd been too embarrassed to confess it, in the face of her evident experience). A virtually celibate adolescence close-guarded by Thorund VIII, a zealous convert to the new Cult of Fafnir; the Grunewald wars, when his conquests had been more martial than amatory; then his accession and marriage, soon after, to Gudrun of lineage and virtue impeccable as his own. To be sure, their early couplings were lusty, if decorous in accordance with Church teachings; but with the repeated misfortunes of child-bed, they had dwindled into stately, dutiful matings as devoid of passion as they were of novelty. So to wed the Kalaia... to have for his own that kaleidoscope of shifting mood, playful, snarling, tender, masterful... the idea was preposterously appealing.

"Ah, Nery," he sighed again, "So you double my grief! This day shall see me bereft of both women I love - how apt that you should arm me to bide my loss in patience." He lifted the *ankh* and pressed it to his lips.

Elinor presented herself as instructed, at half after seventh. She was surprised and vaguely relieved to find Thorund still in his dressing-robe, lingering over coffee and a pipe of Angorian leaf.

"Come, sit ye down, child; take a cup."

Informal, then; she hoped it would not turn into a lengthy harangue of instructions.

"So, Daughter: judging from your hints you've long wished to wed abroad – well, here's your chance! And as a responsible monarch and parent, I must say this afore you go.

'I'm proud of you, Princess – make me prouder! Seize this opportunity with both hands and profit to the utmost by it. Become as a native in the tongue, study their customs and governance, practice state-craft… and be properly grateful. Remember, I'd have given your hand straightaway, if Angor had asked it! But this proposition pleases me better, since you're so young - I lay the Elect has a dozen years on you – and the twelvemonth will give you time to grow- ah, to grow in acquaintance and understanding.

''Tis a fairer deal than you'd come by elsewhere – as well you know, Madam. So spend the time well and wisely, that you might have free choice in respect of their Electhood – not come home premature and perforce, disgraced by having shown yourself unequal to the task. Yet success or failure for Gondarlan does not rest entirely on your shoulders… I'm well disposed to this Angorian alliance, with or without you marry Sol-Lios."

Elinor's heart leapt. That well-nigh amounted to paternal approval of her plans! She nodded meekly, in secret delight.

"I'll try my best, Father."

"Then I'm well pleased – your best is all I can ask." He rose. "Send me word how you do, and if there's aught I can help with," sending on my Wardrobe would be favourite, she thought. "Above all take care of yourself, Daughter; all my prayers shall be on your safe journey. Now, begone; bid farewell to His Grace while I dress to wave you off."

Clasping her shoulders to drop a formal kiss on her brow, the King's robe gaped somewhat at the neck. Elinor caught the scent of her father's body, glimpsed an unfamiliar chain round his throat, and

293

bethinking how little she knew him, her eyes pricked with tears. She ached for him to embrace her, tell her he loved and would miss her; she ached in vain.

"Adieu then, Sire – I'll see you below."

At the Archbishop's door, Elinor braced herself for a sermon and more admonitions.

"Ah, Highness," His Grace was unctuous, "The blessings of Fafnir upon thee, dear Cub, on this morning so doleful for the Pack that loves thee well! A few words afore ye leave our sacred lair, my child, for thy comfort and ah, spiritual guidance... Remember, dear Princess, the Wolf's Eye is ever upon thee! Conduct thyself accordingly; fall not prey to these pa- these people's seductions. O, and how I fear for thee, when I see thee already afflicted – I speak of thy riding-habit, Madam! Tush, most improper - shamefully vulgar!"

"I do but obey My Lord King in humouring his guests," she was stung to retort. "And 'tis how the Empress of Faal-"

"We're not in Faal, Highness – nor yet Angor, thank God!" said Sigismund testily; then recalling his objective, moderated his tone. "But returning to my point: stay uncorrupted, true to Fafnir's Chosen Pack – e'en if it should cause thee a semblance of failure in foreign eyes... For in such undertaking as this, 'twill be no disgrace but rather, redound to thy credit if ye cannot fulfil their disgraceful conditions! We can only pray for thy restoration, in due course, to thy proper place here.

'Therefore is my advice, as custodian of thy soul: co-operate with thy, ah, *hosts*," he injected contempt into the word, "Only so far as is needful! Affect the meekness of a sheep but remain a She-wolf at heart – thus ye may quit the Southron shores unsullied, and Gondarlan be purged of heathen influence."

Elinor bit the inside of her cheek – spiritual dispensation, too! With downcast eyes she gestured helplessly at her costume.

"Holy Father, I'm thankful that mine own inclination be so in accord with your sage advice – which I'll try my best to follow."

"*Try* thy *best*? Nay, child, do not 'try', but succeed! Ahem, I have every faith," he hastily softened the command, "that thy soul will endure, mayhap even be strengthened, by this coming test. Meanwhile *we* must endure the grievous dolour of thy absence... a pain ye might ease for me, belov'd Cub!

'Aye, Highness – pray write often, to my singular comfort! The least little detail of thy journey, of Angor, its country and people

294

and cities… never fear to bore me, I shall treasure thy words till the day ye're safely returned to our bosom."

The Princess nodded. "I shall so write."

"Bless thee, my child!" Sigismund clasped her hand between his own, fat and boneless, repellent as a pail of warm slugs. She fought instinctive recoil but too late, he had sensed it; stretching his lips mirthlessly, he turned the clasp into a pat and released her.

"Then it remains only for me to wish thee Wolf-speed on thy travels, and preservation from the snares and wiles ahead. Come, Daughter, kneel; let us pray…"

At last, suitably shrived, the Princess escaped. Well, she thought, now I know… My royal father wishes me success; my Holy Father wishes the opposite; so which to serve, God or King? Lucky that mine own course lies somewhere betwixt and between – thereby I serve both, to some degree, and myself into the bargain!

At half after eighth, the Kalaios looked up and grinned. Somewhere high overhead Ragnar Thoralson climbed at his behest, for Nikos had ended his Feast of Farewell with a trip to the Mountaineer's chamber to bid him a private good-bye.

"Fain would I offer a more physical demonstration of my affectionate regard, and my sorrow at this untimely sundering of our friendship," he chuckled, "Only I fear to, under the eyes of old Wolfsbane, lest I get you in trouble! Nay, I'm on a different privy errand: to seek a favour of you."

Ragnar looked relieved, if a tinge disappointed. "To be sure, I'll do aught I can."

"Splendid! Then would you climb up the Fang tomorrow morning? 'Twould afford me a measure of consolation to know you were watching from yon tower of fond memory."

The Mountaineer was touched. "Gladly – you'll stay in my eye longer from the Tip than anywhere else."

"Very well – and keep a look-out, for I have a surprise!"

"Eh? What sort of surprise?"

"Un-surprising, if I told you! Nay, you must wait," teased Nikos. He cupped Ragnar's face between his hands, kissed him on the mouth a long moment, and engulfed him in a bear-hug embrace. "But for now, my good friend, I salute thee and bid thee farewell – just remember, tomorrow, look to the ships. You'll know your surprise when you see it."

In the thronged courtyard, King Thorund passed by the ranks of *Kali't'aia*, wishing them each Godspeed. They mounted and broke out the stirrup-cup while he embraced the delegation who then took to their horses, Zafia audibly sniffing. Not for Iris and Hel such public displays of emotion; they did but bow, each to the other, and share a last look before she swung herself up onto Kali and retreated behind mask and cowl.

In due course the King came to Nery. "Ward well our Soldier's Secret," she whispered, as with painful restraint he bestowed the formal kisses. "And remember our rite, my blood-brother... if you're ever in need, call on Nerya Aul'aia."

"But I'm in need now," he whispered back, "And you cannot answer! Ach, that's unfair; pray forgive me. May all our gods go with thee till we meet again."

Last of all, Jehan and Elinor he took by the hands and led to a scaffolding platform draped in the colours of both nations. A fanfare blew; they mounted the steps; Thorund gestured for silence.

"Now comes the hour both dreaded and desired, when our most well-beloved Princess must leave our realm to pursue a place of high honour with our Angorian allies," he cried. "Yestere'en we feasted on farewells; this morning we do but take them quick and clean. And so fare thee well, Sol-"

"Hold hard!" Jehan beckoned to Loric Sorenssen, standing by with two hessian bags. "Afore you dismiss me, O Thorund, a small parting gift - *café* and *cacao* beans – and we've furnished Master Loric with the means for preparation. 'Twill be our pleasure to keep you abundantly supplied... you shall sup your way round the finest strains Centralia can offer."

Thorund slapped Jehan's back heartily. "I'm grateful indeed, Sir – I've quite lost the inclination for small beer with my break-fast. With that, farewell – and mind you look after my child!"

To Elinor he went on, "May Fafnir protect thee, dear Daughter." Embracing her, he kissed both her cheeks. "Be mindful thou art Gondarlan's figurehead abroad - make us proud! So without more ado I'll say, *bon voyage, bien-aimee*, as thy Faalians have it."

The Princess hugged back, stiffly at first. Ironic, she thought bitterly, how he shows more affection in public than private - I suppose 'twould be impolitic to give me a meaner caress than he bestows on these strangers! Then her clasp became convulsive.

"F-f-fare well, Papi," she gulped, burying her face in his shoulder.

"Tush now, Princess – weep not," Thorund chided gently, detaching her grip. "Else I'll be joining thee; and that would never do, now would it, in front of our whole court? Bear up, She-cub – no howling!"

Farewell rang from the ramparts in a mass outbreak of flag-waving, tossing up of caps and tossing off of potations.

Sol-Lios guided Elinor down to the horses. Before mounting, her ladies pulled down her veil and secured it with her cravat, then hastily followed suit, for they made a sorry-looking trio. Fran alone wore the pallor of unrelieved excitement, and hid her glee tactfully, while Berthe was glad to veil a face drawn by misery and the scalding ache in her heart. Loric looked so happy this morning, as if he didn't care one whit... it was too hard to bear, she wished to be gone.

Elinor had blanched in panic; now, chattered her mind, now you must think on it – it's starting! Trumpets blared, drummers drummed, the gates swung open and to a fresh round of cheers, a squadron of Gondaran cavalry led the way through. The Princess cast a despairing glance over her shoulder. Thorund was solemnly waving, courtiers kissing their hands, Ingard beating the butts of their halberds on the cobbles. Her mouth went dry, her legs nerveless; fortunately Luna was wise enough to keep her place in the column unprompted, and set off in step with Sol Invictus.

Through the Outer Bailey they went, then the barbican, whose grim snout progressively muffled the cries of Wolf-bless and God By-ye. Emerging to the relative peace of the Jaw, they clopped down the causeway with frisky seas lapping at their flanks; on, through the Head-gate; and out onto Thorshaven road, where the portcullis shut behind them with a terminal rattle and clang.

It was an exhilarating morning. The graduated blue sky was a-whirl with mewing seagulls, a crimson sun casting long oblique shadows over declivities in the hoary fields and wreathing them in sublime icy mists. High overhead, purple galleons puffed briskly to their foundering on the Central Massif, driven by a strong wind manifest at ground level only as a cheek-tingling breeze, lively with salt. Horses neighed and tossed their heads, Angorians laughed and tossed pleasantries to one another and Loki bristled from his pouch in pop-eyed bliss, Lila temporarily forgotten. On any other day, the Princess would have shared the general elation; she particularly favoured her *Mit'winter* birth-month for its dramatic painted skies. This one, however, made no impression; she stared through it, beyond it, into infinity.

Jehan could not rebuke his company for their cheerful want of tact, yet his heart bled for the Gondaran trio, whose sentiments must perforce be so different. Elinor, for instance, sat frigid as a statue by his side, face fixed blankly ahead; she had spoken no word since those last to her father. He ventured a remark.

"Pray pardon my comrades' excitement, Madam. I hazard they feel same as me – sad to leave, yet avid for home. We've been abroad now these several months, and 'tis hard to be away from kin and country – as I wot you'll shortly discover."

A faint nod was his only reply. He did not press her and they rode on, making with Berthe and Fran a silent island in that merry sea.

Of the more happily affected the Speakers, Iamis and Highest, pleading urgency of shipboard preparations, peeled off for a final gallop across *Thegn* Pavel's acres. Iris meanwhile sat like a dead weight on Kali, trusting that sensible mare to guide herself while she gorged on the scenery, committing every detail to her Eye, torn ever between the cloud-snagged central peaks and the stark contrast of Mount Fang and the Thorsgard's outer defences, ponderous black silhouettes thrusting from the northern horizon. She blessed her dark mask; behind it, tears were running freely.

"I'm heartsick at leaving... all the more that I didn't See it coming! How myopic am I grown, missing a matter so huge?" she berated herself. "That I didn't foretell, didn't expect to- to fall in love – there, I've said it! *Kali-maia*, and how I'm in love...

'Howsoever, I did *not* See it. Am I therefore deficient... or was this, for some divine purpose, hidden from my view...? Hah – therein lies the answer, of course – if I'd Seen, would it have still come to pass? Would I have still come, electing to buy fleeting bliss with a long agony... or asked another to go in my stead, and stayed tranquilly unmated in Aumaia?

'Apparently I was not meant to question, simply to do." Iris sniffed wetly. "So I should commend myself unto Mother's guidance... trust that all occurs as it should, and be consoled."

Her emanations prickled at the back of Zafia's neck. The Healer glanced over her shoulder and smiled; Iris sat like a miniature Fang, as black and erect, as potent with rock-strength. She drew rein and fell back alongside.

"How goes it, Sister?"

"Well enough, now I've reconciled myself. O, but Zafi, it's

hard! I've so lost my heart that henceforth, I shall ne'er again be entirely content to live my life in Angor."

The Healer smiled. "Truly, Lord Hel must be a rare caution to have such an impact on you, love!"

"That he is, and that he has! Aye, my dear: you know me, the things I've Seen and done... and how chary I've been of intimacy, fearing my true nature might taint or discomfit a lover. But to Hel I could give myself fully – he's a Necromancer of highest degree, though he would hardly define it in such terms... and now we've met, there can be but one ending for us - Fusion or death. I look not to See which will come first."

The Healer bowed. "It goes so deep? Then I pray 'twill be Fusion, and before I'm too decrepit to dance at your hand-fast! I do joy for you, Iris, despite your present pain."

"Thanks, love - but it's not only Hel. This *place* has sunk into my heart... and thus is my anguish redoubled! My home-sickness can no longer be entirely cured by going home, when I leave such a part of me here... ah, me." Iris smiled wanly. "Still, the worst moment's past, now our farewells have been said."

The column jogged on down a road increasingly lined with sightseers; where rumour had failed, last night's fireworks had succeeded in alerting folk to their Princess's imminent departure. The nearer they approached to Thorshaven, the more frequent and numerous became these knots of onlookers, coalescing at last into an unbroken line. Others craned from windows hastily re-draped with bunting and banners to see the procession pass. Some few watched in silence; more doffed their caps, waved their kerchiefs and cried their farewells; all, whatever their disposition, got a goodly show – something to cheer, and something to jeer.

Captain Haral rode at the head, holding the royal standard on its sharp-pointed staff at a threatening angle to keep clear the road. A half-dozen Gondaran cavalry trotted behind with a squadron of bill-men sent up from the rear-guard; this latter gradually fell by the wayside as Sergeant Elf ordered pairs to station themselves wherever the crowd looked unduly criminal or boisterous.

Next came the delegation within their *Kali't'aia* phalanx, their multi-hued cloaks and gemstone badges bright in the morning sun, astride their tall steeds. Astride, even the Princess, who was still too stunned to register the gasps of shock or approbation. Then the sharp scent of lavender, tansy and rue, cast into the street and crushed under their hooves, assailed her nostrils. Royal protocol thawed her numbness and she began to bestow a nod here, a gracious wave there. Berthe too revived; painfully conscious of her dignity as one of Elinor's Ladies she straightened her shoulders and held her head high. At her side, Fran's smile of vicarious pride had broadened by the mile; she had even dared a nod or two, preening in her Faali riding suit.

Lastly slogged Elf's infantry remnant, destined for crowd-control at the harbour. Karl and Skala had the honour to lead this contingent through first pick of the cavalry's droppings, their pitiless Sergeant riding behind to drive them on. They panted glumly along, steeled for the next tail to lift, rude laughter and cat-calls ringing in their ears.

Arriving betimes, Nikos had cut through the back streets to a Mermaid bedecked for the occasion, her eponymous carving splendidly repainted and succulently pouting with tail freshly silvered. A blue-painted board had been fixed underneath, with gold-leafed upon it 'Angorian Mission' in characters Upper and Lower; either side hung a painted canvas banner, one red with the black-and-white Wolf's Head, one blue with a red and white Fusion in a yellow sunburst.

He vaulted from the saddle, looped Scylla's reins round a convenient new hitching-rail, and tried his key in the latch. The door was still bolted within. He hammered on it.

"Bestir yourselves, Mermaids – a traveller seeks service."

The bolts shot back seconds later. "Hush, not so loud - I was hoping you'd come! Here," Freya drew him inside, flesh swaying freely in her unfastened robe. "I'll show you what breakfast best suits a lusty tar before his long stretch at sea."

"There, Madam," he panted, rolling off her and thence off the couch in the Snug, after ten frenetic minutes, "That's what we tars call a 'quickie'."

"Not bad," she judiciously replied, mopping up with a thoughtfully-placed kerchief.

"You're too kind – it was somewhat impromptu," he laughed, "For I came but to tell you, alas, that the day has arrived – we're sailing at Zenith. So pray pass it on to the girls – make haste to the ships, if you'd say your final, ahem, good-byes! Aye, come soon – or you can't come at all."

At *Harborplatz,* early visitors were being treated to a novel sight: Angor's Galaia re-boarding their floating barns, variously tripping and waddling over the gangplanks – a pair of nanny-goats and a flock of ducks and geese for each vessel. Little Angor was then emptied and closed up; the crews came aboard with their luggage; and the delegates began trickling in, Iamis and his companions shortly followed by a red-faced Kalaios.

By tenth glass, a rising crescendo of cheers announced the main party's arrival. At the quayside Princess Elinor dismounted, honoured the crowd with a gracious wave, and permitted Sol-Lios to conduct her aboard. She was duly ensconced with Berthe and Fran in seats of honour on the stern-castle, whence they could survey proceedings far removed from the vulgar spectators.

"If you get cold, pray go below at any time," said First Mate Portia. "You'll find *café* and nuncheon already laid. Otherwise, I'll be hard by if you need aught."

Nestled in their cloaks, sipping hot spiced mead, they watched the horses filing down into the hold. The spectacle, the alcohol, the freedom from immediate audience, all conspired to loosen their tongues; anon, Fran could restrain herself no longer.

"Whisht, Loki," she exclaimed, "Sit down, stop pulling – I can't loose you, lest you dive overboard! Look, Madam – there's Luna! Isn't she good, walking all by herself?" She wagged an admonitory finger at the Seekhound. "You might take a lesson from her, sirrah, on how to behave!"

"Ah, leave him be," sympathised Berthe, chucking his chin. "Poor little thing, he's missing Lila, I'll be bound! And getting over-excited with all these new smells, aren't you, sweetheart?"

"Ah-aye," Fran spluttered, "He's all at sea, you might say!"

They dissolved into giggles. Elinor rolled her eyes. "Stop being silly," she hissed, "The townsfolk can see us! Especially now-God's Fur, they're coming aboard! O no, I'm not equal to being stared at like a goldfish in a bowl - we shall go and take coffee until these… lowly persons are put off again."

Her withdrawal was timely; soon both decks were seething with a common ruck of chandlers, craftsmen, ropers, hucksters, sailors and merchants: business acquaintances, some now firm friends, the Angorians had garnered on their stay. Mermaids shoaled everywhere one looked, bedewing the Mariners with brine, professing affectionate thanks; and among them Ferdi Mickelsprech, avid as ever for news.

"So - no dragons, no comets, no sky set a-fire – 'tis what folk are saying, you know. No witches, no eruptions of the Lung - just a mere trifle, a petty contrivance of *thy leaving party*! You might have

301

warned me, is all I can say."

"All you can say – I doubt that!" laughed Nikos, "Least it had better not be, else you're out of a job! But the rebuke's well merited – pray cry our apologies for any alarm."

Ferdi's solemnity cracked. "That I will – fire-works, eh? Hah - I'm not sure they be any less marvel than dragons." He stuck out his hand. "Well, Sir, you certainly gingered things up around here – and I for one am heartily sad to see you go."

Nikos shook the hand and clapped the Crier's broad back.

"As am I, friend Ferdi; be assured, I'll pray most devoutly to return. Meantime I've a rather, ahem, pressing good-bye to attend to," he waggled his eyebrows suggestively, "If you'll excuse me, Master Mickelsprech."

Shortly after eleventh glass, a loud horn sounded on *Quintessence*. Her crew began rushing about, blowing on whistles and calling down hatchways to clear the decks. When the last guests had been ushered back to the *Breath*, the High-ship's sailors cast off from her side and readied their vessel to come about.

"Where's Freya, then?" demanded Else, "I thought you said she'd gone on *Quintessence*?"

Anna shrugged. "She must've come back already – she'll be bidding farewell, *again*, to our Niki, I lay!"

"Nay, he's over there," Freyling sighed. Indeed, there stood the Kalaios alone at the stern, studying Mount Fang through Thorund's telescope. "O God, these last minutes are aching… I can't stand it! I've said him all I can say of good-byes - I think I'll go back to The Mermaid."

"Ho, well I'm not," said Else, "I'm staying to wave the ships off! But someone should go and open up, I dare say we'll get a big rush when they're gone… mayhap that's what Freya's doing."

"Hah – drowning her sorrows, more like," giggled Anna. "She's not been herself by a long chalk this week, one minute laughing and jumping about, next minute crying and sighing! O, I hope she don't mope for months – a long face at the bar's no good for business."

Ragnar Thoralson trained his spy-glass on the great ship wheeling out, graceful as a swan, in the wake of the harbour pilot's row-boat. The other was disgorging a stream of erstwhile passengers to rejoin the milling quayside throng, her masts alive with sailors, her canvas unfurling.

302

Departure was imminent – so where was his surprise? Certainly not in Fang-tip which he had carefully scanned, knowing even as he did so it was pointless; look to the ships, Nikos had said. He had yet seen naught there to astonish; no more fire-works, no hidden messages he could descry among the pennants and flags flapping gaily from the rigging.

Shifting the glass he stiffened. At the stern-rail, tiny but plain as if Ragnar could have reached out a finger and touched him, Nikos was looking his way. Thoralson cranked the window ajar, stuck out his free hand and waved. He saw Nikos wave back; could even see him grin, then hold up an arresting hand and withdraw from sight. A few moments later he reappeared, his telescope once more pointed Tip-wards though the Mountaineer sensed that his friend was no longer looking at him...

Hel! What *was* he looking at? Cold dew broke out on Ragnar's brow. He swept panicked eyes around the chamber, scanning *Fafnirsee* for a surprise invasion fleet. Nothing could be seen but the lively chopping waves and a regatta of cumulus clouds racing in from the north. Blushing at his mistrust, Thoralson redirected his glass.

Nikos was still there, apparently enjoying the aerobatics of the whirling, diving seabirds. The Mountaineer followed his line of vision. Sky, cloud, sky, feathery flash; twist the focus ring – now he had it! Aye, Niki must be watching this gull, this handsome greater black-backed, flying straight towards him, nearer, nearer, until he could make out the shining medallion round its neck...

He laid down his glass with nerveless fingers and fumbled open the window. A moment later came a flurry without.

"Yark!"

"*Ave*," said Ragnar hesitantly, summoning ten per cent of his Angorian vocabulary.

The gull hopped in and onto the bench. Arching its neck, it tapped thrice on the silver yin-yang hanging at its breast, and held forth a scaly yellow leg.

"Yark!"

"Yark yourself!" said Thoralson. He fell to his knees, clumsily unfastened the bird's message tube, drew out a tiny roll of papyrus and unfurled it.

This is Khria, homer to Breath, he read. *In danger or need, tell her 'A Nikos'. She will home to the ship, and the ship will find me. Pray accept her in friendship, or love – what ye will,*

From yr assured servant, N-A, Kalaios

303

"Khria?" said Ragnar, wonderingly.

"Yark – 'rhia," she agreed.

Thoralson laughed. "Well, Khria, I'm Ragnar – your new master, er, keeper, it seems." He scratched her crisp white neck feathers. "And a surprise I've been given, to be sure! But I've never met a homing bird before... mayhap we should try each other out, afore your companions depart."

Scrabbling in a cupboard he found pen and ink. He thought for a moment; smiled; inscribed a few words on the back of Nikos's note and popped it into the tube.

"Let's try it: Khria, 'A Nikos'!"

"Yark!" Off she flew.

Ragnar watched the Kalaios receive her. Message read, Nikos smiled, blew a kiss, took ink-horn and quill from his belt and made an addition. Khria was duly despatched.

To Thoralson's reply, *My thanks. In love – R'* Nikos had subscribed *I wish ye'd told me that last night!*

"So do I," Ragnar sighed. But it was too late, much too late – the *Breath* was under way, moving out into open sea to join her sister, their full heads of sail swelling fat as they heeled into the wind.

Settling Khria on his lap and the spy-glass to his eye, Ragnar Thoralson watched; watched Nikos dwindle to an unrecognisable speck, then disappear altogether as the Angorian ships fleeted away over the southern horizon.

END

Elinor's story continues in Lay of Angor Book 2, *Breath of Gaia*